Memories of You

Benita Brown

The right of Benita Brown to be identified as the Author of
the Work has been asserted by her in accordance with the
Copyright, Designs and Patents Act 1988.

First published in Great Britain in 2011 by
HEADLINE PUBLISHING GROUP

First published in paperback in 2011 by
HEADLINE PUBLISHING GROUP

2

Cataloguing in Publication Data is available from the British Library

ISBN 978 0 7553 5292 0

Typeset in Bembo by Avon DataSet Ltd,
Bidford-on-Avon, Warwickshire

Printed and bound in Great Britain by
Clays Ltd, St Ives plc

Headline's policy is to use papers that are natural, renewable and
recyclable products and made from wood grown in sustainable forests.
The logging and manufacturing processes are expected to conform
to the environmental regulations of the country of origin.

HEADLINE PUBLISHING GROUP
An Hachette UK Company
338 Euston Road
London NW1 3BH

www.headline.co.uk
www.hachette.co.uk

In memory of my mother who because of family circumstances had to leave grammar school at the age of fourteen. Like Helen, she left Newcastle to work in London.

I know she would have enjoyed this story.

Part One

The Beginning

Newcastle, November 1929

Selma stared out at the darkening sky. Wind hurled rain and withered leaves against the window panes. Dr Charles Harris was checking through the papers on the desk in front of him. She heard him clear his throat and she turned to face him.

'As far as I can see from the results of these tests there is no reason why you and Hugh cannot have a baby,' he said. 'You will just have to be patient.'

'Patient! My life is slipping away. I'll soon be middle aged!'

The consultant smiled. 'You married very young, Selma. At twenty-six you are nowhere near middle aged.'

She shrugged impatiently. 'I know. I exaggerate. It's my nature. But Hugh is much older than I am.'

'Hugh is the same age as me. Thirty-seven. Perhaps if you learned to relax you would conceive. Maybe a holiday? Some winter sun? Would you like that?'

Selma sighed and stared down at the gloves she had been twisting round with nervous fingers. 'Perhaps.'

She rose abruptly and her gloves and handbag fell to the floor. Charles hurried round the desk to pick them up, saying, 'I'll have a word with Hugh.'

Selma got the impression that he was glad to be rid of her. Inside the car she stared ahead despondently. 'Take me home, John,' she said.

The chauffeur turned his head towards her. 'We have to collect Mr Partington from Dean Street, madam.'

'Of course. I forgot.'

Soon they had left the leafy avenues behind them and were driving through the town. Selma gazed at lighted shop windows and blurred forms of people hurrying with heads down through the slanting rain. Near Grey's Monument a policeman raised his arms to direct the traffic, his white gloves standing out against the gloom.

The car slowed down as they passed a stationary tramcar. Selma glanced up at the people inside. Those who hadn't found seats were hanging on to the overhead straps, huddled closely together. A boy, his nose pushed sideways as he pressed against the window, stared rudely into the interior of the luxurious car. When he saw that she had noticed him, he stuck out his tongue. Selma turned her head to look back at him. She grinned, stuck out her own tongue and crossed her eyes. She just had time to register his startled expression when there was an almighty thump and the car came to a screeching halt.

Selma was thrown forwards and she banged her head on the seat in front of her. When her head cleared she became aware of John saying over and over again. 'Oh God no . . . Oh God no . . .'

'What happened?'

'She ran straight out between the tram and that car,' the chauffeur said without turning to look at her. His hands gripped the steering wheel. 'I didn't stand a chance. As God is my witness, I didn't stand a chance.'

The traffic had come to a halt and, as a curious crowd gathered, Selma got out of the car.

'Don't, Mrs Partington! Don't look!'

John opened his door and almost fell out on to the road. But Selma was already kneeling to look down at the woman who lay there. There was no obvious injury and Selma reached for her hand.

4

'Don't worry,' she said. 'We'll send for help. I'll stay with you. I won't leave you here alone.'

'Please get back in the car, Mrs Partington,' John said. And then, as if talking to a child, he added, 'You'll spoil your lovely coat kneeling there on the greasy cobbles.'

'That's right, madam.' A policeman had appeared and was standing next to John. 'It's best if you go and sit down.'

John turned to the policeman. 'I didn't stand a chance,' he said again. 'She just ran out straight in front of me.'

'I know, lad. I saw it all and so did many of these folk gathered here.' He turned to the crowd. 'If you've got anything to tell me would you return to the pavement and wait. Otherwise, you've stared your fill and it's time you moved on.' He turned to John. 'Will you help your mistress? This isn't seemly.'

'No,' Selma said. 'I promised her I'd stay with her until help comes.'

The policeman knelt down and, taking off his white gloves, he gently took the woman's hand from Selma. Taking her wrist between finger and thumb he felt for a pulse. The seconds ticked away until eventually he looked up and shook his head.

'No!' Selma cried. 'She can't be!'

'I'm sorry, madam. She's past help.'

Selma got to her feet and stared down at the woman. One shoe had come off and there was a darn in her stocking just above one knee. She stooped swiftly and pulled the woman's coat down. At least I can protect her dignity, she thought.

As she turned to go her foot caught on something and she stumbled. She looked down and to her surprise she saw an orange, a splash of colour on the rain-dark road. A shopping bag lay nearby, the contents spilled and scattered. More oranges, apples, a loaf of bread, a jar of jam, the glass smashed and the red contents oozing out. Selma stared at the jam in horror. She was hurrying home to give her family their tea, she thought. They'll be waiting for her. Wondering what treats she's bringing.

She climbed into the car and sat there hunched and miserable, her own wretchedness momentarily forgotten. She closed her eyes but she was unable to rid herself of the image of the woman with the slightly surprised expression on her pleasant face. A woman whose homely life had been suddenly and wantonly interrupted.

Chapter One

The last few lumps of coal smouldered in the grate and the room was chilly. Helen sat on the sofa with her younger sister Elsie. She put an arm round her and drew her close. The twins Joe and Danny, in their coats and ready to go, stood near the window, brown paper parcels tied with string at their feet. Every now and then Joe pushed the net curtain aside, and looked out at the drenched cobbles and the rain overflowing from the gutters of the houses opposite. Danny kept his head turned away from the window and stared at nothing in particular. Usually so easy-going and happy, the younger boy was now rigid with misery, his face pinched and drawn. Joe, the elder by ten minutes, simply looked angry.

It had been a week since their mother's funeral but Aunt Jane had left it to the evening before to tell them that they were not going to be staying together.

'I haven't got room for all of them,' she'd told their neighbour, Mrs Andrews. 'And I can't afford to take two growing boys. They'd eat me out of house and home. It might have been different if Grace had thought to take out a proper insurance policy. As it is, once the funeral's paid for, that's that.'

Jane Roberts, the widow of a bank manager, had shed no tears for her dead sister; nor had she offered any comfort to her nephews and nieces. She had come when Mrs Andrews had sent for her, and she had done her duty. If she had shown any sign of humanity it had been towards the youngest child. But not many people could resist Elsie. Simply to look at her was to make you draw your breath and wonder at her beauty. Her long hair was angel fair, her blue eyes fringed with dark lashes. Small and fragile, she looked and behaved younger than her nine years.

Aunt Jane had been noticeably gentle with her and had encouraged her to eat the plain food she had provided. But Elsie had only nibbled at her bread and margarine and had pushed aside the plates of gristly stew. Eventually Aunt Jane lost patience with her and ignored her.

Today there was a clean cloth on the table in the front parlour and it was set with a generous plate of ham sandwiches and a sliced fruit cake. Aunt Jane had not come to sit with them as they waited. She had remained in the kitchen with Mrs Andrews. She had explained that she had things to talk about, arrangements to make about handing the keys back to the landlord and the like. Helen wondered if the truth was that their aunt could not face them. Maybe she felt guilty. But if she did, there was no sign of her having changed her mind.

Joe must have been looking the wrong way, for he was as startled as everyone else when there was a loud knock on the front door. A moment later Aunt Jane ushered a tall, thin gentleman into the room. 'This is Mr Jenkins from Haven House,' she said. 'He's come for the boys.'

The last sentence was unnecessary. They all knew very well why Mr Jenkins had come. The gentleman removed his hat and clutched it against his dripping mackintosh. His face was gaunt and his wrists were scrawny. He gazed with hopeful pleasure at the spread on the table.

8

'Have you time for a cup of tea and a sandwich?' Aunt Jane asked him. 'I made the fruit cake myself.'

That was a lie. Helen had made the cake the day before, using up everything that was left in the larder. Mrs Andrews entered the room carrying the teapot. Mr Jenkins' thin features stretched into a smile.

'How kind of you, Mrs Roberts,' he said.

He took a seat at the table and for a moment looked as though he didn't know what to do with his hat until he put it on the floor underneath the seat. He helped himself to a sandwich then looked up and said, 'What about the boys? Are they going to join me?'

'Oh, no, the boys have already eaten.'

Danny and Joe stared at their aunt, disbelief in their eyes. 'We haven't already eaten,' Joe said. 'And I'm hungry.'

'Me too,' Danny added.

Aunt Jane looked flustered. She attempted an amused smile. 'Now really, boys,' she said. 'How can you be hungry after that lovely dinner we had?'

'It wasn't lovely,' Joe said. 'And there wasn't enough.'

An angry flush suffused their aunt's puffy features. 'Ungrateful child!' She turned to Mr Jenkins. 'Their mother spoiled them with fancy foods – more than she could afford, that's what the trouble is. They are completely unaccustomed to good, plain old-fashioned meals.'

Before Mr Jenkins could reply, their neighbour, Mrs Andrews, spoke up. 'I've made up a few sandwiches with the ham that was left over. The boys can eat them on the train,' she said. She looked at Aunt Jane defiantly. 'I hope you don't mind?'

Helen watched the conflicting expressions chase across her aunt's face. 'That's kind of you,' she said. 'Although as it was me that provided the ham, you should have asked.'

Mrs Andrews refused to be intimidated. 'And I've got them a comic each they can read on the journey.'

'I'm not going!' Joe said. 'You can't make me! Danny and I will stay here with Helen and Elsie.'

'I've already told you that's not possible,' Aunt Jane said. 'Helen is only fourteen. She is too young to look after you on your own. And in any case, what do you suppose you would live on? Where would the money come from?'

'I'd get the money!' Joe said. 'I'd get a job.'

'Don't be ridiculous, boy. You are only eleven years old, and even supposing you were allowed to leave school you wouldn't be able to earn enough to keep the four of you.'

'I'll be twelve next April,' Joe said. 'You're allowed to leave school at twelve if you have a proper job.'

'I could work, too,' Danny said. 'We'd make enough between us. Tell, them, Helen. Tell them we want to stay together!'

The boys looked at her beseechingly and Helen felt as though her heart was breaking. 'Aunt Jane is right,' she said. 'She cannot afford to take all of us.'

'She's taking you and Elsie,' Joe said. 'You two will be able to stay together. It's only us that's being sent away!'

'It won't be forever,' Helen said. 'We'll write to each other, won't we? And one day, I promise you, we'll be together again.'

'That's what Grace would have wanted,' Mrs Andrews interjected. Helen saw that their old friend was fighting back tears. '*I* would take the bairns if I could, but now that Albert's on the dole and no prospect of a decent job, it's all I can do to feed the two of us.'

'All I can say is that my sister should have made proper

provision for her children. But she was always feckless. Living from one day to the next without a care to what might happen.'

'What else could she do?' Mrs Andrews asked. 'Grace was the sole breadwinner since Richard died. She spent her days cleaning other people's houses and she spent every penny she earned on the bairns. And she never had any help from anyone except me.'

Helen thought Aunt Jane was going to choke on her own bile. 'My sister married Richard Norton knowing he had a weak constitution. Our parents begged her not to. They wanted her to follow my example and marry a man with prospects and a good pension to provide for his widow when he died. But Grace would have her own way and this is the result.' She glared angrily at Mrs Andrews but their neighbour would not be silenced.

'It's almost as if you blame the poor woman for getting knocked down,' she said.

'She just ran out without looking,' Aunt Jane retorted. 'The driver didn't stand a chance. That's what the policeman said.'

Joe and Danny were white-faced with strain. Elsie was frowning as if she was trying to understand the terrible world she had been thrust into.

'Please stop!' Helen said. 'You're upsetting the children.'

Mrs Andrews was mortified. 'God forgive me,' she said. 'I never meant to upset the bairns.'

'Well, you have,' Aunt Jane said. 'Fancy bringing all that up about the accident in front of them.'

'It's your fault,' Joe exclaimed. 'You started it.'

Aunt Jane turned on him. 'How dare you!' She became aware that Mr Jenkins was watching her. She pursed her lips angrily, then said, 'Let me apologise for this disgraceful scene,

Mr Jenkins. But I'm sure you'll understand how upset we've been since poor Grace was run over.'

Mr Jenkins had had his fill of sandwiches and was on his second piece of fruit cake.

'Would you like another cup of tea?' Aunt Jane asked.

Mr Jenkins cleared his throat and glanced at the clock on the mantel. 'I wouldn't say no to a fill up,' he said. 'I must say, Mrs Roberts, if this is the way you feed these children then they have no cause for complaint. None whatsoever.'

Helen saw the fury in Joe's eyes and she rose quickly and went over to the boys. 'It's all right, Joe,' she said quietly. 'We know the truth of it. Why don't we go to the kitchen and collect those sandwiches that Mrs Andrews has made for you? You'll enjoy them on the train. It will be like a picnic – a day out. Won't it, Mr Jenkins?'

'Erm, ah, yes,' he said and Helen took no comfort from the unfocused look in his eyes.

Helen hurried the twins along to the kitchen with Mrs Andrews following. The sandwiches were in two paper bags on the scrubbed wooden table. Helen took down the string shopping bag from the hook on the larder door and put the sandwiches in it.

'Here you are,' Mrs Andrews said as she put a couple of comic strip papers in with the sandwiches. 'My grandson is finished with them.'

Neither of the boys spoke. Joe looked angrier than ever and Danny had retreated to some lonely place inside himself. The overhead gas mantle flickered, dimmed, then went out. The fire in the range was hardly bright enough to keep the shadows at bay. Helen heard one of the boys sob and was surprised to see that it was Joe; plucky, spirited Joe. She reached out and put her arms round him but he shook her off.

12

Their aunt entered the kitchen. 'It's time for you to go,' she said.

Joe scrubbed at his face angrily with white clenched knuckles but Danny said, 'It's all right, Helen. I understand. We'll write to each other like you say.'

Helen gave him a hug but although he didn't shake her off like Joe had done, he held himself stiffly.

'Mr Jenkins is waiting,' Aunt Jane said impatiently. 'Now come along and get your parcels. You have a train to catch.'

'Goodbye, lads,' Mrs Andrews said. 'I won't come to the door, if you don't mind.' She sank down on to one of the wooden kitchen chairs.

Neither of the twins answered her. They followed their aunt along the passage to the front parlour and picked up the parcels containing all their clothes.

'Don't forget your sandwiches,' Helen said, and Danny held out an arm so that she could slip the string bag over it.

Mr Jenkins rose from the table and got halfway to the door before he remembered the hat he had placed under his chair. Once he had retrieved it he hurried ahead. 'Come along, lads,' he said with an air of hearty cheeriness. It was the first time he had spoken to them directly. He turned to Aunt Jane. 'And I can assure you, Mrs Roberts, that you have done the right thing. Your nephews will be very well looked after at Haven House.'

Suddenly both boys dropped their parcels and rushed back to the sofa where Elsie still sat. They both dropped to their knees and hugged her in turn.

'Goodbye, little'un,' Joe said. 'Promise not to forget me.'

'Nor me,' Danny said.

Elsie, eyes wide but unseeing, nodded mutely. She had not spoken for days. Pain and bewilderment had imprisoned her in a silent world.

13

Mr Jenkins cleared his throat. The boys rose, picked up their parcels and without another word they left the house they had lived in since the day they were born.

Aunt Jane, having seen them off, came back into the front parlour and frowned. 'It's dark in here,' she said. 'I suppose I'll have to put something in the gas meter.'

She left the room and went along to the kitchen where she had left her handbag. A little later Helen heard a coin drop into the meter on the wall behind the front door. One penny, Helen thought. One penny to measure out the time we have left here. She knew they would be going to Aunt Jane's house that very night and she wondered why they weren't setting off straight away, unless their aunt had decided to let them eat up the sandwiches and fruit cake before they left.

Helen heard raised voices from the kitchen. Both the parlour and the kitchen doors were open and the angry words echoed along the passage.

'Do it yourself,' Helen heard Mrs Andrews say at full volume. 'Get your own hands dirty. I'm not your servant, you know. I came to help because Grace was my friend and I love those bairns like they were my own.'

Her aunt did not reply. After a short while she appeared carrying burning coals on a shovel. She must have lifted them from the kitchen range. She knelt down and tipped them into the grate. After arranging them carefully she stood up and sighed. 'There's no more coal,' she said. 'So that will have to do.'

'Are we staying here for tea?' Helen asked.

Her aunt did not reply. Glancing briefly at the clock, she took a taper from the jug in the hearth and lit the gas mantle before closing the curtains and returning to the kitchen. A faint warmth now emanated from the fireplace and, with the curtains drawn against the miserable November evening, the room seemed to give faint echoes of happier times.

Helen gazed into the heart of the fire. She remembered the games they had played trying to see pictures in the fire. As she watched, the coals shifted and settled, sending a shower of ash on to the hearth. She half rose, intending to sweep the hearth clean, but sank back on to the sofa when she realised there was no point.

Aunt Jane returned and went to check her reflection in the mirror hanging on the wall above the fireplace. Her greying brown hair was parted in the centre and scraped back into a bun at the nape of her neck. She tucked a stray wisp behind one ear and then picked up the comb that was kept on the mantelshelf.

'Tidy your hair,' she said to Helen. 'Come here, Elsie. Your ribbons are falling out.'

Not understanding why they should have to do this right now, Helen, nevertheless, went over to the mirror, removed the hairclips that kept her unruly dark blond hair from falling across her face, dragged the comb through it and replaced the clips. By the time she had finished Aunt Jane had retied the blue ribbons in Elsie's hair and had led her to the table.

'Time for tea,' Aunt Jane said and the younger girl looked at her uncomprehendingly. 'Hurry up, Helen,' their aunt added. 'We haven't got all day.'

'You want us to eat the sandwiches and cake?' Helen asked.

'What a silly question. Of course I do. Now sit there with Elsie while I go and get a jug of milk.'

Helen was utterly confused. Mr Jenkins had been given tea, probably so that Aunt Jane could make a good impression – pretend to be the caring aunt. The boys, who might have eaten everything that Mr Jenkins left, had been denied. And now she and Elsie had been prettied up and asked to sit at the table. Was Aunt Jane expecting another visitor or was this gesture simply to impress kind old Mrs Andrews? Helen doubted it.

Elsie was staring at her plate. The best china, Helen realised. Her mother's precious rose-patterned tea set. It wasn't really valuable but it had cost more than they could afford. Her mother had bought it from a stall in the Grainger market week by week, a cup and saucer, a tea plate, the sugar bowl, the milk jug and eventually the teapot. How excited they had all been when their mother had brought that teapot home. She had placed it in the china cabinet along with the rest of the set.

She had stood back and regarded the display with pleasure for a while, then she had said, 'Well, I'm not going to let them sit there all the time. If we have nice things we should use them. And not just for high days and holidays like birthdays or Christmas. We'll get them out each Sunday teatime. Make the day special.'

Aunt Jane was going to take the tea set. She had told Mrs Andrews that most of the things in the house were worthless but, even so, she had arranged for Gardiner's auction rooms to come and collect everything. Everything except the tea set and her sister's few pieces of jewellery.

'Anything Gardiner's won't take you can have,' she'd said condescendingly to Mrs Andrews.

'Good of you,' their neighbour had replied dryly. 'And I suppose you'll be keeping the jewellery for Helen and Elsie?'

Aunt Jane had pursed her lips and nodded and no more had been said.

Mrs Andrews came into the parlour carrying a jug of milk. 'I've warmed it for you,' she said. 'You need a hot drink on a day like this.'

16

While she was pouring the milk into their cups there was a knock at the front door.

'I'll get it,' Aunt Jane called out from the kitchen and Helen heard her hurrying along the passage.

Mrs Andrews saw Helen's enquiring look and shook her head. 'Don't ask me,' she said. 'It's too late in the day for Gardiner's men to come, and the rent collector won't come for the keys until the end of the week.'

They heard the door open and Aunt Jane asking someone to come in. The door closed and a soft voice asked, 'Which way?'

'Just here,' Aunt Jane said. 'The girls are having tea in the front parlour.'

A moment later their aunt ushered the most beautiful woman Helen had ever seen into the room. She felt a moment of guilt because of course their mother had been beautiful – but work and worry had etched sad lines into their mother's gentle face, whereas this woman had the unlined features of a delicate porcelain doll.

She was wearing a belted camel coat with a fur collar, and her silvery-blond hair hung down to her shoulders in a long bob. She looks like the film star Constance Bennett, Helen thought. She remembered the night when Mrs Andrews had looked after the younger children and she had gone to the pictures with her mother to see a film all about spies. They had both been overwhelmed by the leading lady's beauty. Helen looked at their visitor and frowned. Whether or not their visitor reminded her of her mother's favourite film star, she was sure she had seen her before. But she couldn't remember where or when.

Without being asked their visitor had taken a seat at the table. 'The boys have gone?' she asked.

Aunt Jane glanced briefly at Helen and then replied,

17

'You've just missed them. I'm sorry, did you want to see them?'

'Oh, no. That's all right. I just wanted to know that they are safely on their way to Haven House. It's an excellent facility. I know how much you wanted to keep your nephews with you but you won't regret this. They will both continue their education and be trained for some sort of occupation.'

And then Helen remembered where she had seen their guest. It had been on the day of their mother's funeral. She had been sitting at the back of the church but she had not joined the funeral party. When the service was over she had exchanged a brief word with Aunt Jane, but their aunt had never explained the incident.

Now Helen thought she understood. This lady was obviously rich and she was some sort of do-gooder. She had heard of the family's plight. Maybe she had read the report in the newspaper and that was why she had attended the funeral. Their aunt must have gone to meet her one day – the day she had told them she had some legal business to see to – and the arrangements had been made to send the boys to Haven House. But fancy Aunt Jane telling the lady that she didn't want to part with the twins. She must have been overjoyed that what she saw as a burden had been lifted from her shoulders.

'Would you like a cup of tea?' she asked their guest.

'No thank you.'

Helen's frown deepened. For some reason their visitor looked and sounded nervous – but it was an excited kind of nervous, as if something special was about to happen.

'Are you sure?'

'Quite sure. I'll just wait until Elsie has finished eating and then we should go.'

We, not *I*. Helen fought down a feeling of alarm. She

18

glanced at her younger sister. Elsie still had not spoken but she was staring at their visitor with wonder in her eyes. The lady smiled at her. 'Have you had sufficient to eat?' she asked gently.

'She hasn't eaten anything,' Helen said, knowing how hostile she sounded.

'Hasn't she? Oh dear, we shall have to see if we can persuade her.' She smiled encouragingly at Elsie and said, 'I wonder what you would like? How about jelly and ice cream? Would you like that, Elise?'

'Her name's Elsie,' Helen said and was rewarded with a brief impatient frown.

'Oh yes, of course. And what about chocolate biscuits? Would you like that, my dear?'

'She'd just be sick if she had all that, and in any case we haven't got any.'

'Helen, mind your manners!' Aunt Jane said. 'You must talk politely to Mrs Partington.'

'Why?' Helen began to feel frightened. Something was going to happen. Something had been planned and she was filled with a sense of foreboding.

'Because—' Aunt Jane began but Mrs Partington smiled and shook her head.

'It's quite all right, Mrs Roberts. It's natural for the child to be upset at such a time. She will feel better when you're settled in your own comfortable home.'

'I like chocolate biscuits.'

They all turned to stare at Elsie. She was looking at their visitor and smiling shyly.

Mrs Partington was delighted. 'Of course you do. Come here, child. Come and tell me what else you like.'

Elsie slipped down from her chair and went up close to Mrs Partington, who immediately lifted her up on to her

19

knee. Elsie looked up at her wonderingly and then raised a hand to stroke the fur collar of her coat. Their visitor laughed.

'Do you like that?' she asked. 'It's nice and soft, isn't it?'

Elsie nodded shyly.

'Would you like a coat with a fur collar? And perhaps a little fur muff to keep your hands warm?'

'Yes, I would.'

'No!' Helen exclaimed. 'You're going to take her away, aren't you? You're going to take her away from me!'

Mrs Partington put both arms round Elsie and held her close. 'Please don't make a fuss,' she said. 'Your aunt and I have discussed this and we think it would be best for your little sister to come with me. Don't you want her to be happy?'

'Of course I do! But I want her to be happy here with me in the home she loves.'

Mrs Partington looked at Helen over Elsie's head and her blue eyes suddenly looked like chips of ice. 'But you're not staying here, are you? You are going to your aunt's house. Elise has never lived there.' Her soft voice and gently reasonable words belied the look in her eyes as she continued, 'I know you love her, my dear, and what sort of sister would deny this little girl the life that I can give her?'

'You mean because you're rich!'

Mrs Partington's eyes widened as if Helen had said something that no reasonable person could argue with. 'Of course,' she said. 'And now, I think it's time we went home. Do you want to come with me, Elise darling?'

Elsie did not reply and hope leapt in Helen's breast until she saw that her sister had fallen asleep in Mrs Partington's arms. Her head was resting against the soft fur of the coat's collar and she was smiling peacefully. She hadn't smiled like that since before their mother had died.

Mrs Partington rose carefully and looked at Aunt Jane. She spoke in a whisper. 'If you could open the front door for me I'll carry her out to the car.'

Aunt Jane spoke equally softly. 'I'll get the child's clothes. They're all ready in a little suitcase.'

Mrs Partington smiled and shook her head. 'There's no need,' she said. 'Elise won't require them now. We'll just go quickly. The poor child has suffered enough and I don't want her upset by any display of hysterics.' Those last words were spoken directly to Helen.

Aunt Jane fixed Helen with a steely gaze as if to say: *Nothing will make me change my mind.*

She hurried out into the passage. Mrs Partington, carrying Elsie, walked out leaving a subtle waft of floral perfume behind her. Helen hurried to the window and pulled the curtain and the net aside. A large motorcar was parked outside, gleaming wetly in the light from the streetlamps. The house door opened, spilling light on to the glistening pavements, and a man in uniform got out of the car and opened the door.

Mrs Partington slid into the back seat still cradling Elsie in her arms. She nodded to Aunt Jane before the chauffeur closed the door. Aunt Jane hurried back into the house and the car started up and slid away along the street into the enveloping shadows.

Helen heard her aunt hurrying along the passage to the kitchen and then the sound of voices as she and Mrs Andrews held a brief conversation. There was a moment's silence before Aunt Jane left the kitchen and went upstairs. Helen leaned her head against the windowpane, closed her eyes, and began to cry.

'There, there, pet, don't take on so.'

Helen opened her eyes and saw in the reflection of the

room in the window that Mrs Andrews had entered carrying an empty tray.

'Did you know this was going to happen?'

'No, pet. I didn't.' Mrs Andrews began to clear the table. 'And your aunt wants you to get ready to go now. She's gone upstairs to collect her things and then you'll be off to her place.'

'I won't go!'

'You'll have to. I'm clearing the house and handing the keys back to the landlord.'

'I'd find somewhere else.'

'Mebbes you would, but if you ran away and the Welfare found you they'd put you in a home for bad girls, and then when would you see your brothers and sister again? You've promised them that you'll all be together one day, haven't you?'

Helen clenched her fists. 'Yes, I did. And I meant it.'

'There you are, then. And think on this, Helen. Your little sister will be better off living with that kind lady than with your Aunt Jane.'

Chapter Two

They arrived at Newcastle Central Station with fifteen minutes to spare. Just enough time to pop into the station buffet to fortify himself with something stronger than a cup of tea. Mr Jenkins eyed his charges doubtfully. Would they bolt? Certainly on the way here one of them had looked fidgety every time the tram stopped, but Mr Jenkins had taken the precaution of sitting between them on the bench seat at the rear of the carriage. This meant that although it would be easy for one to run for it, he wouldn't be able to communicate with the other and, even if he did manage to, Mr Jenkins would be able to hold on to him. He knew instinctively that one would never leave without the other.

The weather was foul and the deputy head of Haven House thought he had more than done his duty in leaving his cosy private sitting room to take the uncomfortable local train into town in order to collect the Norton lads. Furthermore he didn't think the soft felt of his trilby hat would ever recover properly after the drenching it had received.

Normally it would have been the job of one of the younger teachers to collect the boys, but with the Partingtons' involvement in this matter, the headmaster, Mr Ford, had thought it best to send a senior member of staff. Hugh Partington was immensely rich and even though he must have taken a financial hit just a month ago when the Wall Street Crash affected stock markets worldwide, he was still one of the wealthiest men on Tyneside. Mr Ford was keen to encourage the Partingtons' continued support, so his request that they should take in the Norton brothers could not be refused.

In George Jenkins' opinion, such devotion to duty deserved a little reward. But what would he do with the twins? He scanned the other passengers crossing the concourse and smiled when he saw a familiar face. Constable John Robinson was one of the police officers regularly on duty at the Central Station who were under specific instructions to look out for the unfortunate starvelings, both boys and girls, who pestered travellers with outright begging, or picked their pockets or even ran off with their luggage.

John Robinson had seen George and he smiled as he walked towards him. 'Another two lads for the Haven?'

George nodded.

The constable stared at them and his eyes widened. 'Twins, are they?'

'Yes indeed.'

'I don't think I've ever seen a couple more alike. Peas in a pod, as they say. How on earth will you tell them apart?'

'That's what I was wondering until I noticed that one of them is left-handed and the other right-handed. And look at their hair – those cowlicks are on opposite sides. Now I've just got to attach the appropriate name.'

'So what's the story?'

'Father died years ago, mother was killed in a traffic accident, and their aunt can't cope.'

'Well, I hope they know how lucky they are getting a place in Haven House.'

'I'm not sure if they do. That's why I'd like you to do

24

me a favour and keep an eye on them while I nip into the buffet for something to warm me up.'

'Afraid they might run for it?'

'That's about it.'

'Go on, then. Get yourself a drink.'

'I won't be long.'

Mr Jenkins hurried off to the buffet with alacrity and, although Constable Robinson didn't actually stand over them, he was not far off. If they scarpered Joe guessed that one blast of his whistle would bring the other coppers running. And in any case, where would they go? No doubt by the time they got home Aunt Jane would have gone and taken Helen and Elsie with her. Mrs Andrews was a canny body but she wouldn't be able to take them in. And even if she could she probably wouldn't be allowed to keep them.

He turned to look at Danny to see how he was taking it. All their lives Joe had looked out for his younger twin. He wasn't sure how it had started. He couldn't remember ever making a conscious decision. It had just happened. And if Joe was a natural leader, then Danny seemed happy to follow. So it was all the more surprising to see that Danny, without being told, had taken the sandwiches from the bag.

He sensed Joe's glance and looked up and smiled. 'Ham and pease pudding. Just the ticket. Let's eat them now while we're waiting.'

A minute or two later Constable Robinson glanced over and saw the two boys eating as if they hadn't had a good meal for days. He studied them closely. Eleven or twelve, he thought, about the same as his own son Derek. And they were bonny lads, that was for sure, with their attractive young faces topped by a mop of unruly dark blond hair.

By the look of them they had been well cared for. Loved. They both seemed confident although in different ways. One looked ready to take on the world. The other seemed more easy-going, as if prepared to deal calmly with whatever life threw at him.

He wondered how they would settle in Haven House. The establishment wasn't exactly an orphanage. There were boys there who had been taken away from their families for their own good. Founded by a God-fearing industrialist in the last century, the home aimed to educate the lads sufficiently to make them suitable for employment. Although what employment was to be found in these hard times God alone knew.

Nevertheless, while they were there they would be fed and clothed and if there was no mother's love to be had, at least they would be better off than the hopeless youngsters with pinched, malnourished faces who infested the station.

An impulse took Constable Robinson to the newspaper and confectionery kiosk where he bought a bottle of pop.

'Here you are, lads,' he said a moment later. 'Dandelion and burdock to wash your sandwiches down.'

One twin looked up suspiciously but the other smiled with surprise and said, 'Thank you.' He nudged his brother.

'Oh, yes, thanks,' the other lad said. Then added with a formality that belied his years, 'It's very good of you.'

'Well, then, I'll leave you to it,' the policeman said and, as he walked away, he took out his handkerchief and blew his nose, cursing himself for being a sentimental softy.

'Where did you get that?'

Mr Jenkins stood over them frowning accusingly.

Danny, who had just taken a swig from the bottle, gulped and wiped his mouth with the back of his hand.

'Keep your hair on,' Joe said. 'We didn't nick it if that's what you're thinking. Your pal the copper gave it to us.'

Their inquisitor raised his eyebrows and Joe added, 'Go on – ask him.'

Mr Jenkins took the bottle of pop from Danny and turned to seek out Constable Robinson in the crowded concourse. The policeman caught his glance and, seeing the pop bottle held aloft, grinned and gave the thumbs up.

'All right then, I believe you,' Mr Jenkins said. 'But you must learn to speak to me in a more respectful manner.'

Joe stared up at him. This man who had hardly spoken to them since they had left home and who had seemed so mild-mannered as he sat in the front parlour eating their sandwiches and fruit cake might, after all, be tricky to deal with.

'Well, then?' Mr Jenkins said and, as he leaned over him menacingly, Joe smelled the alcohol on his breath.

'Well what?' Joe asked and received a dig in the ribs from Danny. 'Oh, yes,' he mumbled. 'Sorry.'

'Sorry, *sir*.'

'Sorry, *sir*.' Joe tried his best to keep the belligerence from his tone. For Danny's sake he sensed he must not antagonize this man.

'Very well, then. Pack up your sandwiches. We have to get along to the platform.'

Joe and Danny followed Mr Jenkins over the footbridge over the tracks as their train pulled alongside the platform. As the engine passed under the bridge it sent up a jet of steam that made Joe blink. The soot made his eyes water. At least that was what he told himself. He rubbed at them with closed fists and forced back the howl of anguish that would have revealed to the world that he was not as tough as he had thought himself.

'Hurry up,' Danny said softly. 'We'll eat the rest of our sandwiches on the train and pretend it's a picnic like Helen said we should.'

Joe grinned and nodded. The moment had passed. Whatever lay ahead, Danny would need him to look out for him, wouldn't he? And Joe was determined not to fail him.

Hugh stood with his arm round Selma and looked down at the sleeping child. He caught his breath. Just as Selma had told him he would be, he was stunned by her beauty. The soft light from a pink-shaded bedside lamp revealed eyelashes like dark crescents lying on slightly flushed cheeks. One softly rounded arm lay across the rose-pink eiderdown and all that could be seen of the other was a hand lying palm upwards on the pillow beside her face. There was something about her – an odd sense of familiarity – that both puzzled him and stirred his emotions.

The warm glow from the fire in the hearth pervaded the room which Hugh must now learn to call the nursery. He pulled Selma close and she sighed contentedly as she rested her head in the hollow of his shoulder. Her slender body fitted into the curve of his arms and her hair, brushing against his chin, felt as silky as a baby bird's feathers. She smelled of the light floral perfume that suited her so well.

Her happiness was so intense that Hugh thought it could be felt physically. Nevertheless he was uneasy. He had grown used to how impulsive Selma could be. Lost kittens, rescued dogs; over the years all had been welcomed into the household, and then found other homes if they had been troublesome. Now she had brought home a child. He wondered if she understood what a serious matter this was.

Selma pulled away. 'What is it, Hugh? I sense that you are unhappy.'

'No . . . I'm not unhappy.'

'Uneasy, then?'

'A little. I understand your instinct to help the orphaned family, but bringing one of them into our home is quite a responsibility. Are you sure you've done the right thing?'

'Darling, just look at her! What do you see?'

'A very beautiful child.'

Selma turned to look up at him, eyes bright with eager emotion. 'Yes, yes,' she said impatiently. 'But look closely. Who does she remind you of?'

Of course, that was the thought that had been hovering on the fringes of his mind. The child looked like Selma herself. A young, unformed Selma, but with the same fragile bone structure, dark-fringed blue eyes and silky fair hair. 'You,' he breathed.

'Yes, darling. She could be my daughter.'

Hugh caught his breath. 'Selma . . . you're not proposing that we—'

'Adopt her?' Selma's eyes were shining. 'That's exactly what I'm proposing.'

'But we don't know anything about her.'

'Yes, we do. She's nine years old and she's from a perfectly respectable family.'

'Nine?' Hugh was surprised. 'She looks much younger.'

'I know. Isn't she sweet?'

Hugh controlled a spurt of irritation. 'Selma, *sweet* has nothing to do with it. What do we know about her family?'

She smiled. 'I knew you would ask that. I'm not as simple as you seem to think I am.'

'I don't think you're simple. You are impulsive. Sometimes dangerously so.'

'Hush, we might awaken her.' Selma drew away from the bed. 'I had enquiries made about the family. I knew you would ask.'

'Enquiries?'

'I asked old Arthur to find someone.'

'Arthur Garwood? My solicitor?'

'Who else? I told him the matter was urgent and he obliged by putting an enquiry agent on the case.'

Despite himself Hugh had to smile at his wife's choice of words. 'You sound like someone in a movie,' he said. '*On the case*, indeed.'

'Yes, well, he did.'

'And what exactly did you tell Arthur?'

Selma frowned. 'What do you mean?'

'What reason did you give for wanting to know?'

'I told him the truth, of course. He knew about the accident.'

'No one has suggested that John was in any way responsible.'

'Of course not. But it was our car and in some way that does make us responsible for what happens next. I told Arthur that we wanted to help this family so we needed to find out more about them.'

'You didn't mention adoption?'

'Not at that stage.'

'But you have mentioned it since?'

'Well, of course. Once the report came back saying that the Norton family were poor but utterly respectable I did . . .' she faltered, at last sensing that Hugh might deny her her wish. 'Well . . . I did suggest that we . . .' Selma put her hands on his shoulders and looked up at him beseechingly. 'Oh, Hugh, darling, you're not going to say no, are you?'

He returned her look and his own eyes were troubled. 'And if we have a child of our own?'

She shrugged impatiently and her voice hardened. 'Don't worry. In the unlikely event of that happening, you don't think I would stop loving the child, do you?'

Hugh had spoken to Charles Harris after Selma's recent appointment and his old friend had assured him that there was nothing wrong with either of them. Physically, that was. He had suggested that Selma's deep unhappiness about her childless state might actually be preventing her from conceiving. If adopting this child would make her happy, then so be it. Whether or not they eventually had a child of their own, his wife's happiness was of supreme importance to him.

He saw tears welling in her eyes and he pulled her close again. She slipped her arms around his waist and leaned against him for a moment. Then she pulled away just enough to look up into his face.

'Well, then?' she asked softly.

Even though he still doubted the wisdom of it, Hugh capitulated. 'Very well. You shall have your way.' He took her face in his hands and kissed her.

'Oh, darling. You won't regret this. Just think how wonderful Christmas will be!'

'Christmas?'

'Don't look so puzzled. Yes, Christmas! We shall have holly and mistletoe, and paper garlands and the biggest tree we can find. You shall help decorate it and arrange the presents around the base. And we can build a snowman in the garden and go sledging on the Town Moor!'

At this Hugh laughed.

'What is it? What have I said?'

'I can promise you the tree and the presents, my darling, but only God can send the snow.'

'Well, then, we shall just have to pray! I am determined that Elise will have the best Christmas she's ever had.'

Hugh frowned. 'I thought her name was Elsie.'

Selma smiled. 'Yes, it was. But I have decided to change it to Elise. Elise Partington sounds so much more – well, so much more fitting than Elsie Partington, doesn't it? I mean, *Elsie*! That's so old-fashioned and just a little . . . well, just a little common.'

'I don't agree. My favourite great-aunt is called Elsie.'

'I know, Hugh darling, but the old girl is positively antediluvian. Elise is so much more modern.'

'I suppose so.' Hugh looked doubtful but nevertheless he smiled. Then something occurred to him. 'What if the aunt doesn't agree?'

Selma looked puzzled. 'We needn't tell her that we think her name old-fashioned. Why would we?'

'I didn't mean that aunt. I meant the child's aunt. What if she doesn't agree to the adoption? After all, I suppose she must be the legal guardian if she's the only remaining relative.'

'Oh, she'll agree, all right,' Selma said. 'As long as we pay her enough.'

Hugh looked shocked. 'Pay her? We can't buy a child. I'm sure it must be illegal.'

'No, I didn't mean we would buy her. We will give Mrs Roberts a nice little sum of money to help her to look after the older girl – and to compensate her for having to do so.'

Hugh took hold of his wife's arms and stood back a little as he studied her. 'Where did you learn to be so cynical?'

'I'm not cynical, darling. I'm practical. Now, what's the matter?'

'If you have such a low opinion of the woman why are you happy to leave the older girl with her?'

Selma looked troubled for a moment. 'Do you think I should find her a place with a good family?'

'You mean, ask one of our friends if they want to adopt her?'

'Of course not. Helen Norton is fourteen years old. I meant, find a family to take her in as a domestic.'

'A servant?'

'Yes.' Selma frowned. 'I considered it but apparently the girl is doing well at school and wants to stay on. I couldn't bear to make anyone unhappy.' Her brow cleared and she smiled as if she'd solved a knotty problem. 'So it's altogether best that she stay with her aunt.'

'And the boys? Are you sure they'll be happy at Haven House?'

'Of course. They'll be well looked after – especially as you are giving them such a generous donation. It will ensure that they are clothed, fed and educated. Trained to take up some suitable form of employment.'

'So it seems you have it all arranged.'

Selma looked pleased with herself. 'I have.'

'But nevertheless there is something you may not have thought of.'

'What's that?'

'Elise, as I must call her, might have wished to stay with her siblings.'

'I've told you, that is impossible.'

'You could have found them places in an orphanage where they could stay together.'

'There's no such place. The boys would have been separated from the girls. No, no, this is the best way, I assure you.'

'And what if Elise misses her family? What if she wants to see them?'

'Oh, no. I can't have that. For her own sake I want her to forget all about her humble beginnings.'

33

'Do you think that's possible? She is nine years old.'

For a moment Selma's confidence wavered. Then she said determinedly, 'I'll make sure she does. She's had a perfectly horrid time of it since her mother died. Her aunt told me that she had stopped speaking to anyone. Not a word until she spoke to me. I will make her life so wonderful that she will never want to go back.'

'And how will you do that?'

'Oh . . . you know . . . for a start she will be living in this lovely house, she shall have beautiful clothes, go to a good school – my old school, perhaps – riding lessons, piano lessons, dancing, elocution; all the things that a girl from a good family takes for granted.'

'And what if she doesn't want to ride or dance or go to elocution classes?'

Selma thought for a moment then said, 'Well, I wouldn't insist on the riding but I'm sure she will find dancing agreeable and, as for elocution, that I must insist on. Her manner of speech is not as bad as I thought it would be, but now she must learn to talk like one of us.'

Hugh knew it was pointless to argue with Selma. And in any case, although he had not yet admitted it, the idea of adopting this beautiful child was beginning to appeal to him. He stepped away from her and looked slowly round the room.

'Do you think you may have been a little extravagant buying all these toys?'

Selma looked with satisfaction at the doll's house, the baby doll with real blond hair and eyes that opened and closed lying in the hand-carved cradle, the toy tea cups set out on a little table and the Dutch doll and the Stieff bear sitting on the matching chairs. She had chosen them in Fenwick's toy department only the day before and insisted that they must be delivered immediately.

'Of course I haven't been extravagant. When I was a child I had many more playthings than this. This is just a start. Oh, Hugh, what fun it will be for Elise and me to go shopping together.'

Hugh's feeling of unease returned. His wife was like a child herself. Was she ready to be a mother?

Selma placed her hands on his shoulders and raising herself on her toes she kissed him. 'But now we must leave our little girl and go down for dinner,' she said. 'Come quietly, we mustn't disturb her. We'll leave the bedside light on in case she awakens and is frightened.'

When the door closed behind the man and the woman Elsie opened her eyes and sat up in bed. She had been awake all the time but had lain with her eyes closed trying to make sense of what they had been saying to each other. She realized that the beautiful lady who had brought her here wanted her to stay and that the man had not been entirely happy about it. That made her anxious.

She looked around the room, so comforting in the gentle glow from the fire. She couldn't remember ever being as warm and cosy as this. The bedroom she shared with Helen in her old house had a fireplace, but for as long as she could remember there had never been a fire in it. Their mother would warm their nightdresses over a fireguard by the kitchen range and after a wash at the kitchen sink they would pull them on hastily and hurry upstairs. Once in the bed they shared they pulled the bedclothes over themselves as quickly as they could. On cold nights Helen would cuddle her to keep her warm.

Helen . . . Elsie wondered briefly why the lady hadn't brought Helen here as well. Then she remembered. When they had first arrived at this house she had been asleep, but she had woken up as she was being carried upstairs. In her bewilderment she had called out, 'Helen – where's Helen?'

'Hush, darling,' the lady had whispered. 'Helen is going to live with your Aunt Jane, and she told me that she wants me to look after you.'

'Did she?'

'Yes, and that's exactly what I'm going to do.'

After that Elsie was taken to a bathroom. At home a tin bath was kept under the kitchen bench and on bath night it was dragged out and placed before the range, then her mother or Helen would fill it up with kettlefuls of hot water. Here the lady simply turned on taps. She had poured pink bath salts into the water from a pretty glass jar with the picture of a rose on the front.

Elsie knew about bath salts. Last Christmas they had all saved their pennies and given them to Helen, who had bought some at the chemist shop on the corner. She had bought them loose in a paper bag and put them in an old jam jar, then put on the lid and tied a pink ribbon round it. That had been their Christmas present to their mother.

'Look, darling,' the lady said as she swirled the bath salts around and made pretty pink patterns in the warm water.

Then another lady appeared. She was much older and wore a black dress. At first Elsie thought she might be the lady's grandmother but decided she couldn't be when she asked, 'Do you need any help, madam?'

The conversation that followed had been confusing, mainly because the lady seemed to have muddled up her name with another little girl. A girl whose name was Elise.

'No, that's all right, Mrs Reynolds. I shall bathe Elise myself. However, you can take these clothes away.'

'Do you want them laundered?'

'No. She won't need them any more. Elise is going to start a whole new life here.'

'Very well, madam.'

Elsie thought that Mrs Reynolds pursed her lips and shook her head but her lady didn't notice.

'And tell Susan to bring the tray up in about ten minutes' time.'

After her bath Elsie was dried in a huge soft towel and dressed in a pretty nightdress with a pattern of little rosebuds. The lady looked at her critically and then smiled. 'A perfect fit,' she said. 'I had to guess your size when I ordered your new clothes so I only bought a few essentials. Oh, Elise, darling, we shall have such fun shopping together!' She paused and then asked, 'Why are you frowning? Don't you like your new nightgown?'

'Oh, yes, I do. It's lovely. It's just that my name isn't Elise, you know. It's Elsie.'

The lady smiled. 'I know, my pet, but I decided that as you are going to start a new life you should have a new name and Elise is such a pretty name, don't you think?'

'I suppose so.'

'Well, then, Elise it shall be. Now what is it?'

The lady's smile faded and Elsie found herself desperately wanting to bring it back. 'It's just . . . just that I don't know what to call you.'

'Ah . . . for the moment you should call me Mrs Partington, but soon I hope you will want to call me something else.'

She gave Elsie no time to question her further. She held her hand and led her along a softly carpeted corridor to the room where she lay now.

'I know it's not really bedtime,' she said, 'but you have

had a tiring day. We'll sit by the fire and have milk and bread and butter, and would you like some biscuits?'

'Chocolate biscuits?'

Mrs Partington laughed. 'Of course. That's what I promised you, isn't it?'

A moment later a young woman in a grey dress and a white pinafore appeared with a tray. She laid it on a small table near the fireplace.

'Eat your fill, sweetheart,' Mrs Partington said, 'and then I shall read you a story.' She gestured towards a small bookcase. 'Those are my books,' she said. 'I've had them since I was a child, and now I shall give them to you.'

Elsie looked at the books and for a moment the beautiful room, the comfortable chairs and the warm fire faded as she remembered Helen reading to her by torchlight as they huddled under the bedclothes to keep warm. She remembered that they had been halfway through the latest book that Helen had borrowed from the library. 'Have you got *The Secret Garden*?' she asked.

'Why yes, I have! Do you like that book?'

'I do.'

'How wonderful! That was one of my favourites when I was a little girl. Oh, Elise darling, I see we shall get on famously.'

After she had finished her supper Mrs Partington drew Elsie on to her knee and began to read to her and, although she was interested in the story, the warmth and the confusing events of the day made her yawn.

'Bed for you, my pet,' Mrs Partington said. 'But I promise you I shall go on with the story tomorrow.'

Elsie had been settled amongst the soft pillows and covered with sheets that smelled of lavender, and a silken eiderdown. Mrs Partington leaned over and kissed her brow. 'Go to sleep, little one,' she said and Elsie, wanting to please her, had closed her eyes obediently.

She had heard the door open and she thought Mrs Partington was leaving but instead she'd heard another voice. A man's voice. He and Mrs Partington stood near the bed and talked together then they moved away a little. What she'd heard of the conversation had made Elsie more confused than ever.

Now as she gazed around the room she could hardly believe the pretty lady wanted her to stay here with her. And Helen? What of Helen? Mrs Partington had told her that her sister wanted her to look after her, so it must be all right. Helen would never send her to anywhere where she might be unhappy. She wondered if she would see Helen soon and tell her how lovely this was.

Elsie yawned. She wanted to lie down and go to sleep but there was something missing. Maisie. Maisie the doll that Helen had made for her from a pair of old socks. She had stuffed the socks with scraps of material, embroidered a smiling mouth on the face and sewn on two blue buttons for the eyes. Maisie's plaited hair had been made from yellow wool and her dress from a piece of blue and white gingham left over from the kitchen curtains. Elsie took Maisie to bed with her every night.

Where was she? Surely Helen wouldn't have let her leave without Maisie? Elsie got out of bed and looked all around the room. She even looked under the bed but Maisie wasn't there. She would have to go and ask Mrs Partington. She opened the door hesitantly, stepped out on to the landing and almost bumped into Susan, the young woman who had brought her supper on a tray.

'Goodness, child, where are you going?'

Elsie looked up at her fearfully to see whether she was

cross. She was relieved to discover that Susan was smiling.

'I'm looking for Maisie.'

Susan frowned. 'There isn't a Maisie in this house.'

'Maisie is my doll. Didn't she come with me?'

'No, there was no doll. Just you.'

'Oh.' Elsie thought for a moment. 'Then I'll have to go home and get her.'

'Well, not tonight you're not. Now come along. Let's put you back to bed. It's a good job I came up to collect that tray or you'd be wandering about and making people cross.'

'Would Mrs Partington be cross with me?'

'No, I don't suppose so. But Mrs Reynolds would be.' She saw Elsie's look of puzzlement and continued, 'Mrs Reynolds is the housekeeper and she's an old termagant.'

Elsie remembered Mrs Reynolds. She was the older lady dressed in black who had come into the bathroom. She wasn't sure what a termagant was but she suspected it wasn't very nice.

Susan looked around the room. 'If you want to take a doll to bed with you how about this one?' She took the baby doll from the cradle then frowned and put it back again. 'Perhaps not. If it fell out of bed its pretty china face might break. What about Gretel, here?' She picked up the wooden doll dressed like a little Dutch girl.

Elsie looked at the doll solemnly. 'She wouldn't be very cuddly, would she?'

'I suppose not. Well, how about the teddy bear?'

Elsie nodded.

'Right. Back into bed with you. I'll tuck you in.'

Susan built up the fire a little and placed a cinder guard before the fireplace. 'Night, night,' she said. Then she picked up the tray and left the room, closing the door after her.

Elsie pulled the teddy bear towards her and discovered that it was not at all cuddly. It might have nice silky fur but its limbs and body were stiff. She pushed it away from her and hoped that it wouldn't be too long before she was reunited with Maisie.

Chapter Three

Aunt Jane led the way upstairs. Helen noticed how she had to grip the banister rail and that she was out of breath by the time they reached the top. Her aunt opened one of the bedroom doors and stood back to allow Helen to enter. 'This is your room. Unpack your things then come down for a bite of supper. And get that look off your face. You'd think you'd be over the moon to have a lovely room to yourself in a house like this.' Not waiting for an answer she hurried along the landing and down the stairs.

Helen put her suitcase down, looked around and saw nothing that was lovely. The faded oversized cabbage roses on the wallpaper made the small room look even smaller. The matching curtains didn't quite reach the windowsill. Helen guessed they must have shrunk in the wash, and judging by the whiff of household soap they hadn't been rinsed properly.

She pushed the net curtain aside and looked out into the shadowy street of semi-detached houses. Streetlamps shed pools of light on the pavement between the bare-branched trees. Low brick walls and neat privet hedges enclosed small gardens. Porch lights above some of the front doors shone a welcome for people arriving home from work. This was what was known as a respectable suburb. It was only a few miles away and yet it was so different from the rows of old houses tumbling down the steep hill towards the river where Helen had been born and spent all her life so far.

She had been happy there. Her mother had kept their small house clean and warm. She had seen to it that there was always sufficient coal, at least for the fire in the kitchen range if not the parlour, and enough pennies for the meter so that the gas lamps could shed their warm glow on a winter night. Helen shivered. Her aunt's house was cold and this room above the porch probably the coldest in it. The electric light with its dim bulb and frosted glass shade did nothing to disperse the chill.

Smoky mist had begun to curl its way along the avenue and the houses opposite became vague outlines. Somehow they looked less solid, suggesting to Helen's overwrought senses that this was only a dream. She stared out for a moment longer and then sighed. This wasn't a dream; she wasn't going to wake up and find her mother presiding over the teapot at the kitchen table and her brothers, her sister and herself eating bread and jam and talking about what had happened at their different schools that day.

Helen drew the curtains. She turned to face the room and tried to take in the reality of her new life. The single bed was pushed up against one wall and an old-fashioned wardrobe took up most of the wall opposite leaving only a narrow space between. The wardrobe must once have stood in a much larger room. The matching chest of drawers squeezed in between the wardrobe and the window was equally clumsy and just as hideous. An old mirror, the silver spotted, hung above the chest and reflected the picture opposite.

Helen turned and looked at the picture of two rosy winged cherubs suspended in a blue sky dotted with fluffy white clouds. They were holding a garland of flowers between them. She knew the picture to be overly sentimental but nevertheless it brought an ache of grief to her throat. Her mother, her gentle, tender-hearted mother, would have loved it. She was surprised that it had found a home in Aunt Jane's gloomy house. The paintings she had glimpsed in the entrance hall and on the dark panelled walls as she ascended the stairs were of sailing ships ploughing through stormy seas, and murky landscapes peopled with men in Highland dress and alarmed-looking stags.

She looked down at the suitcase that had been her mother's. It was dark blue with a soft leather top. It was old and battered but it must have been expensive once. The case had been a present from one of the ladies Helen's mother worked for and it had not been empty. The lady had filled it with clothes she no longer wanted. Her mother had been thrilled to own such fashionable garments even though they were second-hand. Helen knew that Aunt Jane had commandeered any of the clothes that had caught her fancy although heaven knew what they would look like on her shapeless form.

Helen lifted the case on to the faded green eiderdown that covered the bed, opened it and began to unpack. It didn't take long. Her underwear, socks, jumpers and blouses only filled three drawers of the chest and her few skirts and dresses hung forlornly in the cavernous space of the wardrobe. She took particular care of her school uniform, smoothing the gymslip and shaking out a school shirt to drape over a hanger.

She remembered how proud her mother had been when at the age of eleven she had passed the scholarship that would take her to the grammar school. Aunt Jane had disapproved. She had told her sister that Helen should remain at the elementary school, leave when she was fourteen then find a job. In Aunt Jane's opinion Helen ought to find a job as soon as she could and bring some money in, rather than cause her mother the extra expense of buying the uniform and books that were needed.

But Grace Norton had refused to listen to her elder sister. She'd told her that with a proper education Helen would one day find a much better job and it was worth every effort to keep her on at school.

'And what if the twins pass the scholarship, too?' Aunt Jane had asked. 'How will you manage then?'

'I'll manage somehow,' Grace had replied, but Helen could see how worried she was.

As it happened she had not had to face that problem. Even though Joe and Danny were far from stupid they had failed to gain a scholarship. 'Don't worry, Mrs Norton,' the headmaster had reassured her. 'When the time comes we'll find them good apprenticeships. They'll be a credit to you yet.'

And what would their future be now? Helen wondered. Would the superintendant of Haven House make sure they found good apprenticeships once they reached the age of fourteen? She could only hope so. In the meantime she would keep in touch with them and supply any encouragement that was needed.

After she had put her clothes away Helen took her school satchel out of the case and stowed it in the bottom of the wardrobe. Then she lifted out her precious supply of books. Some of them were her own, bought with her pocket money from the second-hand book stall in the Grainger Market, and two of them had been borrowed from the library. She intended to take the library books back even though she had not finished reading *The Secret Garden*. She knew she couldn't bear to go on with it now that she couldn't share it with Elsie. She looked around for somewhere to put the books and decided to keep them on top of the chest. Perhaps her aunt might have a pair of bookends.

She stared down into the suitcase. The lining was of maroon silk and there was an elasticated pocket sewn along the back. Helen reached into the pocket and took out the doll she had made from a pair of socks. After Mrs Partington had taken Elsie away Helen had gone up to the bedroom she had shared with her small sister to collect her own things and had been distressed to find Maisie on the floor.

She had run downstairs to show her aunt. 'Can we send this to Elsie?' she'd asked.

Aunt Jane had looked at her scornfully. 'Don't be silly. What would Elsie want with that old thing now that she can have any toy she wants? Just throw it away.'

But Helen hadn't thrown it away. She had put Maisie in her case. She was sure that no matter how many new toys Elsie had she would want her doll and, somehow, she would find a way to get it to her. She put Maisie in one of the empty drawers of the chest and closed the suitcase.

She looked around for somewhere to store it. The logical place was on top of the wardrobe but she couldn't reach that far. So she kneeled down and slid the case under the bed. As she rose to her feet there was a knock on the door. Surprised, Helen opened it to find a tall, sallow-faced girl standing there. She didn't look much older than Helen herself but she was wearing a grubby white apron over a grey woollen dress and a white cap was clipped to her lank brown hair. Helen had not known that Aunt Jane had a maid.

'The missus says are you coming down?' the girl asked. 'I've taken a tray in to your aunt but you're to have summat in the kitchen with me before I go home. I'm Eva by the way.'

'Oh – I'm pleased to meet you, Eva. I'm Helen.'

The girl sniffed. 'I know your name. Now, are you coming? I want to get away home.' She turned and began to walk away.

Helen couldn't make up her mind whether Eva had been pleased to welcome her or not. Her words had been polite enough but there had been no smile. She followed her aunt's maid down the stairs. The doors of the rooms downstairs were all closed except for the one which led into the kitchen at the back of the house.

'Hawway in and shut the door,' Eva said. 'The missus goes mad if any cooking smells get into the rest of the house, and she had a nice pair of kippers for her tea. Kippers and brown bread and butter – but don't think that's what you're going to get.'

Helen closed the door quickly and looked around the kitchen. It was surprisingly small, but a half-open door on the far wall gave a glimpse of a scullery. A fire burned in the range and a pulley clothes airer hung from the ceiling. An electric light hung above a table covered in blue-and-white checked oilcloth. The table was set with tea plates and cups and saucers for two.

'I take it you divven't mind sitting down with me?' Eva said challengingly.

'Of course not.' Helen surveyed the table which was otherwise bare and added, 'Can I help you?'

'Help me? What do you mean?'

'Make the tea?'

The maid laughed. 'I divven't need help to spread margarine on a few slices of bread but you can make a pot of tea for us, if you like. You'll find everything you need on the dresser and the kettle's boiling on the range. The milk's in the larder back there.' Eva nodded towards the scullery.

Bread and margarine, Helen thought. Not much of a

supper. She wondered if there would be any jam. There wasn't. But before Eva sat down she said, 'There's a bit of cheese left, if you like.'

'Yes, please.'

'It's nothing fancy, mind. It's what me ma calls best mousetrap.' Eva actually smiled when she said this. She produced a lump of orange cheese wrapped in greaseproof paper and set it down next to the plate of bread and margarine. 'We'll not bother with a cheese dish. There's only you and me.'

The two girls sat silently while they ate, neither knowing what to say to the other.

As Eva poured herself a second cup of tea she asked, 'That won't give you nightmares, will it?'

Helen looked puzzled.

'Eating cheese before you go to bed.'

'I shouldn't think so.'

Helen didn't realize how despondent she must have sounded so she was taken by surprise when Eva's attitude seemed to soften. 'Lost yer ma, haven't you?' she said.

'Yes.'

'I'm really sorry for you. But at least your aunt's taken you in. No matter what she's like it must be better than an orphanage.'

The girl sounded truly sympathetic, which was probably why Helen blurted out, 'But that's not the worst of it!'

'What do you mean?'

'There are four of us. I've a sister and two brothers. We've never ever been apart, ever in our lives, and now I just don't know when I'll see them again.'

Eva was silent. The fire crackled in the hearth and the kettle hissed gently on the range. She reached for the teapot and topped up Helen's cup. 'There you are, pet,' she said.

'Help yourself to sugar. Now, if you don't mind I'll have to go. I've stayed late because of you.'

'I'm sorry.'

'Divven't be. The moment I get home I'll have to start work again helping with me young sisters and brothers.' Helen choked back a sob and Eva said, 'I shouldn't hev said that. I opened me mouth and put me foot in it, didn't I?'

'It's all right.'

Eva reached for her coat which was hanging on the back of the door. When she was ready she said, 'Look, I'm going to take the rest of the cheese home. You won't say anything, will you?'

'Of course not.'

'And would you mind clearing up and washing the dishes? The missus said that you were to help me.'

'No, I don't mind.'

'I'll be off, then.'

'Wait!' Helen looked up at the older girl. 'What am I supposed to do?'

'What do you mean?'

'After you've gone. Am I supposed to sit here in the kitchen until I go to bed?'

Eva looked troubled. 'I don't know. Mrs Roberts never told me. When you go in for her tray you'd best ask her.'

'Her tray?'

'Aye. She'll be finished her meal by now. She said you could wash up.'

Helen tried to take in all this new information and suddenly felt overwhelmed. Eva looked troubled so Helen tried to smile. 'You'd better go. Your mother will be waiting.'

'You'll be all right?'

'Yes.'

49

'Goodnight, then. I'll see you first thing in the morning.'

Eva put the cheese in her bag. A moment later Helen heard the back door closing behind her. She sat and sipped her tea, staring out of the window which the dark sky had turned into a mirror to reflect the room. She was not used to being completely alone like this. Even the reflection of the fire did not cheer her. The house was deathly quiet; so unlike the cheerful hubbub of home.

But that much-loved house wasn't home any more; not to Helen nor to her sister and brothers. From the dreadful moment she had learned of her mother's fatal accident Helen had tried to remain strong for the sake of the younger children but now that her family had been torn asunder and she was completely alone she found she could no longer contain her anguish. She pushed aside the plates on the table, lowered her head on to her arms and wept until her throat ached.

Eventually her sobs subsided. Her head was aching and she felt slightly feverish. She became aware once more of the crackle of coals and the ticking of the clock on the mantelpiece but she did not hear the kitchen door open, and it wasn't until she felt a cold draught of air on her back and saw a shadow fall across the table that she realized someone had entered the kitchen.

Helen's hair had fallen forward and she pushed it back from her face as she raised her head to find her aunt staring down at her. Aunt Jane's expression was unfathomable. Helen wiped the tears away with the back of her hand. It must have been obvious how distressed she was but there was no sympathy forthcoming.

'I can see you're tired, Helen,' her aunt said. 'Perhaps you'd better go up to bed – after you've washed the dishes, that is. You'll find mine on the tray in the sitting room. Come, I'll show you.'

Wordlessly Helen rose and followed her aunt to a room at the front of the house. She looked around the over-furnished room with surprise. She had not expected such an austere individual as her aunt to indulge in creature comforts, but the carpet was thick, the velvet-covered settee and easy chairs well padded and the matching maroon and gold curtains overpoweringly luxurious for a small sitting room. A fire blazed in the hearth set into a fireplace decorated with exotically patterned tiles and the mantelpiece was crowded with what Helen guessed to be Dresden figurines.

Helen became aware that Aunt Jane was staring at her expectantly. She realized that her aunt was waiting for her to say something. She hesitated, not knowing quite what was expected.

'Well?' Aunt Jane said, her arms folded over her body. 'What do you think?'

'Of the room?'

'Of course of the room! Have you ever seen anything like it before?'

'No.'

'So?'

'It's . . . very nice.'

'Very nice? Is that all you can manage? You with your superior education?'

Helen thought the room suffocating and unappealing but decided she should keep that opinion to herself. But neither would she express an admiration she did not feel. 'It's . . . opulent,' she said, deciding that that didn't necessarily mean she approved.

Aunt Jane narrowed her eyes and looked at Helen suspiciously. Helen adapted an expression of wide-eyed wonder and had to control an urge to laugh when she realized that Aunt Jane had no idea what the word meant.

51

She frowned and pursed her lips. 'Well, then, there's the tray,' she said, pointing to a low table that stood by one of the armchairs. 'When you've washed the dishes you can make cocoa for us and bring it in.'

When Helen returned Aunt Jane was sitting by the fire flicking through a magazine. 'Just put my cup down on this little table,' she said. 'But haven't you made one for yourself?'

'I have. But I wasn't sure whether I was supposed to sit in here with you.'

'Of course you can. It will be a real treat for you. Bring your cup in and sit by the fire for a while before you go to bed.'

She did as she was told, thinking that perhaps her aunt wanted to talk to her. But Aunt Jane didn't even look up from her magazine when she came back into the room. Apparently just being here was a privilege. Helen sat by the fire gratefully enough but she felt entirely out of place and longed for home. As soon as she had finished her drink she rose and said, 'I'm very tired, I think I'll go to bed.'

Aunt Jane looked up as though she had forgotten Helen's existence. 'Oh, of course,' she said. 'You can wash these cups before you go up, and do you know how to see to the fire in the range? Build it up just enough to make sure it keeps going through the night so that there will be hot water in the morning.'

'Yes, I can do that.'

'And put the milk bottles out.'

It didn't take Helen long to wash the cups. She rinsed the pint and the half-pint milk bottles and put them out on the front doorstep. Then uncertainly she opened the door to the sitting room. 'Goodnight, Aunt Jane,' she said.

Her aunt didn't even look up from her magazine. 'Goodnight, Helen.'

Upstairs was cold and the air felt slightly damp. Helen found her way to the bathroom and got into her pyjamas as quickly as she could, but as soon as she was in bed she realized that no matter how tired she was she was not going to be able to sleep. She wondered if her sister and brothers were sleeping, or were they lying awake like she was?

Joe and Danny . . . were the beds in the home warm and comfortable? Was the food good? Had the other boys there welcomed them? And did anyone care if they were happy or not? But at least the twins had each other. They had never been separated since they were born. They had always been in the same class at school and had always sat next to each other in the classroom. And Joe . . . Joe was resourceful and good-hearted. He would always look out for Danny and in doing so would always make the best of things.

And what of Elsie? There was no doubt that she would be warm and comfortable tonight. The Partingtons' house must be truly luxurious. As she grew she would be well nourished, well dressed and lovingly cared for. Elsie was young enough to adapt to her new life. But Helen prayed that in doing so her little sister would not forget her real home and how happy she had been there. Mrs Partington would be kind to her, would love her, and for that Helen was grateful, but she was afraid that Elsie would forget all the wonderful times they had had when their mother was alive.

Helen thought back to the summer days when they would take the train to the seaside and have a picnic on the beach. And how their mother, like a child herself, would take off her shoes and stockings and paddle with them, dodging the incoming waves and laughing if she got caught. And the winter nights sitting together by the fire and looking for pictures made by the burning coals.

Elsie had never known their father; he had succumbed to Spanish flu before she was born. Richard Norton had been a tall, good-looking man but he had never been strong. He was fit only for clerical work but he had always done his best for his wife and children and he had been a kind and loving father. Helen wondered if the boys remembered him. They had been barely walking when he died but he had happily crawled along the floor with them, playing with their toys and minding them when their mother left the house for the cleaning job she had in a department store each evening.

And now their mother had gone. Helen wondered if what they told the children at Sunday school was true. Had her parents met up in heaven and were they looking down on their children now? If they were, surely their mother's heart would break to see them separated like this.

We were so happy, Helen thought. I will cherish those memories all my life. But what about Joe and Danny and Elsie – particularly Elsie? As the years go by will they forget? I can't let that happen, Helen thought. No matter that we have been parted, I must find a way to bring us all together again. And until then I must remember every little detail of our life together.

Shivering in the damp air, Helen got out of bed and switched on the light. Her schoolbag contained a pack of exercise books that her mother had bought for her at Woolworths. She took one of the books and a pencil, got back into bed and, sitting hunched against the pillow and with her knees up, she began to write.

Chapter Four

Joe had not found it easy to get to sleep. All his life he had shared a bed with Danny, and even though this had become more and more uncomfortable as they grew, given a bed of his own he felt as though he had lost a limb. But sheer exhaustion had claimed him and he had been sleeping deeply until a moment ago. Surely it couldn't be morning? He stirred reluctantly and opened his eyes only to close them again immediately. A bright light shone in his face, hurting his eyes, and all around the source of light there was darkness.

'What the—' he began.

'Shut up!' someone whispered urgently and the light dipped, vanished for a moment then swivelled round to reveal a face barely a foot away from his own. 'It's me, Ginger. I was on your table at supper, remember?' The boy moved the torch down until it no longer glared in either of their faces and just gave enough light for them to see each other, a small pool of light in the shadowy vastness of the dormitory.

Joe's heart was pounding from the sudden awakening. He stared nervously at the thin, freckled face topped by a mop of ginger curls. The boy grinned and Joe relaxed a little but remained wary. 'What do you want?' he asked.

'Just a chat. Which one are you?'

'What are you talking about?'

Ginger grinned. 'I've told you, keep your voice down. You know what I mean. You must have been asked it a hundred times or more. Are you Joe or are you Danny?'

'Why do you want to know?'

A spasm of irritation drew Ginger's brows together. 'Because I like to know who I'm talking to, that's why.'

'And why do you want to talk to me in the middle of the night?'

'I just want to fill you in about one or two things you should know if you want to keep out of trouble. I want to help you and your brother.'

'Why should you want to help us?'

'God knows. And do you know what? I've gone right off the idea. I'm going back to bed before I catch me death. It's bloody freezing in here.' He turned to walk away.

'No – wait,' Joe breathed. 'I'm sorry. Stay and talk. Tell me things I ought to know.'

Ginger came back. He was obviously of a forgiving nature. 'Well, for a start, was it you who took that last bit of cake?'

'It was mine.'

'Makes no difference. Don't ever cross Tod Walker. He likes to think he's the boss round here.'

'You're kidding, right?'

'Why should I be kidding?'

'Because he's just a big dozy lump.'

Ginger drew his breath in and shook his head. 'Don't be fooled by the look of him. He may look like Billy Bunter but he's no fat owl. He's as strong as an ox and surprisingly quick on his feet. Like I said, keep out of his way and try not to annoy him or he could make it difficult for you. There's a bunch of them will do anything he tells them.'

Joe peered at Ginger and saw that he was in earnest. 'OK,' he said. 'Now what else should I know?'

'Mr Jenkins. He looks harmless enough and most of the time he is. But after he's had one of his secret tipples he's mean-tempered and vicious.'

'Yeah, I think I've already worked that out.'

'Have you?' Ginger looked puzzled.

'He was as nice as ninepence when he came to collect us but then he had a drink at the station bar and he turned sour.'

Ginger nodded. 'There you are then.'

'Anything else?'

'Nothing major. But if you keep on my right side I'll see you're OK.'

'Thanks, pal. Good of you to bother. Let's shake on it.'

Ginger looked at him quizzically then said, 'Are you taking the mick?'

'Nah, why should I?'

'I dunno. There's something about you. And you still haven't told me which one you are.'

Joe grinned. 'You'll work it out.'

'You mean there's a way to tell the difference?'

'Yep, but if you figure it out don't let on to anyone else, OK?'

Ginger looked at him searchingly for a moment and then returned his grin. 'OK.'

'Now go back to bed and let me sleep. I'm fair whacked.'

Keeping his torch pointed down at the floor, Ginger left without further comment and made his way across the dormitory to the bed opposite Joe's. Joe heard the bedsprings creak and a rustle of bedclothes. Then all was silent. He lay back and tried to sleep but the talk with Ginger had unsettled him.

When they had arrived at Haven House Mr Jenkins had taken them straight to the headmaster's study. After he had knocked and received the summons to enter he had ushered them into a book-lined room with a large desk dominating the floor space. A thin scarecrow of a man stood warming his backside at the fire. He looked at them over the top of half-moon spectacles perched near the end of his nose.

'Ah, yes, the Norton boys,' Mr Ridley said, 'Joseph and Daniel.' He paused as if trying to remember what he should say next. 'Um – I hope you will be happy here. If you work hard and follow the rules there is no reason why you should not be.' And then the air of geniality gave way to stern admonition. 'But if you are disobedient and cause trouble of any kind you will be dealt with accordingly.'

Joe had not been sure exactly what that meant but he didn't think it would be pleasant.

Mr Ridley cleared his throat. 'But I'm – ah – sure that any boys recommended by Mr Partington will fit in here admirably.' After bestowing a vague smile the headmaster seemed to lose track of things again. 'Now then, Mr Jenkins, what shall we do with them? Have they missed supper?'

'No, sir, the boys are just going in.'

'Well – ah – that's good.'

Mr Ridley walked over to his desk looking relieved that everything was settled, and Mr Jenkins shepherded them out and shut the door behind them. 'I'll take you up to your dormitory first,' he said. 'Just leave your bundles on your beds. You can stow your things in your lockers later.'

They hadn't had much time to take in the long, high-ceilinged room and the narrow, iron-framed beds before Mr Jenkins hurried them down to the dining room, found places for them at one of the long tables, introduced them perfunctorily – 'Joseph and Daniel Norton' – then abandoned them. The boys already seated there looked at them curiously. Joe heard someone mutter, 'Peas in a pod', but no one spoke to them until a red-haired lad with a freckled face pushed a plate of bread and butter across the table towards them.

'Help yourselves,' he said. 'It's butter, not marge. You can have as much as you want. You can even ask for more up at the hatch there, but there's only one piece of cake each.'

Despite the sandwiches they had eaten on the train, both Joe and Danny had healthy appetites and they began to eat thick slices of bread and butter while a woman in a white overall came round the table with a large enamel jug and filled everyone's beaker with warm milk.

'Ugh,' the ginger-top said. 'I hate warm milk.'

'You don't know how lucky you are,' the woman retorted. 'Think of all those poor starving children in China.'

'I do think about them,' he replied. 'I've thought and thought but I still don't know how me drinking warm milk can help them.'

The lads each side of him giggled and the woman shook her head and moved on. No one spoke very much and if they did they kept their voices down. A young man in a shabby suit whom Joe presumed to be one of the teachers walked up and down the room to make sure everyone was behaving. Soon the woman in the white overall came round again and placed plates of sliced cake at intervals on the tables.

As they finished their bread and butter the other boys began to reach for the cake. Soon there were only two slices left on the nearest plate and Joe made sure that Danny got a piece before reaching for his own.

'That's mine,' a wheezy voice said. 'Pass it over.'

Joe looked across the table and saw an overweight, pasty-looking boy sitting a little further down. There was already a piece of cake on the boy's plate. 'You've got a piece,' Joe said. 'This is mine.'

He heard an intake of breath and was aware that the boys nearest to him had stopped talking. The fat lad scowled but didn't say anything so Joe ate his cake and didn't think any more about it at the time.

Back in the dormitory Joe and Danny had hardly unpacked their belongings, stowing them in their bedside lockers, when the same teacher who had patrolled the dining room came in and called, 'Lights out in five minutes. If you want the bathroom be quick about it.'

There had been a scramble and soon everyone was in bed. After lights out there was some subdued whispering and Joe realized that Danny had hardly spoken since they had arrived at Haven House.

'You all right, Danny?' he'd said quietly.

'Yep. What about you?'

'Yeah – I think we'll be OK here.'

Now, reflecting on his talk with Ginger, he realized he had said that to reassure his brother. He wasn't sure if it was true. He'd already taken Mr Jenkins' measure. The headmaster was a strange one but Joe didn't think he'd be too much of a problem, there was enough food and the beds were clean and reasonably comfortable, so all in all he couldn't figure out why he felt so uneasy.

When Helen woke up she knew she had been dreaming but all that remained of the dream was a profound feeling of loss. She had no idea what time it was but faint noises from downstairs told her that someone was up and stirring. She got up, made her bed and washed and dressed hurriedly before going downstairs, taking her coat and her schoolbag with her. Eva was in the kitchen seeing to the fire in the range. She turned her head and looked over her shoulder as Helen entered.

'My, you're up early,' she said. 'It's just past seven. If you expect me to make your breakfast you'll have to wait until I've seen to this fire.'

'That's all right. I can get my own breakfast.'

'Suit yourself.' Eva shrugged and turned her attention back to the range.

Helen watched her for a moment and then said, 'What am I to have?'

Eva sat back on her heels, wiped her forehead with the back of an arm, and sticking out her lower lip she blew upwards to shift a stray lock of hair. 'Whatever you like,' she said, then noticing Helen's perplexity she grinned. 'What do you usually have?'

'Depends – depended on what we had in the pantry. Porridge, bread and dripping, toast, a cup of Bovril, tea . . .'

'Well, you could have any of those, even the porridge if you can be bothered to make it yourself and if you make it with water. I usually has a thick slice of bread and dripping myself. I'll join you as soon as I've washed me hands.'

'You have breakfast here?'

'Aye, all me meals. That works out cheaper for her than paying me a respectable wage.'

Eva rose to her feet as the kettle began to boil. 'I'll make us a pot of tea. You go and get the milk and for God's sake be quiet. There'll be hell to pay if you wakes her up.'

Helen slipped her school coat over the back of a chair and tucked her schoolbag underneath it. She heeded Eva's warning as she tiptoed through the gloomy hall to the front door. The milk was waiting on the step. Back in the kitchen she found that Eva had already placed the teapot on the table and was reaching for cups and plates from the dresser.

'What's it to be then?' the older girl said.

'I'll have the same as you.'

'Go on then – get the dripping from the pantry in the scullery. There's a new loaf in the bread bin, I always buys it on the way to work, but it's not for us. Bring what's left of yesterday's.'

The two girls sat companionably at the table. The tea was hot and sweet and the jelly at the bottom of the bowl of dripping was rich and dark. 'Put plenty pepper on,' Eva said. 'I do.'

When they had finished Helen rose and carried her dishes to the sink. 'Leave them,' Eva said. 'You'd best get off to school. It will be a long walk for you, won't it?'

'Yes . . .' Helen put her coat on, picked up her bag then hesitated at the door.

'What is it?'

'What am I supposed to do at lunchtime?'

'Oh – I quite forgot. The missus says you're not to come home and she's left you ninepence to get a pie or something at the nearest baker's shop.'

'Ninepence?'

Eva raised her eyebrows. 'What's wrong with that? Ninepence is far too much for a bit lunch, if you ask my opinion. Not that it's any of my business.'

'No, you don't understand – I'm not complaining. It's just – well – I'm surprised.'

'Here . . .' Eva rose from the table and crossed to the dresser. She opened one of the drawers and took out a sixpence and a threepenny bit. 'It's a good job you asked. Sorry,' she added a little awkwardly as she gave Helen the coins. 'Mrs Roberts will give you the same every school day – and I must say, the old skinflint's being very generous for a change. I don't know what's come over her. But after all, you are family and she wouldn't want people to think she was neglecting you. If anyone ever asked, that is.'

Helen would have liked to say that the only person who might ask was their old neighbour Mrs Andrews and that was unlikely. Furthermore she didn't feel a bit like family. However she just smiled her thanks and slipped the coins into her pocket.

'You'd better go out the back door,' Eva told her. 'Can't have the sound of the front door closing and waking her majesty up.' Suddenly she gave a genuine smile. 'To tell you the truth, the hour or two I have to myself in the mornings is the only good thing about this job. Keeps me sane.' Suddenly she looked rueful. 'There's never any peace and quiet at home, you know. Last week I actually missed coming here, especially as I didn't get paid, but she said she didn't need me while she was at your place.'

'I'm sorry.'

'There's no need to be. It was hardly your fault. Now get away with you or you'll be late for school. Oh, hang on a minute – how did she manage?'

'Manage?'

'Your aunt – with the cooking and the cleaning?'

'I did the cleaning and as for my aunt's cooking . . . well . . . I suppose she must be out of practice.'

'Nuff said!'

The two girls grinned at each other and Helen left for school.

It was just past eight o'clock and the school bell would ring at quarter to nine. In the past Helen's walk to the girls' grammar school had taken about ten minutes but now she had much further to go. The air was chill and damp and it was still quite dark. As she sped along the suburban avenues the streetlamps went off, leaving the way ahead smoky with mist. Helen could hear the footfalls of other early morning pedestrians but all she could see was silhouetted figures hunched against the cold as they hurried along.

She remembered a poem they had learned at school:

> No sun – no moon!
> No morn – no noon –
> No dawn – no dusk – no proper time of day.
> No warmth, no cheerfulness, no healthful ease,
> No comfortable feel in any member –
> No shade, no shine, no butterflies, no bees,
> No fruits, no flowers, no leaves, no birds!
> November!

The poem suited her mood exactly and she wondered, as she often did, how poets – men and women who had never met you – could express exactly what you were feeling. She loved reading poems and had tried to write them but, although her mother had thought them wonderful, Helen knew in her heart that they would never be good enough to be published anywhere except the school magazine.

She reached school just as the doors were thrown open and a senior prefect appeared on the steps and rang the bell. This was quite unnecessary on a day like this. No one was keen to linger in the yard.

'Where were you last week?' one of the girls in the same class as Helen asked. 'Have you been playing truant?'

'Hush,' Eileen Hall said. 'Don't you know? Her mother died.'

The first girl looked aghast. 'Oh, Helen, I'm so sorry.'

'That's all right,' Helen said then she looked at the sympathetic faces of the other girls who had crowded round.

She realized that none of them knew what to say to her. 'Look,' she said, 'do you mind if we don't talk about it?'

Most of them looked relieved and when Eileen hugged her they began to walk away. 'I understand,' Eileen said. 'But if you do want to talk there's always your faithful old friend Eileen.'

Monday morning for Helen's class started with double Maths with the headmistress. Miss Forster swept into the classroom clutching a pile of exercise books to her chest, her gown billowing out behind her.

'Good morning, girls,' she said briskly and even as they answered in unison Miss Forster began to walk up and down the aisles between the desks, swiftly tossing each book in the direction of its owner, calling out the owner's name as she did so. The class had seen this many times but they remained transfixed, waiting for at least one of the books flying over their heads to miss the desk aimed for and fall to the floor, but this never happened. Helen had often wondered if Miss Forster did this deliberately, a small joke to liven them up and catch their attention, but as soon as the books were delivered she would sweep back to her desk quite unsmilingly.

'Helen, your last homework was all correct but you've got some work to catch up. See me at break time,' Miss Forster said. Her tone was matter-of-fact but Helen couldn't help noticing it was rather more subdued than usual. However, she didn't have time to wonder why, because with her usual efficiency Miss Forster launched straight into the lesson.

At break time she cleaned the blackboard with swift, vigorous strokes and sent the girls out to the yard. They went reluctantly and Helen imagined that many of them would hide behind the coat racks and talk quietly in order not to attract the attention of a patrolling prefect.

Helen remained seated until Miss Forster had cleaned the board to her satisfaction and sat down at her desk. Miss Forster beckoned her and Helen rose and made her way forward. The headmistress was uncharacteristically hesitant. Then she said awkwardly, 'I'm so sorry about your mother, Helen.' She paused, took her spectacles off and wiped them with a clean handkerchief. 'I – erm – I was wondering how you are coping now. I mean, you have a younger sister and brothers, don't you?'

'Yes.'

'And who is going to look after you? What arrangements have been made?'

'My sister is to be adopted by a wealthy couple, my brothers are going to Haven House and I am living with my Aunt Jane.'

Miss Forster detected Helen's brusque antipathy and frowned. 'But that is very satisfactory, isn't it? Your sister will have every advantage, Haven House is an excellent institution and you are with a relative. In this sad situation that must be better than you hoped for.'

'I hoped that we would all remain together.'

'Oh, my dear, I do understand, but the alternative might have been an orphanage where you still might have been separated. And you would probably have had to leave school and find employment.'

Helen stared down at the desk. 'If there had been any way for us to stay in the house I would gladly have left school and worked to keep us together.'

'If your mother could hear you say that she would be most distressed.'

Helen looked up in astonishment. 'Are you saying that my mother would not want us to remain a family?'

'No, my dear, I'm sure she would have wished for that if

it were possible, but she would be heartbroken to think that you had to leave school. She was so proud when you passed the scholarship and she was determined that you should have a good education. You know that is true, don't you?'

'Yes . . . I do.'

'I want you to know that if you play your part I will do all I can to help make your mother's dream come true.'

Helen did not know what to say. She had always liked and respected Miss Forster but she had never known her to breach the necessary barrier between teacher and pupil before. And now that she looked at her she realized that Miss Forster herself seemed discomforted by the moment of intimacy and was retreating quickly to her customary position behind a barricade of stiff formality.

'Very well, Helen,' she said in a more matter-of-fact way, 'you had better go and enjoy what is left of break time. No doubt Eileen will be waiting for you.' Miss Forster rose and left the classroom swiftly and Helen followed reluctantly. She knew Eileen would be waiting for her and that she would offer sympathy and support, and she didn't yet know how to cope with that.

Fortunately Eileen sensed her mood and was happy just to walk with her around the schoolyard in the short time they had left. The girls, subdued by the miserable weather, were all muffled up in their coats and scarves. Small snatches of conversation were muted by the oppressive dampness and there was none of the usual animated gossip and laughter. Everyone seemed glad when the bell summoned them back for the rest of the morning session.

At lunchtime they hurried home and as soon as the last girl had left the building the door was shut behind them. Helen had managed to avoid Eileen in the crush; she had no desire to explain her lunch arrangements. She guessed that her friend would probably feel sorry for her and she would have had to explain that there was no need to be. Ninepence would buy her a much better lunch than anything served up by Eva in the dismal confines of Aunt Jane's kitchen.

There was a row of shops not far from the school with a small café tucked between a baker's and a greengrocer. When Helen entered in her school uniform she attracted curious glances. She wasn't quite sure what to do. Should she go to the counter to order or should she sit and wait at a table? As she stood there uncertainly a waitress pushed past with a loaded tray and said somewhat impatiently, 'Take the table over there. Look at the menu and I'll be with you in a tick.'

Helen was pleased and surprised to see what her ninepence would buy her. She decided on a plate of shepherd's pie and peas followed by a cup of tea, and there would still be a few pennies change – unless she decided to have a pudding. When the waitress had taken her order she looked around at the other tables. Many of the other customers were young women who looked like clerical staff. They wore inexpensive but smart outfits with fashionable little hats perched on bobbed permed hair.

Most of them chatted cheerfully but one or two were more subdued as if they had a lot to think about. One girl in particular only picked at her food and kept glancing at her watch then looking out of the window. Helen found herself imagining what story lay behind the anxious expression on the young woman's face. Different scenarios presented themselves to her imagination. Influenced by the romantic books and films her mother had so enjoyed, she decided the most likely cause of the young woman's distress would be a man, a sweetheart whom she suspected had abandoned her. Or perhaps it was more sinister than that; had she stolen something at work – money . . . secret plans – and was fearful that the police might arrive at any minute to arrest her?

Maybe she would write a story about the girl and invent a satisfying ending to the tale . . .

When the waitress arrived with her plate of shepherd's pie Helen was smiling at her own fanciful ideas, but the harassed woman took it as a cheery greeting and smiled in return. 'There you are, pet,' she said. 'I hope you enjoy it.'

Suddenly Helen realized that despite all the grief she had suffered since her mother had died, and the pain caused by being separated from her sister and brothers, she had begun if not to enjoy at least to appreciate the new situation she found herself in. Her aunt's ninepence a day would buy her a strange but precious kind of independence.

Chapter Five

'Which one are you?'

Joe woke to the echo of the question that Ginger had asked him in the middle of the night. But this time there was a hint of menace in the voice. He opened his eyes and sat up quickly to find Tod Walker standing over Danny's bed.

'Why do you want to know?' Joe asked before Danny had a chance to answer.

'Stands to reason,' he said. 'Got to know who I'm talking to. And in this case I want to know who it was who took my piece of cake. But whatever your name is,' he turned to stare at Joe, 'I'm guessing it was you.'

'What makes you think that?'

'Because you're the cocky one.' He indicated Danny with a sideways nod of the head. 'He's the softy.'

Joe suppressed an angry retort. Tod sounded pleased with himself – and that was bad, wasn't it?

'Yes, I reckon this one,' he pointed a thumb over his shoulder, 'wouldn't have dared take that last piece of cake. Not when I said it was mine.'

'Is that what this is about? A flipping bit of cake, you big greedy baby? Now go away and leave my brother and me alone.'

Joe had been unable to conceal his scorn. He was aware of an air of shock: it was as if everyone had breathed in simultaneously, leaving the dormitory airless. Then the tension eased and somebody giggled, and another boy laughed out loud. Tod Walker, his eyes blazing in his pasty face, turned round furiously and surveyed the watching boys. They fell silent. Someone coughed nervously. No one, not even Ginger, could look Tod in the eyes.

One by one the boys turned away and began to get dressed and make their beds. Tod Walker stood glowering for a moment, fists clenched, then turned to Joe and said, 'Think you're clever, don't you? Well, you're not. Just wait and see.'

Joe's fists were clenched as he watched Tod walk away. Danny got out of bed and touched him on the shoulder. 'Forget it,' he said. 'No harm done.'

'He's trouble.'

'I know, but I can look after myself. Really I can.'

Joe turned to look at his more gentle brother. He doubted that very much, but he didn't want to undermine Danny's confidence by saying so. 'Of course you can.' He forced a grin. 'Now let's get dressed and get these beds made, then we can see what they serve up for breakfast here.'

Joe watched the others surreptitiously and saw how neatly they made the beds. Danny and he had never made their bed at home. They had simply pulled down the covers to air the sheets and someone – their mother or Helen – tidied their room and made the bed for them.

'That won't do. That won't do at all.'

Joe turned from his struggle with the bedclothes to see Ginger watching him.

'Why not?'

'Because it's like the army here. Or a hospital. Have you ever heard of hospital corners? Here, I'll show you.'

Ginger took over and soon had Joe's bed looking neat

71

and tidy. Then he turned to help Danny but was surprised to find that Joe's brother had already finished.

'Not bad,' Ginger said. 'You're catching on quick.'

All the while they had been talking Joe was aware that they were being watched. And now a group of boys hurried down the dormitory towards them, seized the bed covers on his and Danny's bed and pulled them off, throwing them to the floor.

The lads ran off laughing, then Tod Walker strolled towards them. 'Oh, dear,' he said. 'You'll have to do that all over again.'

Joe clenched his fists in fury. 'Pathetic,' he said. 'You're just pathetic.'

Tod raised his eyebrows. 'Really? That's what you think? Well, you'll just have to find out how *pathetic* I am, won't you? Now clear off, Ginger. Leave your new friends to sort this out themselves.'

For a moment it looked as though Ginger might defy Tod but Joe shook his head slightly and Ginger backed away.

Tod laughed and followed him out of the dormitory. At the door he turned and said, 'You'd better not take too long about it. Those who are late for breakfast don't get any.'

Joe was so angry that he was all fingers and thumbs as his mother used to say, and it was Danny who made both beds. 'Don't let him get to you,' he said. 'That's just what he wants.'

'I know. Don't worry. We'll just have to outsmart him.'

With the beds made they hurried along the landing to the stairs and as they went down Joe was relieved to see that the orderly queue of boys was still filing into the dining room. They were the last in and when they took the only two seats remaining they found that Tod Walker was sitting directly opposite. Joe was pretty sure that Tod had arranged that somehow but it made him all the more determined that he wouldn't get the better of him.

When Elsie woke up she stretched an arm across the bed and was surprised to find that she was alone. Helen must have got up early to help with the breakfast, she thought. She closed her eyes and tried to go back to sleep but soon a gentle crackling sound began to puzzle her. It was the sound of coals burning in the grate. She frowned. They had never had a fire in their bedroom. And during the bitter winter months, even with Helen to hold her close, she had always felt cold.

Now she was warm, warm as toast, and the bedclothes didn't just smell clean as they did at home, they smelled of flowers as well. For of course she wasn't at home with Helen and her brothers. The beautiful lady, Mrs Partington, had brought her here and as far as Elsie could understand it she wanted her to stay here. Forever.

'Hello, sleepyhead.'

Elsie looked up to see Mrs Partington standing over her. She gave a start of surprise.

'Oh, darling, did I frighten you? I came in quietly so that I wouldn't disturb you. But now that you're awake, shall we have breakfast together? I'll ring for Susan. Now just this once I'm going to help you get dressed.'

Elsie sat up. 'I can put my own clothes on. I do every morning.'

'Of course you can, Elise, but Susan will help you in future. That's the way we do things. And this morning I want to help you myself. I want to dress you in your nice

73

new clothes. First of all put on this sweet little dressing gown while we go along to the bathroom.'

By the time they came back from the bathroom a small table had been placed before the fire and Susan had just finished laying out the breakfast.

'Here we are,' Mrs Partington said brightly. 'Eggs and toast soldiers. Will you like that?'

'Yes.'

'Yes, what, darling?'

'Yes, thank you.'

'Good girl. It won't take you long to learn proper manners.'

Elsie was embarrassed. She would have liked to have told Mrs Partington that she already knew how to say please and thank you, that her mother had always insisted on proper manners and that it was her own fault that she hadn't remembered them this morning, but Mrs Partington had turned her attention to the table.

'Very good, Susan,' she said. 'Just bring a pot of coffee for me. Now, Elise, keep your dressing gown on while you eat your breakfast, we don't want everything to go cold, especially the milk. I used to hate that when I was a little girl.'

'You hated milk?'

'No, sweetheart, I meant I hated the skin that formed on the top if you left the milk too long. Now come along, let's enjoy our first morning here together.'

While Elsie started on her breakfast Susan returned with a pot of coffee for Mrs Partington. She was followed into the room by Mr Partington.

'So, I'm to breakfast alone,' he said.

Although he was smiling there was something about his tone that made Elsie look at him anxiously. Was he cross?

'Oh, Hugh, don't be peevish,' Mrs Partington said. 'You

74

often breakfast alone simply because you insist on getting up at such an unearthly hour to get to the office.'

'And you have your breakfast in bed.'

'That's right. Well, this morning I thought I would take breakfast with Elise, here by the fire. It's nice and cosy.'

'You couldn't resist playing with your new toy.'

'Hugh!' Mrs Partington sounded shocked. '*Pas devant!* You must not talk like that. I do not regard Elise as a toy. I regard her as a daughter.'

'Forgive me, sweetheart. That was thoughtless. It seems I must get used to having a child in the house.'

'Yes, you must.' She smiled up at him. 'Have you had your breakfast?'

'A very good one, thank you. A pair of Craster kippers on the bone, nice and smoky, and with a couple of poached eggs on top.'

'Ugh! Are you surprised that I don't take breakfast with you more often?'

'No, my love, but I do miss your company.'

'Well, why don't I ring for Susan and get her to bring you a cup and a fresh pot of coffee. We can sit here together like a proper little family.'

'Very well. Anything to please you, my darling.'

Elsie had listened wide-eyed, fascinated by the way they talked. They called each other *my love*, *my darling* and *sweetheart* and behaved almost as though they were children rather than proper grown-up people.

Once Susan had brought the coffee for Mr Partington they seemed to forget about her. Mrs Partington began to tease her husband about the time he spent at somewhere called the office. 'Honestly, Hugh, dawn till dusk every day.'

'A slight exaggeration, Selma, and in any case I only do

it for you, to make sure that we can afford anything your heart desires.'

'But why do you have to do everything yourself? Surely you must learn to delegate.'

Mr Partington laughed. 'Delegate? Where did you learn such a big word?'

His wife smiled but Elsie thought she was just a little bit cross when she replied. 'I wish you wouldn't think of me as a complete fool,' she said. 'I do have a brain in my head and believe it or not I actually read the stuffy newspapers that you have delivered.'

'No, I don't think of you as a fool, Selma. It is I who am the fool for not wishing to see you as you are. I like the illusion of a dear little wife to be protected from the hurly-burly of the world.'

'Oh, you can protect me all you like. I don't mind that. Just remember now and then that I'm a grown-up, not a sweet little child-wife.'

Elsie was beginning to get bored. She had drunk her milk and eaten her egg and all the toast soldiers. It had been a good breakfast but she realized she was still hungry. She wondered if she was allowed to ring for Susan and ask for more. There was a bell pull at the side of the fireplace. She was staring at it when Mrs Partington suddenly noticed that all the plates were empty.

'Oh, what a good little girl,' she said. 'To eat up all her breakfast like that. Would you like some more toast, Elise? And perhaps some apricot preserve.'

Elsie wasn't sure what apricot preserve was but she guessed it would be something like marmalade. And no doubt the toast would be hot and spread with butter. They had rarely had butter on their toast at home although her mother sometimes mixed some in with the margarine. But for breakfast most mornings they had mostly had bread and dripping or porridge made with water and just a little milk to pour on and cool it down.

'Yes, please,' she said. 'And may I ring the bell for Susan?'

Mrs Partington raised her eyebrows and laughed. 'Of course you may, my pet. Isn't she just too sweet, Hugh? Have you time for another pot of coffee?'

'Not really but it's so cosy here by the fire with you that I think I'll say yes.'

'There you are. I knew you would like us being a proper family.'

'Is that what we are?'

'Of course. You, me and our daughter, Elise. A proper family.'

Elsie stared at them but they were looking at each other in the sort of way her brother Joe would have called soppy. For the moment she was excluded and she wasn't sure if she liked that. Mrs Partington was so beautiful and so kind and she had brought her here to this lovely house where she was to live forever and ever and it seemed that she was to be their daughter.

She didn't find that strange. After all she had no mother now and she couldn't remember their father at all. And everybody should have a mother and father, shouldn't they? She wondered briefly if her brothers would find a new father and mother. Surely they would want to have the same ones. And Helen. What about Helen? Perhaps not. After all, she was nearly grown up and Elsie wasn't sure if grown-ups needed parents the way children did.

She tucked into the toast and apricot preserve. She decided it was delicious. And Susan had brought some more hot milk. The milk was all right but she wondered if she would be allowed to have coffee. Her mother had sometimes made what she called a coffee dash by adding something from a bottle to a cup of warm milk. The bottle had a label showing two men sitting by a camp fire drinking coffee. One was dressed in a kilt so he must be Scottish and the other had a funny cloth wrapped round his head. Joe had told her that this was a turban and the men were soldiers and this was what soldiers drank to keep their strength up.

Helen had laughed at this. 'That's what they want you to think, Joe,' she'd said. 'Don't be fooled by the advertising.'

That conversation had been above Elsie's head but she remembered it fondly and she wondered if the coffee that Mr and Mrs Partington had would taste just as delicious. Now they were talking about someone called Miss Chambers and someone else called Miss Barton. Apparently these two ladies were coming today and Mrs Partington was going to interview them – whatever that meant.

She was just spreading apricot preserve on the last piece of toast when she realized they had stopped talking. She looked up to find them smiling at her.

'Mr Partington is going to work now,' Mrs Partington said. 'But he wanted to ask you something.'

For a moment Elsie was alarmed. She remembered that Mr Partington had not seemed as keen to have her here as his wife had been. Was this going to be some sort of test and if she didn't give the right answers she would have to leave?

'What is it?' she asked.

'Don't look so worried, moppet,' he said. 'I only want to know if you think you'll be happy here.'

'Oh, yes,' Elsie said. 'I'm sure I shall be.'

'Right then. Duty calls.' He rose and to Elsie's

embarrassment he pulled his wife up into his arms and kissed her.

When he had gone Mrs Partington sat down again and poured herself the last of the coffee. She took a sip and then leaned forward. 'We've started well, haven't we, Elise?'

'Yes,' Elsie said although she wasn't quite sure what Mrs Partington meant.

'And you do understand that I want you to think of yourself as Elise from now on? Elise Partington sounds much better than Elsie Partington, doesn't it?'

'Yes, I suppose so.'

'There's no suppose about it. Take my word for it, it does.' In saying this Mrs Partington revealed that quick flash of impatience that Elsie had noticed before and which had so worried her. She stared down at her empty plate on the table and wondered how she could make Mrs Partington smile again.

'I'm glad you're going to call me Elise,' she said. 'But what am I to call you? You said you would tell me.'

Mrs Partington's smile returned and she leaned forward. 'You are going to live here as our little girl. My husband and I already think of you as our daughter. What do you think you should call me?'

Elsie hesitated. When her real mother had been alive she had called her Mam or Ma but somehow that didn't seem right for Mrs Partington. And then something stirred in her memory, something from the storybooks that Helen had read to her. Books about children who lived in big houses and whose parents had servants just like the Partingtons did. Her face cleared.

'Mama,' she said. 'Shall I call you Mama?'

The smile on Mrs Partington's face was the only answer Elsie needed.

The following week Helen was having breakfast with Eva. They were talking quietly because Aunt Jane had scolded them, saying their morning chatter carried all the way upstairs and woke her up too soon.

'You could always look them up in the telephone directory. People like that are bound to have a telephone,' Eva said.

'But so will all the other Partingtons.'

'There can't be that many with a telephone, and in any case from the sounds of it all you'll hev to do is look out for the grandest address in town.'

Helen and Eva sat companionably at the table in the kitchen. This morning Eva had made porridge and had livened it up with a spoonful of black treacle. In the short while Helen had been at her aunt's house the two girls had become friends. Well, almost friends, Helen thought. They could be chatting quite happily about nothing in particular when suddenly Eva would close her mouth, thin her lips and go silent.

After a while Helen realized this usually occurred after one of Eva's regular tirades about 'the missus'. She remembers I am her niece, Helen thought, but surely she can't think I am cut from the same cloth. However, this morning her aunt's maid was in a friendly mood.

'Another cup of tea?' she asked. 'Hot and sweet to warm your cockles on a cold morning.'

'Where would I find a telephone directory? In the library?'

'I daresay. But why not try a telephone box?'

'Of course.'

'Eeh, sometimes you're not very bright for a girl that gans to the grammar school, are you?'

80

Helen laughed. 'No, I'm not. I'm certainly not as sensible as you are.'

'Get away with you! But now that you mention it I don't think what you propose to do is at all sensible. Or right for that matter.'

'Why not?'

'Lissen to me. Your little sister has been taken in by very rich people. Her life is going to be very different from yours and mine. And you said yourself that she seemed to take to Mrs Partington when she came to get her.'

'Well, yes, she did. But I haven't seen her since then, have I?'

'Nor should you. For once I agree with your aunt. It would only upset little Elsie if you suddenly reminded her of things she can't have any more.'

'Things she can't have?'

'Your mam and you and your brothers all together in your snug little house. The bairn is young enough to let those memories fade.'

'But I don't want them to!'

'Can't you see that's cruel? I'm not saying your little sister will forget everything entirely. She hev happy memories that she'll bring out and hev a look at now and then. But meanwhile if you really love her you'll let her get on with her new life.'

Helen stared at Eva. The girl's homely young face seemed to take on the aspect of a kindly old woman. 'You're very wise, Eva,' she said.

'Aye, I'm a pupil from the school of life, me. Now drink up your tea and haddaway. You divven't want to be late for school, do you?'

'No.'

'Shall I put that doll back in your room?'

'No.'

'What do you mean, "No"? Surely after all that's been said you don't still plan to take it to your sister, do you?'

'Perhaps not. But I have to be sure. I know it's only an old doll but I made it for her and she must be missing her.'

'Mebbe she did at first – until she got used to all the new dolls she'll hev now. And hevn't you listened to a single word I've said? For God's sake let it be, Helen, and let the bairn get on with her new life.'

Eva rose abruptly and clattered the dirty dishes into the sink. Helen stuffed Maisie into her school satchel and slipping on her coat she left without another word. She was sorry that she and Eva were at odds with each other, and on the way to school she went over everything they had talked about. She thought about it again all morning at school and twice was scolded for being inattentive. By the time lunchtime came she had almost made her mind up but she had to be sure. And there was only one way of achieving that.

Instead of staying in the café for lunch, Helen bought a sandwich to take out and hurried along to the nearest telephone box to consult the directory. Eva had been right; there weren't many Partingtons with telephones. The two who looked the most likely had the initials E and H. They didn't live very far from each other and if she dashed she would just have time to at least look at the houses before hurrying back to school.

Not much later she found herself lurking in the gravelled driveway of a house opposite what surely must be the grandest house in Newcastle. Set a little way back from the road, surrounded by gardens that looked more like a municipal park, the Partington residence was more country mansion than townhouse.

The first Partington address she had passed had been grand

enough – a tall terraced house with steps leading up to the front door and another set leading down to an area below the level of the pavement where no doubt the servants' entrance was. Helen had stopped briefly to look at it and then hurried on. The grand terrace gave way to large villas with highly cultivated gardens and finally she had arrived at Redebank, the address listed in the phone directory as being that of H. Partington.

But what should she do? March up to the door and ask to see Mrs Partington? Then ask her to give Elsie her doll? Her aunt had told her that on no account must she do that. Helen remembered her aunt's anger when she had asked if she could have the Partingtons' address.

'Why do you want it? You're not planning to go and see her, are you, after everything that's been said? After all the arrangements that have been made?'

'And what exactly are those arrangements?'

'How dare you set yourself up against me!'

'I'm not. I genuinely want to know what you and Mrs Partington have agreed to.'

'Why?'

'Because Elsie is my sister. And I need to know that she will be taken care of.'

'What are you accusing me of? Do you think I would hand her over to someone who would treat her badly? Mrs Partington will care for her as if she were her own daughter and the child will have every advantage in life. You may be her sister but you could never provide for her, admit it.'

Helen stared down at her aunt who was sitting by the fire in the stuffy and overheated front parlour. Jane Roberts' cheeks were blotched red with anger, which made her almost comical to look at, but Helen did not feel like laughing.

'I thought you understood all this from the beginning,

Helen,' her aunt went on. 'I distinctly remember telling you that Mrs Partington does not want Elsie to have any contact with her family. Even me. There are to be no visits, no letters and certainly no parcels containing a grubby old doll.'

'Maisie is not grubby!'

'For goodness' sake. If only you could see yourself. Any minute now you're going to start crying like a big baby. I've had enough of this. Instead of being grateful for everything I've done for you it seems you are determined to cause trouble and upset me. Go to bed now, Helen, and I refuse to discuss this matter with you ever again.'

That had been the evening before. Helen had accepted defeat because there was nothing else she could do. It sickened her to hear her aunt talk as if she really cared what happened to them and it had crossed her mind that money must have changed hands. The Partingtons were very rich and money could buy just about anything. Even a child.

The air was frosty and the ground iron-hard. Helen realized that her toes were so cold that she could hardly feel them. She glanced at her wristwatch. It had been a present from her mother when she had passed the scholarship exam to go to grammar school. She had stayed too long. Even if she ran all the way she was going to be late for afternoon school. That meant detention. Not that Helen cared. She would rather stay at school for an extra half-hour and sit in the classroom to do her homework than go back to her aunt's gloomy home any sooner than she had to.

Just as she had decided to leave she heard voices – a woman's voice and that of a child. She stepped back into the shadow of the large stone gatepost and waited, holding her breath as she watched the house opposite. The voices got nearer and eventually two figures appeared, rounding a curve in the drive. The child was running and the woman behind her lumbered along awkwardly, steams of breath misting in the air as she tried to catch up.

'Miss Elise,' the unfortunate woman called, 'will you please slow down a little!'

The little girl stopped and turned round laughing to face the round figure approaching her. 'Hurry up, Barty,' she said.

It took Helen every ounce of self-control not to leave the sanctuary of the tall hedge and run across the road towards her sister. For Elsie it was, even though the woman with her had called her Elise.

Her sister was wearing a heather-coloured tweed coat with a velvet collar that would have been fit for little Princess Elizabeth. A matching beret was trimmed with white fur. Her gloves and stockings were white and she wore shiny black patent leather shoes. She looked beautiful; she was like a child in a film about high society. Except that Elsie was more beautiful than any child film star Helen had ever seen. But most of all she looked happy.

And it was that that caused Helen the most pain. She was immediately ashamed of herself. Surely she hadn't wanted Elsie to be miserable? Had she been hoping to see her sister's face awash with misery and tears? How selfish I am, she thought.

The woman – whoever she was, she certainly wasn't the sophisticated Mrs Partington – had caught up with Elsie and was standing on the pavement trying to catch her breath. She was dressed in a brown tweed coat and a matching felt hat. Helen had a surreal moment thinking that it was the belt of her coat that kept this cumbersome figure safely parcelled up.

'That was naughty of you, Miss Elise,' the poor woman

said. 'You know I can't run as fast as you can. And anyway, you're supposed to hold my hand when we go out.'

'But I had to run to keep warm.'

'You really shouldn't answer back like that. You are supposed to do as I tell you.'

The woman Elsie had called Barty suddenly gave a grimace of pain and stooped to rub at one ankle.

'What's the matter?' Elsie asked.

'I went over on it while I was running.'

'Did it hurt?'

'Yes, it did.'

'I'm sorry, Miss Barton. That was my fault. I shouldn't have made you run like that.'

The woman, who had been visibly irritated, suddenly melted. 'There, there, I dare say I'll soon be as good as new. Now, will you take my hand and we'll get along to the Dene for our nature walk.'

When they turned to go Helen edged back until she was behind the gatepost. She knew with certainty that she didn't want Elsie to see her. It would be quite wrong to upset this happy, confident child just now when she was so obviously adapting to a new way of life. Mrs Andrews had been right; Eva was right. What could Helen offer Elsie now?

But one day, Helen thought as she watched the child and the woman walk away, one day we'll be together again, all of us: Joe, Danny, you and me. I promise you this, Elsie, and I can only pray that you will not have forgotten all about us.

Helen accepted her detention cheerfully and dealt with Eva's grumbles when she was late home for tea. That night she wrapped Maisie in an old scarf – the first scarf she had ever knitted when she was not much older than Elsie was now – and put the doll in her suitcase. She couldn't bear to throw her away.

Besides, she thought, no matter how many beautiful toys Elsie has now, I'm sure she'll be glad to see Maisie again. One day.

A yelp of pain woke everyone up. The boys sat up in their beds and looked down the dormitory to see Tod Hunter lying on the floor with one of the twins kneeling over him and apparently throttling him. Ginger sprang out of bed and raced towards the struggling boys, and while the other twin was still yawning and getting out of bed he tried to pull the figures apart.

'Whatever he did, leave him alone. Now. You've given him a bloody nose. That's enough.'

The twin allowed Ginger to pull him up and then nodded towards the bed. 'Look at that,' he said. 'A whole pisspot. He's drenched me, too, the dirty bastard.'

'Don't use language, it's not allowed here,' Ginger responded automatically, but when he saw the bed his nose wrinkled in disgust. 'Pooh, it stinks – and you do, too. He must have been saving it for days.'

Tod, dabbing his nose with a handkerchief, sniggered as he began to get up. 'Thanks for dragging him off me, Ginger, but I didn't need any help. I'd soon have got the better of him.'

'Yeah, I'm sure,' the twin said.

Tod began to stroll away. He turned and said, 'You'd better go and ask Matron for some clean sheets. Tell her you've pissed the bed like the dirty little slum kid that you are.'

The twin looked as though he was going to retaliate but Ginger grabbed a fistful of his pyjamas and held him back.

'Let it go, Joe,' he said, and he looked straight into his eyes.

When Tod was out of earshot the twin said softly so that no one else could hear, 'You know, don't you?'

Ginger leaned in towards him and spoke just as quietly. 'Yeah, you swapped beds. You've been doing that regularly. You guessed that Tod would go after Danny and you wanted to fool him as long as you could. You knew I would work it out, didn't you? Danny's left-handed and you're right-handed. Easy. Have to tell you some of the others have noticed, and even Tod won't be fooled much longer. You're going to have to teach Danny to stick up for himself.'

A mutinous look crossed Joe's face and Ginger let go of his pyjamas. He sniffed his hand and wrinkled his nose in disgust. 'Now you've got me smelling like cat's piss,' he said. 'Hawway, grab a quick shower and if you get some clean bedclothes, I'll help you make your bed. What is it?'

'Will Matron be angry?'

'Very. Are you bothered?'

'No.'

'Don't lie. Not to me.'

'Well, yes, I am. What shall I say?'

'Well, you can't tell her the truth. No one tells tales, not even on Tod Hunter. You'll just have to take it like a man. Can you do that?'

Joe suddenly grinned. 'I reckon I can.'

Before they went to the bathroom Joe and Ginger stripped the bed. As Joe picked the sheets up from the floor he found the enamel chamber pot that Tod had left behind. He looked inside and saw that it was not quite empty. He walked down the dormitory until he reached his tormentor's bed.

'This is your property, I think,' he said. He emptied the

remains over Tod's slippers then tossed the chamber pot on the bed before carrying on his way to the bathroom.

'Bad move,' Ginger said to him when they got there. 'For all his bluster I think he was beginning to realize he was on a loser trying to better you. Now you'll only have made him worse than ever.'

Chapter Six

Dear Danny and Joe,

I hope you have settled in by now and that all is going well for you. I think about you all the time and I'd like you to write and tell me all about Haven House; whether it's comfortable, whether you are well fed and what sort of lessons you are doing. You know our mother was proud of you both and the progress you were making at school so I hope you will continue to work hard. Does that sound bossy? Sorry.

Have you made any friends? I hope you have, because although you'll always have each other, it's good to have other people, too. Remember Mother used to tell you that you should both have a life of your own instead of behaving like carbon copies of each other. Even though you look so alike you don't always think and behave the same way, do you? And that's a good thing. Everyone should be an individual with a personality of his own. Do you know what I mean? Or will you just say, 'There goes our Helen spouting from the dictionary again!'

If you've been wondering about Elsie and me I'd better tell you that we are not both living with Aunt Jane. After you had left for Haven House a rich lady called Mrs Partington came and took Elsie away with her. It was the same lady who came to the church on the day of our mother's funeral. Do you remember her? She sat in the back pew and then she talked to Aunt Jane after the service. She found out that we would be alone and she wanted to help. In fact it was her husband who got you places in Haven House. As for Elsie, you mustn't worry about her. This lady has no children and she wants Elsie to be her own little daughter.

Now don't start worrying about this. The lady is really kind and Elsie seemed happy to go with her. And although I miss her as much as I miss you I believe she's better off with the Partingtons than with Aunt Jane. I went along to see where Elsie is living and I could see that she was happy and well-cared for. And I promise you I'll always keep an eye on things. And one day we will all be together again.

As for me, I'm living in Aunt Jane's posh house and I'm going to school as usual. And here's a thing: Aunt Jane doesn't want me to come home at lunchtime so the old skinflint actually gives me ninepence a day to get something for myself. Imagine ninepence! I've found a nice little café not far from school. It's called the Cosy Café, which is a good name for it, because it's a friendly place. I treat myself just about every day to a proper dinner and sometimes a pudding too. Imagine your big sister sitting in a café like Lady Muck ordering dinner from a menu and having her meal brought to the table by a waitress!

I've got to know the waitress, who is called Margery. She has one daughter, Dorothy, who is also a waitress but she's working in London.

Some of the regular customers are quite interesting

91

and one or two have started to say 'hello' to me. The office girls think it's funny to see me sitting there in my school uniform but they are quite friendly.

I don't spend much time with Aunt Jane but I have made friends with Eva, her maid-of-all-work. She's a funny sort of girl. Sometimes friendly, sometimes sulky, but I really like her and we often have a laugh together. She says she doesn't mind coming to work so much now that I'm here to have a good old chinwag with and we certainly can talk when we get started!

Helen put her pen down on the blotting paper. She was sitting at the table in the kitchen. The skies outside were dark and when Eva had opened the back door to go home a gust of wind blew in, bringing with it the smell of soot mixed with something else. Eva said it was the smell of snow. She was convinced there would be snow by morning and she had shovelled more coal on the fire in the range than she ought to have done so that Helen would be warm and cosy.

Neither of the girls thought it likely that 'the missus' would venture into the kitchen that evening, not now that she had instructed Helen to answer the call of the bell just like Eva did. It suited Helen very well to stay in the kitchen on her own. She could spread her school books on the table and get on with her homework.

She got up and warmed a pan of milk. It was time to take Aunt Jane her cup of cocoa. She also made one for herself and, duty done, she returned to her letter. She had mixed feelings about what she had written. She knew she had not been entirely candid. She had led her brothers to believe that she was happier about Elsie's situation than she was.

Everything their old neighbour Mrs Andrews and her new friend Eva had said was true. Elsie would be much better off with the Partingtons than with Aunt Jane. But this would never compensate for the fact that she missed her little sister dreadfully and she believed with all her heart that she should have found a way for the family to remain together.

She did not feel guilty about making light of her own situation. All she had said was true. She had found a friend in Eva, and although Aunt Jane could sometimes behave like a wicked stepmother in a fairy tale, she wasn't actually cruel in any physical sense. She was simply totally uncaring. Helen suspected that the Partingtons were paying her aunt some sort of allowance and that might explain the ninepence a day for her lunch. If that were true she ought to be grateful. She *was* grateful, she supposed.

Ninepence a day was more than ample. She had begun to put a little bit by towards buying Christmas presents. Her list was small: her brothers, Mrs Andrews, Eva, and her school friend Eileen. She had agonized over whether she could send anything to Elsie and had decided that she couldn't. Then finally she had added Aunt Jane's name. After all, Christmas was Christmas.

Helen picked up her pen, dipped it in the bottle of ink, and resumed writing. She sent the boys her love and urged them to write to her as soon as they could. To encourage them to do this, she slipped a couple of pages of writing paper and a stamped envelope in with the letter. Not wanting to risk more conflict with Aunt Jane, she had gone back to the telephone kiosk to find the address of Haven House. She would post her letter on the way to school in the morning.

Helen wiped the pen, put it in her pencil box, put the top back on the bottle of ink and put them in her schoolbag along with the writing pad, blotting paper and her books. She put out the milk bottles, banked up the fire and went to bed. She did not say goodnight to Aunt Jane. Eva would deal with the used cup in the morning.

Her brothers' answering letter came only a few days later. Helen blessed the fact that the postman called long before her aunt was up in the morning. She didn't have time to read it before she went to school and at break time she was on cloakroom duty, so the letter had to wait until she was seated at her usual place in the Cosy Café.

The writing on the envelope was near perfect. Danny's, Helen guessed. Even though the younger twin was left-handed, his writing was much neater than impetuous Joe's. Maybe it was because Danny had had to try harder when learning to write from left to right across the page. She opened the envelope and had to tug at the pages to get them out. The boys had filled not just the sheets of writing paper she had sent for them but had obviously torn pages from a school exercise book, too. Helen hoped they wouldn't get into trouble for it.

She glanced through the letter quickly and smiled when she realized what they had done. They had taken turns, and even if the handwriting had not been so different it would have been easy to tell which boy was writing at the time.

Dear Helen, (Joe began)

We were really pleased to hear from you. Well, you needn't worry about us. No, not at all. The beds are clean, there's plenty of grub and the lessons are just like at our old school. The teachers are pretty much the same as teachers anywhere but the headmaster, Mr Ridley, is a bit of a curious old coot. He wears his gown all the time just like the beaks in the comics and he never seems to know quite what is going on, or what he's supposed to say. Sometimes he opens the

94

door of a classroom, everybody stands up, but he doesn't say anything. He just blinks and stares for a moment and looks as though he's forgotten why he's there then he leaves again. What a hoot! That rhymes with coot!

Mr Ridley is what you would call an eccentric. (Danny had taken over.) I think he is one of those very clever people who don't quite fit into everyday life. He leaves a lot of the running of the school to the deputy headmaster, Mr Jenkins. Mr Jenkins is the chap who came to collect us. He's OK most of the time but he has a problem. He likes a little tipple and when the drink takes him it's almost as if he becomes a different person. He can get quite nasty. But don't worry about that, Helen. It's never anything personal, and the other boys here have learned how to deal with it. Personally I think it's because he's very unhappy. I don't think this is the sort of life he planned for himself.

Yeah, (Joe again) Jenkins is one to avoid when he's been shut up in his room with his friend the bottle, but we've all learned to scarper when we see him coming and we make extra sure that he won't find anything to complain about. I'm sure you'll be pleased to hear that! Now over to Danny who wants to tell you a bit about the surroundings.

It's really nice here on the coast. About a hundred years ago a rich ship owner built Haven House for himself and his family. The trouble was, all his sons and daughters died before he did, so he left the house to a charity to set up a school for boys. The house is at the far end of the town on the way to the lighthouse and from the upstairs windows there is a marvellous view of the sea. You would love it, Helen. On fine days the water seems to sparkle and on dull days the sky and the sea seem to merge into each other so you can't tell which is which. And as for stormy days! Joe is just about to snatch the pen. There, he did it! The ink blots are his fault!

Had to stop him before he went all soppy! (Joe wrote.) But he's right. This is a grand place to live and we're not exactly prisoners here. We can spend any free time we have exploring the cliffs and the beach and the caves. One fly in the ointment is that once a week we all have to go out for a run, no matter what the weather. Some of the lads are really keen to be first one back. Not because they don't enjoy the run. They do! It's because they want to be the winner. The one who gets back first the most times gets a trophy cup at the end of each term. Honestly! Who wants a cup that you can't keep? And in any case, once it's handed over Ginger says that they just lock it up in old Ridley's study again. They don't even put your name on it. He says that even though we'll never be toffs, they're trying to run the place like a public school. Whatever that is. Over to Danny, who will try and explain.

Joe's friend, Ginger, said that rich boys who go to something called public schools have it much harder than we do. They have to have cold showers and the food is terrible and their parents pay a fortune for this. Furthermore the older boys are allowed to beat them. At least we only get caned by the headmaster. I don't mean that's a regular occurrence here! As Joe said before, this is just like any school except we can't go home at night.

And also we have to work for our keep! (Joe had

taken over again.) Well, not exactly our keep. We have to do jobs in the house, like cleaning windows or peeling spuds, and in the gardens. There's a front garden to keep tidy and a massive kitchen garden. There are greenhouses too. Some of the boys really like this and want to get jobs as gardeners when they leave. Some lads hate having to do anything at all and there's one lazy waster called Tod Walker who gets away with it. He persuades other boys to do his work for him and then has the nerve to take half the pay as well. Oh, yes, we get paid for this work. It's supposed to teach us that you work for what you get in life. We don't get very much, but it's like getting pocket money. Danny and I are planning to go into town and do some Christmas shopping in Woolworths. I'm handing over to Danny to sign off.

We'd better go now; we've got some homework to do. Please write again soon, Helen. We really miss you and Elsie but we're sure we'll be together again one day just like you promised.

Love,

Your brothers Danny and Joe

Helen was torn between laughter and tears as she folded the letter and put it back in the envelope. Laughter because the different characters of her brothers were so plainly revealed in how and what they had written, and tears because no matter what they wrote they were determined to show her they were making the best of it.

She was glad that they had made at least one friend. Or had they? Danny had referred to the boy they called Ginger as 'Joe's friend', not his own. But of course Danny, for all his quiet ways, had always been the more self-sufficient of the two, content to stay in the background and let Joe lead the way.

Then what was she to make of this boy called Tod who 'persuaded' other boys to do his chores and then kept half their pay? That didn't sound good at all. She couldn't imagine Joe ever consenting to an arrangement like this and neither would he allow Danny to be bullied. Was this lad a bully? Helen hoped not, and then tried to console herself with the thought that even if he was, Joe would be able to deal with it.

'You've let your rice pudding go cold.' Helen looked up to see Margery standing over her. 'Must have been a very interesting letter. From your boyfriend, is it?'

Helen smiled. 'I haven't got a boyfriend. It's from my brothers.'

'Don't they live at home with you?'

'No. After our mother died we were . . . well, we had to be split up.'

'Oh, I'm sorry, pet. Listen, give me that pudding and I'll pour some warm milk on it. And how about a spoonful of jam to jazz it up a bit?'

Helen smiled her thanks and as soon as she had finished she hurried back to school. She found it hard to concentrate on the afternoon's lessons. As Joe and Danny had reminded her, Christmas was coming and she didn't know how she would be able to bear this first Christmas without her family around her.

On Saturday the twenty-first of December Helen got up early and took the tram into the town centre. Eva was put out that they didn't have time for what she called their regular 'chinwag', but Helen wanted to be out of the house before Aunt Jane came down for breakfast and found some task for her to do or an errand for her to run. Mostly the tasks were sewing and mending or going to the shops for such items as buttons, elastic, hairnets, or fancy cakes for the Sunday teatime treat. Aunt Jane had never actually said that Helen couldn't go out on errands of her own, although she was sure if she asked there would be some objection. So she left the house early to avoid a confrontation.

Helen loved going to the Grainger Market. The huge covered market was an endless source of delight with interesting people in every alleyway and arcade of shops. Even though she had arrived early the market was in full swing. She hurried through the butchers' quarter with its strong smells of blood mingled with sawdust to the greengrocers' stalls already stacked high with fresh fruit and vegetables. Helen breathed in the wonderful tang of the oranges and marvelled at the varieties of nuts all ready to be bought for the Christmas table.

Some of the stalls had Christmas trees for sale. Helen remembered one Christmas when their mother had told them they couldn't afford a tree. They had been disappointed but, not wanting to upset her, they had made the best of the bunches of holly and mistletoe she had bought in this very market. Then, on Christmas morning, they had come downstairs to a wonderful sight. Perhaps it was the smallest Christmas tree ever but there it was, in the front parlour, the light from the fire reflecting on the coloured spheres of glass. Their mother never told them how she had managed to do this. She insisted it must have been Father Christmas who found he had one left on his sledge so decided to leave it for the Norton family.

Helen and the twins no longer believed in Father Christmas but they had kept up the pretence for Elsie's sake. Elsie . . . What sort of Christmas would she have? Helen was sure Mrs Partington would do her best to make it a wonderful time for her. And what of Joe and Danny? From their letter Haven House didn't sound such a bad place. She hoped there would be a party of some sort and that the boys might even be given presents. They would certainly get presents from her.

Reluctant to go back to Aunt Jane's house, Helen mingled with the crowd and found herself listening to snatches of conversation and imagining the stories behind them. She decided to treat herself to a cup of tea and a toasted teacake in the mezzanine café, and as soon as she was settled at a table where she could look down on the busy scene below she took her notebook and pencil from her pocket and started making notes about anything or anyone who interested her or caught her eye. She couldn't remember when she had started doing this, but often these snippets developed into full-blown stories.

Her mother had encouraged her in this and would often say things like, 'Go on, Helen, what happened next?' or 'What was she wearing? Was she really beautiful?' Or 'No, I didn't think she would do that.' She used to joke that listening to Helen's stories was as good as going to the pictures and that she could enjoy them in front of her own cosy fire.

When she realized a queue was forming for the tables, Helen reluctantly drained her cup and set off to do her shopping. She had her list and she knew where she was going. First she would go to Marks and Spencer's Penny Bazaar and then she would go to the book stalls where she would have time to linger just a little longer.

On Sunday after lunch Helen told her aunt she was going for a walk. There was a moment of silence when Helen could see Aunt Jane was trying to think of some reason why she couldn't go, but eventually she said, 'Well, just make sure you help Eva with the dishes first. It's her half-day today, you know.'

On Sundays Aunt Jane and Helen had lunch in the dark little dining room at the back of the house. 'Get along with you,' Eva said as the two girls cleared the table. 'I'll have these washed up in no time and I can see you're dying to break out of here even on a day like this.'

It was bitterly cold. 'Too cold for snow,' Eva said, although Helen failed to see the logic in that. She walked briskly and by the time she reached the old familiar streets her cheeks were glowing.

'How bonny you look,' were Mrs Andrews' first words as she welcomed her into the house next door to where Helen had grown up. They went straight through to the kitchen where Mr Andrews was snoring gently by the fire. 'Don't mind him,' their old friend said. 'And don't worry. We won't wake him up with our chatter. He's as deaf as a post.'

Strangely, once they were seated at the table they didn't chatter very much. In fact both found it hard to say anything at all as they sipped the hot sweet tea and gazed pensively into the glowing flames.

Eventually Helen roused herself and asked, 'What are your new neighbours like?'

'Nice young couple. He works at the bakery, comes home covered in flour and looking like a ghost. She's a dressmaker of a sort. Alterations and mending. She's expecting. It'll be nice to have a bairn next door again.'

Helen couldn't speak.

'Eeh, I'm sorry, lass. That was thoughtless of me.'

'No, it's all right. Life moves on.'

Mrs Andrews gazed at her speculatively. 'Yes, it does, and

101

whatever happens I have the feeling that you will cope with it.'

They fell into a reflective silence again and after a while Helen had the urge to go. It wasn't that she wanted to leave her old friend so much as that she no longer felt at home here. It nearly broke her heart to acknowledge this but it was true. Before she left she took a small packet wrapped in Christmas paper from her pocket and put it on the table.

'Oh, no, Helen,' Mrs Andrews said. That's not for me, is it? I haven't got you anything this year.'

'I wasn't expecting anything. And it's not really from me. It's something my mother would have wanted you to have. Go on, you needn't wait until Christmas Day. Open it now.'

Mrs Andrews' work-roughened hands were trembling as she tore off the wrapping paper. When she saw what was inside she cried out, 'The little blackbird!' She stared at the pie funnel with delight.

'You always liked it.'

'Yes, I did. He looked so cocky there in the middle of your mother's pies, just as if he was saying he'd done it all himself. But how did you manage to save it from – I mean . . .'

'Aunt Jane wouldn't have wanted it. I took it from the drawer in the kitchen table even before she had a look around.'

'I can't take it, Helen. You should keep it yourself.'

'No. I want you to have it. And I know my mother would want that too. Every time you make a pie you'll remember old times and happy days.'

Helen didn't get much sense out of their old neighbour after that and soon she left to go back to Aunt Jane's house and see what Eva had left for her to serve up for tea.

On the Monday, the day before Christmas Eve, the school term came to an end. Although the teachers insisted that lessons should go on as usual until the last minute, the atmosphere was light-hearted with the girls finding any opportunity to laugh and some of the younger teachers joining in the fun. School friends exchanged presents before they left for home, including Helen and her friend Eileen. Sitting on the shoe lockers in the cloakroom, they agreed to open their presents then and there and laughed when they saw what had happened. They had bought each other identical pairs of red and white Fair Isle woollen mittens.

'I know where you bought these!' Helen exclaimed. 'The Penny Bazaar!'

'Well, I certainly didn't knit them!' Eileen replied and they laughed until their smiles faded.

'I suppose I'd better be going home,' Helen said reluctantly.

'You must come to our house whenever you want to,' Eileen said. 'You don't have to wait to be asked.'

'I will,' Helen replied, but again she had that strange feeling that life was moving on.

Once outside it was too cold to linger and they hurried away in different directions along the pavements where frost sparkled in the fading light of the winter's day.

On Christmas morning the postman called with a small parcel for Helen. Aunt Jane was still in bed so Helen took it up to her room to open it. Joe and Danny had sent her a box of vanilla fudge and it had got squashed in the post. Each square had merged into the next one, but Helen knew she would enjoy it more than any fudge she had ever eaten. She left it on top of the dresser and went down to help Eva in the kitchen.

Helen wondered what Aunt Jane would have done if she had not been living there. Would she have had her Christmas dinner all alone, waited on by Eva and greeted by no one?

'Last Christmas the missus invited a friend along from her bridge club,' Eva told her, 'but a few days later the woman died.'

The two girls stared at each other through the steam rising from the pudding pan and tried not to laugh. It was no use. Eva cracked up first. 'And before you say anything it wasn't my cooking!'

'I wouldn't even suggest it,' Helen said. 'But has my aunt no other friends?'

'They come and go but she's always picking quarrels with them. If she's not careful she's going to be a very lonely old woman.'

Aunt Jane insisted that Helen accompany her to church and it was true that not many people greeted her cheerily. They did not stay to gossip after the service.

When they got home the table had been set with the best damask tablecloth, the best silver-plated cutlery, and there was even a cut-glass vase in the centre holding a sprig of holly. There was also a bottle of port wine and two glasses. When Eva had brought the food and gone back to the kitchen Aunt Jane poured herself a glassful of the wine and filled half a glass for Helen.

'Well, then, Helen,' she said with an air of smug complacency. 'I'm sure this will be the best Christmas dinner you've ever had.' She set about carving slices from the capon and indicated that Helen was to help herself to the vegetables and the gravy.

They ate in silence. By the time Eva came in with the pudding Aunt Jane had had another two glasses of wine and her face was flushed. 'That was very nice, Eva,' she said and her maid-of-all-work raised her eyebrows at the unexpected praise. 'Now make yourself up a plate of dinner from what's left of the vegetables and take yourself a slice of the capon. Put the rest in the pantry for tomorrow.'

Eva wasn't coming to work on Boxing Day. Aunt Helen had given her the day off – without pay, of course. She said Helen and she could manage perfectly well on their own. She meant Helen, naturally. She would probably sit by the fire as usual reading her magazines and being waited on hand and foot.

'When you've finished, wash up what you can,' Aunt Jane added. 'Helen will do the rest.'

Before Eva left Helen slipped into the kitchen to give her her present. 'You shouldn't hev!' Eva said as without waiting to be told she tore off the wrapping paper. Her eyes shone as she stared at her gift. 'A bottle of scent. What is it?'

'Muguet des Bois.'

'Come again?'

'Lilies of the Valley. But it's not Coty. It's a copy, I'm afraid.'

'I haven't a clue what you're talking about, but thank you, anyway. I've never owned a bottle of scent in me whole life.'

'Everybody should have a little luxury now and then. That's what my mother used to say.'

'She was a wise woman,' Eva said. 'But now, if you don't mind, I'll be off to the madhouse to help me ma with all those dratted kids.'

Eva was only pretending to complain. Helen could see how eager she was to get home and she envied her, for Helen herself faced a long, dreary day with her aunt. She was to make sandwiches at teatime and put up a couple of plates of cold meat and pickle for supper. By the time she had finished in the kitchen Aunt Jane had taken herself and her bottle of port wine to the front parlour.

'Do sit down, Helen,' she said. 'Although, wait a minute, you'd better see to the fire first. It's chilly, isn't it?'

Personally Helen thought her aunt kept this room far too warm and the rest of the house too cold, but she did as she was told and sat at the other side of the hearth. Her aunt had already nodded off and Helen had to restrain her giggles at the little piggy noises she was making. She stared at her mother's sister, the coarse features and the network of broken veins on her cheeks, and wondered how on earth they could have been related. Perhaps her mother had been a changeling, a child substituted for another by the fairies. Or perhaps a wicked witch had left her own daughter in Aunt Jane's cradle.

She stared at the woman glumly and remembered how that morning she had given her aunt her present at the breakfast table. Her aunt had raised her eyebrows as she opened the wrapping paper and gazed at the pair of embroidered Swiss handkerchiefs. There was a moment's silence. Perhaps Aunt Jane had actually been embarrassed, but if so she didn't give it away when she said, 'Very nice, Helen, and I'm sure it's right for you to show your gratitude, but we don't give presents in this house.'

With those words she had dampened any Christmas joy there might have been before the day had properly begun. Well, at least, Helen thought, I can escape into a book for a while. Sighing with an emotion that was akin to contentment, Helen settled back in her chair and opened *The Constant Nymph* by Margaret Kennedy, one of the books she had treated herself to from the bookstall in the market.

Soon, along with the book's heroine, fourteen-year-old Tessa, Helen was living in a rambling chalet high in the

Austrian Alps and falling in love with Lewis Dodd, a gifted composer, and worrying dreadfully that her beautiful cousin Florence was going to steal him away . . .

On Christmas morning, straight after breakfast, Joe and Danny were among a small group of boys summoned to Mr Ridley's study. Straight away Joe's eyes were drawn to the pile of brightly wrapped presents on the headmaster's desk.

'Ah . . . um . . . Merry Christmas, boys,' Mr Ridley said.

'Same to you, sir,' the boys replied in unison.

'As those of you who have been with us for some while know, most of the boys here do not get Christmas presents sent from outside. There is – ah – no one to send them. But a lucky few of you do have people who remember you.' He paused and eyed the pile of presents sadly. Joe wondered if he was going to tell them that they could not have them. The headmaster's next words seemed to confirm the suspicion. 'We have discussed whether in all fairness we should pass these on to you . . .'

So why show them to us? Joe wondered.

'But we decided that we should.'

Then why not get on with it?

'However, as in previous years I must ask you not to flaunt these presents,' Mr Ridley continued. 'You may take them up to your dormitory and put them in your lockers. But be quick about it. You can open them later. You must come down and join the other boys in the hall as soon as possible.'

Mr Ridley handed out the presents and the boys hurried upstairs as they were told. Once in the dormitory not one of the boys could resist opening their presents and there were exclamations of delight and disappointment. Joe could see from the shape of the parcels that Helen had sent them a

107

book each – he knew the presents would be from Helen; who else was there to remember them?

'What have you got?' he asked Danny.

'*Coral Island.*'

Joe grinned. 'I've got an island too. *Treasure Island.*'

'We can read them and swap.'

'I'm sure Helen meant us to.'

'What have you got here then?'

Joe looked up to see Tod staring at them. He didn't answer.

'Books, is it? Don't see the point of books.'

'Well, why would you when you can't read?' Joe said and saw the flicker of dismay in Danny's eyes.

'What did you say?' Tod asked.

'My brother was joking,' Danny said.

'No, he wasn't,' Tod retorted. 'He was suggesting that I'm ignorant. Well, let me tell you I'm not.'

Joe would have retorted further but Danny took his arm and tried to pull him back. He might have succeeded if Joe had not noticed that Tod was carrying two Christmas presents. 'How did you get those?' he asked.

Tod grinned. 'Sent to me, weren't they? Some kind person remembered me just like someone remembered you.'

'You're lying.'

Tod's small eyes narrowed even further. 'I'm what?' he asked quietly.

'You're lying. You didn't come to Mr Ridley's study with the rest of us. You've stolen those from two other boys.'

'So now you're calling me a thief?'

'It's as good as thieving, what you do. So yes, you are a thief and you're a bully, too.'

108

The two boys stared at each other and Joe was aware that Danny had become very still. Oh, no, he thought. I should have kept my mouth shut. Whatever Tod does next he's bound to take it out on Danny, too. He was ready to defend his brother physically when to his surprise Tod simply shrugged and walked away.

When they went down to the hall they found that a long queue of boys had formed to receive presents provided by the charity board and handed out by Mr Ridley. There were jigsaws, board games, sketch pads, boxes of crayons and some totally unsuitable presents in Joe's opinion, like socks and handkerchiefs. The distribution was indiscriminate and once the parcels were opened a lot of swapping went on.

Ginger was over the moon with his game of draughts and Joe and Danny decided to be content with their socks. After all, they had the presents that Helen had sent them. For the rest of the morning they were given free time. Many of the lads wanted to stay indoors with their presents but one of the younger teachers encouraged a group to go with him for a game of football on the beach. Joe and Danny went along.

'That's dangerous,' Joe said as he stared up at the gash in the cliff face above him. He had been sent to collect the ball when it landed amongst a pile of rocks at the foot of the sandstone cliffs. At first he couldn't find it and the rest of the boys began to shout impatiently. Danny had come over to help him.

'Erosion,' Danny said.

Joe grinned. 'If you say so.'

'The sea crashes against the cliff face until it crumbles,' Danny said as he peered up to where the top of the cliff was hanging over without any visible support. 'It's worse than when we went for a run last week. A spot to avoid, I think.'

The Christmas dinner was good and everyone would have been happy if they hadn't had to join in the 'party' afterwards. This started with team games leading up to teatime with sandwiches and mince pies, followed by carol singing before they had the usual supper of hot milk and bread and butter, and went to bed.

'Well, that wasn't too bad,' Joe remarked to Danny as they climbed the stairs. 'We'll be able to write and tell Helen that we enjoyed ourselves. We don't want her fretting, do we?'

Danny didn't answer. He was staring down at the pieces of paper that littered the top landing.

'What are they?' Joe asked but he already knew the answer. They were the torn and crumpled pages of a book.

He knew what he'd find when he picked them up but he gathered them up all the same and followed the trail to their beds in the dormitory. Both of their books had been destroyed. Only the empty covers remained on the beds.

He became aware of the silence and that the other boys were staring at them. Even Ginger didn't have anything to say.

Then Danny took hold of his arm and said quietly, 'Pick all the pages up and we'll put them in our lockers.'

'What's the point? We'll never be able to put the books together again.'

'Maybe we will and maybe we won't, but at least we'll still have Helen's presents. And listen, Joe, that's all we're going to do. We're not going to say anything to anyone. Right?'

Joe looked at his twin and something about his determined expression surprised him. Danny had changed since he had come here and, he wasn't sure why, but this time he was happy to follow his younger brother's lead. He helped Danny pick up the torn pages, ignoring the sniggers of Tod's cronies – for who else but Tod Walker would have done this? Or ordered it to be done? But when he went to bed he couldn't sleep for the anger that raged through him, burning almost like a fever. Tod Walker would pay for this. One way or another he would pay.

Selma Partington couldn't remember when she had had such a happy Christmas. Probably not since she had been a child herself. I mean, it's been marvellous the way Hugh has spoiled me, she thought, but I'm not the important one now. Elise is. I'm a mother and we have our own darling little daughter to make our family complete.

However, Christmas this year would not be quite the same as Christmases she had planned for the future. Despite the fact that Miss Barton had already taken the matter of Elise's way of talking in hand, the child was still not quite 'one of them'.

Next year she would have a party. No, two parties. One for a select group of friends and their children and another for Hugh's employees' children. Hugh would dress as Santa Claus and Elise would be a dear little elf to help him give out the presents. Nevertheless this year they would go to the pantomime. Hugh had asked her if she would like to go to their London house for a while and take Elise to the Lyceum to see *Puss in Boots*.

'It would be fun,' he'd said, and although Selma was truly touched by his enthusiasm she had refused the offer.

'No, darling,' she'd said, 'we'll see what Newcastle has to offer.'

Secretly she was already dreaming of sitting in the box at the theatre and being noticed with Elise. Hugh would be with them and they would smile and laugh like the happy family they were. Everyone who saw them would admire them and would talk about the beautiful child who seemed to be so devoted to Selma Partington.

Selma thought her dreams quite modest for her first Christmas with Elise and they all came true. But even before the tinsel and the decorations had been taken down and put away for another year things went horribly wrong.

Chapter Seven

Ginger was the only witness. Most of the boys had grumbled at being forced to turn out for a run on New Year's Day. Only the really keen types stripped to their running shorts and vests without complaint and set off along the cliff top path as usual. Ginger wasn't a runner. He was small and slight, and malnutrition as a baby had weakened his bones and drained his energy. He was usually one of the last to return to Haven House along with Tod Walker.

Here was at least one thing that Tod could not bully someone else into doing for him. He had to complete the run along with everyone else and by the time he returned he would be in a state of complete fury. The others had learned to keep out of his way.

Ginger always hung back to avoid Tod and today was no different. Except that with the swirling mist coming in from the sea the way ahead was obscured and it was hard to tell who exactly was in front of him. This was really spooky, Ginger thought, like a Sherlock Holmes story he'd read, but he didn't expect that he would see a murder.

The mist thickened and Ginger slowed down. He bent over and grasped his knees when he began to cough. This will be the death of me, he thought, and when the coughing spasm passed he straightened up and rubbed at his watery eyes with cold fingers. By the time he could see again the mist ahead had cleared and there, just like in the story, two figures were struggling on the very edge of the cliff.

Ginger blinked and stared at them. It was Tod and Joe . . . or was it Danny? From this distance he couldn't tell the difference. It shouldn't have been either of them. Both twins were reasonably fit and they usually got back to Haven House long before the likes of Tod Walker. Then, while he was still puzzling over this, it happened. Did Tod scream in terror as he went over the cliff or was it the eerie screech of a startled gull?

The mist swirled in again and Ginger remained where he was, trembling with fright. By the time the way ahead had cleared there was nothing to see, no one on the path ahead of him, and he set off fearfully, half-convinced that he had imagined it all. But then he came to a place where the turf was scuffed and he paused and inched towards the edge of the path. He looked down towards the beach, already knowing what he would see.

Tod Walker lay in a crumpled heap amongst the boulders. His eyes were open and he was staring upwards but Ginger knew that he couldn't see anything. Nor would he ever see anything again. What must his last visions have been? The lowering sky? The cliff face hurtling upwards as he plunged towards the rocks below? The silhouetted figure of another boy looking down on him?

Ginger began to tremble uncontrollably as he tried to make sense of what he had witnessed a few short moments ago. Joe . . . Danny . . . Which one of them did this? And had it been an accident or something more sinister?

He had taken to the Norton twins straight away – lively Joe and quiet, thoughtful Danny. Nice lads, both of them, and Ginger couldn't believe there was a bad bone in their bodies.

It must have been an accident. Ginger edged back from the cliff top and when he could no longer see the horror of what lay below the trembling subsided. The best thing he could do was to get back sharpish and see what was up. But whatever had happened he decided it wasn't his place to land either of the twins in trouble.

By the time he got back to Haven House just about everybody had had their showers and they were filing into the dining room for tea. Ginger climbed the stairs slowly. As he reached the landing Joe and Danny came towards him.

'Tail end as usual?' Joe said.

Ginger thought Danny's smile was strained when he said, 'Don't tease him, Joe, can't you see he's whacked?'

Their expressions didn't give anything away. What was happening here? What had happened on the cliff top? Had Tod had a go at Danny and had Danny had to defend himself? Or had the bully boy picked a fight with Joe and Joe had got the better of him? Whatever the truth of it was Ginger baulked at asking them. He realized that for the sake of friendship he didn't want to ask any questions in case he didn't like the answers.

But when was anyone going to notice that Tod Walker had not returned?

The answer to that came just as Ginger was taking his place at the table. At last one of the teachers spotted that Tod had not signed in and Mr Jenkins, in a very bad humour, started questioning everybody. Joe and Danny shook their heads and professed ignorance like everybody else and Ginger kept quiet. Whatever had happened on the cliff top he was prepared to give the twins the benefit of the doubt, so the best thing to do was wait to see how things developed.

It didn't take the search party long and by the end of the meal Mr Ridley called for silence and told the boys that there

115

had been a tragic accident. Accident, Ginger thought. It could have been, couldn't it? Perhaps Joe or Danny didn't mean Tod to go over the cliff. By now he had convinced himself that was the truth of the matter and his spirits revived. He decided that he wouldn't have to say anything. He would let things take their course. After all, it was sad but true that no one, not even his bunch of cronies, was going to grieve over Tod Walker. He looked across the table to where the twins were sitting next to each other, smiled at them hesitantly and then turned his attention to his supper.

'I think Ginger saw what happened,' Danny said later when the dormitory was silent. He had come to perch on Joe's bed and he kept his voice low, so as not to risk waking anyone else.

'Why do you say that?'

'Well, think about it. He was the last home so he must have been behind us.'

'Doesn't mean he saw anything.'

'What about the way he was looking at us at suppertime? Sort of worried and thoughtful. What was that about?'

'You're right. That was odd.' Thoroughly alert now, Joe sat up.

'Do you think he'll say anything?' Danny asked.

'He would have said by now.'

'Maybe not to the teachers, but when the police come. He wouldn't want to lie to them, would he?'

'I'm not sure. He's been a pal, remember.'

'Yes,' Danny said. 'But can we count on that? After all, this is serious.'

They both sat silently for a while, taking in the gravity of the situation. The enormity of what had happened. Nothing in their young lives had prepared them for this. Instinctively they drew together, each wanting to protect the other.

Then Joe said, 'I think it's time to go.'

'Where? To Helen?'

'First place they'll look. Besides, Aunt Jane would turn us in.'

'Helen will worry.'

'We'll have to send word somehow.'

'But we can't tell her what happened.'

'No.' Joe sounded grim.

'We can't ever go home, can we?' Danny said bleakly.

'We haven't got a home. But no, we can't.'

'What will we do?'

'I'll think of something. And remember, Danny. Whatever happens, I'll always look after you.'

When Hugh came home the house was in uproar. Servants hurried up and down the stairs and there was already a pile of luggage in the hall. He found Selma emptying the contents of her wardrobes on to her bed.

'What's happening?' he asked. 'Are we going somewhere?'

'Of course we are. We can't stay here.'

'Why ever not?'

'You saw the letter. You know what's happened.' She stopped what she was doing and faced him angrily. 'And you didn't even tell me. You just went to the office and left it for me to find and read by myself.'

'I went out early. I didn't want to disturb you. And besides, it's sad but there's nothing we can do.'

'About the wretched boys, no. They've run away from the best chance life gave them like ungrateful little guttersnipes. But it's not them I'm worried about.'

'What, then?'

117

'The girl, of course. Their elder sister, Helen.'

'But why? What has she done?'

'Hugh! Did you actually read this letter?' Selma picked it up from her dressing table.

'Yes.'

'And also the letter that came with the belongings they left behind?'

'No, I didn't.'

'If you had you would know why we are leaving.'

'Let me see.'

Hugh sat down on the chair by the dressing table and read the letter that Selma thrust in his hand.

'So?' Selma said. 'Do you see what she told them?'

'She told them a lot of things.'

'Including the fact that she came here to spy on us.'

'That's a bit strong. She probably just wanted to see if her little sister was all right. That's natural, isn't it?'

'I told her aunt there must be no contact whatsoever.'

'And at the time I thought that was a little harsh. I mean, why stop them seeing each other?'

'Because Elise has settled in so well here and I want her to forget about her former life completely. I want her to become our daughter – think how unsettling it would be for her to have all those memories dragged up.'

'I suppose so.'

'I'm sure of it. So that's why we're going to London.'

Hugh turned to look in the mirrors of the dressing-table. The reflection of his wife moved about the room feverishly. It crossed his mind that she looked almost demented.

'Selma, sit down a minute,' he said.

She stopped and looked at him impatiently. 'Why?'

'What you propose to do . . .' he gestured towards the

heap of clothes on the bed, the tumble of shoes and handbags on the floor, '. . . all this is a little drastic, isn't it?'

She frowned, lost in thought, and then gave him her full attention. 'You're right, Hugh, darling,' she said and for a moment he thought sanity had returned. She smiled. 'Why on earth should I bother to take any but my favourites? I can buy whatever I want in London both for me and for Elise.'

Hugh's spirits sank again. 'I didn't mean that. I mean this running away business. It isn't sa— I mean it isn't sensible.' He had almost said 'sane'. 'Just go and see the children's aunt.'

'I intend to.'

'Go and see her and tell her what has happened and that she must make sure that Helen doesn't come near our house again.'

Selma shook her head. 'That won't do.'

'Why not?'

'Because I don't trust her.'

'Mrs Roberts?'

'No, the girl. She didn't want me to take Elise, that was quite obvious, and didn't you read what she said in her letter?'

'That she'd keep an eye on things?'

'How dare she! But worse than that, she's promised the boys that one day they will all be together again. Oh, Hugh, don't you see? She intends to take Elise away from us!'

Selma suddenly collapsed on top of the pile of clothes on the bed and, heedless of the fact that the garment she sat next to was pure silk, she lifted up the sleeve and tried to stem her tears. Hugh was truly alarmed. He had accepted that his young wife was devoted to the child and he had been both pleased and amused when she encouraged him to enjoy the role of father. But this was more than devotion, it was obsession. He must face the prospect that Selma was mentally ill – or dangerously near to it.

He got up and went over to the bed, then sat beside her, taking her in his arms. She turned towards him and wept in earnest. He waited until her anguished sobs subsided then said gently, 'Of course, my pet, you are right; we must go to live in London.'

She moved away from him and looked up through brimming tears. 'And you will come with us?'

'Of course. Why shouldn't I?'

'You like living here. And there's the wretched office.'

He smiled at her. 'I admit I am very firmly attached to my roots in the North Country, but I am even more attached to you, and as for the office, I can assure you that the premises in London are just as suitable for me to run the business from. In fact the board of directors would prefer it.'

'Good.' Like a butterfly emerging from a chrysalis, Selma cast off her misery. She looked around at the chaos she had created. 'Oh, dear, I've been very silly, haven't I?'

'I wouldn't dream of saying such a thing.'

'Of course you wouldn't. But I have. And now that everything is agreed between us I must go about this in a more organized way.'

Like a good child, Selma began to fold her clothes and hang them away again.

'Leave that, darling,' Hugh said. 'You don't have to do that. Isn't it time you popped along to the nursery to see if Elise has had her supper?'

'Goodness – yes! She'll be waiting for her bedtime story.'

Selma darted out of the room without a backward glance, leaving Hugh feeling very anxious indeed. He accepted that he was so in love with her that he would do anything in his power to make her happy, but in agreeing that they should take this child in the first place had he unwittingly led them into dangerous waters?

The years of longing for and failing to conceive a child might have seriously affected her already fragile personality. They would go to London, it was the only way to calm her, but he would have to see Charles Harris before they left. Although he would not tell Selma.

Ignoring Selma's rule that he must not smoke in the bedroom, he took a cigarette from his case, lit up and took a long drag from it. When he exhaled he stared glumly through the bluish smoke. There was a question that had been haunting him from the moment Elise had come into their lives, darling Elise, whom he had found no difficulty in giving his heart to. She gave every indication of being happy with them, but what would happen if in years to come, when she was old enough to understand what had happened, she found out that it was their car that had run down and killed her mother?

At first Jane Roberts felt pleased and honoured when Eva announced that there was a Mrs Partington at the door. 'Well, show her in here, girl. You mustn't keep a lady like that waiting on the step.'

In the short interval before Mrs Partington swept into the room, Helen's aunt hurried to the window, edged the lace curtain aside and looked with satisfaction at the expensive motor car parked in the street outside her house. She hoped earnestly that the neighbours were watching.

'In here, madam,' she heard Eva say.

She moved away from the window quickly. 'Mrs Partington,' she said, 'how nice of you to call.'

Her guest didn't respond but simply regarded her coldly.

'Erm . . . Can I offer you a cup of tea?'

121

'No. And for goodness' sake tell the girl to leave us.'

Eva was standing in the doorway, wide-eyed as she regarded the slim, elegantly dressed woman who was, she had just decided, the most beautiful creature she had ever seen – even if she did have a temper on her. For Eva had realized, even if it had not dawned on the missus yet, that this woman was wound up tight with fury.

'Off you go, Eva,' Jane Roberts said. 'I'll – erm – I'll ring if you are needed.'

Reluctantly the maid withdrew.

'Well, what have you to say for yourself?' Mrs Partington said as soon as the door clicked shut.

'Say for myself? I'm not sure what you mean.'

Selma Partington glared at her. 'The boys – those wretched twins. Surely you know they have run away?'

Jane Roberts experienced what people called a sinking feeling. Something had gone terribly wrong and she sensed that there was more to come. Suddenly her breath caught in her throat. She stumbled towards an armchair and sank down. With great effort she remembered her manners and waved vaguely towards the other chair. 'Forgive me,' she said. 'Won't you sit?'

'I prefer to stand.'

That was a pity. It meant that Jane had to crane her neck and look up at the terrifying woman who was standing over her. 'What have they done?' she asked and when Mrs Partington simply scowled at her she said, 'The boys, what have they done?'

'I've told you. They've run away from Haven House.'

'Nobody told me. But why? Have they . . . have they done something wrong? Have they stolen something?' She shrank into herself when she saw that Mrs Partington was growing even angrier.

'I have no idea why they ran away. As far as I know, they have committed no crime or we would have been told. It's what they left at Haven House that is important.'

'Left?'

'Apparently they went in such a hurry that they left everything behind them. When their lockers were searched this letter was found.' Mrs Partington opened her handbag, took out a letter and handed it over. 'Read it.'

'Yes – thank you – but you're, erm . . . standing in my light.'

To Jane's enormous relief her visitor at last sat down in the chair opposite to her, but Mrs Partington never took her gaze from her as she fumbled with the envelope and began to read the letter. She saw her own address on the first page. 'But I didn't . . .' she began.

'Turn to the last page. Look at the signature.'

'It's from Helen,' Jane Roberts said. 'I didn't know she'd written to them. Is that why you're angry?'

'Read it.'

It didn't take her long to realize why Mrs Partington was so angry. 'She came to your house,' she said.

'I told you specifically that there was to be no contact.'

'I know. I agreed. I hope you don't think I put her up to it.'

'Actually I don't.'

Jane Roberts breathed a sigh of relief but the respite was short-lived.

'But nevertheless I hold you responsible. She actually told her brothers that she would continue to "keep an eye on things" as she put it.'

'I'm sorry. I'll see to it that it doesn't happen again.'

'It's no use. You obviously can't control the girl. Our arrangement must come to an end.'

123

Ginger faced Mr Ridley, Mr Jenkins and a large policeman in uniform in the headmaster's study. He had been the last to be called. That was because he had been the last to sign in after the run. He knew from the gossip that no one else had any idea what had happened and he had his story ready.

'So you're absolutely sure you saw nothing?' the policeman asked.

'No, sir. Well . . .' he hesitated as he had planned.

'Well?' Mr Jenkins asked impatiently.

'I did see Tod Walker ahead of me. Then I didn't.'

'Make sense, boy!'

'The mist was coming and going. At one point he was there. The mist came in. I stopped – and when the mist cleared again he wasn't there. I thought he must have gone on while I was coughing.'

'Coughing?'

'Yes, sir. You know I have a bad chest.'

'And you saw no one else?'

'No one, sir. Tod and me are usually the last home. I thought he'd beaten me to it this time.'

'What about the Norton boys?'

'The twins? Oh, they're pretty fit. They would be among the first home.' Well, what he said hadn't been a lie, he thought, and they didn't seem to realize that he hadn't really answered the question. And then he wondered again which twin it had been whom he had seen scuffling with Tod Walker, and how they had arranged to sign in. Probably whoever got home first had signed for both of them. Knowing those two that would have been easy enough to arrange.

'And what did you think when you realized he hadn't returned?' the policeman asked.

'Who?'

'Tod Walker, of course,' Mr Jenkins barked.

'I didn't think anything. I mean, I just didn't know, did I?'

Ginger put on what he hoped was a gormless look and was rewarded with an impatient shake of the head by Mr Jenkins and a weary sigh from Mr Ridley. The policeman closed his notebook and said, 'Well, I think that's about it. You can go now, lad.'

'An accident, then?' Mr Ridley said to Mr Jenkins after the policeman had gone.

'It seems so.'

'We will still attract censure.'

'Why?'

'We shouldn't have sent them out in such conditions.'

'No.'

'And the Norton boys?'

'Runaways. It happens. They didn't realize how lucky they were. Good riddance to them.'

Mr Ridley didn't reply. He was thinking about the sum of money that Hugh Partington would no longer contribute. He eyed his assistant headmaster thoughtfully. He knew himself to be totally unfitted to run such an establishment as Haven House and he wondered if it was time to find someone more dedicated than Jenkins to be his deputy. It probably was.

'You stupid, stupid girl! What were you thinking of?'

Aunt Jane had stormed into the kitchen, taken hold of Helen's arm and dragged her from her chair and then across the hall into the front parlour. She slammed the door behind them and turned to face Helen, breathing heavily.

'What is it? What's the matter?' Helen rubbed her arm and stared at her aunt in alarm. The broken veins on her face had purpled and her eyes were almost popping from their sockets.

'I've just had a visit from Mrs Partington.'

'I know. Eva told me.'

'And why do you think she came here? Why do you think a great lady like her bothered to come to my little home?'

'I . . . I don't know.'

'You went to visit your sister. That's why. Even though you were told not to. Ever.'

'I didn't visit her. I just went to . . . to have a look at where she was living.'

'Nevertheless you saw her.'

'I didn't speak to her. She didn't see me.'

Aunt Jane suddenly clutched at her throat. She began to gasp and Helen thought she saw a flicker of fear in her eyes, but after a moment her aunt's breathing eased and the fury returned.

'But you would have done eventually. You told your brothers in your letter. That's how the Partingtons knew you'd been there.'

'My brothers? Letter?' Helen was confused. 'How do you know about the letter?'

'Because the ungrateful brats have run away, that's how, and they left most of their things behind them. Well, they needn't think they can turn up here, that's all I can say. And as for you, you needn't think you're going back to school. I should put you out. That's what you deserve. But I've decided it's time you made yourself useful around here.'

Chapter Eight

Helen gripped her pencil and stared at the blank page in front of her. The kitchen was quiet; her aunt had gone to bed hours ago, but Helen could not sleep. Even though she would have to rise early the next morning to get to work she had taken her notebook and gone down to make herself a cup of tea. It was no use. No words came. The page remained blank. As it had since the beginning of January when her world had changed once more.

She had always taken comfort in recording small events, describing people and moments that she wanted to remember, and since she had come to live with her aunt she had had the added purpose of keeping any precious memories for the sake of her sister and brothers, for she had deluded herself that one day they would all be together again.

What was the point of writing anything now? What had she to record? Oh, yes, her birthday in February. Her fifteenth birthday. There had been a card from Eileen and an invitation to tea which Helen had ignored. How could she bear to go to her old school friend's house now that she had been forced to leave school and abandon all the hopes that her mother had had for her?

Unsurprisingly there had been no card from her aunt, only a reminder that it was time she found a job and that she had better get along to the employment exchange. Aunt Jane had grudgingly acknowledged that Helen might qualify for a job in an office rather than have to settle for shop work, although she wasn't sure if it would be well paid enough for her to make a meaningful contribution towards her board and lodging.

Helen hadn't even told Eva it was her birthday. What was the point? They were barely speaking. Aunt Jane had cut Eva's hours almost by half, saying that once the rough work was done and the lunch prepared, Helen was quite capable of doing anything else such as dusting, bed-making, and seeing to the tea and supper.

Work was hard to come by, even domestic work, so although Eva had begun to look for a position elsewhere, winter, spring and early summer went by and she hadn't found a decent paying job within walking distance of her home and family.

'Might have to settle for factory work,' she told Helen, although both girls knew that not many places were taking on new hands.

So Eva and Helen had passed from an easy-going friendship into awkwardness on Helen's part and a barely disguised state of resentment on Eva's.

During those first dreadful weeks after Mrs Partington had called to see her aunt, Helen had been up early every morning, waiting for the postman in the hopes that she would hear from her brothers. The letter when it came was welcome but far from reassuring. For a start there was no stamp on it, which meant Helen had to pay the postman, but that also meant there was no postmark, so she had no idea where it had come from.

The message was brief:

Dear Helen, (Joe wrote)

Sorry we upped and left but don't worry about us. We'll be OK. We can look after each other.

Joe has found a job, (Danny added) and I help out.

Love,

Joe and Danny

That was all. They hadn't told her where they were, what the job was or why they had run away in the first place. For weeks Helen waited for another letter, but one never came, and by the end of a hot dusty summer she had accepted that she might never hear from them again.

As for Elsie, despite her aunt's explicit instructions that she should never go near the Partington house again, Helen could not resist it. She had gone one morning when she was supposed to be going to the employment exchange. She had stood in the gateway opposite all morning and had seen nothing at all. No one came or went. Eventually, unable to stop herself, she had crossed the road and walked up the long drive to the house. Daringly she stared in through one of the windows. As she had suspected, the furniture was covered with dust sheets. The Partingtons had gone away.

'What do you think you're doing?'

An angry voice behind her startled her and she spun round to face a man who looked like the gardener.

'Nothing . . . I just wanted to know where they were.'

'If by "they" you mean Mr and Mrs Partington, what's it to do with you?'

Helen had no answer.

'Now get along with you,' the man said. 'And there's no need to think that just because the family isn't in residence there isn't someone looking after the place. So it's no use going back and telling your father that there's rich pickings here. That's what you are, isn't it? A thief's nark. I've seen your like before. Dressed all respectable so you think you won't be noticed in this part of town but dishonest as they come. Now clear off before I call the police.'

Helen was mortified but she tried to leave with dignity. It crossed her mind that the gardener, or whoever he was, might report that a girl had been looking in the house and that Mrs Partington would guess who it was. But what could she do? The damage had already been done and it would only make the Partingtons more determined to stay away and keep Elsie to themselves. When she got back her aunt asked her if she'd had any luck at the employment exchange.

'No,' she had replied. 'No luck at all.'

Then she had been offered a job in the office of a pickle factory. After the first day she realized that rather than a clerk she was just a general dogsbody. She wasn't going to learn anything and furthermore she went home smelling of vinegar. But her wages were just enough to allow her to put a little by every week even after her aunt had taken what she considered to be a fair contribution towards household expenses.

She wasn't too sure what she was saving for. She only knew that during the weeks she had been given ninepence a day she had also been given a measure of independence. She had learned that it was good to have a little money of your own.

Helen stared once more at the blank page, then she closed her notebook and leaned forward on the table, resting her head in her hands. She would rest here a little before she went back to bed.

'What the hell are you doing?'

Helen looked up startled to find Eva standing over her.

'You look bloody awful. Have you been down here all night?'

'I suppose I must have been.'

'And now you're going to go to work?'

'Of course. How could I miss another fun day at the pickle factory?'

'You poor, poor thing!' Helen had never seen Eva so angry. 'How dare you complain? You've got a job when hundreds of people haven't and if it isn't exactly what you consider good enough for you then just think on what exactly you're good for!'

Helen stared up in astonishment.

'You don't know what I'm talking about, do you? Not the faintest idea! Listen, Helen, I felt sorry for you when you first came here – being parted from your family and all. And I felt sorry about what happened next, I mean, you must be worried sick about your brothers running away. But all this moping on about your little sister when anyone would tell you she's really fallen on her feet. And you – look at you. Feeling sorry for yourself all the time.'

Helen was stung into replying, 'I don't feel sorry for myself.'

'Oh, yes, you do. You go on as if you're the only person in the world who has troubles. You can't see further than your own nose. I don't think I've ever come across anyone so self-centred!'

'Self-centred?'

'Yes, self-centred. And don't just sit there staring at me. I've no sympathy for you. I'll make you a bit of toast while you hev yourself a wash and then for God's sake get out of here and get on with your life.'

The two girls didn't speak again that morning. Helen was surprised and hurt by Eva's outburst but after the initial shock she realized immediately that she deserved it. She tried to put

131

herself in Eva's shoes. Her friend's family worked hard and struggled to survive. Eva herself had left school at the age of twelve and had worked ever since. As far as Helen could see, Eva had no prospect of bettering herself whereas she, Helen, had at least had a good schooling up till now and it was entirely up to her what she made of it.

On Friday, with her pay packet safely in her pocket, Helen didn't go straight home after work. She knew her aunt would complain if her tea was late but she didn't care. Why should she? She knew by now that Aunt Jane would not turn her out. She had become too useful, not just because she had taken over much of the housework but also because she had come to perform the countless small duties demanded by a lonely woman who was increasingly fussy about her health. Helen had not been able to make up her mind about whether Aunt Jane was really ill or whether she was becoming a hypochondriac.

Margery was wiping the tables down and she looked up in surprise when Helen walked into the Cosy Café. 'My, my, stranger. Where have you been?'

'Have you missed me?' Helen smiled as she took a seat at a table by the window and looked at the menu.

'Well, yes, I have. Did you leave school, then?'

'I'm a working girl now.'

'Right-ho, madam. What can I get you?'

'A pot of tea and poached egg on toast, please.'

'Coming up.'

While Helen waited she looked around at the other tables. The café didn't remain open in the evening and one or two customers were finishing their meals. By the time Margery got back with her poached egg she was the only one left. She'd brought two cups with the pot of tea.

'Mind if I sit with you?' she asked.

'I hoped you would.'

Margery reached into the pocket of her pinafore and took out a packet of Craven "A" and a box of matches. 'Like one?' she asked.

'I don't smoke.'

'I did at your age. Helps the nerves.'

'But what about your throat? I mean, you're taking in hot smoke, aren't you?'

'No worry about that.' Margery opened the pack and took out one cigarette. 'Look, it's got a cork tip – it's specially designed to prevent sore throats. In fact it may be good for them. That's what Dot told me last time she was home.'

'Dot?'

'My daughter. Dorothy.'

Helen knew very well who Dorothy was but she said, 'Of course. How is she? Does she like working in London? Why don't you tell me all about it?'

Mabel Norris peered through rheumy eyes out of her kitchen window as the lad trudged across the yard towards the path that led down to the stream. A year or two ago she would have gone with him. Taken her bread and cheese and apples and a flask of milk and sat on the bank for a while, and maybe even had a little snooze before getting back to work. But now her arthritis had made her a prisoner, confined her to within a very short distance of the farmhouse.

She would have liked a bit of company. She'd told him often enough that he was welcome to sit at her table but who could blame him for wanting to be outside on a day like this? Even on rainy days, she reflected, he seemed uneasy to stay inside for too long and didn't even sleep here. He was quite happy to take the blankets she had given him and sleep in the barn.

Funny lad, she thought. Never says much, but works hard even though he sometimes has to be told twice what to do. Jake, he calls himself. She closed her eyes a moment and tried to remember what the rest of his name was. Had he told her? She wasn't sure. But if he had it would come back to her, wouldn't it? When she was having a good day.

It had been a bitter cold day in January when Jake had arrived. She'd been on the point of selling up when she'd heard the commotion the hens were making that morning. It must be a fox. She grabbed her walking stick and hurried painfully across to the nesting boxes. It was no fox. She'd seen the lad running away and climbing over the wall. A bairn, she thought. Another hungry bairn from the town, and she never knew why she did it but she called out, 'Come back. Don't be frightened. You can sit by the fire and I'll make you a pot of tea and bread and butter and boil one of those eggs if you like. As long as you leave some for me.'

To her astonishment his head popped up over the wall. He surveyed her guardedly and then he climbed over.

'Bread and butter?' he said and she nodded.

More than a bairn, she thought. He's almost a grown lad. Probably can't find a job. Who can these days? And that's when it came to her. If she took him on she might be able to hold out at least one more year. Who knew, maybe longer? This smallholding was the only life she'd ever known. The pittance she might get if she sold up would hardly provide for a comfortable old age. With any luck she would be able to carry on until she dropped dead. Then she would never have to leave.

Jake had seemed grateful to be offered a job but he was a funny lad. Changeable. One day he would be guarded but chirpy, another day very quiet, even dreamy. He was almost like two different people. Mabel Norris didn't live long enough to discover why.

By the time the autumn term was about to begin Selma decided that Elise could be sent to school. Miss Barton had done her best with the child's accent, and as any good girls' school would teach elocution as well as deportment, any remaining little mispronunciations would soon be ironed out.

Elise was playing croquet in the garden with Barty when Hugh came home to find Selma sitting in the conservatory going through a pile of prospectuses. The day was warm and he longed for a shower and a Pimm's – maybe not in that order – but he flopped down beside his wife and picked up some of the prospectuses from the floor where they had been discarded. Selma smiled at him briefly and started flicking through the pages again.

After a moment he said, 'So I take it she's not going to go away to school.'

'Of course not.'

'I thought you wanted the very best for Elise.'

'The very best doesn't have to be a boarding school. There are some good day schools in London.'

'With waiting lists, no doubt. I mean, haven't we left it a bit late for the coming term?'

Selma gave him a pitying look. 'Really, Hugh. Have you forgotten who you are?'

'Do you mean have I forgotten *what* I am?'

She frowned. 'What are you saying?'

'What you meant is that I am a rich man. A very rich man. And you are prepared to use that fact to get what you want.'

'What we both want.'

'Both want?'

'For Elise. For our daughter. Surely you would do anything to get the best for Elise?'

Hugh looked out into the garden at the beautiful child moving so gracefully across the lawn and admitted to himself that he was as enchanted as Selma was. But in his case he hoped the enchantment stopped short of obsession. Maybe he should insist that the child go away to school. Maybe that would be good for Selma. Then he looked at his wife's eager face, saw her happiness, and knew that he couldn't do it. Elise would go to whatever school Selma chose; he had neither the will nor the heart to deny her that.

'Leaving? What do you mean you're leaving?' There was a sheen of perspiration on Jane Roberts' brow as she looked up at Helen in alarmed astonishment. Helen had just placed her aunt's tray on her knee and it wobbled precariously.

'Be careful, you'll spill your tea.'

'Don't speak to me like that.' Her aunt gripped the handles of the tray. 'And how dare you come in here and say that you're leaving me after all that I've done for you?'

'I would have thought you'd be glad to get rid of me. After all, you have made it plain what an expense I am.'

'That's true. As well as feeding you I've bought you clothes and shoes.'

'A skirt for work and one pair of shoes. And surely you had money left from the sum Mrs Partington gave you?'

Aunt Jane's eyes narrowed but she didn't deny it. The room was too warm as usual and Helen longed to open the windows, even though the evening air outside was dusty with summer heat.

'Have you no gratitude?' Aunt Jane said.

'I should be grateful?'

'Of course. I took you in when your mother died. Where else would you have gone?'

Helen regarded her aunt solemnly. 'That's true. You gave me a home, but I think it suited you. You have no children of your own and you wanted someone to look after you as you grow older, and even take over some of the housework because you are too mean to pay Eva a proper wage.'

The teacup rattled as the tray on her aunt's knee slipped to one side. 'Viper!' Aunt Jane gasped. 'I have t-taken a ver . . . ver . . . viper to my b . . . bosom!'

Helen would have laughed except that something strange seemed to be happening to Aunt Jane's face. It was slipping sideways, just like the tray. Helen stepped forward but she was too late. The tray crashed to the floor, spilling the contents on the hearthrug: tea, sugar, milk and cucumber sandwiches.

Her aunt was trying to get up. 'Hel—' she began and Helen never knew whether she had been about to say her name or whether she was asking for help, for a moment later she sank down again and simply looked up at Helen with one startled eye.

Helen didn't even stay to clear the mess from the floor. She ran to fetch the doctor.

'A stroke,' Dr Salkeld said. 'But not too bad. With care and attention she ought to make a reasonably good recovery. It's a good job she's got you. Niece, aren't you?'

'Yes.'

'Right then. I'll call in tomorrow morning, but how are you going to get her up to bed?'

'I can't. Not until tomorrow when her maid arrives.'

'You'll sit with her?'

'Yes.'

137

'Good girl. I'll be off then.'

As soon as Dr Salkeld had gone Helen cleared the mess from the carpet and took the tray through to the kitchen. Her own sandwiches were waiting on the kitchen table and she was tempted to stay there and eat them, but breathing a sigh of resignation, she took them through to the front parlour and tried to enjoy them as Aunt Jane stared at her with a comically crooked air of reproach. It was as if she was trying to convey that this was all Helen's fault. And that would have been easier to bear if only there hadn't been an undeniable expression of panic in the one eye she had open.

You can't leave me now, Helen, she seemed to be saying. *Surely you won't leave me now.*

In later years Joe still prayed and hoped that the dairyman's lad had gone to investigate as soon as he'd discovered that the milk churn wasn't waiting by the stile the next morning. Not only because someone would have to take care of the livestock but also because he didn't like to think of Mrs Norris lying all alone by the nesting boxes with the hens pecking around and treating her body as if it were just something to perch on. He and Danny had been with her for over a year and she had been good to them – although she had never discovered there were two of them.

They had made that decision straight away. 'They'll be looking for two lads,' Joe had told Danny. 'So one lad we'll have to be.'

Not that anyone had ever come near Mrs Norris's smallholding. She had no friends or family that Joe knew of, and if anyone did come by, both twins kept out of the way. Even the dairyman didn't know anyone was there as Joe or Danny – whichever one was 'Jake' that day – was always

138

careful to leave the churn and the basket of eggs and scarper before anyone arrived.

Joe tried not to think about the fact that they had just left her lying there. 'If we take her into the house it could be a while before she's found,' he had said to Danny.

They had entered the house themselves. The first time they had been in there together and filled a knapsack with any food that would travel. They felt no compunction about that. They both knew that Mrs Norris would want Jake to have anything he found useful. Joe glanced at the Rington's tea caddy on a shelf of the dresser. He had a good idea of what was in there. He took it down, opened it and emptied the money it contained on to the table. His eyes widened.

'More than I thought,' he said. 'This will do us for a while.' It never crossed his mind that this was dishonest. After all, if they didn't take it who would? No one that Mrs Norris would like to have it, he was sure of that.

'How far will that get us?' Danny asked.

'London if you like, and there'll still be lots left over.'

'London?'

'Yeah, I reckon that's far enough away and it's big enough to get lost in. But it's getting there that might be tricky.'

'Why?'

'They could still be looking for two of us.'

'After all this time?'

'Depends whether they decided that Tod went over the cliff by accident or not.'

They looked at each other solemnly.

'So what will we do?' Danny asked.

'We'll travel separately and meet up when we get there.'

'Where?'

'King's Cross. That's a railway station. Whoever arrives

139

there first must wait for the other.'

'We're going by train?'

'I don't see why not. We've got enough money to buy tickets and some left over. So my plan is that we part now and hitch to the station at Darlington or York or wherever we can get a ride to.'

'King's Cross must be a big station. How will we find each other?'

'There's got to be a waiting room, hasn't there? And a refreshment room where we can buy food.'

After thinking it over Danny agreed, and they took a pack of cards from the dresser and cut to see who should go first. Joe drew the high card. 'I'll be off,' he said. 'Give me two hours' start.' Then, trying not to look at Mrs Norris lying amongst the clucking hens, he slipped away.

Danny watched the old clock on the mantelshelf and waited for two hours as Joe had told him to do. Outside the sky darkened and it began to rain. By the time Danny decided he could go the rain was torrential. He hesitated at the door, but looking up at the skies he didn't think it was going to ease off for a while, and he wanted to get away before nightfall.

He glanced over his shoulder at the fire in the hearth regretfully. Leaving the door open so that the wind blew the rain across the stone-paved floor, he made a run for it, pausing only briefly to look down at Mrs Norris and the raindrops streaming down her face like tears.

Joe had found a cosy billet in a waiting room just as he'd said he would, but he soon learned that if the policemen in Newcastle Central Station were fierce, the London bobbies were worse.

He was moved along every time a copper spotted him.

140

Who do they think I am? he asked himself indignantly. A criminal of some kind? Then he caught sight of himself in a mirror in the men's lavatories. A right little tramp, he thought. No wonder they don't like the look of me. He paid sixpence for a wash and brush-up. The attendant, a tall, lugubrious man, gave him a bar of soap and a nice clean towel and showed him into one of the little white-tiled cubicles.

When Joe emerged the attendant eyed him speculatively. 'All alone in town?' he asked.

Joe said he was and could have kicked himself when he saw the narrowing of the man's eyes. 'But that's just for the moment,' he added quickly. 'I'm meeting my brother, my elder brother. That's why I thought I'd better smarten up a bit. He's – erm – he's been on business in the North and he's been delayed.'

The man raised his eyebrows. Joe knew he didn't believe a word of it but he must have decided it wasn't worth pursuing. He shrugged and walked away. Joe returned to sit by the fire in the waiting room. Someone had left a newspaper on the bench seat. It was open and folded over to show the Situations Vacant column. Joe glanced at the jobs advertised and grinned: bank clerk; travelling salesman; live-in chauffeur and handyman. London might be the land of opportunity – didn't they say the streets were paved with gold? – but there was nothing there for him. And then he saw a job that would be just the ticket; furthermore, according to the times given, he could go along right now and apply for it.

What should he do? Sitting there he could hear the announcements of trains leaving and arriving. Was there still a chance that Danny would arrive today? Then the time came when the next arrival from the North wouldn't be until the next morning. He knew he wouldn't be allowed to stay in the station overnight and in any case he didn't want to. With an anxious look at the clock above the fireplace he grabbed the newspaper, shoved his hand in his pocket and pulled out the cash he had left. No worries there. He headed for the taxi stand.

He was back bright and early the next morning. When Danny arrived he looked tired and ill. He was coughing. 'Got soaked,' he explained, 'and no one wanted to stop to give me a lift in that weather.' It had taken him all night to walk to Darlington, where he'd had to wait at least an hour for the London train.

'What do we do now?' he added somewhat forlornly.

'We get a taxi and I take you home,' Joe told him.

'Home?' Danny, his face pale, his eyes swimming, looked bewildered.

'Yes, mate. That's what they say here. Call each other mate. Yes, home. I've got myself a job and better still a nice cosy billet is part of the deal. We can both stay there and if I prove satisfactory they might take you on too.'

Joe was so full of his own achievement that he didn't notice how ill Danny looked until he realized that he had fallen asleep in the taxi. A good meal and a warm bed is what he needs, Joe thought. He'll soon be right again. For the rest of the journey he looked out of the windows as the streets flew by. Last night when he had come this way it had been dark. He would have to learn his way around. Taxis were expensive. But they were here and they were together, and whatever happened he would look after Danny. There was no question about that.

A month after Helen's sixteenth birthday she decided that her aunt had recovered enough for her to leave her. Jane Roberts had been lucky in that the stroke had only affected

142

her left side. During the day she was looked after by a nurse recommended by Doctor Salkeld and Helen took over when she got back from work. As Aunt Jane recovered she began to resent the weekly cheques she was writing for the nurse and she told Helen that she was going to dismiss her.

'Then who will look after you?' Helen asked.

'You, of course.'

'But I'm at work all day.'

Jane Roberts managed a lopsided sneer. 'In a per-pickle factory.'

'In the office.' Helen didn't think much of her job but that didn't mean that her aunt should belittle it.

'We are family. Your place is here with me.'

Helen was aghast. Was she really expected to stay here in this miserable house tied to this unpleasant woman forever? She examined her conscience and decided that she owed her mother's sister nothing. The week before the nurse was due to leave she told her aunt that she had indeed given notice at work but that she was going to leave as she had originally intended.

'But don't worry,' she said, not giving her aunt time to react. 'I've thought of everything. You won't have to pay a private nurse. You'll be looked after.'

Aunt Jane opened her good eye wide. 'Ll-lurlooked after? Who by?'

'Eva.'

Aunt Jane looked as though she was going to protest vigorously so Helen hurried on. 'I've spoken to her and she's willing to come back and work full-time. She'll even live in if that's what you would like. She can sleep in my room and be on call during the night. You'll have to pay her a proper wage, of course – if you want to keep her.'

143

Aunt Jane began to shake her head and she put on what Helen called her 'pitiful look'.

'Wh–who would have thought,' she said. 'My own f-flesh and blood. A viper, to my bosom.'

The words were the same as she'd uttered before but the fight seemed to have gone out of her. Helen almost felt sorry for her but she had prepared herself for this moment.

'I've been to your bank,' she said.

'How d-dare you!' The old spark had returned. 'My business!'

'Don't worry. I don't suppose they would have told me details of your account even if I had asked. I told the manager your situation and that you would authorize Miss Evans – that's Eva, your maid,' Helen added when she saw the puzzled look on her aunt's face, 'to do any business you require. He remembers your husband and he's agreed to come along and see you and help you in any way he can. You can use your right hand so you'll be able to sign cheques as you have been doing and sign any letters or instructions.'

Her aunt was staring at her almost as if she was frightened of what she saw. 'Wh–who would have thought,' she said. 'Own flesh and blood . . . viper . . . viper to my bosom.' She began to shake her head slowly from side to side and to Helen's dismay it looked as though her aunt's eyes were filling with tears.

Helen left the room quietly. She didn't say goodbye. Eva was waiting in the kitchen. 'I've told her,' Helen said. 'And she's agreed.' This wasn't strictly true but Helen knew that her aunt was in no position to make any objection.

'Thank you, you're a real pal,' Eva said. 'Fancy having the chance to hev a bed to meself!'

'Nevertheless, looking after my aunt will be a thankless task.'

'I know. But I need the job. And I'll write to you and let you know what's going on like you asked.'

'Are you sure you don't mind?'

'It will give me a chance to practise me writing. I won a pencil box at school, you know, for composition and me fair hand.'

They smiled at each other. 'Time for a cuppa?' Eva asked.

Helen nodded and sat down. She sipped her tea and then looked up at Eva. Without much hope she said, 'If a letter comes . . .'

'Don't worry. I'll send it on.'

There were tears in both girls' eyes when they said goodbye.

Part Two

The London Years

Chapter Nine

13th March 1931

Am I superstitious? Should I have travelled to London on Friday the thirteenth? Well, I did, and I'm here, and to prove it to myself, if no one else, I am actually writing it down in my diary.

The journey from Newcastle to King's Cross took nearly six hours and I was the only passenger who remained in the compartment for the whole journey. Other people came and went and it was fun imagining why they were travelling, where they were going and whether their journeys were happy or sad.

Eva had made some sandwiches for me and a couple of times I bought myself a cup of tea on the train. From where I was standing in the tea bar I could see through to the dining car where people were sitting at tables having proper meals. Imagine that! The tables were set beautifully with white cloths and jugs of water; the meals looked good but the knives and the forks and the glasses rattled as the train went over the points. Over the points . . . I think that's the term.

Some of the other travellers were quite chatty but I didn't really want to talk. I was thinking of London and what it would be like. Of course it's our capital city and the King and the Queen live there in Buckingham

Palace, but according to my lessons at school London is also the hub of our great Empire. Bustling, busy, important, and yet all I could think about was fog!

Surely everybody in the civilized world knows about the London fog. At least they do if they read novels and go to the pictures. What was I expecting? To arrive in a shrouded city with footsteps echoing on the cobblestones, where Sherlock Holmes could be seen hurrying back to his lodgings in Baker Street or, terrifyingly, Jack the Ripper might materialize before my very eyes?

One of the last films my mother and I saw together was called *The Lodger*. Ivor Novello was in it. A murderer is on the loose in London and Daisy, a beautiful blonde fashion model, finds that her parents have taken in a new tenant who leaves the house at night and keeps his cupboard locked. Daisy's sweetheart is a policeman who becomes convinced that the lodger is the man they are after. But Daisy is not so sure . . .

What a laugh we had on the way home that night, Mother and I linking arms and hurrying nervously through the streets and clinging on to each other and pretending to be frightened every time we heard footsteps! We went to the fish and chip shop and bought enough chips and batter to make it up to the small fry that they hadn't been allowed to come with us.

Just before the train reached King's Cross it slowed down and went through a series of tunnels. The other passengers in my compartment leapt up and took their luggage from the overhead rack and hurried out into the corridor. Everybody, it seemed, wanted to leave the train first. I got my case but then I sat down again. Suddenly I was struck by the enormity of what I had done. I had left the city where I had lived since I was born and decided to make a new life for myself. Well, at least, not completely new. Wherever I went and whatever happened to me, I knew that I would never give up hope of being reunited with my brothers and sister one day and salvaging what I could of the precious years we had spent together.

Dorothy Sutton was waiting for me on the platform. She came forward as soon as I stepped off the train. She had seen all the passengers hurrying by, the scramble for porters and the queues for taxis, and had begun to wonder if I had missed the train or changed my mind.

'Helen Norton?' she asked challengingly as she approached me.

'Yes.'

I stared at a young woman dressed in the height of fashion. Her belted coat had a little false cloak at the top of each sleeve and her cloche hat had no brim at all. Margery had told me that her daughter spent all her money on clothes and that she looked like a proper lady. Well, she did, but at that moment she was a very cross lady.

'I had to buy a platform ticket,' she said. 'I couldn't turn round and go home without making sure. So that's a penny you owe me.'

'I'm sorry.'

She looked me up and down and her expression changed. 'My Gawd, what has Mam sent me?' she said. 'You look like a school kid.'

'I'm sixteen.'

'Well, you don't dress sixteen, do you?'

'I suppose not.'

She's right. I don't. My old school coat is the only coat I have and my shoes were bought for comfort rather than fashion.

151

Dorothy shrugged and put on a long-suffering look. 'I told Mam that I'd be happy to have a girl from home to share my digs. I didn't say I was prepared to look after a kid.'

All the time she was talking train doors were slamming, people were shouting and steam was hissing up from the gap between the wheels and the platform. To my horror I thought I was going to cry, but suddenly Dorothy grinned.

'Although come to think of it, I might enjoy that.'

'What?' I asked, bewildered by her change of mood as well as her words.

'Looking after you. Showing you the ropes. Passing on my valuable knowledge and experience. Well, we can't stand here gassing all night; I'd better get you back to the diggings. Can you manage that?' she asked, giving my case a cursory glance, and turned to hurry away without waiting for my answer. 'I'll buy your ticket, you can settle up with me later.'

My first ride on the underground! Going down the moving staircase everyone else looked so casual, chatting, looking bored, looking cross, anything but impressed that they were being carried down into the underworld! I was scared on the platform and wished that Dorothy wouldn't stand so near the edge. Then there was a rumbling sound, a rush of warm air and the train hurtled into the station. There were no seats and I almost became separated from Dorothy as people pushed and shoved and got on and off the train at different stations. But my reluctant new friend took charge and brought me safely to Kilburn and what she called 'the diggings'. And here I am writing it all down before I forget a moment of it.

I am alone. Dorothy had a date with Mr Barker, her

gentleman friend, so she showed me the room that was to be my own, the tiny kitchen, the bathroom we share with the flat downstairs, and told me to get an early night as she would be taking me into work with her early tomorrow to the restaurant in Soho to see if Stefano would take me on.

Tomorrow . . . I can't sleep for thinking about it.

Several exercise books had been filled since that night when Helen had arrived in London. She didn't make an entry every day. Sometimes she was too exhausted when she got home from work at the restaurant and sometimes she made the editorial decision that the events of the day simply weren't interesting enough to record for history.

Over the months Helen would get the exercise books out and flick through the pages, going over days she had enjoyed and days she had hated, and trying to decide what exactly – or rather who exactly – she was writing this for. She had borrowed the works of diarists from the library. Some of them were also writers, such as Louisa May Alcott and Beatrix Potter. Then there was Dorothy Wordsworth, sister of William, to whose notes and observations Helen decided the famous poet owed much, especially his poem 'Daffodils'.

These diaries were fascinating because they revealed more about interesting people. Who would ever want to read about the daily life of a waitress? Helen wondered. What's so fascinating about endlessly clearing and wiping down tables, taking orders from the table d'hôte menu or pushing the more expensive à la carte? Or explaining tactfully to customers that you couldn't just order a cup of tea at the busiest time of the day and that you had to have a sandwich at least?

Even though Helen suspected that no one else would

ever read her diaries, she had found the writing of them compulsive. So she had gone on writing with pen and ink in school exercise books even after she had bought herself a second-hand typewriter at the market in Portobello Road. The typewriter was for writing of a different sort altogether.

16th July 1931

I've been in London for four months now. Dorothy has been as good as her word and looked after me. She persuaded Stefano to take me on as she'd promised. 'Go on,' she'd said, 'you know how hard we northern lasses work,' and he had to agree.

I like working at Stefano's. Being a waitress is incredibly hard work but it's so interesting. Stefano is a pet lamb but Marina, his wife, is a tartar. Here in Greek Street the customers are a varied bunch, much more diverse than the clientele of the Cosy Café at home in Newcastle.

Living with Dorothy can be trying at times. She isn't the world's best housewife – or anywhere near. Sometimes I tease her, asking her what she will do if Mr Barker asks her to marry him.

'Oh, I shan't have to do any cooking or housework,' is her usual answer. 'I shall be living in a nice house in Pinner and I shall have a maid and a cook and someone to come in and do the washing and ironing.'

She makes a joke of it but a long time ago I suspected that Mr Barker, whom I've never actually met, is never going to make an honest woman of her because he is already married. But, even though we are the best of friends, I've never felt able to ask Dorothy about this.

Dorothy and I seldom go out together. She spends as much time as possible with Mr Barker and, in any case, we very rarely have the same days off work. So I explore London on my own. I bought maps and guide books just like a tourist. I go to look at interesting buildings, I visit museums and art galleries, I love the old markets, and I go to the pictures.

I've recorded all this in my daily jottings, but what I haven't admitted until now is that as I'm walking along busy streets I'm not just taking in the passing show. I know the Partingtons are here because I see pieces about Mrs Partington's social life in the society pages of the newspapers that customers leave in the restaurant. I haven't found out where they live. They aren't listed in the telephone directories – there are so many for London – but it seems that you don't have to be if you choose not to.

So I go into the most fashionable shops and look at rich women buying clothes for themselves and their daughters. Elsie will be twelve years old now. Perhaps she no longer looks like a child but I'll recognize her. Of course I will. The question is, will she recognize me, and if she does what will I do? The likelihood of bumping into them in a shop like this is far-fetched, I know, but I spend hours imagining it might happen.

Could Joe and Danny have come to London? This is a place where they would be able to vanish if they wanted to. But why would they want to vanish? Why didn't they just come to me when they ran away from Haven House? What happened there? Whatever it was, didn't they know that I would have done anything in my power to help them?

But of course they didn't know that. How could they? What use had I been to them? I had allowed the family to be split up and the only promise I had given was that

155

one day we would be together again. I don't blame them for not putting much faith in that. Wherever they are, I'm sure that Joe will take care of things. At least that's what I tell myself.

What if they aren't in London? What if they aren't even in the British Isles? They could have gone to Liverpool and made for America. That's one of my worst fears. I try not to think about it.

25th December 1931

The second Christmas without my sister and brothers, but I haven't had time to brood. Stefano kept the restaurant open and I was amazed at how busy it was. What sort of people would prefer to eat in a restaurant rather than at home on Christmas Day?

Well, some people have to work, Christmas Day or not. A lively bunch of girls from one of the theatres came in and ordered the full Christmas dinner. How on earth were they going to do their high kicks, Dorothy wondered, when they were full of turkey and roast potatoes, stuffing and plum pudding? All the while the girls were eating they kept glancing hopefully at a couple of serious-looking men at the next table. The men were dressed in pinstripe suits and they were obviously discussing business. Dorothy said they had an office in Wardour Street and were part of a film company.

Then there were some of the usual bunch of reporters, men and women who work in Fleet Street. *He* was there – Matthew Renshaw, they call him, he doesn't come in often. I think he works abroad a lot. Dorothy showed me a report in a newspaper that he had written from Berlin. It was serious stuff. Political. All about the Nazi party winning one hundred and seven seats in the Reichstag, that's the German parliament, and it was obvious from the way Matthew had written his report that he didn't think that was a good thing.

When he does come to the restaurant he looks as though he's got a lot on his mind. Even when he gives his order from the menu he barely glances at you. He's tall and not exactly skinny but looks as though he could do with a few more good meals. He wears a tweed jacket with leather patches on the elbows and Dorothy says he looks like a schoolmaster or a socialist. His face is interesting rather than handsome, and a swoop of dark hair sort of flops over his forehead. Sometimes I wonder how much he can actually see through the lenses of those owlish glasses of his. I'm pretty sure he wouldn't recognize me if we met outside the restaurant and I try not to let this bother me. Why should it?

Today he didn't seem to notice what he was eating, even though he emptied his plate. I would have taken him seconds at no extra cost if only he had smiled at me.

As well as the workers there are the lonely people, who haven't got a proper home to go to, and there are a lot of people like that in London. They live in flats and bedsitting rooms in rundown houses that were once grand mansions with whatever possessions they have managed to bring with them. There are always rumours that some of them have smuggled the family jewels out by stitching them into their clothing. Particularly the Russians. Well, if they have, good luck to them. How else are they going to live?

All over Europe, it seems, there are people leaving their homes and walking for miles until they find somewhere safer to live. 'DPs', Stefano calls them, Displaced

157

Persons who just happen to be the wrong religion or race, even if their ancestors have lived in their towns or villages for hundreds of years.

Groups form like little social clubs and they come to Stefano's at their own special time on their own special day and discuss in their own languages the news from home. Stefano says that none of them will ever go home again and, what's more, it's going to get much worse before it gets better – if it ever does. From reading Matthew's report it would seem that he agrees with him.

Everyone was very jolly until they started singing and then people began to cry. Songs from their homelands, I suppose, which brought back painful memories. Marina was having none of it. 'For God's sake, this is Christmas Day!' she announced in that smoky voice of hers. 'We're supposed to be rejoicing.' She said that we would sing some proper carols and she persuaded, well, let's be honest, ordered, Stefano to take the lead.

What a surprise. Our boss has the most haunting tenor voice; his customers listened in amazement and Marina's purpose to jolly everyone up was defeated when people started to cry again at the sheer beauty of it.

Nevertheless everyone was agreed that we'd had a good time. The tips were generous and Dorothy, as the senior waitress, shared them out equally between the girls, even though she was entitled to keep a little extra for herself.

I got a taxi home. Dorothy has gone to some West End Club or other with Mr Barker. I wonder how he has managed to get away from his wife – I'm sure he has one – on Christmas Day. Perhaps she's an invalid and he dopes her to the eyeballs when he sneaks out of the house . . . Perhaps he murdered her a long time ago and he's hidden her body in the cellar of his house in Pinner . . . Do the houses in Pinner have cellars?

Oh dear, maybe I'm too full of the Christmas spirit to write any more. I only had one glass of red wine. Why am I feeling guilty? Perhaps it's because I've suddenly realized that in spite of the circumstances, I actually enjoyed myself today.

15th October 1932
Dear Helen,

Well, here's my monthly report although I don't have much to tell you. Your aunt doesn't change. She still complains about everything and she is making no effort to help herself. In my opinion she could do a lot more than she does but she likes to play the martyr. Dr Salkeld calls on her every week – sometimes twice – and then sends in his bill, no doubt.

And there's the chemist, too. Whenever your aunt reads of some miracle potion or pill in one of her magazines, some newly discovered vitamin or other, she sends me along to buy whatever it is. Honestly, Helen, you should see her bedside table. And the smell of some of those bottles is disgusting. All they seem to do is make her fatter. My mam says lying around in bed or on the sofa all day and eating as much as she does will kill her rather than the stroke she had.

At least she doesn't interfere with the way I run the house. So long as I keep serving up good grub and doing the basic housework, she doesn't complain too much. Mind you, she keeps me on the hop, so now my younger sister, Louie, calls by when she can to run errands for me. I've got to be honest with you, Helen, when Louie calls she often stays to eat with me. I hope you don't think that's dishonest – particularly as your aunt doesn't know about it.

Well, Helen, that's it for this month. I look forward to your reply as ever. News from the big city and all!

As usual I end by saying there haven't been any letters for you. You know I would forward them if there had been.

Yours truly,

Eva

Helen had saved the letter to read when she came back from work. She had lit the gas fire and it popped and spurted complainingly as she drew up the battered armchair to make the most of its grudging warmth. The restaurant had been busy but, as usual, Stefano had made sure the girls had a good supper before he locked up so all Helen wanted was a cup of tea before falling into bed. Even though Stefano had stumped up for a taxi, Dorothy had not come home. Again. Helen wasn't privy to where her friend went most nights or how she managed to turn up at work each morning and work as hard as ever.

Before going to bed Helen put Eva's letter into the old shoebox with the others. When they had started writing to each other Helen had asked how her aunt was and how Eva was coping and, somehow, this had developed into what Eva called her monthly reports. Do I care? Helen wondered. Do I really want to know how my Aunt Jane is, or am I suffering from guilt because she and I really are family? Was there ever a time when she and my mother were loving sisters, and did they share memories just as precious as those my sister and brothers and I have?

Eva never told her whether her aunt mentioned her.

Perhaps Aunt Jane had decided to forget her, or perhaps what she said was too hurtful for Eva to report. Remembering how her aunt had called her a viper, Helen smiled. If that was still how she referred to her, Eva might think it tactful not to say anything.

Helen thought for a moment about what Eva had told her about Louie. It was wrong of Eva not to let Aunt Jane know and yet what harm could it do? Her little sister being there to help meant that Eva could devote more of her time to her mistress. But it must be on Eva's conscience all the same, Helen thought. Otherwise she wouldn't have told me.

She put the lid on the shoebox and placed it back on the shelf in her wardrobe. A little later when she climbed into bed a gust of wind blew a spattering of rain against the ill-fitting window and the curtains billowed out in the draught. She was tired enough but for a while she lay awake, fretting as she often did that there still hadn't been a letter from Joe and Danny. Was she foolish to hope that one day there would be?

Chapter Ten

August to December 1933

Joe trudged back across the crowded beach clutching two ice cream cones in one hand. The Bank Holiday crowd had streamed out of London and it seemed they had all made for Brighton. Joe had to pick his way carefully between the family groups and he earned a few cross glances.

Before he had gone far the ice cream began to melt and drip down on to his hand and wrist. It was hot. People were saying this was a heatwave, and perhaps he should have listened to Myra and stayed in London today, but old Doc Balodis had said that Danny should get away from London as often as he could, that he needed fresh air. And Joe would do anything to make Danny better.

Danny had never really been well since he had arrived in London and Joe had often wondered what would have happened if he had sent his brother off first and he had stayed at Mrs Norris's for an extra hour or two. Then he would have been the one to get caught in the rain, and he might have had more sense than Danny and made for somewhere warm and dry to wait it out.

Well, it was warm and dry here on the beach and Danny could relax on the deckchair while Joe brought him whatever he needed. Not that Danny ever made many demands. It was part of his easy-going nature to accept whatever life brought and he often told Joe how grateful he was for everything he did for him.

'Here you are,' Joe said when he reached the deckchairs placed side by side, and Danny looked up and grinned.

'What a mess,' he said. 'Look at your sleeve.'

'I know. My new jacket. The first time I've worn it.'

'You should have taken it off and left it with me. I told you.'

'You're right. You usually are. Now take this and eat it before I drop it on your head!'

The brothers smiled at each other and Joe settled down to eat his ice cream – or what was left of it. He did this in record time and then fished a clean handkerchief from his pocket and cleaned the mess from his jacket and his arm. Danny's suggestion that he leave his jacket behind had been entirely reasonable but Joe couldn't have risked Danny going to sleep and someone walking off with it.

It wasn't just that the jacket was new; it was the inside pocket stuffed with fivers that Joe was worried about. Joe never left their money in their room at the lodging house. Never. So wherever he went their stash went too. He wasn't sure if Danny knew this. He wasn't even sure if Danny knew how much they were worth. Or how it was that a kennel lad could afford to look after him the way he did.

And if Danny ever did find out about the money and asked where it came from, Joe wondered if he would be able to look his twin brother in the eye while he explained.

After finishing his ice cream Danny wiped his hands fastidiously on his own handkerchief then opened up the newspaper and spread it across his face before lying back and announcing his intention of having forty winks.

163

'Wait a minute,' Joe said. 'Let me have the racing pages. Now shut your eyes for a while and when you feel like it we'll find a decent café and have a good meal before we go back.'

It was habit to look down the list of names to check up on which dogs were racing tonight. Not that Joe ever had a bet himself. Knowing what he did, it would be too dangerous. If he started winning regularly there would be those who would say he had inside information and they might investigate. He couldn't have that. Raymond had made that very clear to him.

At first sight Raymond looked like a harmless little bloke: overweight, pockmarked, a sharp suit and a trilby hat pulled low over his jutting brows. He was always smiling but Joe had noticed long ago that the smile rarely reached his close-set eyes and even the first time they'd met, his sense of self-preservation had kicked in and told him to beware.

The taxi driver had looked at him curiously when he'd picked the cab up at King's Cross that first night in London, but apart from telling Joe that, yes, he knew where to take him he hadn't said much. Joe had had to take a cab even though the fare would eat into the money he had left. He hadn't a clue how to get to his destination otherwise and he wanted to make sure that he was in time to get one of the jobs advertised in the evening paper.

Joe knew they were nearly there when he heard people shouting. The shouts rose to a crescendo and then died away and then started up again. When the cab pulled up the driver said, 'You after a job, then?'

'Yes.'

'Good luck to you. But don't you think you're a bit young to be going to the dogs?' Laughing at his own joke, he pulled away.

Raymond had interviewed him in his glass-sided office that looked down on the track. 'Any experience with dogs?' he'd asked.

'Only farm dogs.'

'Country boy?'

'Something like that.'

'Secrets, eh?'

'No.'

The answer came out too abruptly and Raymond laughed. 'Well, so long as the rozzers aren't after you.'

Joe scowled and Raymond laughed. 'I like the look of you,' he said. 'I'll give you a trial.'

'The paper said "jobs",' Joe said. 'More than one.'

'So?'

'I've got a brother.'

'The pair of you get on?'

'What do you mean?'

'Brotherly love and all that. No fighting.'

'We're twins. We're the best of pals.'

'Where is he?'

'He'll be arriving in London tomorrow.' Joe had hoped fervently that that was true.

'OK. I'll take you both on. One pound and fifteen shillings a week each, but all found at Myra's. She's a friend of mine and she keeps a decent lodging house. You won't starve there.'

And they hadn't gone hungry even though it soon became obvious that Danny wasn't strong enough to work. The sawdust and the straw in the kennels and the dust raised at the end of the race when the dogs were fighting over the snare sent Danny off into terrifying coughing fits.

To Joe's surprise Raymond hadn't sacked them. Instead he'd arranged for Danny to see Doctor Balodis and told Joe that there was a way he could make a little extra money, enough money to pay the doctor's bills and for Danny's board and lodging.

If Joe's conscience had ever been bothered by what he was doing he consoled himself by saying that he had never actually hurt a dog; he'd never put a bit of straw under a dog's eyelid as some did. He liked the dogs, their sleek coats, their long, powerfully muscled legs, their trusting eyes. If he had thought for one moment that the capsules he added to the dogs' food had a lasting effect on them he couldn't have done it. Or so he told himself. Then Danny and he would have had to move on, find something else. And where else could he earn an extra five pounds a week just for making sure that the right dog won the race – or lost it?

When Danny woke up he looked rested and fitter than he had done for months. The hot summer had given him a light tan. Joe had seen the glances from the girls in their bathing suits and he knew that Danny looked older than his years; they had turned sixteen that April. He was also handsome and Joe supposed that meant he was, too.

Although he didn't have a job Danny never seemed to be bored with life. In town he would take a book – he always had a book of some kind – and he would sit in a park, or go further afield to somewhere like Richmond and walk by the river. He knew how to fill his days and always seemed contented.

Now he sat forward in the chair, folded the newspaper, stood up and announced that he was starving.

Joe gave the deckchair tickets to a couple of girls who had been sitting on the sand nearby. They giggled and one of them said, 'Thanks, I'm sure. A true gent.'

The other asked if they would be coming back and

Joe shook his head. He and Danny set off to find fish and chips.

'Your mother is just *too* wonderful, isn't she?'

Elise opened her eyes reluctantly and squinted up to see Ernestine, one hand shading her eyes, gazing intently at the group of women sitting on the terrace. This was a last get-together at Shirley's house before the start of the autumn term. It was supposed to be a tennis party but the summer heat had lingered and it was much too hot to play. The girls had abandoned their game to flop down under the trees at the far end of the court whilst their mothers sat at a table shaded by an awning and chatted idly as they drank something long and cool and pink from glasses full of bits of fruit.

Shirley and Annette, lying prone just a short distance away, had heard Ernestine's remark and giggled. Ernestine was known for the intensity of her attachments, and her attachment to Elise Partington extended to Selma, her mother.

Elise propped herself up on her elbows and looked across at her mother then pretended to look puzzled. 'Too wonderful for what?' she asked.

Ernestine frowned. 'What do you mean?'

'I'm asking you what *you* mean. You've just said my mother is *too* wonderful. I mean, you can say someone is too fat to wear the latest style, or too clumsy to be a good dancer, but what exactly is it that my mother is *too* wonderful for?'

Ernestine's podgy face began to colour with embarrassment and Shirley, her thin, clever features expressing exasperated impatience, said, 'Do stop teasing her, Elise. You know very well that she was simply exaggerating – it's her way. She meant that your mother is beautiful and fashionable and so much more fun than all the other mothers. And as for you, sometimes it could be said that you are too clever for your own good.'

'Are we quarrelling?' Annette asked. She rolled over on to her back and covered her freckled face with one arm. 'It's too hot to quarrel. Wake me up when you've stopped.'

'No, we're not quarrelling,' Shirley said. 'I was merely, in my own officious way, asking Elise to be a little kinder than she is to her faithful devotee.'

Elise knew that some response was called for. 'Look, Ernestine,' she said, 'I'm sorry. I shouldn't have teased you. In fact I'm jolly pleased that you admire my mother. And yes, she is wonderful. And it's *too* kind of you to say so.'

Annette smothered a giggle and Ernestine didn't know whether she was still being teased or not, but when she saw the way Elise was looking at her, so kindly and so sincerely, she decided to give her idol the benefit of the doubt. 'That's all right,' she said. 'I know I shouldn't gush. It's a bad habit of mine.'

Elise lay back and closed her eyes again. It was pleasant lying here under the trees with a slight breeze nudging the leaves casting dappled shadows on the faces of the four girls. They were friends at school: Shirley Chapman, Annette Saunders, Ernestine Fry and Elise Partington, an elite little clique drawn together not so much by common interests as the fact that their fathers were extremely rich men. Or in Ernestine's case it was she herself who was rich. Her parents were dead and she was heiress to a respectable fortune. She lived with her guardian, a grim old aunt who disapproved of just about everything to do with modern life. It was no wonder she idolised Selma Partington.

My mother, Elise thought, is beautiful, fashionable, witty, energetic, always ready to discover new entertainments, new delights and share them with me. Elise adored her mother and felt sorry for girls who did not have such complete relationships – girls, happy enough, who lived on the margins of their parents' social lives and sometimes did not see their mothers for weeks on end.

And, of course, there was the secret. Or rather the thing that must never be mentioned. Sometimes when she was alone Elise allowed herself to think about it and tears would come to her eyes – tears of gratitude that Selma Partington loved her so much that she had taken her into her house as a daughter and made her life whole again.

Elise must have slept for a while because when she next opened her eyes it was a little cooler. She sat up and saw that Ernestine had moved back far enough to sit propped up against a tree. Shirley and Annette were no longer there.

'They've gone to the summer house,' Ernestine told her. 'There are refreshments laid on there. They said not to wake you.'

'Why ever not?' Elise didn't know whether she should feel excluded. Shirley and Annette were more what you could call 'best friends', whereas she always made up a threesome or a foursome. Never a twosome.

'They made some joke about Sleeping Beauty needing her beauty sleep, but I guess they just want to gossip together about boys.' She paused and moved forward to sit next to Elise. 'It's sickening, isn't it?'

'Sickening?'

'The way they go on. As if boys were important.'

'Aren't they?'

Ernestine looked at Elise in surprise, saw her smile and relaxed. 'You're teasing again, aren't you?'

'Yes, I am. Now why don't we go along to the summer house and spoil their little tête-à-tête? I could do with a cool drink, and despite this wretched heat I'm hungry.'

Shirley's older brother Tom and his friend Perry Wallace had taken over the court and were playing a desultory game of tennis. Perry paused before serving to wipe his forehead with the back of his wrist and then stared at the girls walking across the lawn.

'My God, who's that?' he asked.

'Who? Where?'

Perry smiled his attractive, raffish smile. Tom often wondered if he practised his expressions in front of a mirror each night. Sturdy and muscular in an unromantic way, Tom was confident enough not to envy his friend's lanky elegance and his undoubted good looks.

'Don't pretend you didn't notice her,' Perry said. 'I mean that vision of utter delight who has just walked into the summer house.'

'There were two of them. Which one do you mean?'

'You know very well which one I mean. The blonde, although to call her that doesn't do her justice.'

'What would you call her, then?'

'The angel? The form divine? The goddess?'

'A baby goddess as yet, I think,' Tom said.

'So you do know which one I mean?'

'Of course. No one could ever refer to poor lumpen Ernestine as a form divine – or any of those other hyperboles you've just uttered.'

'So?'

'The beautiful child is Elise Partington. She's at school with my sister.'

'Child?'

'I'm afraid so. She is thirteen, maybe fourteen at the most.'

'She looks older.'

170

'Oh . . . do you think so? Her face is that of a child.'

'And may always be so,' Perry said. 'Some women are like that. It can be devilishly attractive. But her figure, those delicious curves . . . the way she walks . . .'

Tom's puritanical instincts caused him to flush. 'I say, hold on, old chap. I don't like the way this conversation is going.'

'In some countries – even in some parts of America – she could be married by now.'

'But here in England you could go to jail for what I suspect your intentions are.'

Tom tried to make a joke of it but Perry sensed his disapproval. He opened his eyes wide as if shocked at whatever Tom was suggesting. 'My intentions are entirely honourable.'

'That's a first.'

Perry ignored the taunt and said, 'Partington?'

'Yes.'

'Hugh Partington's daughter?'

'No other.'

'And Elise is an only child, isn't she?'

'Yes, but how do you know that?'

'Everybody in society knows that the beautiful Selma Partington has one child on whom she dotes, and that Hugh Partington would spend his entire fortune on making her happy.'

'That last is an exaggeration. Partington is very astute and he would never contemplate Elise marrying someone he didn't think was suitable. If that's what you have in mind.'

At that Perry tossed a ball up into the air and aimed a shot directly at Tom. It caught his friend in the midriff.

'Oomph! What was that for?'

'For reminding me that I am not, as you put it, "suitable".

171

I am cultured, expensively educated, some say charming, and I am from a very good family, but although I will inherit a country estate and a gloomy mansion, I am poor. Some fathers might be impressed by my background but not, I imagine, Hugh Partington.'

'Miss Fry might be.'

'Miss Fry?'

'The orphaned Ernestine's guardian. Ernestine is heir to a considerable fortune.'

'Poor Ernestine.'

'Why do you say that?'

'Because looking as she does she will realize one day that anyone who shows an interest in her must be a fortune hunter.'

'You can be very cruel, Perry.'

'No, just realistic. And at the moment I'm also very thirsty. I suggest we go to the summer house and refresh ourselves.'

From her seat on the terrace Selma had observed the way Tom Chapman and his handsome friend had stopped playing tennis when the girls had walked towards the summer house. She was too far away to hear what they were saying but the way they were looking at the girls raised a prickle of unease. Tom Chapman was eighteen and having just left school he was due to go into the army. Selma did not know what Perry Wallace was going to do, but she hoped that whatever it was would take him away from London.

She had no idea why she suddenly knew this was important. Perhaps it was a mother's instinct – something telling her that her precious child was in danger of some sort. She tried to shake the uncomfortable feeling off and reached for her cigarette case which was lying on the table next to her drink.

172

When she lit her cigarette her hands were shaking slightly. She decided that as soon as it was polite to do so she would thank Shirley's mother and say it was time to go home.

The hot weather dragged on into autumn. Working in a busy restaurant in the heart of London was exhausting and Helen cherished every day off when she could escape to the seaside, where at least she might find a cool breeze blowing in from the sea. Sometimes she took a trip into the country instead. She would buy a ticket at the coach station in Poland Street and take a Green Line bus to any destination that happened to take her fancy.

She was always amazed and delighted by how rural the country could be within thirty miles of London – villages with duck ponds, ancient inns, woodland walks, and everything so mellow and different from the harsh beauty of her native north country.

Sometimes she would see an old house, a dwelling that must have stood there for centuries, and she would daydream about the people who had lived there. One day, looking at such a house through the tangled stems of roses in its neglected garden, her imagination took flight. I want to write about this house, she thought. Not a history book, I'm not clever enough for that. I want to write a story about it, how it changed and grew, and what it meant to the generations who lived here over the years. Maybe it would be the same family . . . maybe not . . .

On the coach on the way back to London she began to make notes in the little notebook she carried with her wherever she went. But by the time the country lanes had given way to busy roads, and the clear, lucent light of the country sky had clouded over with the smoke and dust of the city, Helen closed her notebook and put it away in her bag. I'm an eighteen-year-old waitress, she thought. What on earth made me think I could write a whole novel? And even if I did, who would want to publish it? Something written by a complete unknown? No, perhaps I'd better forget about writing a novel for a while and set my sights a little lower.

Once she was back in her room she wrote a brief account of the day's events in the latest exercise book which, added to the pile of exercise books in the cupboard, became the latest instalment of what she jokingly thought of as *The Journal of Helen Norton, The Everyday Doings of an Ordinary Girl.*

Then, after making tea and toast for herself, she got her second-hand typewriter from its hiding place under the bed and fed two sheets of foolscap separated by a piece of carbon paper into the roller. She consulted some scribbled notes and began to write something different altogether.

Helen could only do this when Dorothy was not at home. She did not want anyone to know what she was writing and she knew that the sound of the typewriter would bring her curious flatmate to her room. But as Dorothy seldom came home early, and even stayed out all night now and then, keeping her secret was easy. The difficult part was knowing when to stop. Or knowing if what she was writing was any good. There was only one way to find out, and the time was approaching when she would have to do something about it or put away her dreams.

I'll set myself a deadline, she thought. It's the only way. I'll put this lot in a big envelope and make sure to post it before Christmas. Or maybe I should take it round personally. No, they might think that was presumptuous of me, and in any case I'm hardly the type of person they would expect to walk into their office. One look at me and someone would take the envelope, tell me they would be in touch and dump it in the wastepaper basket as soon as I'd walked out the door.

Helen kept her promise to herself, and once the restaurant began to get busy over the Christmas holiday season she had hardly any time to brood about the lack of response from the magazine she had finally chosen to send her manuscripts to. In fact what caused her more anguish was the absence of Matthew Renshaw.

According to Dorothy, Matthew had gone to Spain where some anarchists were causing trouble in Catalonia and Aragon.

'How do you know this?' Helen said.

'Simple, I asked one of the other reporters. Honestly, Helen, I guessed long ago that you're sweet on him but you'll get nowhere unless you learn to put yourself forward a bit more.'

For the rest of Helen's shift that day and long into the night, Helen didn't know whether to be more upset that her feelings for Matthew had been so obvious or that the man himself was in Spain and probably risking life and limb reporting on a bunch of lawless people who, rightly or wrongly, wanted to overthrow their government.

Chapter Eleven

1934

Helen had always kept up to date with the news by reading the newspapers that customers left behind. But recently she had started buying her own newspaper – the paper Matthew worked for, of course – and scanning it quickly for reports from 'our foreign correspondent'.

If Matthew had returned to London after he had been to Spain, he had not come into the restaurant. But then why should he? Stefano's wasn't the only good restaurant in the area and Matthew, like some of the other customers, might like to try somewhere different for a while such as the new Pizza Paradiso in Store Street or an Indian meal at Veeraswamy's.

She read his reports and learned that, no longer in Spain, he was still risking life and limb covering such events as the riots in Paris, where there was a political crisis, and then he went on to Austria where there was actually a civil war. Talk at the tables in the restaurant often turned to the events in Europe these days, especially amongst the refugees. There was gloomy speculation that the maelstrom of turbulence and destruction was in danger of plunging the whole world into another war.

Helen's nineteenth birthday passed and still she hadn't heard from the magazine she'd submitted her work to. She'd first come across *Potpourri* some time ago when a customer had left it in the restaurant. Dorothy had found it first and after glancing through it during her tea break she'd passed it on to Helen.

'Not bad,' she'd said. 'But I don't get why they've called it after a bowl of dried flower petals.'

'Potpourri can also mean odds and ends,' Helen told her. 'A miscellaneous mixture of things.'

'If that means it's a hotchpotch then it's just the right name for it. I mean, personally I like something like the *Woman's Illustrated*. For threepence – that's half the price of what *Potpourri* is – you get a bit of fashion, a nice recipe and a romantic story or two – oh, and the readers' letters, of course; some of them are good for a laugh. This *Potpourri* has all of those, I give you that, but it's also got more serious stuff. I mean, people discussing things.'

'What things?'

'There's an article about working in a cotton mill in a northern town and another one about town life versus country life. I mean, as if it isn't a foregone conclusion! Who would want to live in the country? But here, see for yourself.'

Helen had saved the magazine to read that night and she'd enjoyed every page. She couldn't remember when she had first had the idea that she could write something for the magazine and send it in, but she did know that if she did it wouldn't be a romantic story. She had another idea. There was something she was bursting to write about and, conceited or not, she thought the readers of *Potpourri* would be interested.

She had a vague idea that any submission would have to

be typed rather than handwritten and a trip to the library, where she consulted the *Writers' And Artists' Yearbook*, confirmed this. So she'd bought her second-hand typewriter, a box of foolscap and a box of carbon paper. The *Yearbook* had also advised that the writer should keep a copy. The first box of foolscap had been used, and one or two more, before the day Helen decided she was ready to send something in, making Christmas her deadline. Finally, in the New Year, a month after her nineteenth birthday, the postman delivered a large envelope. Her work had been returned.

For a whole week Helen didn't even open the envelope. She had put it under the bed alongside the typewriter and brooded about it. All my hopes dashed, she thought dramatically. And then she remembered another piece of advice offered by the *Yearbook*: *Read your rejections carefully. The editor, although not wanting your work, might have found the time to offer suggestions on how to improve it.* So, one night after a busy day at the restaurant, she opened the envelope and after reading the letter that was enclosed with her typescript she remained sleepless for the rest of the night.

She had already wasted a week and now she had to wait for her day off before she could go to the magazine's premises in Russell Square. The office was on the very top floor of a large old house which had once been the home of a well-to-do family. This was probably where the most junior maid slept, Helen thought as she climbed the seemingly endless flights of stairs.

Long before she reached the top landing she could hear the sound of typing, and judging by the rhythm it sounded much more professional than her own. The door was ajar. Helen paused before she knocked. She had no idea what to expect but imagined the room might look like one in a film she'd seen about a plucky girl reporter who had battled with the editor and finally won his heart, as well as making her point.

'Come in, come in!' someone shouted just as she was about to knock. 'I can see you hovering there. Do come in, we don't bite.'

What she saw was nothing like the film set. It was simply an untidy room with two desks positioned opposite each other under the sloping eaves and any spare bit of wall lined with filing cabinets and bookshelves.

'Ah, there you are,' the voice continued, and Helen turned to face a jolly-looking girl with a mass of curly hair who was sitting at one of the desks. She looked far too young to be the editor of a magazine. In fact she didn't look much older than Helen herself.

'I take it from that envelope you're clutching that you want us to read some of your work?'

'Yes . . . I mean, no. You've already read it. You asked me to come and discuss it. I'm Helen Norton.'

'Ah, yes.' The girl smiled brightly. 'Lovely to meet you. I'm Charlotte. Charlotte Street. Isn't that a hoot?'

'A hoot?'

'My name. Charlotte *Street*!'

Remembering the route she had taken to get here, Helen smiled.

'My mother has no sense of humour whatsoever so I can only presume she's rather dim,' Charlotte said. 'I like to get that over with at the start,' she added. 'And we won't mention it again if you don't mind.'

'Of course not.'

'And now you'd better meet my boss who is also my aunt. She's my mother's sister but she's not a bit dim, are you, Jocelyn dear?'

Charlotte smiled across the room at the woman sitting

opposite her. Helen was flustered. She'd been so taken up by Charlotte's eccentric greeting that she hadn't turned to look at the occupant of the other desk. She did so now and saw a woman who was as thin as Charlotte was plump, and who was rather beautiful in a faded but distinguished way.

'Jocelyn Graves,' the editor introduced herself, 'and I'm glad you came, Helen. I think we have something very promising here. But do sit down. Charlotte, shift that pile of paper off that chair, will you, and brew up a pot of tea.'

Charlotte took the papers from the chair, stood and looked round indecisively for a moment and then dumped them on the floor. She dragged the chair closer to her aunt's desk and then left the room. Moments later she was back with a tray of tea and biscuits and the discussion began.

'I have to admit you are younger than I imagined,' Jocelyn Graves began. 'You have a very confident style.'

'Do I?'

'No false modesty, please. You must know that you're good.'

Helen flushed. She wasn't pretending to be modest; she was genuinely surprised. However, she thought it best not to say anything when things seemed to be going well.

Charlotte had taken her tea to her own desk and resumed her typing. Outside a wind had risen and was hurling rain against the windows. Helen became aware that the room was chilly and she glanced at the hearth and saw that a fire had been there recently but that it had died. The coal scuttle was empty.

Jocelyn Graves saw her momentary puzzlement and laughed. 'We operate by the skin of our teeth here,' she said. 'I put my own money into this venture, and although we're not exactly broke I won't be able to pay you very much.'

'Pay me? You mean you're going to publish my articles?'

'I do indeed, my dear, but I asked you to come and talk to me because you will have to make some changes.'

'Of course! Anything!' I shouldn't have said that, Helen thought immediately, she might want me to make changes I don't agree with.

Miss Graves smiled when she noticed Helen's frown. 'Don't worry,' she said. 'Nothing major. But I take it Stefano's is a real restaurant?'

'Yes.'

'And Stefano is the owner and Marina is his wife?'

Helen nodded.

'And Dorothy? She's an interesting character. She's real?'

Helen smiled. 'Absolutely.'

'Well, you'll have to change all the names. We don't want to be sued.'

'Sued? But I haven't written anything that isn't true – or anything too dreadful about anyone.'

'You can never tell what will cause offence.' Miss Graves smiled. 'And also we don't want the readers to identify the place. They will try to, of course. That will be part of the fun. Usually they will get it wrong, but if anybody guesses and asks you, you must deny it. Also you'll have to keep your own secret. If anyone suspects that you are writing these pieces it will all be over. No one will act naturally in your presence again.'

'I didn't think of that.'

'Don't worry. I'll keep you right. By the way, these incidents you write about, they are true, aren't they? I mean they are fact, not fiction?'

'I didn't make them up.'

181

'Or even embellish them a little?'

Helen thought for a moment and then said, 'I didn't embellish but I did edit.'

Jocelyn Graves raised her eyebrows. 'Good answer. Here, let me see.' She reached across the desk for the envelope Helen was holding. She took the sheets of foolscap out and read through them quickly. 'This shouldn't take much work,' she said. She shuffled the papers and added, 'These four can go in with only the changes I mentioned. The other two need cutting. Each piece should be about a thousand words. But before we go ahead I have to ask if you can keep this up. Can you write something about your life as a waitress in London every week or have you put all your heart and soul and all your experience into the pieces I have here?'

'No . . . things happen every day, I'm always taking note – interesting people, the things they say; I've kept a diary for years just so that I could remember everything.'

'Good. Now if I make some notes will you take these home and work on them?'

'I'll bring them back tomorrow!'

Jocelyn Graves laughed. 'Well, if you can. But we haven't mentioned your fee, have we?' She sighed. 'I'm afraid all I can offer you is seven guineas. Will that do, or do you want to take your work elsewhere? I'm sure it will be accepted.'

'No, I sent it to you because I think *Potpourri* is just the right place for it. And seven guineas will do very nicely. Although . . . is that . . . . I mean . . .'

'What are you trying to say?'

'Is that for all six of them, or only for the four that don't need much work?'

Miss Graves opened her eyes wide and then smiled. 'Oh, my dear girl, I don't approve of slave labour. I mean seven guineas for each piece, paid on acceptance.'

'Each piece?'

'Yes.'

'Seven guineas?'

'Yes, and from the looks of you right now I think I should ask Charlotte to make another pot of tea, or better still let's celebrate with a glass of good Scotch whisky, a bottle of which I just happen to keep in the top drawer of my desk.'

Without being asked, Charlotte bustled over with three mismatched glasses. 'Good-oh!' she said. Then, 'Down the hatch!' as the three of them raised their glasses and drank a toast to Helen's future as a feature writer for *Potpourri*.

Helen had never had whisky before – or anything stronger than a glass of wine if Stefano was feeling generous and Marina was in a good mood. After she had caught her breath she decided that it probably wouldn't be the drink of her choice but nevertheless it was fitting that this moment in her life should be celebrated.

Miss Graves decided they would make the minor changes to four of the manuscripts there and then and the windows were dark by the time Helen left the office. Charlotte was busy tidying up. If lifting piles of papers from one place and putting them down in another could be called tidying.

'By the way,' Miss Graves said as she was slipping on her coat. 'The title. I'm going to stay with the one you've given it – "À la carte" – I don't think I could have thought of a better one myself.'

On the way home Helen called at Eli's, a delicatessen not far from where she lived, and bought a couple of crusty bread rolls, some really smelly cheese, a few slices of salami, olives and a pickled cucumber from the barrel beneath the counter. She also bought herself a large slice of almond cheesecake. Coffee, she thought, a really good coffee, not the bottle of coffee essence I usually settle for. She perched on the high chair beside the counter and waited while Eli ground the beans. She savoured the different aromas and the atmosphere of the shop, at the same time delighting in the variety of customers who called there.

Alone in her room she set her private banquet out picnic-fashion on a tablecloth on the floor, lit the gas fire and threw down some cushions to sit on. It didn't bother her in the slightest that she had no one to share her feast with, or to share her triumph. She would write about it in her diary later, try to record for posterity what it was like to have a dream come true, but tonight, as well as feeling pleased by her success, she couldn't help thinking what this would mean to her financially.

Seven guineas for each article. Was it really true? At the restaurant she earned thirty shillings a week plus tips. Most customers were generous and sometimes the tips added up to more than her wages. She wasn't exactly starving, especially as Stefano gave the staff at least one good meal every day. But an extra seven guineas a week was more than she had ever dreamt of earning. Her life could change dramatically.

Or could it? Not really, she thought. I can't give up my job; I need it if I'm going to go on writing about the life of a waitress. And I can't suddenly move out of here and find a better place to live – a modest little apartment, for example. Dorothy would want to know why – and how I could afford it. If she saw the articles in *Potpourri* she would put two and two together straight away, and Miss Graves said I must remain anonymous.

Helen stared at the gas fire which had begun to splutter and pop as the money in the meter ran out. Well, at least I'll be able to keep that little monster fed with pennies, she thought, and if I can't buy myself some nice new clothes I could at least buy some luxurious lingerie, sheer and lightweight instead of sensible and serviceable. No one would ever see my underwear. She laughed nervously. What on earth put that idea into my head? She stared at the half of the pickled cucumber left on her plate. Could the vinegar have fermented? Could she be drunk?

By the time Helen had cleared up and gone to bed she knew exactly what she was going to do with any money she earned. She was going to open a bank account and save as much as she could. She remembered how her aunt's ninepence a day had given her a satisfying sense of independence. Well, how much more independence would seven guineas a week give her?

One day, she thought, in two or three years' time, perhaps, I may have saved enough money to buy a house of my own. Somewhere for me to live with my sister and my brothers when we are all together again.

Helen worked on her features for *Potpourri* and opened a bank account as she had planned. She kept her word to herself and saved almost all of the money she earned from her writing, but she did discover a hitherto unexpected side of her character. Now that she could afford it she craved a little luxury, so she gave in and indulged herself in the luxurious silk underwear that she was sure no one would ever see.

She also, much more sensibly, had her eyes tested and bought herself a pair of spectacles. The lenses were round and the frames were of faux tortoiseshell. She wore them at home when she was writing but also took them to work to wear in her lunch or tea breaks when she might read the paper.

When Dorothy first saw her wearing them she told Helen

that she looked like a schoolteacher or a socialist. This was a favourite expression of hers. Helen remembered that that was how Dorothy had referred to Matthew. Then she had been joking but now when she said it to Helen, there was a slight hint of disapproval.

'Well, what's wrong with that?' Helen asked.

Dorothy sighed. 'Honestly, Helen, you have no idea at all, do you? I mean, you'd be quite attractive if you tried harder but you just don't seem to care.'

Helen smiled and tried to laugh it off, and looked away so that Dorothy would not see how hurt she was. *Quite* attractive. Was that all she was? And was that why Matthew Renshaw never seemed to have noticed her as a real live person?

She glanced back at Dorothy. No one could say that she didn't make the best of herself. Her hair was always cut and styled in the latest fashion and every spare penny was spent on cheap copies of the latest collections from Paris. And what had this brought her? It had brought a relationship with a man who either didn't want or wasn't able to commit to her. There were things Helen could say to Dorothy that might be just as hurtful. But she wouldn't say them. She knew she would never be able to say anything that might destroy another person's dreams.

Danny liked to take a book and sit in a park or a garden square. Joe encouraged him to do this, saying the fresh air and the sunshine would be good for him. He had his favourite places but he also liked to discover somewhere new. This was the first time he had come to Russell Square, which made what happened all the more amazing.

He had treated himself to a cup of tea and a Chelsea bun at the café in the garden and then settled on one of the benches to read his book about unsolved London murders. They were all true stories and Danny was fascinated by them. He decided that he would visit the various locations himself and try to put himself in the detective's shoes. Or those of the murderer . . .

Perhaps he would do this when the weather got a little cooler. The late September sun still held some warmth but a nippy little breeze was already stirring the leaves of the sheltering trees.

Then something made him look up from the page. He couldn't see anyone at first, but something, he never knew what, made him turn his head and look at the young woman hurrying along the path that wound towards him. Taller than he remembered, still slim, and still with that determinedly hopeful manner. It was Helen.

Normally so in control of his emotions, Danny felt a surge of joy. His first instinct was to leap up and hurry towards her, put his arms around her and hug her, but immediately all the reasons why Joe and he had decided it would be better not to get in touch with her came flooding back.

First of all there was what had happened on the cliff top at Haven House. How could they ever tell Helen the truth of it? And if they didn't, how could they lie to her?

Then there were other things they wouldn't be able to tell her about . . . Essentially, everything that had happened since they came to London. Joe didn't think Danny knew about his taking money to dope the dogs. Sometimes Danny felt offended that his brother should think him so naïve and unquestioning about the fact that he could afford to pay for board and lodgings for both of them from a kennel lad's pay. Danny knew about Joe's secret stash of cash. There was nothing much he didn't know about the late-night callers at Myra's house and what went on at the dog track.

Any moment now Helen will be near enough to recognize me if she looks my way . . .

As his sister came within calling distance Danny fought down the urge to get up and run towards her. Hesitant after the years apart, he decided to leave it to fate. I'll go on reading, he thought. If she glances my way and recognizes me then this was meant to be. If not I'll stay silent. His nerves stretched agonizingly tight, and unable to hold his gaze, he looked down at his book. His heart began to beat erratically; he could feel his temples throbbing. He held his breath.

Then when Helen's sensible shoes entered his field of vision he looked up. But his sister hurried by. She had not bothered to glance at the solitary figure sitting there with a book. She looked eager and purposeful as she left the garden and crossed the road.

Danny let his breath out in a long, regretful sigh. So that's that, he thought. It wasn't meant to be. But nevertheless he got up and hurried after her. He stood on the pavement and watched as she entered one of the houses, and after a moment he followed and read and memorized the names on the various brass plates near the front door. Business premises, he thought. Helen doesn't live here.

By the time she came out again the streetlamps were lit, and away from the pathways there were mysterious areas of darkness in the garden. As Helen hurried along the path she never noticed the figure that detached himself from the shadows and followed her home.

Chapter Twelve

31st October 1934

Halloween. A crowd of bright young people came into the restaurant this evening. They were dressed as witches and ghosties. This must have been one of the coldest days of the year so far and some of the poor girls in their silky costumes were shivering with cold and had red noses and goose pimples they hadn't bargained for. None of them stayed long. They were all on their way to clubs or private parties where the festivities would go on until midnight and probably long into the early hours of the morning. Stefano joked that in the morning the street cleaners would be sweeping up drunken hobgoblins along with the rubbish.

One or two of the merrymakers were carrying pumpkin lanterns which they lit when they left the restaurant. Some of them had fortified themselves against the cold with a drink or two, and as they lurched off down the streets their lanterns swayed violently, the candles sputtering and smoking.

As I watched them I was overcome with a nostalgia so strong that I was almost transported back in time. Back to the kitchen in our old home where I was helping my mother make lanterns from four turnips. Turnips because they were cheap and also because we could cook the bits we'd hollowed out. Turnip with potato to make soup, or mashed up with carrots and butter and seasoned with pepper. I wonder if Stefano knows how delicious this humble root vegetable can be.

When Joe and Danny were old enough to be trusted with a knife they were allowed to help. Joe would attack his turnip enthusiastically, eating bits of raw turnip as he went. Danny was good at making the faces: slanted eyes, a triangular nose and a scary mouth with teeth like fangs. Elsie never made her own lantern. She would sit and watch while Mother or I made it for her and she always wanted it to be 'pretty'. I don't think anything we made ever lived up to her expectations.

With the candles secured inside the lanterns off we would go, wearing witches' hats made from rolled-up paper and cloaks fashioned from old tablecloths or curtains. Now that I remember, we didn't do much more than run up and down the street whooping wildly, and the only creatures we frightened were the neighbourhood cats. But when we went home Mother would have the soup on the table and either a toffee apple each or a big plateful of cinder toffee.

Once Elsie was in bed we would put the light out and sit by the fire and tell ghost stories. We all had a turn. Mother and I tried not to make our stories too frightening but we needn't have worried. Neither of the boys took them seriously. Joe's stories were usually a mixture of comic book horror and farce, and Danny's were fantastical rather than bloodcurdling.

So what shall I do tonight? It is almost midnight. Dorothy will not be coming home, she hardly ever does these days, and I must face the witching hour alone. Well, I am not completely unprepared. I shall sit by the fire drinking hot spiced cider and eating the large slice of gingerbread I bought at Eli's. And I shall open the book I have borrowed from the library, *The Best Ghost Stories of Algernon Blackwood*. But no matter how engrossing the stories, it will be difficult to banish the memories of those four children in their home-made costumes running up and down the street with their turnip lanterns all those years ago.

One of the other kennel lads had brought a pumpkin lantern to work and Raymond had raised the roof. 'Do you want to start a fire and burn the place down?' he'd yelled. 'Get it out of here and don't bother to come back. I can't afford to employ halfwits!'

The lad, Alfie, was only fourteen and this was his first job. As he turned to go there were tears in his eyes but he didn't attempt to plead with Raymond. That would do no good at all, everyone knew that.

Joe slipped out after him. 'Wait,' he said. 'What will you do?'

'Go home, I suppose, although I don't know what I'm going to tell them.'

'You'll have to tell them you've been sacked. There's no getting round that, but you can say you're after another job.'

Alfie looked puzzled. 'But I'm not.' He sniffed loudly and wiped his nose on his sleeve.

'Don't do that,' Joe couldn't help saying. 'Whatever job you go after you don't want to present yourself with snot all over your sleeve.' Joe reached into his pocket and drew out all the coins he had there. 'Here you are,' he said. 'Go on, take it.'

'What this for?' Alfie asked but he held out his hand uncertainly.

191

Joe tipped the coins into the lad's palm. 'First go and buy yourself an evening paper. Then go to the nearest café, get yourself whatever you want to eat and go through the jobs column. You might strike lucky – even if the only job you can find is an errand boy.'

Alfie looked uncertain.

'Go on,' Joe said. 'It's worth a try. That's what I did when I arrived here without anywhere to sleep even.'

'Yeah, but we all know how clever you are. Raymond's top lad.' There was a hint of a sneer in Alfie's tone. 'I'm just a halfwit, remember.'

Controlling a spurt of annoyance, Joe said, 'You will be if you don't take my advice. That's the best chance you have coming to you tonight. Now get out of here and take that stupid pumpkin with you.'

Joe watched him go. He didn't really hold out much hope for the lad. Times were hard and Alfie didn't do much to help himself. But at least he had given him a chance. And he wasn't sure why. Had it been the pumpkin? Had the sight of it brought back memories of the Halloweens they had all enjoyed together as children with their turnip lanterns and the cinder toffee their mother or Helen had made for them?

He wished he wasn't working tonight. He wished he could take off with Danny. Perhaps the pair of them could go up west and watch the silly sods with more money than sense making fools of themselves with the drink. Then he would take Danny to a nice restaurant and treat both of them to the best the menu could offer.

He wondered what Elsie would be doing tonight. Would her rich adoptive parents have a party for her? They probably would. And Helen. What would Helen be doing? And who would she be with? Suddenly he felt sorry for both his sisters.

Wherever they were they were not together, whereas he had Danny. He and his twin would never be parted if Joe had anything to do with it, and as soon as work was over tonight he would get Danny from their shared room, where he would be reading as usual, and take him along to the all-night café next to the station. Sid's Caf might not compare to a West End restaurant but the food was good and the helpings generous. And these days Joe had money to spare.

Before Tom Chapman was allowed to go out with his friends his mother persuaded him that it was his duty to help out at the party she always gave for Shirley. Tom knew that persuade was hardly the right word for it. No one ever mistook Darlene Chapman's polite requests for anything other than an order from on high. In this case he was perfectly agreeable. He was actually fond of his younger sister and he thought her friends a jolly bunch of girls, especially as most of them seemed inclined to hero worship as far as he was concerned. It did a chap no harm at all to know that he was appreciated by the fair sex. So long as he didn't let it go to his head and start behaving like a rotter. Like some people he knew.

When he told Perry, his friend, rather than being put out, offered to come along and help. Tom accepted the offer gratefully, not remembering until it was too late that Perry had an ulterior motive. He behaved himself well enough, helping out with the games, soothing those who got muddled or upset and fetching cool drinks for the overheated. But Tom would have been blind or stupid if he had not noticed the way Perry's eyes followed Elise Partington's every move. Annoyingly he didn't put a foot wrong so there was nothing Tom could say.

Then, to his surprise, when Perry did make a move, it was another girl altogether that he set out to charm.

During the game of ducking for apples Ernestine Fry managed to soak not just her face and her hair but her clothes as well. When she stood up triumphantly clasping the stalk of the apple between her teeth everybody laughed. Poor Ernestine sensed that the laughter was not exactly friendly, dropped the apple, looked down at herself and began to cry. Perry snatched a napkin from the buffet table and hurried forward. He led her away and helped her to dry herself, all the time keeping up a flow of conversation as if what had happened was perfectly normal.

By the time Darlene Chapman had sent a maidservant over with a towel Ernestine was smiling again and looking up at Perry adoringly. Ernestine was led away to find a dress of Shirley's that would fit her. Difficult, Tom thought, when Ernestine was on the chubby side of sturdy and his sister was so athletic and trim. However, that was not his problem.

What happened next took him by surprise. He was on his way over to speak to Perry when Elise Partington forestalled him.

'That was very kind of you,' Tom heard her say.

'Kind?'

'To comfort Ernestine like that.'

'I only did what anyone would have done.'

'But no one else did anything. That's my point. They were just laughing at her.'

'I got there first, that's all.'

'Perhaps. But people can be so cruel, can't they?'

Perry looked at Elise intently. 'Yes, they can. But never to you, I think.'

Tom was just about to cut in; he thought the conversation had gone far enough, when to his surprise it was Perry who broke away. 'Well, I must get back to my duties,' he told Elise. 'I think we have to get some sort of team game going.

A pumpkin relay. Ah, there you are, Tom. I'm ready for duty. Lead the way.'

Perry didn't look back, neither did he approach Elise again that night, but Tom knew the damage had been done. He had observed the way Elise looked at Perry while he walked away and he had seen that rather startled expression as if she had suddenly become aware of some emotion within herself. Some emotion she did not yet understand.

When Elise arrived home at one o'clock in the morning her mother was waiting for her by the fire in her own little sitting room. She smiled up at her and then asked the maid to bring them hot milk and biscuits for them to enjoy while they had a little chat. Elise didn't want milk and biscuits but she took them and said thank you because she didn't want to disappoint her mother.

'Your poor old father has gone to bed,' Selma said when they were alone, 'but I wanted to wait up for you. Did you have a lovely time?'

'Yes, I suppose so.'

'Only suppose so? What's the matter? Are you tired? I mean, I know this is late but Shirley's mother did want you all to stay for what she calls the "witching hour".'

'No, I'm not tired. It's just that . . .'

'What is it, then?'

Selma's tone was impatient and Elise looked at her just in time to catch a flash of irritation in her eyes.

'No, really, it was fun. Mrs Chapman always goes to great lengths to entertain us. But this party was the same as every other Halloween party I've been to at that house.'

'And that's not good enough?' Again that slight impatience.

'Oh, yes,' Elise assured Selma. 'Nothing but the best at

the Chapman house.' She smiled, hoping to make her mother smile in response.

'But? I sense there's a "but" coming.'

'Well, blame the witch, the ghost and the mummy!'

Elise looked anxiously at her mother and saw with relief that she had caused her to smile.

'You'll have to explain.'

'It's the games we play. Pin the wart on the witch, Guess the ghost, Wrap the mummy, and the scary stories that aren't really scary. The same old games as last year and the year before that and the year before that . . . and well, they're kid's games, aren't they? Honestly, Mum, we're not kids any more, are we?'

Her mother's smile vanished as quickly as it had come. She put her mug of warm milk on the tray on the small table. Elise noticed that she hadn't drunk any of it and a skin had formed on top. 'No, Elise,' Selma Partington said thoughtfully. 'I don't suppose you are.'

Thoroughly unsettled by her dissatisfaction with the party and disconcerted by her mother's strange mood, Elise took a long time to get to sleep. She tried to think of nice things – new clothes, days out with her mother; that sort of thing usually worked – but this time it was half-forgotten images that came to mind: a witch's hat made from rolled-up paper, a cloak which had once been a curtain, and a turnip lantern swinging, the cut-out pattern of its face chasing across the pavement as she ran down the street saying 'Boo!' to anyone who might be lurking in the shadows.

14th November 1934
Dear Helen,
    I'd better come straight out with it. On Saturday

Donald and I got married. You know I've told you about him. The family moved in next door to my mam and I would see him when I went home for a visit. Now don't get worried. I'm not going to leave your aunt in the lurch. I'm not going to set up a home of my own. The truth is, Donald is out of work and we couldn't afford to on what the assistance pays.

No, I'm not leaving. Far from it. Donald is moving in here with me and your aunt will be even better looked after. I mean, you need a man about the house, don't you? Donald and I will take the back bedroom and Louie is going to have the little room that used to be yours.

Your aunt is pretty much the same as ever. She likes her magazines and she listens to the wireless. She eats every scrap of whatever I cook for her – and lots of cakes and sweeties in between – but she doesn't seem to want to make the effort to do much else. Doctor Salkeld calls at least once a week, I'm sure I don't know why. I hope you don't mind, but I've made it plain to him that I don't think his visits are necessary.

Yours truly,

Eva

15th November 1934

Eva's latest report arrived this morning. She doesn't write so often now because, really, there is very little to say. Aunt Jane seems to have opted for the life of an invalid although I'm pretty sure there's no need for it. Perhaps I've been careless, perhaps I haven't bothered to read Eva's letters properly and perhaps I should have noticed the change in her attitude, but this letter has disturbed me.

197

Why? Aunt Jane is being looked after. I'm sure the meals will be good and the house will be clean. But did she ever know that Eva's little sister, Louie, was spending so much time there? And now it seems she has moved in. And so has Eva's husband. Can my aunt have agreed to this?

And after all that happened after my mother died, why should I care? Nevertheless, maybe I should write to Doctor Salkeld.

3rd December 1934

I shall never forget that moment when he looked up, our eyes met and I knew he was seeing me properly for the first time. At last, I thought, as I saw him smile in wonderment. I knew that the waiting was over.

If I were writing a romantic novel that is how I might begin to describe what happened today. But I'm not. I'm recording the event in my everyday diary and the truth of it is it was more like farce than romance. Let's be honest, it was complete slapstick and I didn't behave like a romantic heroine, I behaved like a clown.

It was so long since Matthew had been to Stefano's that I was beginning to think that I would never see him again. The last report I read of his had been from Afghanistan some time ago. Surely he had come back to London but, if so, why hadn't he been in for a meal? Perhaps he had found somewhere better to go. Then today, at lunchtime, there he was.

My heart stood still!

No, it didn't, it was my feet that came to a duck-toed stop. I was carrying a couple of Fruit Surprises for the two ladies sitting at the table just beyond where he was sitting. I recognized him from the back. The dark hair, the tweed jacket that he always wore, and the way he held the menu up to scrutinize it as if it was some sort of important document. I saw all this but I didn't see the walking stick that he had left carelessly jutting out into the aisle between the tables. How could I have known that he had a walking stick?

One of the ladies was smiling expectantly as she saw me approaching and then I think I registered her surprised expression just before I realized that I had stumbled and was about to fall. With a Fruit Surprise in each hand there was no way of saving myself unless I let one of them go. I did. You can guess which one. The one nearest to Matthew. I watched in horror as the tall sundae glass tipped then fell on to his unsuspecting head.

I heard someone gasp and then badly stifled laughter coming from the nearby customers, and some inane instinct made me dash forward and place the remaining Fruit Surprise on the table in front of one of the ladies. Then I turned to look at Matthew and was appalled. Fruit, jelly and custard covered his hair and dripped down on to his spectacles. He looked up blindly and put out a groping hand to take up the napkin from the table. He began to wipe the lenses of his glasses as if cleaning the windscreen of a motor car.

A hopeless task. Eventually he took them off, looked at them in a puzzled fashion that would have made me laugh if I was not so near to crying, then he looked up slowly and saw me. His eyes widened – at least they widened as far as they were able with custard dripping down his brow on to his eyelashes.

I held my breath just like a heroine in a love story. I really did. I was waiting for the bellow of outrage, the justifiable fury of the outraged hero. Time stood still, as they say, and then, I could hardly believe it, he began to laugh. At that I really did cry; I blubbered like a baby first of all with relief then with apprehension as I saw Marina bearing down towards me.

'I'm so sorry, Mr Renshaw,' she said. 'Please accept our most humble apologies.' She picked up the empty sundae glass from the table. 'Needless to say, there will be no charge for whatever you order today. And as for you,' she turned to face me but before she could say anything Matthew stopped her.

'What happened is entirely my fault,' he said. 'Look.' He took up his walking stick and showed it to Marina. 'It was very careless of me. It is I who should apologize to Helen.'

He knew my name! Even though I was overjoyed I was annoyed with myself and, let's admit it, with him too. Why shouldn't he know my name? I had been waiting on him at the table long enough. I had a moment of sheer resentment at his detached attitude but I didn't have time to brood. I was dispatched to the kitchen to fetch another Fruit Surprise for my patient lady customer while Marina helped Matthew clean himself up then took his order. She told him she would bring his meal herself.

I thought that was the end of it, the end of our brief affair, but when he had finished his meal he sat for longer than he usually did over his coffee. He kept glancing my way until the time came that I had to pass by his table.

'Helen,' he said. 'I really am sorry. I haven't got used to this damn stick. I hope you won't be in too much trouble with Marina.'

'Oh, I shouldn't think so,' I lied.

'Well, in any case, that's the best laugh I've had for a long time.'

'You thought it funny?'

'Didn't you?' He smiled.

This is where my romantic heroine would have been speechless with joy but in reality I giggled like a schoolgirl. We laughed together but at the same time I noticed the dark hollows under his eyes and that the lines of his face were more severe than they used to be.

Then he stopped laughing. 'Come for a drink with me?' he said.

'When?'

'Tonight when you finish work.'

He must have seen my surprise because he looked embarrassed.

'I can't,' I said. 'I'm on a split shift today and I won't finish until nearly midnight.'

'Oh, I'm sorry.'

'But it's my day off tomorrow.'

Now it was my turn to be embarrassed.

His smile returned. 'A whole day, then! We'll meet for lunch, then perhaps the cinema. Have you seen *The Count of Monte Cristo*?'

'No, but I'd like to. I think it's my favourite novel of all time. And as for Robert Donat . . .'

Matthew smiled. 'Well, according to my mother Mr Donat will not disappoint you, but she tells me that the film is a little different from the book.'

'Oh, that doesn't matter at all.' Did I sound too eager?

'Tomorrow then,' he said. 'Erm . . . shall we meet at eleven o'clock by the statue of Eros?'

He didn't need to say where the statue of Eros was. Everyone knows that Piccadilly Circus is where you find the god of love.

When Matthew got back to his parents' house he found his sister Patricia waiting for him.

'Shouldn't you be at home making a meal for your new husband?' he asked.

'George is working late. And in any case, I've prepared everything. Only got to throw it into the pots and pans and light the gas.'

'Efficient as ever.'

'That's me. Mum and Dad aren't back from the matinee yet, so come into the kitchen, sit down, have this cup of tea I'm just about to pour for you and tell me what happened.' Patricia placed his tea in front of him, poured one for herself and took the chair facing him. 'Now, then. Talk.'

'And just as bossy,' Matthew said.

'Matthew! I'm serious. What happened at work today?'

'They've agreed I can come back to work – so long as the doc agrees – but I won't be travelling very far for a while.'

'I should think not. No more globetrotting for you, young man. So what will you do?'

'Well, they seem to think I'm a pretty good reporter.'

'Of course you are!'

'And the only reason I can't go abroad is because I still have to report to the hospital.'

'I'm not going to like what's coming next, am I?'

'Jim Dacre is just about to retire.'

'Jim Dacre?' Patricia frowned and when her brows cleared she looked anxious. 'Jim Dacre is a crime reporter. Isn't that another dangerous job?'

'Maybe. But I'm not so likely to stop a bullet here in London.'

'Oh, darling brother, that's not true. You may not have

to consort with rebellious tribesmen who are armed to the back teeth, but some of the criminal fraternity in London here are just as dangerous if not more so.'

'It's not all like that, you know.'

'What do you mean?'

'A lot of the crimes I'll be covering will be the petty stuff. Thieves, fraudsters, men who murder their wives when they come home and find their dinner isn't ready.'

He grinned and Patricia shook her head. 'Go on, make a joke of it. But I don't know what the old folks will think.'

'Father will accept that it's what I want to do and Mother will go along with whatever he says.'

Patricia put both hands on the table and pushed herself to her feet. 'You're right. And I'm not going to nag you because I can see that whatever was said today it has made you happy. You know you've been like a bear with a sore head since you came home?'

Matthew shook his head.

'What is it?' Patricia asked.

'I'm saddened by your use of cliché.'

His sister grinned. 'You really have cheered up, haven't you? And I understand. I know you were in pain – still are – and I know how dreadful it must make you feel that your leg will never be completely right again. So getting back to work is just what you need.' Patricia looked at her watch. 'I'd better go and make myself pretty for George. No, don't get up. I can see myself out.' She dropped a kiss on his head and straightened up. 'What's that smell?'

'Smell?'

She wrinkled her nose. 'Vanilla . . . ? Are you using some new kind of brilliantine? If so I don't like it. It smells like custard.'

Without waiting for a response, Patricia hurried through

to the hall and a moment later Matthew heard the front door close. After she had gone he realized that he was still smiling. He wondered what Patricia would have said if he'd told her why his hair smelled of custard. And also what the outcome of that farcical incident at Stefano's had been.

Had he really been so difficult to live with since he'd come home wounded from Afghanistan? He supposed he had. It wasn't just the pain; it was the memories of what he'd seen there. Then today, completely out of the blue, an unfortunate girl had dropped a mess of custard and jelly on his head and he'd looked up at her and seen her properly for the first time. Usually so analytical, he couldn't explain to himself why that moment had been so important. All he knew was that for the first time for months he was looking forward to tomorrow.

Chapter Thirteen

Selma loved shopping for Christmas. Not just for presents for friends and family but also for the house. Every year she would succumb to the latest fashion in decorations to be found in Harrods or Gamages. She would supervise the decking of the halls, as she called it, herself, and then on Twelfth Night everything would be taken down, packed away and stored in boxes along with the trunks and the unused knick-knacks in a room on the top floor.

Hugh didn't know why Selma bothered to keep them. They were never used again. Then one day he realized that each box was labelled with the date. It was as if his wife was making a record of the Christmases they had enjoyed together. Maybe she would look at them in later years to remind herself that their enjoyment had been real. Her dreams of family Christmases had been fulfilled. He found this endearing and, as he could well afford it, he encouraged her to spend whatever she liked if it would make her happy; for her happiness was essential to his own.

In the middle of December, he realized that this year she hadn't even mentioned Christmas. Nothing had been ordered, no plans had been made, or if they had it had all been done in secret. Was she planning some big surprise? Were he and Elise going to be first teased into thinking that she had forgotten and then whisked up into some last-minute extravaganza that would take their breath away?

One morning he found her flicking listlessly through the Army & Navy Store catalogue.

'Looking for something special?' he asked.

She smiled wanly. 'Christmas decorations, actually. I thought I might just order everything from a catalogue this year.'

This surprised him. 'But I thought you loved going to see the displays, visiting the elves' grottoes, gazing at the Christmas windows on Oxford Street?'

'Well, yes, I do . . . or rather, I did.'

'What has changed?'

'Elise. She's growing up. She doesn't find that sort of thing fun any more.'

'Has she said so?'

'Not exactly.'

'Selma darling, please explain.'

'Well, after the Chapmans' Halloween party she complained that that sort of thing was for kids and that she was no longer a child.'

'She was right, wasn't she?'

Selma's eyes widened. 'You agree with her?'

'Of course. She isn't a child but neither is she old enough to be admitted into the grown-up world. She is at an awkward age, darling, and you'll have to allow for a mood or two.'

'Oh, no, she's not moody. In fact she tries her best to please me, always. It's just that . . . oh, dear . . . she is no longer my little girl.'

Hugh smiled. 'Well, little girl or big girl, I can guarantee that she will be disappointed if you don't make Christmas as special as you always do. And, furthermore, so will I. Now put that catalogue aside. I have decided to devote my whole day to you. We shall go to whatever shop you want to go to and buy our Christmas decorations together.'

Selma seemed cheered by his words and she went with him happily enough, but Hugh couldn't help noticing a certain lack of energy. Then, seeing her revealed in the bright lights inside the store, he saw suddenly that the lines of her lovely face were more sharply drawn and that there were faint violet-coloured smudges under her eyes. He drew in his breath and fear gripped his heart.

This mood of hers isn't just about Elise, he thought. Selma is ill. I pray God it isn't serious, because I don't know how I could live without her.

20th December 1934

Marina was no match for Matthew. As well as being utterly disarming, he managed most subtly to remind her of the Fruit Surprise incident and, with what could be called a combination of charm and threat, he persuaded her to give me Christmas Day off and a half-day on Boxing Day. I owe him thanks but I have to admit that he might not have been successful if Dorothy, who had been listening to the conversation, had not intervened. As senior waitress Dorothy helps make up the rotas, and she pointed out that there would be no problem getting other girls to work because on days like that the tips would be good, and some of the regular customers even brought Christmas presents for the staff.

And now, perversely, I am half wishing that Matthew had not been successful for I have been invited to spend Christmas with his family in Wimbledon. His mother, his father, his sister and his sister's husband will be there. The Renshaws are not rich but they are more than comfortable. His father, retired now, worked for a long-established tea

207

company and his mother, unusually for a woman from a privileged but non-academic background, went to university. Matthew's sister, Patricia, taught Physical Education at an independent girls' school before she married a chap who works for the BBC. What will such a family make of me?

'What on earth do you find to write about all the time?'

Helen looked up in surprise. If Dorothy had knocked she hadn't heard her. She blotted the page and closed the exercise book quickly. 'It's a diary,' she said. 'I jot down things that have happened each day.'

'I know what a diary is,' Dorothy said irritably. 'And I know you keep one. But I just can't imagine that your days can be interesting enough to use up all that ink.'

Helen was outraged. 'Do you know how hurtful that sounds? How unkind you can be at times?'

Dorothy, unused to Helen going on the offensive, stared at her in surprise and then said, 'I'm sorry. You're right. It's a bad habit of mine to speak without thinking first. Cyril often tells me so.'

'Cyril?' Helen smiled. 'So that's his name.'

'Have I never mentioned it before?'

'You haven't. You always refer to your gentleman friend as "Mr Barker", like a character in a Victorian novel. And anyway, what are you doing home so early?'

'It's past midnight.'

'Maybe so, but that's early for you.'

'I know. I've come home because I wanted to talk to you. But first let's put the kettle on and make a pot of tea.'

Helen made the tea and they sat on cushions by the fire. The flickering gas flame illuminated Dorothy's face and Helen could see that she looked uneasy. She wondered if her flatmate had changed her mind about the Christmas work rota. Still intimidated by the thought of meeting Matthew's family, she was half hoping this was true when the older girl's announcement took her completely by surprise.

'Cyril and I are going to get married,' she said.

Helen stared at Dorothy's troubled face and wondered if she had heard aright. 'Married?' she repeated.

'Yes.'

'But that's marvellous, isn't it?'

'Of course.'

'Then why aren't you smiling?'

Dorothy sighed. 'It's complicated.'

'Explain.'

'The divorce will take ages.'

'I guessed there was a wife.'

'She put a detective on to us so Cyril is the guilty party all right and he hasn't got a leg to stand on. He can't defend himself.'

'Why should he? Surely he wants to marry you, doesn't he?'

Dorothy looked defiant. 'Of course. It's just that Geraldine will get everything she wants, even custody of the children.'

'Children?' This surprised Helen. Somehow she had never thought there were children involved.

Dorothy laughed. 'Not that I care. I mean, you can't imagine me with a houseful of spoiled little brats, can you?'

'Houseful?'

'Well, two. Jane is thirteen and Jonathon is eleven. Honestly, Helen, you know me. I'm not the motherly type, am I?'

'No, I don't suppose you are. But how does Cyril feel about it?'

209

'Oh, I don't suppose she'll stop him visiting them now and then so long as he keeps up with the payments. And that's the problem. What with maintenance and school fees etc. we're going to be as poor as church mice.' Dorothy paused and gazed down into her cup of tea, then she looked up and tried a tentative smile. 'Here, top this up for me, will you?'

Helen obliged. 'You were saying?'

Dorothy sipped her tea, paused for even longer and then said, 'Helen, we've decided that now it's all in the open we might as well just live together at the apartment.'

'The apartment?'

'It belongs to Cyril's brother who works in Singapore. We've been using it for . . . well, you know . . .'

'Yes, I know.'

'His brother has agreed that we can stay there until we've sorted ourselves out.'

'That's good, isn't it?'

'Yes, it is, for us. But not for you.'

'I don't understand.'

'You'll have to find someone to take my place here.'

'Why?'

'Don't be dim. The rent. How could you afford to pay double what you're paying now?'

'Oh, of course.'

'Helen, I'm really sorry. I know what a pain it will be to find someone suitable. I had all kinds of girls sharing and then moving on until you came.' She looked up and smiled. 'You and I worked out quite well, didn't we?'

'We did. And don't worry. I'll . . . I'll find someone.'

Even as she said so Helen knew that she wouldn't. She didn't need help with the rent but she could not tell Dorothy that. Nobody knew that she was earning good money from her writing – not just for her weekly piece about life as a waitress in a London restaurant; she had also started doing book reviews and the occasional play review for the magazine.

She had even been sent along to a fashion show, although Charlotte had been doubtful about that and had told her aunt that Helen might be a little too sensible to appreciate such things as the importance of a hemline. Helen had wondered whether Charlotte had really meant 'dowdy' and had taken consolation from the fact that whatever her outside appearance was, her underpinnings were sensational.

'Do you want me to help you?' Dorothy asked. 'Help find someone to take my place, I mean.'

'No, that's OK. I'll manage. Perhaps I won't stay here.'

'Where would you go?'

'I might look for a place where I can afford the rent on my own.'

'That would either be the size of a rabbit hutch or in an area where you wouldn't want to walk home alone at night.'

Helen grinned. 'Then I'll go for the rabbit hutch. But stop worrying about me. I'm a big girl now, really I am.'

Dorothy looked at her thoughtfully. 'Yes, you are, aren't you? When I think of the funny little kid I met at King's Cross just over three years ago I can hardly credit you're the same person.'

'I'm not a kid any more.'

'It's not just that. You've grown up, yes, but you've changed as well.'

'For the better, I hope.'

'I think so.'

'You don't sound sure.'

'Well, I'm not. I mean, there's nothing actually wrong with you.'

'Thanks a lot!'

'It's just that you're so . . . so . . . guarded, not to say secretive. You come back here after work and you write in your diary and that's about it. You never have a good gossip with the rest of us.'

'That's not true! We have many a laugh at work and I enjoy the banter as much as anyone else.'

Dorothy looked at her speculatively. 'Yes, you do. But I always get the impression that you're watching and remembering things, and I bet you anything you like that you write it all down in that blessed diary.' Dorothy's eyes widened and she laughed. 'Why, you might even be a secret agent of some sort. A spy. Stefano's would be just the place to send you.'

'What on earth do you mean?'

'All the people who meet there. The refugees from all over Europe. They're not all friendly or grateful to be here. Cyril said some of them are positively subversive. He says these are troubled times we're living in. Storm clouds gathering over Europe and all that.'

'He may be right, but I assure you I'm not a spy.'

Even as she said this Helen wondered if that was true. She certainly wasn't a foreign agent but in a funny way she was spying on her fellow human beings. She had done this as long as she could remember. She was an onlooker, someone who maybe felt slightly like an outsider, different enough to be able to observe and record all the terrible and wonderful things that people did.

'Well, I must say, Helen, you've taken this well.'

'Why shouldn't I? I'm really pleased for you.'

And I am, Helen thought. But I'm also wondering about the present Mrs Barker and whether she still loves her errant husband. And the children . . . how will they feel about their father leaving home?

'I meant that you've taken it well that I'm leaving the flat,' Dorothy said.

'When will you be going?'

'As soon as possible. And that's another thing, I wonder if you'd mind helping me pack up.'

'Of course I'll help.'

'I'm not taking everything. I won't need the pots and pans. And I'll be leaving some of my clothes. Some of them are a little outdated. You can have them if you like.'

'Your outdated clothes?'

'Don't look like that. I didn't mean to offend you. Just an alteration here and there and you could bring them bang up-to-date. You know I've said it before, I wish you would care more about your appearance. Especially now that Matthew Renshaw has taken notice of you at last. Although, come to think of it, he's not exactly a fashion plate, is he, in his schoolmasterly tweed jacket with its leather patches?'

Helen would have liked to have said that in her opinion Matthew's jacket was made from very good tweed and that furthermore she didn't think there was anything wrong with her own appearance, and that Dorothy's taste in fashion was not hers. However, she decided not to take offence. After all, if she was going to live on her own there was no reason now why she could not spend some of her earnings on really good clothes. Dorothy would never see them.

Something occurred to Helen. 'Will you continue to work at Stefano's?'

'For a while, but once we're married Cyril doesn't really want his wife to be working as a waitress. In fact he doesn't want me to work at all. The aim is to find a nice little house in a respectable neighbourhood and be Mr and Mrs Suburbia. That's how he puts it. He wants us to be respectable.' Suddenly Dorothy couldn't meet Helen's eyes.

213

'Is that what you want?'

'Of course. What kind of girl do you take me for? I haven't just been having a good time, you know. I really love him.'

'Of course you do.'

Dorothy yawned. 'I'm beat. I'll have an early night – early for me, I mean.' She grinned. 'And no doubt you'll want to get back to your scribbling.' She got up and headed for the door where she paused. 'Goodnight, Helen. We'll start sorting things out tomorrow.'

That conversation took place on the Wednesday and Dorothy was gone by Saturday. She had taken the next two days off work and she spent Christmas Eve settling into her new home. Helen wasn't invited – not then nor for some nebulous date in the future. It seemed as though Dorothy was already cutting ties with the life she wanted to leave behind.

Helen had worked a split shift on the Saturday and during her time off she walked along Oxford Street to shop for clothes. She had no intention of altering and adapting the clothes Dorothy had left behind. They would all go to the Salvation Army or one of the Refugee Centres.

She took her cheque book with her but she had no real idea of what sort of clothes she would need for a visit to Matthew's house. His sister had been a sports teacher; was her taste spare and spartan? His mother was something of an academic; did she favour cardigans and yet more tweed? No, Matthew had told her that Mrs Renshaw frequented the theatre and the cinema and that she and his father loved to dine in good restaurants.

Dine! Oh, no. Did the wretched family change for dinner? In despair she thought of Charlotte. Jocelyn Graves' niece might dress casually for work but she came from the kind of background where the women would know exactly what to wear at any time of day and for any sort of visit. Glancing at her watch, Helen hurried along to the office in Russell Square and raced up the stairs.

Charlotte and Jocelyn were testing a cake recipe. That is, they were just about to cut into a pink confection that Charlotte had baked the night before. Charlotte looked up and grinned. 'Want a piece?' she asked. 'If it's any good Jocelyn is going to let me have a cookery column.'

'I haven't time,' Helen said. 'I want you to come shopping with me.'

When Helen explained her dilemma Jocelyn smiled and said, 'Charlotte, you'll have to go. We'll sample the cake later. I promise I'll wait for you.'

Charlotte took control. 'How much do you want to spend?' she asked.

'Whatever it takes.'

'A girl after my own heart. Let's go!'

Charlotte grabbed her coat and on the way down the stairs she said, 'We haven't time to go from shop to shop, so I suggest we go to Selfridges where we can get everything you need and where the customer is always right. Is that OK?'

Helen smiled her agreement.

Just a little later as they entered the store Charlotte asked Helen what she knew about the Renshaws and Helen could only repeat the sparse details she knew.

'Never mind,' Charlotte said. 'That will do. You want a classic day dress, something a little longer than you usually wear and of a very simple cut. Smoky blue, I think, to match your eyes. They won't be expecting you to change for dinner otherwise your beau would have told you.'

Helen flushed. 'He's not my beau and I wouldn't bank

on him having told me. He can be a little absent-minded.'

'Even so, he will have had instructions from his mother. I'm guessing he's been well brought up.'

When they were both satisfied with the dress Charlotte said, 'And now the coat. I take it you're not going to turn up in that serviceable flannel you usually wear?'

Helen shook her head.

'Good, because the dress we've chosen has a coat to go with it. We won't have to agonize over what will be a good match.'

The coat was a wrap-over with wide revers and a belt. When Helen tried it on Charlotte stepped forward and showed her how to turn the collar up behind, 'To frame your face,' she said. 'Hurry up, handbag and shoes next, and why not treat yourself to a pack of silk stockings? Gosh, Helen, I'm enjoying this.'

When Charlotte was satisfied that they had thought of everything she left Helen to pay for her purchases and, excusing herself, said she had to go to the powder room. But when she came back she handed Helen a small leather case. 'Present from me,' she said.

Helen opened it to find a simple string of pearls with matching clip-on stud earrings.

'Don't say anything daft like, "You shouldn't have done!"' Charlotte instructed. 'And now you'd better ask them to send this lot along to the office. You obviously won't want them to be delivered to Stefano's. You can pick them up tomorrow. See you later,' she added. 'I'll save some cake for you.'

When she was back at work Helen began to wonder whether she should have bought presents for Matthew's family but decided that that might seem a little presumptuous. After all,

Matthew was not her beau as Charlotte had called him. She wasn't quite sure what he was. Certainly a friend, and he definitely didn't seem to have any other woman in his life. Or if he did, that woman would surely have complained by now about the amount of time he was spending with Helen.

He took her to the pictures, they visited art galleries and museums, they sat in coffee shops and watched the world go by as they talked, but apart from holding her hand and kissing her forehead or her cheek when he took her home, Matthew had never attempted to take the romance any further. Once when she had asked him in for coffee he had smiled and murmured, 'Better not.'

She had been so embarrassed, so worried that he would think her forward, that she had not asked him again. What was she to make of it? All she knew was that, unsatisfactory as this state of affairs was, she would be totally bereft if he did not seek her company.

When Helen went to the office in Russell Square to collect her new clothes she asked Charlotte's advice again. 'Why don't you take something along for the table,' Charlotte said. 'Flowers, chocolates, a bottle of wine are the usual sort of things, but you can be more original than that.'

'Can I?'

'Buy some of those nutty cinnamon biscuits dipped in spiced honey that Stefano serves with coffee. The ones you've brought here now and then. Put them in a cake box and scatter a bit of icing sugar over them. That will do very nicely. And, Helen, do try to enjoy yourself. You look as though you're going to the gallows rather than a jolly good lunch on Christmas Day.'

Jocelyn laughed and Charlotte asked her why.

'We don't know what the lunch will be like, do we? But

217

I can understand why Helen is apprehensive. You feel out of your depth, don't you?' she asked Helen directly.

'I do. I'm not sure if I'll know how to behave.'

'Of course you will,' Jocelyn said. 'You will simply be yourself. You are intelligent, observant and adaptable enough to deal with any situation you find yourself in. I'm sure Matthew's family will be charmed with you. Oh, I've been meaning to ask you.' Her supportive smile changed into a frown.

'What is it?'

'Have you told Matthew that you write for us?'

'No. You said I must remain anonymous.'

'I did, but that was before you had a boyfriend.'

'He's not my boyfriend.'

'You sound uncertain about that. But anyway, he's a friend. You must have been tempted to tell him more about yourself.'

'I've thought about it but somehow it would seem like boasting, wouldn't it?'

Jocelyn smiled. 'Helen, you're priceless. But I'm glad you haven't told him yet, although one day I suppose you must. When you're more certain about whether he's your boyfriend, that is.'

Before she left the office Charlotte bemoaned the fact that she would have to spend Christmas helping with a clutch of small brothers, sisters and cousins at the family home in Kensington. Jocelyn sympathized and announced smugly that she was going for three days to her cottage in Cornwall with a hamper from Harrods, a bottle of good Scotch and a clutch of detective novels, including the latest by Margery Allingham and Dorothy L. Sayers. It didn't occur to Helen until much later to wonder whether Jocelyn Graves would be going to her cottage alone.

There was no dog racing on Christmas Day and Myra cooked dinner not only for her lodgers but also for one or two of Raymond's friends, including Dr Balodis. Danny had never been able to work out whether Myra and Raymond were actually married. Certainly the owner of the dog track spent a lot of time at the boarding house and when he did they shared a bedroom, but there were also periods when he went missing. Although he always turned up at the track in time for the night's events.

He must have told Myra that he wouldn't be there on Christmas Day, so on the Sunday she started taking a drink or two to console herself. She wasn't a miserable drunk; on the contrary she got merrier and merrier, so by the next day, which was Christmas Eve, there was a party atmosphere in the house as she dragooned anyone who arrived to help with the preparations for the grand feast she was preparing. A feast that Raymond would always regret having missed, she declared.

Myra got Joe to start making the sausage meat and apple stuffing, and when Danny saw how his brother responded to Myra's motherly ways he ached with longing for the years gone by when the food had not been so plentiful but their mother's love had been all-encompassing.

Dr Balodis's contribution to the occasion was a Christmas tree. While Danny helped him decorate it with wooden angels and tinsel, the doctor told him his name was Alberts – with an 's' – and that Livonia was the home of the first Christmas tree. Danny remembered learning at school that the first Christmas tree had been put up in Riga, the capital of Latvia, hundreds of years ago, but the history of that part of the world was so complicated that he decided to give the doctor the benefit of the doubt.

On Christmas morning he heard Myra go downstairs very early, no doubt to put the pudding on to steam. He waited until he heard her tottering back upstairs and then, while Joe slept on, he got dressed and slipped out of the house. He made his way to Kilburn. It was still dark and Danny was used to taking advantage of the shadows. He was waiting in a doorway opposite the house where Helen had her flat when Helen's friend called for her. He had come in a car. Helen didn't invite him up – it seemed she never did – but she was dressed and ready to go when she opened the door.

Danny caught his breath when he saw Helen illumined by the hall light behind her. How beautiful she looked, how stylish – and how like their mother. He watched as the man opened the door of the passenger seat and saw Helen in just like a gentleman should do.

He didn't know where they were going, but the night before, when the man had brought her home, Danny had heard him say as he turned to walk away, 'I'll see you in the morning, nice and early.'

The car drove away and Danny felt hollow inside as he watched it go. He knew it wasn't fair to blame Helen. It had been his and Joe's decision not to contact her, but he couldn't help wondering whether she missed them as much as they missed her. That was why he was here, standing alone and miserable in the frosty dawn. He just wanted to catch sight of her on Christmas Day.

And then he raised a smile. At least I have Joe, he thought. My twin brother, the other half of me, the person I would do anything for. I'd die for him if necessary. Danny began to cough. The early morning air, full of soot as Londoners lit their fires, was not good for his chest. He wrapped his muffler firmly round his lower face and set off on the journey back to Myra's. He and Joe would make the best of it.

Fleetingly he wondered what sort of Christmas Elsie would have. Adopted by such rich people, her life would be very different from everything that had gone before. Living in luxury as she must, he wondered if she ever remembered the Christmases she had spent with her family. And if she did, would she long for those days to return or would she have changed too much by now? Whatever the answer was, he hoped that their little sister would be happy.

Chapter Fourteen

On Christmas morning Hugh and Elise went to church alone. Selma told them she was tired after the dinner party they had given the night before. She would have breakfast in bed and would come down when they returned. Then they could open the presents that were waiting under the tree.

To Hugh Elise seemed no different from usual. She greeted him with a smile and joined in the pretence that Father Christmas must have called. Hugh knew Selma would not have imagined the changes in their daughter's behaviour and he accepted that girls reacted differently to their fathers, especially fathers as doting as he was. This caused him no worries.

What had kept him awake at night and what was eating into his soul was the suspicion that Selma was ill. His wife had never been the sort of woman to 'soldier on'. She wasn't exactly a hypochondriac but she believed in being safe rather than sorry, and as everybody knew the best consultants in the world were in Harley Street, she took full advantage of them both for herself and Elise.

If she has felt at all unwell she will have been to see someone, Hugh thought. And if she has, surely she would have told me. Unless this is really serious and she wants to keep it to herself until after Christmas. Much as it cost him he decided to go along with that.

After the decorations they had chosen together had been delivered, Selma told him that she was engaging a 'clever little woman', an interior designer, to actually put them up.

'She's marvellous, darling,' Selma said. 'And she just happens to have time to fit us in between other engagements.'

'But you've always made a grand job of it,' Hugh told her. 'And it's such fun doing it together.'

'Well, not this year,' Selma said irritably, and Hugh had felt himself dismissed as though he were an importunate child.

Selma was up and dressed by the time Hugh and Elise returned from church and she seemed very much like the old Selma, excited about the presents, pulling crackers, and hoping like any child to be the one who found the silver sixpence in the plum pudding. Hugh was pleased to see how tender she was with Elise. If they had been having any mother and daughter problems Selma seemed to be coping, and the day passed peacefully.

On Boxing Day Selma broke another family tradition. They did not go as a family to the pantomime. 'I've taken a box at the Theatre Royal and I'm sending Elise off with those three chums of hers,' Selma told him. 'They'll have much more fun on their own and the entertainment is supposed to be spectacular this year. I've heard one of the scenes is a vast lake with an army of girls entering the water and marching down and down until they are entirely submerged beneath the surface. I read in the newspaper that in one of the rehearsals a bathing cap was found floating on the water. You can imagine there was great panic until it was discovered that the owner of the cap was safely ashore and simply lost her cap in transit.'

As she recited this her eyes sparkled with amusement and

for a moment she was the old Selma. 'You know, I can't imagine how they're going to get a lake on the stage and what on earth any of this has to do with *Cinderella*!'

'Doesn't it make you want to go along and see for yourself?' Hugh asked.

'No, darling. I would rather have a peaceful day with you.'

When Matthew returned from taking Helen home at the end of Christmas Day he found his sister waiting for him.

'This is getting to be a habit,' he said.

'What do you mean?'

Patricia and her husband, George, were staying the night and she was already dressed for bed in pyjamas and dressing gown, with a scarf tied round her head like a turban, through which Matthew could catch a glimpse of metal curlers.

'Can you actually sleep with those instruments of torture all over your scalp?' he asked.

She frowned and shrugged impatiently. 'I asked you what you meant when you said this is getting to be a habit.'

'Waylaying me in the kitchen. What do you want to know this time?'

'Cocoa?'

'Surely you haven't waited up when everyone else is slumbering just to make me a cup of cocoa?'

'Oh, do be serious, Matthew. I meant, shall we have a cup of cocoa while we talk.'

'If talk we must, then yes, for goodness' sake let's have a cup of cocoa.'

Patricia had already begun to warm a pan of milk and soon brother and sister were sitting at the table eating slices of Christmas cake.

'Well, then?' Matthew asked.

'It's about Helen.'

'I thought it would be.'

'She's very nice.'

'Of course she is.'

'I didn't know what to expect when you said she was a waitress.'

'I never thought of you as a snob, Patricia.'

'I'm not. At least, to be perfectly honest I have to work at it, and you are my brother, and . . . oh, dear . . .'

Matthew decided to rescue her. 'It's all right, I know that you're basically a good sort and I never had any doubt that you would like Helen no matter what her background.'

'That's strange, isn't it?'

'Helen's background?'

'I mean the fact that you can't really tell what it is. She's . . . well . . . she's clever and rather ladylike, isn't she? And she has such good manners. I could tell the old folk were taken with her even if she was rather subdued at first.'

'Of course she was subdued. She'd never met any of you before; she probably didn't know what to expect.'

'Of course not. But I very soon got the feeling that she was observing us keenly and almost assessing us. Storing away the information for future reference if you like.'

'You make her sound quite cold and calculating.'

'Oh no, not that. Just, well, I don't know, a bit analytical, perhaps. But nevertheless I was impressed. She was quite a surprise.'

'And is this why you are denying yourself George's warm embrace, just because you want to tell me you were impressed by Helen?'

Patricia didn't answer straight away. 'Would you like a mince pie?' she asked. 'Or there's some trifle left. I'm rather peckish, aren't you?'

'No thanks,' Matthew said. 'You can't be hungry after the amount we've eaten today. You're just procrastinating.'

'Well, all right. I do like Helen but I hope you're not serious about her. There, I've said it.'

'Serious? In what way?'

'Don't be dim. Helen is an attractive girl. You've been taking her out. You've brought her home to meet your family – on Christmas Day! Isn't that getting serious?'

Matthew stared at his sister. He didn't know what to say because he didn't have an answer. He liked being with Helen. He thought she was funny and bright as well as being attractive in an unshowy way. They enjoyed the same books and films and could always find something to talk about. But was this a romance? He couldn't help but be aware that Helen would like it to be and he was certainly attracted to her. So why was he holding back? Was it because he knew deep inside that if he got too close to her, this witty, attractive, intelligent girl had the power to break his heart?

'How old is Helen, Matthew?' his sister asked. 'Nineteen?'

He nodded.

'You're twenty-seven.'

'That hardly makes me an old man.'

'Of course not. And some girls are fully-fledged grown-up females at Helen's age, but she isn't. I really don't think it would be fair to her to rush her into a grown-up relationship.'

Matthew smiled.

'What is it?'

'Perhaps I'm the one that isn't ready for a grown-up relationship. I've never had one, you know. After all, what sort of woman would put up with my erratic lifestyle? It just wouldn't be fair. But don't worry, sister mine. I promise I won't do anything that would hurt Helen. I care too much for her to do that.'

Patricia had to be satisfied with that but she was annoyed with herself for not telling Matthew of her other concern. Something that was niggling away at the fringes of her mind. Patricia was sure there was more to Helen than she was telling anyone. Was it a case of still waters running deep, or was there something specific that the girl didn't want anyone – even Matthew – to know?

At lunchtime the next day every table at Stefano's was taken and a cheerful crowd of would-be diners who had not had the foresight to book in advance waited in the lounge bar area. Helen knew that most of these people were going to the matinee performances of the pantomimes and other Christmas entertainments. Some of them had come into town in good time for the early evening performances and intended to linger over a good meal.

This made things difficult for Stefano who was loath to move them on and free a table. Marina was made of sterner stuff and with the greatest of charm she persuaded those who had finished their meal to retire to the bar where the rising tide of cheerful voices made any real conversation almost impossible.

Helen preferred the restaurant to be busy. Slow days, especially when the weather was foul, were boring and made her wonder sometimes what on earth she was doing here. Today she was glad that she didn't have too much time to think. She had been nervous about meeting Matthew's family but she thought it had gone well. His mother and father obviously adored him and their welcome had been warm and friendly.

His brother-in-law George, who worked in the sub-basement control room at Broadcasting House, was quiet but droll and at times during the day he had caught her eye and sent complicit looks as if to say, 'I know, we're both outsiders to this charmed circle but they're all right, really.'

Helen decided she liked him a lot, especially when she saw how patient he was with his rather bossy wife, Matthew's sister, Patricia. Patricia had taught physical education before she married and she reminded Helen of the sports teacher at her own old school. She was fit and hearty and inclined to organize people even when there was no need to do so. At one point when she had organized Helen, George and Matthew into helping her set the table for lunch she actually said, 'Shall we get into two teams?'

'Splendid idea,' her husband had responded. 'Did you bring your whistle?'

After a moment of puzzlement when Patricia obviously couldn't understand why the others were laughing, she smiled and laughed herself. Not a bad sort, Helen decided, but as the day wore on she realized that jolly though she was, Patricia was not entirely happy about her being there.

The meal had been wonderful, the conversation interesting, and Matthew attentive. The drive home through the frosty streets with brightly lit Christmas trees displayed in suburban windows had been magical. In the warm confines of the car Helen had never felt so close to Matthew. They didn't talk much but what he did say made her feel part of his world, his life; so it was all the more disappointing when they arrived at her flat and he made no attempt to take her in his arms and kiss her with passion rather than the gentle kiss he dropped on her forehead when he saw her to the front door.

Lying awake later she tried to understand what it was she meant to him. Did he want friendship, or something more?

But whatever it was she was prepared to wait and find out. After all, there was no denying the fact that she was deeply and hopelessly in love with him.

On Boxing Day Matthew's parents kept open house for friends and neighbours, and Patricia saw to it that he did his duty, serving drinks and socializing. Some of the guests had known Patricia and Matthew since they were children and the men, particularly, were fascinated by his work and wanted to talk about the dangers he had faced in what they referred to as 'foreign parts'.

Matthew found this a strain but at least it kept him occupied and gave his sister no chance to take up the previous night's conversation. When he had gone to bed he had thought long and hard about what she had said. By morning he knew that his feelings for Helen were much deeper than he had wanted to acknowledge to himself. People made jokes about war-hardened foreign reporters, saying that they were cold-blooded and heartless. They had to be if they were going to remain sane enough to report without prejudice some of the situations they found themselves in.

But Matthew wasn't heartless. That was the problem. His solution had been to detach himself from the world around him. There were those on the paper who called him a loner. And he'd been happy with that until that crazy incident at Stefano's when Helen had dropped the mess of jelly and fruit all over him. The shock had made him look up and see an appalled young girl. Her expression of comic dismay had gone straight to his heart. His instinct had been to reassure her. To try and make things up to her. After all, it was his fault he had left his wretched walking stick in the way. That was the reason he had asked her out. Or so he had told himself.

She was funny and intelligent and remarkably good company. How could he have known how much she would come to mean to him in such a short time? He had promised Patricia that he would do nothing to hurt Helen. Well, he wouldn't. But neither could he give her up.

He smiled as he poured the drinks and chatted to friends and neighbours. He avoided Patricia's pointed glances. When duty was done he hugged his mother and set off cheerfully. He was going to see Helen, the girl he loved.

When Matthew arrived at Stefano's Helen was still working. Marina recognized him and asked him to wait in the bar. Before he knew it someone had put a paper hat on his head and a young woman held a spray of mistletoe over him and kissed him enthusiastically. Marina gave him a complimentary glass of festive punch and told him she would see that Helen was relieved of serving duties immediately.

A little later, when Helen appeared, he was surprised to see that she was wearing her serviceable old coat. Instructed by his mother and dressed in his best himself, he had imagined that Helen would wear the attractive outfit she had worn the day before. She smiled a little wanly, he thought, and they made their way to the door.

Once outside Helen paused and turned to face him. 'Sorry about this,' she said as she glanced down at the way she was dressed. 'But I didn't want to take my good clothes to the restaurant. They end up smelling of food.'

'Wise decision.' He glanced at his watch. 'Let's go. I want to get to the theatre in time to order refreshments for the interval and to buy the biggest box of chocolates they can provide. It's years since I've been to a pantomime and I intend to enjoy myself.'

Matthew had chosen to bring her to see *Cinderella* because

everyone was talking about the amazing scene at the lake. He was of the opinion that the story about the floating bathing cap found during a rehearsal and the chorus girl they had feared drowned was a publicity stunt to draw in the audience. Not that that was needed considering the starry and popular cast.

Helen had mixed feelings about the choice of pantomime. *Cinderella* was the last Christmas show her mother had taken them to at the Theatre Royal in Newcastle. There they had had seats in the gods, the highest balcony of all where the slope was precipitous but the seats were cheap. Sitting there they had seemed a long way from the stage but her mother had laughingly told her that the actors would appear more beautiful and the costumes more gorgeous if you couldn't see them too closely.

Now, here they were in the front row of the grand circle where theatregoers traditionally wore evening dress at the evening performances. Even here at the matinee some of them were very expensively and fashionably dressed. She hoped Matthew wouldn't be ashamed of her. What she had told him was perfectly true. The staff cloakroom was next to the kitchen and any garment left there would carry home the rich aroma of the day's dishes, but there was another reason she could not have taken her new clothes there. She did not want to explain to anyone how she could afford them.

Families in the audience were greeting old friends and making arrangements to meet for refreshments during the intervals. When the house lights dimmed the good-humoured chatter faded, people settled back and looked expectantly towards the stage. Lights went on in the orchestra pit and the musicians began to tune up. The conductor took his place but before raising his baton he looked up at one of the boxes where the occupants were still talking and laughing quite loudly. He rapped his baton on his music stand and said, 'Young ladies, if you please!'

Not a bit abashed, one of them leaned forward and called out, 'So sorry,' and she smiled engagingly, winning an indulgent smile in return.

Helen leaned forward and gripped the padded velvet-covered edge of the balcony. Her heart thudded painfully and her breath caught in her throat.

'What is it?' Matthew whispered as he leaned forward and took her arm. 'Are you ill?'

Helen shook her head.

'Are you sure?'

Someone behind them said, 'Sshh!' and Matthew turned and frowned.

'I'm all right, really, I am,' she said quietly.

'Good,' Matthew took hold of her hand. 'Then let's enjoy the show.'

Matthew was surprised at how tightly Helen returned his grip. He could have no idea of the emotions the sight of that beautiful girl in the box had aroused within her. Or that that girl was Helen's sister.

Myra had insisted on a box. They had come to the matinee because there was a meeting tonight at the track and Joe would have to be at work in the kennels. They made a strange party, Myra, Dr Balodis, and the twins. Their landlady was wearing her fur coat and a hat shaped like a dinner plate that tipped forward over one eye. Danny wondered how she could see properly. Dr Balodis wore a belted camel coat and on his head a large fedora that made him look like a secret agent in a movie. That was Danny's opinion.

Danny and Joe were dressed in their new suits: square-shouldered and double-breasted, navy blue with vertical white stripes. Myra said the suits made them look like proper little men. Danny thought they made them look like gangsters, but Joe had set his heart on them and Danny would do anything that would make Joe happy.

Myra had wanted to see the show because she was a fan of Revnell and West, a popular music hall act known as 'the long and the short of it'. Ethel Revnell, at just over six foot tall, and Gracie West, at just over four foot, played two evil schoolgirls in the variety halls. Myra thought they were the perfect choice to play the ugly sisters.

Their landlady was making much of the fact that they were in a box. She tipped the usherette generously and ordered ice creams for the boys and drinks for her and the doctor to be brought during both intervals. Before the lights dimmed she leaned forward and observed the audience keenly, pointing out people she considered to be of importance in the stalls and the dress circle. None of this meant anything to Dr Balodis who sat blinking in the shadows and wondering why he had allowed himself to be dragooned into accompanying her.

'Cheeky young madams,' Myra whispered sotto voce when the conductor reprimanded the four girls in the box directly opposite.

A moment later the music began. After a short medley of popular tunes the curtains rose and Joe, Myra and Dr Balodis turned their attention to the stage and the gaily dressed dancers. Danny, however, was still staring at the girl in the box opposite. The girl who, although he hadn't seen her since she was nine years old, was unquestionably his sister Elsie. He had already seen Helen sitting with that man in the front row of the grand circle; he had spotted her when they had first arrived.

And now, here they all were, Helen, Elsie, Joe and Danny,

together at the theatre after all these years. And he was the only one who knew.

After the show Joe had to get away quickly. The meeting at the track that night was a big one, with some heavy betting expected. Myra and Dr Balodis went off to a club she knew and Danny said he might stay up west for a while and take in the sights.

What he did was to mingle with the crowds on the pavement outside the theatre and wait until his younger sister and her friends emerged from the brightly lit foyer. They were in high spirits. He watched and he listened and he learned their names. He frowned when he realized that Elsie seemed to have become Elise. He saw from the girls' confident attitude that their families must be very rich indeed. They are indulged and spoiled, he thought, their young lives a round of pleasure.

Very soon a motor car pulled up and a young man who turned out to be the brother of the one called Shirley approached them.

'Tom, there you are!'

'Good time?' he asked.

'Brilliant!' his sister said.

'Well, let me tell you the night isn't over yet. Mama has hired a film projector and some Charlie Chaplin films. Perry and I are going to give you your own private screening after you've eaten the banquet that awaits you.'

'Your lordly friend, Perry, actually wants to hang around with us kids?' Shirley asked.

'He's setting up the screen and sorting the reels as we speak.'

'But no doubt you two will be going out later?'

'Of course.'

'Not fair.'

'Don't worry, little sister. Your time will come. Now, let's go.'

Tom Chapman ushered the girls into the luxurious depths of the Lagonda and then he pulled away through the crowded streets. Danny made a decision. Smiling quietly to himself and feeling like a character in a movie, he hailed a taxi and told the driver to 'Follow that car!'

By the end of this evening at least he would know where one of Elsie's friends lived.

The theatre was half empty by the time Matthew and Helen left their seats in the front row of the grand circle. 'Let them all go,' he had told her quietly. 'We don't need to join in the rush.'

Helen nodded but didn't speak. She was staring ahead raptly at nothing in particular as far as Matthew could tell.

'Did you enjoy the show?' he asked.

'Very much.'

She sounded as though she meant it but she seemed strangely detached. Perhaps she's still lost in fairyland, Matthew thought fancifully, swimming in the magic lake or dancing with Prince Charming at the ball. You didn't have to be a child to be caught up in the magic of the theatre.

The cleaners were already working in the row behind them, tipping up the seats and removing empty chocolate boxes and sweet wrappers, getting the auditorium ready for the evening's performance.

'Let's go now, sweetheart,' Matthew whispered and marvelled at how easily the endearment had slipped out.

Helen turned her head towards him and her eyes widened but, although her smile was one of surprise, she still had that oddly detached air. Matthew wondered if she was tired and

235

worried that she might reject his suggestion of going on somewhere for supper. But she agreed, merely asking if what she was wearing would pass muster.

'Don't worry,' he said. 'The place I have in mind is not the sort of place where you have to dress up. It's a little club in a basement in Soho where we can get a so-so bottle of wine with an adequate meal, but listen to some very good music.'

Once out on the crowded pavement Matthew put his arm round Helen and held her close to save her from the thoughtless jostling of people out to have a good time.

The club was crowded but a generous tip to the head waiter secured them a table far enough away from the swing door that led to the kitchen and not too near the band. As they waited for their meal they watched the couples on the small dance floor. Matthew was longing to ask Helen to dance so that he could hold her in his arms but her unaccustomed air of reserve had placed a barrier between them.

What could be wrong, he asked himself. Can she have decided that she doesn't want to see me any more just as I have realized how much she means to me? But when he reached for her hand across the table she didn't withdraw it. She allowed him to order their meal, spaghetti bolognese accompanied by a bottle of Chianti in a straw flask. That made her smile but her mood remained passive.

At last, after the meal, and feeling like a schoolboy with his first crush, Matthew asked her to dance and felt his heart pounding when he held her close and discovered how fluidly they moved together to the dreamy beat of the music. Helen was just the right height to rest her head on his shoulder. He found this satisfying and he let it lie there although this meant that he couldn't see the expression on her face.

When they left the club they walked, holding hands like lovers, to where he had left his car in Soho Square. When he drew up outside her flat in Kilburn he took her in his arms and kissed her as he had never kissed her before. He could have sworn that she was as moved as he was and yet she was content to say goodnight and leave him without inviting him to come in. Just as well, he thought. It's early days and I am going to have to get used to coming a-courting.

26th December 1934

Matthew kissed me tonight. Kissed me in a way I have wanted him to do for a long time. And it was wonderful. If I were the heroine of a romantic novel my heart would be singing and I would be overcome with joy. Well, I am overcome, but not just with the knowledge that he feels something for me.

Why did it have to happen now? Why did he have to make his feelings plain on the night when I saw my darling sister for the first time since she was a child? She has grown so beautiful and she looks so happy. For the first time I have serious doubts about the effect it would have on her to remind her of the past. I would not want to be the one to threaten her secure if precious little world.

So tonight when I should be lying in bed and reliving the wonderful sensation of being in Matthew's arms, I am torn between relishing my love for him and the bittersweet joy of having seen my sister.

Hugh found Selma in her own private sitting room, the little room she called her boudoir. She was sitting by the fire when he entered the room and she rose to hurry towards him. The deceptively simple grey silk dress clung to her figure, emphasizing the curve of her breasts, and her hair was softly permed to form soft waves framing her face.

'We'll eat in here tonight,' she said and gestured towards the small table set for two. Hugh looked and saw quail's eggs, smoked salmon, Stilton cheese, soft white rolls, Florentines, fruit cake, and an ice bucket containing champagne.

'Fortnum and Mason?'

'Mmm.' She smiled and nodded.

'Are we celebrating?'

'We are.'

'Something special?'

'Very special. That's why I sent Elise to the pantomime. And she's going to stay with Shirley Chapman tonight. Shirley's brother will be collecting them.'

'You didn't want Elise to share the celebration?'

'No, darling, I didn't. You see, we are going to have a baby. At last you and I are going to have a child of our own.'

Part Three

A Year Later

Chapter Fifteen

26th December 1935

I can hardly believe that a year has gone by since I first met Matthew's parents and that I was so apprehensive of spending Christmas Day with them. This time I actually stayed overnight so I have two days' diary entries to write up.

The restaurant was so busy that Marina said I had to work on Christmas Day. Well, I didn't have to but I felt sorry for Stefano. However, I only stayed until the lunch menu was over. Once I'd helped set up the tables for the evening meals I made a dash for home to bathe and change into my glad rags. Matthew was already waiting, sitting in his car outside the flat, working on some notes for his column. He was pleased to see me, as ever, but he seemed a little distracted.

'What is it? Won't the right words come?' I asked him before I headed for the bathroom.

'No, it's nothing to do with my work.'

'That doesn't sound very convincing.'

'Well, perhaps it is. But on the other hand I could just be imagining things.'

'Oh, Matthew,' I said, 'fancy starting to tell me something like this now! Look, your mother has been good enough to have the meal later than usual, just so that

I can join you. I'll have to get ready, but promise me we'll talk in the car on the way there.'

We did. Matthew told me he thought he was being followed. If that was the case it would almost certainly be something to do with his job as a crime reporter. I mean, he isn't being dunned for debt or anything! And his description of the person that he thought was following him didn't seem to fit that of a debt collector.

A young man, he told me. Little more than a boy. From the glimpses he'd caught of him the youth was good-looking and well dressed in a slightly flash way. I knew that Matthew is far too astute to make connections where there are none so I took what he said seriously. I asked him if he thought it could be connected with any of the crime stories he was investigating. Any one of them, he told me, but the thing that worried him most was that he had caught sight of the youth in the street where my flat was.

When we pulled up outside his parents' house he took me in his arms and said, 'I would never forgive myself if harm came to you because of me. When Christmas is over we'll have to have a serious talk about this.'

Patricia had done most of the cooking this year and she was gratified when I told her how much I had enjoyed the meal. It was true, she was as good at cooking as she was at everything else, and I'm sure the baby she is expecting will have the perfect mother.

I think she has accepted that Matthew and I are a couple but I'm not sure if she has accepted me.

That night I stayed with them and I had the distinct impression that Patricia was patrolling the corridors to make sure that Matthew did not sneak along to my room. She needn't have worried. We haven't done 'that' yet.

Not because I wouldn't but because he has this idea that he would be taking advantage of a girl so much younger than he is. He wants to wait until I'm sure. Sometimes I fantasize that I'll have my hand-embroidered silk underwear decorated all over with the slogan, 'I'm sure!'

This morning was a bit of a trial. The Renshaws held their usual Boxing Day open house and I had to meet their friends and neighbours. Most of the women glanced at my bare wedding finger and I knew that Mrs Renshaw would have loved to introduce me as her son's fiancée but, as yet, we are not officially engaged. Matthew has this crazy idea that I am still young enough to meet someone else and change my mind. That's something else I want to discuss after Christmas!

I had the whole day off from work today but we didn't go to a pantomime this year. We went to the pictures to see *Scrooge*. It was all right, I suppose, although Seymour Hicks was far too old to play the part of the young Scrooge as well as the old, and I was disappointed that we didn't see the ghosts, only heard their voices. There was no excuse to cuddle up to Matthew and shiver with pretend fright.

We came back here for supper. Mrs Renshaw had packed a hamper for us and I'm sure it was as luxurious as anything to be found at Fortnum and Mason. As we nibbled brandy mince pies and sipped glasses of my favourite Madeira wine, we had our serious talk. Matthew tried to persuade me, as he has before, that I should move. He says that his friends at the office are good at nosing out reasonably low-cost accommodation in what he deems the better parts of town and he would help me find somewhere. He can't understand why I am so reluctant to move. Neither can I if the truth be told.

This flat is far from lovely. It isn't even particularly comfortable. Perhaps I stay because it's the first home I made for myself after my mother died. Leaving the house I had grown up in and moving to Aunt Jane's was unspeakably cruel. Here in London Dorothy made me welcome in her carelessly welcoming way and I suppose I made a little nest for myself. The fact that she spent so little time here made the place my own.

So, whatever Matthew says, here I will stay. Until the time comes to look for a place we can live in together, that is.

Note to self: Be observant. When I leave the flat look out for good-looking young man who may be watching the place.

Note to self: Just realized I haven't heard from Eva for a while. Must go back over her letters and check the date. I shouldn't think much has changed at Aunt Jane's house but I suppose I ought to make sure that everything is all right. (I'm sure I don't know why!)

Danny waited until Helen's lights went out and began his walk home. He liked keeping an eye on his older sister, often being there just as she came home from work and seeing her draw the curtains and put the lights on in her upstairs flat.

He daydreamed sometimes that he would knock on her door and after a moment of shock she would invite him in. They would both cry – and laugh – and cry again, and then they would sit down and tell each other what had happened over the years since their mother had died.

He would be able to tell Helen that Elsie was safe and well. That he had discovered where she lived, where she went to school, who her friends were, and that he had been watching her just as assiduously as he had been watching

Helen herself. Maybe Elsie didn't look as happy these days and maybe that was because she was no longer the centre of attention since Mrs Partington had given birth to a little boy in June. Danny had watched as the nursemaid wheeled the pram out to the park and had seen how reluctantly Elsie had sometimes accompanied them.

Although she was sweet-natured, even when Elsie had been a little girl she had liked to be the centre of attention and they had all been happy to spoil her. They would have a laugh about that.

But it would never happen. Not only could Helen never be told about what had occurred at Haven House but in the years since then Joe, loyal stalwart Joe, had been drawn further and further into a life of shady dealings and crime that could no longer be called petty. And what about me? Danny asked himself. I've done nothing to stop him. I am just as bad as he is, no, I'm worse, because I'm happy to live off the money he earns.

Tonight he had realized that Matthew Renshaw had spotted him. Helen's friend had been sitting in his car making notes but suddenly he had looked up and stared straight at him. Danny had continued to walk casually along the street and round the corner. He had waited a while, then returned when Helen's curtains were drawn and her lights switched on.

Once, long ago, someone had tried to make something of the garden of the house opposite Helen's flat. The house was now divided into bedsitting rooms and no one seemed to be responsible for the garden. The lawn was overgrown, the flowerbeds choked with weeds and the rustic wooden bench splintered and peeling. The dusty privet hedge had grown so high that Danny could sit on the bench without being seen from the street and look upwards to the windows of Helen's top-floor flat in the house opposite. During the winter months the shadows were deep enough to hide him.

Nevertheless he knew he would have to be more careful in future. Especially if he wanted to keep an eye on Matthew Renshaw. And apart from the fact that the man was courting Helen, there was a very good reason why he should.

1st January 1936

I've told him. After a hectic night at Stefano's Matthew and I went back to my little flat in time to greet the New Year together with a bottle of pink champagne. We put the wireless on and as soon as Big Ben had stopped striking Matthew kissed me and then opened the champagne. He filled the glasses, and after the first delicious sip of the sparkling wine he wanted to kiss me again but I stepped back.

'It's time you knew,' I said. 'I've been leading a double life.'

He looked puzzled and not a little worried so I hurried on to tell him that as well as being a waitress in Stefano's, I was also a writer and that I had a regular column in a magazine called *Potpourri*.

I wish I'd had a camera to record his reactions. But I remember every expression that crossed his face and every word he spoke. Surprise was quickly followed by delight. And then he gave a shout of triumph. 'I've seen that magazine!' he said. 'Don't tell me – you must be the writer of the À La Carte feature. You are, aren't you?'

I nodded.

'I should have guessed.'

'I'm glad you didn't,' I said. 'I was told to keep it secret.'

Then Matthew took my champagne glass from my

hand and put it down, along with his, on the table. 'My clever, clever darling,' he said and he began to kiss me over and over again.

Every time I drew breath I tried to tell him that he must keep this revelation to himself and that I must remain anonymous.

'Of course I'll keep your secret,' he said at last. 'Although it will be very hard. I'd like the whole world to know how accomplished you are.'

And then he demanded to see all the back numbers of *Potpourri* that I had and he settled down in front of the fire to read the À La Carte pieces and various other features that I'd written. We finished the champagne and nibbled the canapés Stefano had given me but we hardly spoke to each other. Every now and then Matthew would laugh or exclaim with delight. I could not have wished for a more appreciative critic. He read for hours until at last he said that as I had to go to work in a few hours' time he would tear himself away.

He hugged me tenderly and told me to try and get some sleep. It was not the way I had wanted the evening to end.

Daily Chronicle, 23rd January 1936
DOG TRACK GAMBLING RING?
Matthew Renshaw
Crime Correspondent

Questions are being asked by bookmakers about a number of suspicious bets. For some time now there has been a series of unusual and highly risky wagers. For example, at one dog track several punters placed bets on two races and named dogs in each to come first and second. The named dogs duly came first and second.

Urine samples were taken from the dogs and proved to be negative. They had not been doped. Not this time. But the police remain convinced that some other method had been used to nobble the dogs and so does this reporter.

Big money is involved here, attracting gangsters and casting a shadow over what should be a harmless enough night out for working people.

In his office high above the track Raymond tossed the newspaper down in disgust. 'We'll have to play it straight for a while, Joe. Can't have that nosy reporter finding anything that could send you off to prison.'

'Prison? Me?'

'Yeah, I reckon you'd get at least eighteen months, and prison wouldn't be kind to a lad like you.'

'But why would I go to prison? You told me to do it.'

'Can you prove that? I'd simply deny all knowledge. I'd say you were bribed by gangsters. After all, this is a respectable dog track. Why would I muddy my own pitch?'

'That's something I've never understood.' Raymond and Joe looked over to where Dr Balodis was sitting in the corner. He leaned over and picked up the newspaper from the floor. 'Why do you do it, Raymond? You make a good living here. Why get involved with crooked trainers – and worse?'

'You know why. Why do you supply the drugs? The money's good, very good. I don't see you saying no.'

'You're right. I am as bad as you. But the lad here, you wouldn't – how shall I put it? – throw him to the dogs, would you?'

'He's no innocent. And he didn't take much persuading. So there's no need to feel sorry for him. And besides, if we keep our noses clean until the heat dies down I don't see there's going to be any trouble.'

'Except from your masters.'

'What are you talking about?'

'The men who come to see you late at night. The men who bring you your orders.'

Raymond got up from his desk and went to stand by the window. The lights were still on, flooding the track below. The punters had gone and the bookmakers were packing up their stands. 'They'll understand,' he said. They'll just have to wait until the heat dies down. We can't risk any dogs being tested.'

'When big money is involved people tend to get impatient.'

'Pack it in, Balodis. If you can't say anything helpful just keep your trap shut.'

Dr Balodis smiled. 'Well, you'll get nothing from me for a while but there are other ways to nobble the dogs, aren't there, Joe? A big bowl of water or a couple of steak and kidney pies will slow a dog down and there'd be nothing to show for it.'

Raymond shook his head. 'So long as that reporter is hanging about there'll be nothing doing. And that means there'll be nothing extra in your pay packet, understand, Joe?'

Joe nodded but he resented the way Raymond was talking as though he'd ever been keen to do this. He looked around the room: the walls covered with yellowing posters, the battered office furniture, the cracked lino, all illumined by a single bulb without a shade. The ashtray on the desk was overflowing and the room smelled of stale tobacco and the lingering aroma of pies and chips drenched in vinegar.

Suddenly Joe felt sick and not just physically. He was sick with himself and the grubby way he had been living. He had gone along with it because of the money, the money he had needed to look after himself and Danny.

Now he wondered if there was any way out of this. But when he thought of the shady characters that Dr Balodis referred to as Raymond's masters he was filled with foreboding. He knew too much, that was the problem. They would never let him go.

21st March 1936

Today is my sister's sixteenth birthday. How I wish I could send her a card! No doubt she will be having a party and it will be very grand. I wonder if there will be any pictures of it in the *Tatler*. Or whether a young girl's birthday party, no matter how rich the guests are, will not be quite as newsworthy as the usual high society balls.

Charlotte likes to read the *Tatler* even though Jocelyn mocks her gently for being so interested in the charity events, the race meetings, the shooting parties and most of all, the gossip.

'But I was at school with some of these girls,' Charlotte will say, and then Jocelyn reminds her that at the time Charlotte complained she had nothing in common with them.

Nevertheless, Charlotte brings the magazine into the office with her every week and Jocelyn herself is not above looking at the fashion pages. Then she passes it on to me. I still have the photograph I cut out showing Elsie with her mother and father on the ski slopes at Gstaad. How beautiful she and Mrs Partington are, and how lovingly they are smiling at each other. I often look at the photograph just to remind myself of how happy Elsie must be.

How I wish I could tell Matthew that this beautiful girl is my sister. Perhaps I will one day, but it seems at the moment that I have got into the habit of keeping silent about my past.

'Isn't she lovely?' Shirley said wistfully.

She and Annette watched as Elise glided gracefully across the ice. 'Oh, for sure,' Annette said. 'In her white boots and that cute fur-trimmed skating dress she looks just like Sonja Henie. It'll be off to Hollywood next.'

Shirley laughed. 'Do I detect a note of sarcasm?'

Annette sighed. 'I'm sorry to say you do. But don't you ever get tired of hearing people say how beautiful Elise is?'

'No, I don't. It's a fact of life. Elise is beautiful, you with your blue eyes and your freckles are delightfully wholesome and I am — well, I am good old Shirley. I always will be.'

Annette looked at her fondly. 'You are attractive, you know.'

'Don't feel you have to say so.'

'But it's true. Your complexion is good; you have a good figure and a fine head of hair.'

Shirley burst out laughing. 'You make me sound like some sort of farm animal you are about to send to market.'

The two friends fell silent for a moment as they watched Elise glide along to the music.

'I'm sorry I was so begrudging before,' Annette said. 'She is lovely. But do you realize, neither of us has mentioned Ernestine?'

'Ah, Ernestine. I still can't believe it.'

Suddenly Elise swirled towards them across the ice. She was smiling. 'Are you going to stand there all day?' she asked. 'Or are you going to come and join me? After all, this is my party, you know.' When she saw their serious expressions her smile faded. 'What's the matter? Aren't you enjoying yourselves? Was this a bad idea, just me and my best friends coming to the ice rink?'

'No,' Shirley said quickly. 'It was a very fun idea, much

251

better than a kids' party, and as soon as we get our courage up we'll be joining you on the ice. We were just thinking of Ernestine and how she should be here with us. That's all.'

'Oh, Ernestine. I still can't believe it,' Elise said, echoing what had just been said before.

'What on earth made her do it?' Annette said.

'Her aunt,' Shirley said. 'She's her guardian. She's in control.'

'But Ernestine could have said no,' Annette protested. 'I mean, no one can make you get married if you don't want to, can they?'

'Perhaps she did want to,' Elise said.

'I don't believe it. She's sixteen. He's old enough to be her father – no, her grandfather! And have you seen him?'

'I saw the wedding photographs in the *Tatler*.'

'They're almost indecent. Him so stooped and wrinkled and so . . .'

'Royal,' Annette interjected.

'Royal?' Shirley said indignantly. 'What is he? A potty little prince of a potty little kingdom somewhere in Europe. A kingdom that probably won't even exist after the war everyone says is coming.'

'He's an archduke,' Annette said. 'His family go back to the days of the Holy Roman Empire. Didn't you read the article that went with the pictures? He has all kinds of titles and Ernestine will share some of them.'

'While old Otto helps himself to her fortune in an attempt to keep his kingdom afloat.'

Elise had been listening quietly. 'A wedding should be a happy occasion and you both make it sound so sad, sordid even. Whilst I suspect you're right about Otto I just can't believe Ernestine would marry someone just for a few royal titles.'

252

'Surely you don't think she could possibly be in love with him?' Shirley challenged.

'Well, you never know. She has a pretty miserable life with her aunt. Perhaps her new husband is kind and indulgent and . . . and . . .'

'Fatherly?' Annette said. She was smiling.

'Yes – no – oh, I don't know what I meant. I just want Ernestine to be happy.'

'Oh dear, Elise, you believe in romantic love, don't you?'

'What's wrong with that?'

'Oh, there's nothing wrong with it,' Annette said. 'I mean, we can all have our dreams but there are other reasons why people like us get married.'

'People like us?'

'Rich people. We have to marry other rich people, or important people, or as Ernestine has done, aristocratic people. None of our fathers, no matter how indulgent, would take kindly to us marrying some poor man who just happened to be in love with us.'

'They would think he was after our money,' Shirley added.

'But that's dreadful,' Elise said.

'No, it isn't,' Shirley replied. 'I mean, we're all vulnerable. There are men out there who are simply fortune hunters. How could we ever be sure he was sincere? But cheer up; it's not the Dark Ages. We can still choose someone we could be happy with and you never know, we may actually make a love match. But I can't believe Ernestine will be happy with that old crock. Can you?'

The three friends looked at each other and then Annette said, 'It may not be for long.'

'What do you mean?' Shirley asked.

253

'She's bound to outlive him and then she'll be a merry widow with her titles and her money, and next time she can marry anyone she chooses to, even someone totally unsuitable like a racing driver, or a crooner, or a film star.'

Shirley stared at Annette for a moment and laughed. 'I hadn't realized you were so cynical.'

'Not cynical. Just realistic.'

'Well, let's hope if it happens her Archduke won't have squandered her entire fortune. But look, we've shocked Elise; she's actually shivering with horror.'

'I'm not horrified, I'm cold,' Elise said, 'and it's time you two monsters stepped out on to the ice. Come on, take my hands, one of you at each side of me, we'll go around together.'

The three friends set off to the strains of a Viennese waltz, Shirley and Annette clumsy but enthusiastic, laughing as they tried to match Elise's sure movements. Elise, looking even more graceful in comparison to her friends, tried to smile but she had been truly shocked by Annette and Shirley's views on love and marriage.

She tried to imagine what her father's attitude would be. He had married for love and his bride had not been from a truly wealthy family. But Elise supposed it was different for men. If it was the man with the fortune rather than the woman he could probably marry anyone he pleased.

Unless you were the King of England, of course. Elise, like all the other girls, had joined in the gossip at school about the handsome young king and the divorced American woman he wanted to marry. Some of the girls were scandalized and wanted Wallis Simpson to be locked up in the tower or sent home to America forthwith. Other girls were taken up by the romance of it all and were hoping that the King would be able to marry the woman he loved. Elise knew very well which side her two friends would take but she would never agree with them. When it came to marriage, surely love was the most important consideration of all.

When they had had enough of skating they changed out of their fashionable skating clothes and went to the restaurant. A table had been reserved for them and there was a feast of sandwiches and cream cakes.

Shirley smiled her approval then sat down and said, 'Now I suppose it's the right time to give you this.'

She pushed a small gift-wrapped box across the table. Elise opened it to find a bracelet of gold links.

'It's a charm bracelet,' Shirley said. 'They're all the rage and I know you wanted one. But a charm bracelet is no use unless it has charms.'

'So here you are,' Annette said as she handed Elise an even smaller box. 'Look, I've started you off with one charm.' Inside the box was an exquisite little golden ballerina. 'All the charms have meanings, you know,' Annette said.

'Well, they do if you believe in that sort of thing,' Shirley interjected. She laughed.

Annette gave her a mock frown and carried on. 'A ballerina means your dreams will come true. I found this little book all about charm bracelets. I think my mother got it from Tiffany's or Cartier's when she was a girl. The three of us chose our gifts together.'

'Three of you?'

'Yes, Ernestine as well. And when I think about it, she must have known at the time that she wouldn't be here for your birthday. What a sly puss she turned out to be!'

Annette handed Elise another box and inside this one was a golden flower. 'That means love will blossom for you soon. Gosh, I've just thought, did Ernestine choose that one because love had already blossomed for her? Or at least she

255

imagined it had. Oh, but look. Is that coming our way?'

The three friends turned to see a waitress carrying a cake towards their table. The pink and white confection was ablaze with birthday candles. Heads turned, people smiled and someone started singing, 'Happy Birthday'. Soon everyone had joined in and as the waitress placed the cake on their table someone said, 'Blow the candles out! Make a wish!'

Elise was pink-faced with embarrassment but her friends laughingly urged her to stand up and oblige. She managed it with one deep breath. Everyone applauded as she sat down again and the waitress, who had been standing by, asked her if she wanted her to cut the cake.

'No, let me look at it for a moment,' Elise said. 'Leave the knife. I'll cut it myself.'

The three friends stared at it. Sixteen pink and white candles, eight of each colour, were set into silver rosebud holders on the top and all round the sides there was a pattern of pink and white rosebuds.

'Oh, look!' Annette exclaimed. 'There's a little skater in amongst the candles!'

'Very sweet,' Shirley said. 'You're still Mummy's little girl!' She laughed.

'Well, I think it's lovely,' Annette said. 'But from the look on your face you weren't expecting that, were you, Elise?'

'No, I wasn't.'

She remembered how preoccupied her mother had been that morning. 'You'll enjoy the skating rink, won't you Elise?' she had said.

'Yes, thank you.'

'John will take you. He'll pick up your friends en route and then I'll send him back later.'

'Are we coming back here for tea?'

'No, darling. I've booked a table in the restaurant for you.' She had smiled distractedly. 'It will be fun. You can watch the skaters through a sort of glass wall.'

'Are you going to join us for the meal?'

Selma frowned. 'No, I thought I'd made that clear. You know I like to be here for little Bertie's teatime. I don't approve of these mothers who never set foot in the nursery and just leave everything to the nursemaid. Now off you go. Everything has been arranged.'

At the time Elise had thought ungraciously that her mother had been glad to get rid of her. Since her baby brother had been born the previous June Selma had spent very little time with her daughter. Elise supposed that was normal when a new baby arrived and she had tried very hard not to be hurt. But a birthday was a special day, wasn't it? Couldn't little Bertie have been left to have tea with the nursemaid just for once?

But perhaps she had been too harsh. The cake was a lovely gesture. Her mother must have ordered it specially and she had wanted it to be a surprise.

'Are you just going to sit there and look at that cake?' Shirley asked. 'Or are you going to cut it up and offer us some? Here, I'll help you take the candles out.'

'We can't possibly eat all this,' Annette said. 'What will you do with it? Take it home?'

'No,' Elise said. 'Look around you. Look at the children on the other tables. They'd love a piece of cake, I'm sure of it!'

Elise beckoned the waitress over and told her what to do. The young woman cut the cake into small squares, making sure each piece was topped with icing, then she offered the plate to all the children in the restaurant.

'It's like a proper party, now,' Shirley said. 'All we need are some party hats and some of those cardboard trumpets.'

The waitress overheard her. 'Oh, we have some of those, miss,' she said. 'We cater for all sorts of parties here. Would you like me to get some?'

Shirley grinned at Elise. 'It's your party. What do you think?'

'Oh, yes please,' Elise said. 'By all means get the party favours out. And have you any crackers?'

'Of course.'

'And streamers?'

'Definitely!'

Elise, confident in the belief that her parents would not mind these extras being added to the account, watched happily as an ordinary outing to the ice rink turned into something more special for the children there. And all because of the cake she had not been expecting.

Some of the children came over to wish Elise 'Happy Birthday', paper hats askew and trailing streamers. The parents thanked her before they left. The waitresses started clearing the tables and preparing them for the crowd that would come to the rink for the evening session.

'I suppose we'd better go,' Elise said. 'John will be waiting to take us home.'

'Oh, didn't I tell you?' Shirley asked. 'I don't need a lift. We're going to the coast this weekend. The parents went last night and I have to join them. Actually,' she looked slightly embarrassed, 'Annette's coming too.'

'Oh, I see,' Elise said. But she didn't. The Chapmans had a lovely second home in Sussex and she had spent many a weekend there as their guest along with Shirley's other school friends, Annette and Ernestine.

'You could have come,' Shirley said, 'but we were sure

your parents would be doing something special this weekend. I mean, dinner or the theatre or something.'

'Oh, right, of course,' Elise said quickly, hoping that she was hiding her hurt and disappointment that her parents had not planned anything at all. Unless there was another surprise waiting, she thought. Like the birthday cake.

'Tom's coming for us,' Shirley said. 'And speak of the devil, here he is now.'

The girls looked up as Shirley's older brother made his way through the tables towards them. He was not alone; close behind him was his friend Peregrine Wallace, known as Perry.

Elise had seen Perry often over the years. Sometimes he seemed to have taken up residence at the Chapmans' house – and their seaside house, too. He was so different from Tom Chapman that Elise had occasionally wondered why they remained friends. Tom was stocky and rather ordinary to look at whereas Perry was tall and rather dashing, and maybe he wore his fair hair just a little too long. Tom was good-natured and practical whereas Perry's moods and behaviour could never be relied on; or so Shirley had told her. Now and then he had led Tom into the most awful scrapes.

'And he's just about penniless, you know,' Shirley had declared as if that was the ultimate judgement of a man's character.

But no matter what others thought of Perry Wallace, Elise had never been able to forget how kind he had been to Ernestine when she'd made a fool of herself at the Halloween party.

'Had a good time, girls?' Tom asked.

'Super,' his sister replied.

'Well, jolly good. And are you ready to go now?'

'We are, but haven't you forgotten something?'

Tom frowned. 'Forgotten something? I don't think so. The cases are in the car.'

'Tom! Can you remember why we came here today?'

'Why . . . ? Oh, yes. Elise's birthday. Many Happy Returns and all that.' He grinned good-naturedly.

Shirley shook her head in mock despair. 'Now that my idiot brother has minded his manners,' she said, 'I suppose we'd better go.'

Shirley and Annette rose from the table and Elise thought they seemed rather embarrassed as they took their leave. Perhaps they had guessed from Elise's subdued reaction that nothing further had been planned to celebrate her birthday.

Perry, who had not spoken until then, lingered as the others made their way between the tables.

'Did you have fun?' he asked.

Elise considered the question. 'Yes, we did.'

'So you're sixteen now.'

'Yes.'

'You know the saying, "Sweet sixteen and never been kissed".'

'I've heard it.'

'And?'

Elise was overcome with embarrassment.

'It's all right. You don't have to answer that!' He smiled at her. 'I'm sorry.'

'That's all right.'

'Well, I'd better go before they send a search party.'

Suddenly Elise didn't want him to go. 'Are you . . . ?' she began.

'Am I what?'

'Are you going with them to the sea?'

'Yes. I wish you were coming, too. I thought you might

be, you know, but I suppose your parents will have something special planned for tonight.'

'I suppose so.'

For no reason that she could easily define Elise felt hot tears pricking at the back of her eyes and now just as much as she had wanted Perry to stay, she wanted him to go and leave her to her thoughts.

'Goodbye, then, Elise,' he said. 'Oh, and here's my card. I forgot to give it to the waitress.'

Perry handed her an envelope and left her puzzling slightly over his words. When he had gone she opened the envelope to find a birthday card with an illustration of a birthday cake on the front. Inside was written: 'Hope you like it. Thought this would be a fun thing to do!' Then at the bottom was a telephone number. That was all.

Elise stared at the card for a moment before she realized the significance of what was written there. Her mother hadn't ordered the cake, Perry had. And now he had gone and she hadn't thanked him. She had no idea where he lived so she couldn't send a thank-you letter, but he had given her his telephone number. Even as she resolved to phone him as soon as the weekend was over she knew that it would not just be to thank him for the cake. She wanted to see him again and she hoped that he wanted to see her.

Chapter Sixteen

June 1936

'My, you've certainly jazzed this place up!'

Dorothy stood in the middle of Helen's sitting room and looked round approvingly at the colourful new curtains, the matching cushions and the pictures on the walls.

'Are those paintings original?' she asked.

'No, I'd never be able to afford them if they were. They're prints.' Helen saw from Dorothy's expression that she had no idea of the value of the prints and was relieved. To Dorothy, as to everyone except Matthew, she was supposed to be existing on a waitress's pay.

'Well, I certainly admire you for making the place so nice. You can't have much left after paying the rent, I know I didn't. And anything I had left I spent on clothes whereas you don't seem to mind if the fashions change.'

It irked Helen not to be able to respond to this but in the interest of keeping her double life secret she let it go. She thought how well her former flatmate looked. Dorothy was fashionably dressed in a navy and white linen dress and a matching jacket. A small white hat about the size of a saucer tilted forward over her expensively permed hair and her make-up was skilfully applied. But most of all she looked happy. And there was an air of excitement.

'I hope you don't mind my calling like this,' Dorothy said. 'I phoned the restaurant and Marina said you were on a split shift so I took the chance and came over.'

'No, I don't mind you calling. I'm pleased to see you.'

'Well, go on, put the kettle on!'

While Helen made a pot of tea Dorothy took a seat and eased off her shoes. 'Don't mind me,' she said. 'They're new and I'm breaking them in although Cyril says I should be saving all my new stuff for when we go.'

'On holiday?' Helen asked her.

'No, not a holiday. We're going to live abroad. Singapore. Everything's arranged.' She glanced across to see what effect her words had had and must have been pleased with Helen's suitably wide-eyed expression.

'Singapore? When are you going?'

'Next month.' Suddenly Dorothy's smile faded. 'It's a little daunting, isn't it?'

'I suppose it must be.'

'That's why I've come, really. I needed to talk to someone, not to ask advice, you understand, just to convince myself that it's really happening.'

'So it wasn't because you felt you had to see an old friend before you go.'

'Don't be like that, Helen. Of course there was that too.'

'Of course. So tell me why you're going to Singapore.'

'Well, you know Cyril's brother lives there?'

'Yes. That's why you were able to have his apartment in town.'

'He's found Cyril a job. A good job with a cold storage company. It means we won't have such a struggle to pay the maintenance and the school fees. You see, everything is so much cheaper there and even on a moderate salary you can live very comfortably. A nice house and garden, a gardener, a cook, a maid, everything.' Dorothy's eyes were shining.

'Like in a story by Somerset Maugham,' Helen said.

'Don't show off. You know I don't read very much.'

'Sorry. And I'm pleased for you. Really I am. And I'm glad you came to say goodbye.'

'Goodbye . . .' Dorothy said and suddenly she looked strained.

'What is it?'

'It's my mother. She thinks she's never going to see me again. I said she could come out and visit but she says she would just embarrass me.'

'Why does she think that?'

'Well, she says she's only a waitress and she could never pass for anything else, and the kind of people we'll be mixing with will probably be—'

'Outrageous snobs.'

Dorothy looked uncomfortable. 'Well, that's what she thinks.'

'And Cyril? What does he have to say?'

'Cyril says she's very welcome.'

'I'm glad to hear it.'

'But she's made her mind up, I'm afraid. And I'm worried about her. She's lived on her own since Dad died and I think she's getting pretty weary of working in that café.' Dorothy sighed. 'But the rent has to be paid and even if it didn't she says going out to work is better than sitting at home alone all day.'

Dorothy stared ahead bleakly and Helen felt truly sorry for her. She remembered Margery very well; how kind she had been when Helen was a schoolgirl going to the Cosy Café for her lunch with her ninepence a day. It was because of Margery that Helen had found this very flat when she came to London. She wished there was something she could do.

'I think you'll just have to go on trying to persuade her,' she told Dorothy. 'And you must write every week. You know that.'

'Yes, I do, and I'm ashamed to admit I haven't been writing to her regularly up until now. I'm not like you, forever scribbling away.' She smiled. 'Shall I write to you? I mean, if I did, would you answer my letters?'

'Of course I would.'

'I will then. I shall order a leather writing case from the Army and Navy Stores and I shall sit on the veranda of my new home with a cool drink and when I've finished the letters and sealed the envelopes I shall give them to the houseboy to take to the post office. There's always a houseboy in the movies, isn't there?'

Helen looked at her former flatmate speculatively. 'Dorothy,' she said, 'promise me you won't become an outrageous snob yourself.'

Dorothy laughed. 'I promise.'

Helen wasn't so sure.

The talk of letters reminded Helen that Aunt Jane's maid, Eva, had not replied to her own letters for some time now. She had no idea why this bothered her. After all, Aunt Jane meant nothing to her, did she? At work that evening her mind kept returning to those unhappy days after her mother had died. Her mother's sister had shown no true sympathy. Neither had she shown any love for the children; she had simply done her duty and, what's more, had probably profited from her arrangement with the Partingtons. Helen tried to convince herself that she should leave the matter alone but, annoyingly, her conscience wouldn't let her.

By the time she got home that night she had decided what she was going to do.

A sudden shower had sent the customers at the outside tables hurrying into the café in the park. Some carried their own cups and plates; some left everything for the waitresses. Elise took a table near the window and smiled up at Perry, who was still holding the cake stand he had rescued. He sat down and proffered the cakes.

'Another cream cake, Elise?'

'Yes, please.'

'The meringue, the chocolate éclair, or the strawberry tart?'

'Oh, the meringue. I love them!'

'So it seems. I think you've had one every day this week. But what will your mother say if you can't eat your tea?'

'Nothing at all. She'll be in the nursery with Bertie. I don't think she's even noticed that I'm taking longer to get home from school.'

'You're not taking much longer,' Perry protested. His smile was rueful. 'I get little more than an hour of your company and then you have to go, just like Cinderella.'

'Except I'm not wearing a ball gown and glass slippers. Only this foul school uniform and sensible shoes.'

'But you still look enchanting!'

'Don't talk like that. It's embarrassing.'

'But why? It's true, you know.'

Elise looked down at her plate and, putting her cake fork aside, she took the meringue in her hands and broke it gently into two sugar-spun halves to reveal the generous dollop of cream in the middle.

'Go on,' Perry said. 'Eat the cream with your teaspoon. I know you want to.'

Elise savoured the cream for a moment and then continued.

266

'I never know whether you're serious or just making fun of me.'

'Why on earth would I make fun of you?'

'Oh, I don't know. It's the way you are. Shirley says you're very much the joker and that you take nothing seriously. You never have.'

'That's true. Until now. You're a really sweet kid, Elise. I would never make fun of you.'

'A kid? A child? Is that the way you see me?'

'I use the term loosely,' he said. And then he was silent for so long that Elise began to regret asking the question. When he spoke he reached across the table for her hand and said, 'I don't see you as a child. I see you for what you are. A beautiful young woman.'

Elise looked down at his hand resting on hers. It was a large hand with long, well-manicured fingers. Underneath its gentle pressure she curled her own hand up, worrying about the traces of paint she had not removed successfully after the art class. Suddenly Perry's grasp became more firm.

'You haven't told Shirley that we're meeting, have you?'

'No. I've told no one. If my mother found out she'd only try to stop me seeing you.'

Perry withdrew his hand. 'And why is that?'

'Well, you know . . . she'd say that I was too young to have . . . I mean . . .'

'A boyfriend?'

Elise, who didn't know if Perry regarded himself as her boyfriend or not, was overcome with embarrassment. She managed to whisper, 'Yes,' and then, her courage returning, she added, 'If that's what you are?'

'Elise, look at me.' He was smiling. 'Is that what you'd like me to be?'

'That's not fair!'

267

'Why not?'

'You're asking me to say what I want without saying what you want.'

'Elise, I'm nearly six years older than you are.'

'That's nothing.'

'Yes it is when you are only sixteen. And no matter what I want, I have to make sure that you know what you're doing.'

'I do.'

Perry didn't say anything. He called the waitress over and ordered another pot of tea. Elise watched how the woman reacted to him. Wherever they went he got admiring glances and smiles from women, some of them old enough to be his mother. He flirted with them; Elise didn't think he could help himself, that's why it had been difficult for her to take him seriously.

Even so she believed she was wiser than he gave her credit for. She wondered if he knew the other reason she had wanted to keep their meetings secret. Whether or not her parents considered her to be old enough to have a boyfriend, there remained the fact that they would probably not consider the impecunious Perry Wallace remotely suitable. She didn't want to hurt him by telling him so.

The shower was brief but it had been heavy enough to refresh the leaves of the trees and the flowerbeds in the dusty park. Raindrops still ran down the window of the café, their reflections making patterns on the tablecloth. Perry glanced at his wristwatch.

'You'd better take a taxi,' he said. 'We're a little later than usual.'

'I don't have any money with me,' Elise replied.

'For goodness' sake, I wouldn't expect you to pay your own cab fare. What do you take me for?'

Perry summoned the waitress and settled the bill, then they left the café and hurried along the rain-washed paths to the entrance of the park. It didn't take long to hail a cab and, to Elise's surprise, Perry got in with her. He gave the driver the name of a street that was just round the corner from where Elise lived.

'Just to be safe,' he said as he settled back to sit beside her.

She stared straight ahead. He had told her he was her boyfriend. It was official. What would he do? Would he try to kiss her? Did she want him to kiss her? To her relief all he did was take her hand and hold it tightly. When the cab drew up he said quietly, 'Tomorrow as usual?'

'Mmm.'

'My own little darling,' he said, then he leaned towards her and brushed her lips very softly with his own.

Elise stared after the cab as it drove away. Her heart was racing and she was slightly out of breath. She began to walk home slowly, savouring the feeling of excitement the kiss had aroused within her. She wondered where and when Perry would kiss her again.

Perry paid off the cab as soon as he saw an underground station. Money was shorter than ever and he had spent more than his budget could stand on the simple treats of afternoon teas in the modest cafés and teashops he and Elise had visited since they had started seeing each other.

In the past, in pursuit of older, more sophisticated females, he had had to cough up for dinner, the theatre, nightclubs and even trips to Paris, so he shouldn't really complain. Except that now he was under a great deal of pressure to settle certain gambling debts. He had promised those concerned that his situation was about to change and that if

269

they only gave him time he would be able to pay back everything he owed.

The problem was that she was far too young. Not too young to get married legally but too young to be judged by her family and friends to be capable of making a sensible choice. When he had first thought of Elise Partington as a suitable bride he had imagined a gradual courtship, waiting to propose if necessary until she was twenty-one and could marry without her parents' consent.

But the matter had become urgent. And as Hugh Partington would never agree to their marriage, there were only two things Perry could do: get her pregnant, or elope to Gretna Green and present her parents with a fait accompli.

Even though a romantic elopement would involve another input of cash that he didn't have, he favoured that rather than the caddish act of simply seducing the poor girl. She was so dammed innocent. When he had kissed her just now he had felt nothing. She was so beautiful and yet he found she did not appeal to his senses in the slightest. He was used to older, more experienced women; he could not remember when he had last made love to a virgin, or even if he had. As far as Perry was concerned Elise Partington was beautiful without being in the least desirable, and yet he would have to forge ahead with his plan, and much sooner than he had wanted to. Otherwise he thought it no exaggeration to speculate that his life could be in danger.

Matthew heard the laughter as he climbed the stairs leading to the office on the top floor. Now that he knew Helen's secret he was an approved visitor to the offices of *Potpourri*. He liked the editor Jocelyn Graves very much and he thought her niece Charlotte great fun. It hadn't taken him long to see how fond Helen was of both of them. In fact they seemed to have taken the place of the family she never talked about.

The magazine was doing well and a visit to the office was usually a jolly affair. When Charlotte was trying out new recipes for her cookery column he was offered cakes or savouries, and sometimes even some sort of casserole put together in their tiny kitchen on an ancient gas cooker which must have been in the house since the top floor was given over to the maidservants.

Today he could hear the tinkle of glasses and he hoped he wasn't going to be asked to sample one of Charlotte's dreadful homemade wines. Then, just before he reached the top step, he heard the unmistakeable pop of a champagne cork and the exuberant cheers of whoever was in the room.

The door was ajar as usual and he pushed it open to see Charlotte pouring the sparkling wine into a set of champagne flutes set out on an old tin tray which itself was perched precariously on top of a pile of manuscripts on her desk. She turned her head as he entered and, seeing who it was, grinned happily.

'Come in, Matthew,' she said. 'You're just in time to join the celebration.'

Matthew looked round the room and saw that Jocelyn and Helen were smiling fondly at Charlotte, as was a tall, rather formally dressed young man he had never seen before. 'That's Edward, by the way,' Charlotte said, waving the bottle in his direction. 'Matthew Renshaw, allow me to introduce Edward Gough.' She paused and then said a touch dramatically, 'My fiancé.'

As a somewhat breathless Charlotte handed round the glasses she reminded Matthew of a friendly Labrador puppy eager for approval. When everybody had one there was an awkward pause while Charlotte and her fiancé smiled at each other rather foolishly.

Then Jocelyn said, 'I suppose I'd better propose the toast. So, raise your glasses everyone and join me in wishing Charlotte and Edward a long and happy marriage!'

'To Charlotte and Edward!' everybody said in unison.

Then, rather self-consciously, Charlotte placed a hand on Edward's arm and said, 'I think you're supposed to say something now.'

Matthew noticed the solitaire on her engagement finger and wondered if she had made that gesture deliberately.

'Am I?' Edward said. 'Oh, well, yes. I'd like to say how happy I am that Charlotte has agreed to marry me.' Duty done he retreated behind an embarrassed smile.

Charlotte topped up their glasses until the bottle was empty, then Jocelyn put the cover on her typewriter and took her handbag from one of the drawers in her desk.

'Let's go,' she said. 'Bertorelli's. Large plates of pasta and as much Chianti as you can drink. My treat. You too, Matthew and Helen. I insist.'

It was only after Jocelyn had locked the office door and they were all clattering down the stairs that Matthew realized that the only words that Helen had uttered were when they had toasted the engaged couple. Once they had reached the pavement he took her hand. 'Are you happy for Charlotte?' he said.

'Why do you ask?'

'You seem subdued.'

'Just tired. Stefano's was busy today.'

She would say no more but once they were in the restaurant and the conversation began to flow her rather cool manner warmed a little. Matthew learned that Charlotte and

Edward had met at a family wedding, that he was, according to his besotted fiancée, exceedingly clever and that he was a junior civil servant in the Foreign Office.

'Very junior,' Charlotte said, 'and paid a pittance in spite of all the languages he speaks. So I'll not be deserting my desk at the magazine for a while yet.'

Despite his skills as a linguist it seemed that Edward had very little to say in his native tongue and was happy to leave all the talking to Charlotte. Charlotte, rosy with wine, was equally happy to oblige.

When they left the restaurant Edward stepped forward to hail a taxi and as he did so Charlotte took hold of Matthew's arm. 'Don't wait too long,' she told him.

'What do you mean?'

'Do you really not know? Oh, Matthew, you're perfect for each other. For goodness' sake marry the girl before she gets tired of waiting for you.'

Matthew, embarrassed to be spoken to like this, glanced quickly at Helen. He was relieved to see that she was talking to Jocelyn and did not appear to have heard what Charlotte had said.

Charlotte gripped his arm more tightly. 'Oh, I know you think you're doing the right thing,' she said. 'You're older than she is and when you met she was completely inexperienced. But think about it. Do you really want her to go off with someone else? I don't think so. So, Matthew old chum, bloody well get on with it!'

When the others had driven off in the taxi Matthew and Helen walked to where he had parked his car. Helen was quiet on the way back to the flat but she seemed happy.

'I'm going to be a bridesmaid,' she told him. 'The family are quite grand but in an impoverished sort of way. Charlotte's father will probably be left penniless after this wedding.'

'Seriously?'

'Well, not exactly penniless but Charlotte says it's a good job she doesn't have any sisters to marry off and her elder brother has been through university and started working in the bank. That's why I'm going to be a bridesmaid, you know.'

'Because Charlotte's brother works in a bank?'

Helen nudged his arm. 'Don't be daft. Because she has no sisters and apparently very few suitable cousins.'

'You like Charlotte, don't you?'

'Very much.'

'I suppose she's like a sister to you?' Matthew didn't know why he had said that but even though he couldn't see Helen's face he sensed the change in her expression.

'No,' she said. 'We're very close but she's not like a sister.'

After that Helen was quiet and when they got back to her flat he didn't stay for very long. He longed to ask Helen about her own family, but when he had tried to in the past he had been rebuffed. He knew she came from Newcastle and that she had had to leave school earlier than she would have wanted. But she never explained why. She had told him that her mother was dead, and when he had asked her if there was any other family she had simply said, 'No, I have no family.'

He had sensed a great sadness when she said those words and had often wondered if there had been some kind of tragedy in her past. But if so, and whatever it was, she had obviously buried it deep inside her. Maybe one day she would tell him, but until then he would just have to be patient.

The onset of night had brought a cold wind and her windows were not exactly draught-proof. When Matthew had gone Helen drew the curtains. Too full of Chianti to want anything more to drink, she simply sat and listened to the hiss and pop of the gas fire.

After a while sheer habit took her to her desk where she sat down and opened her diary. She took the cap off her fountain pen and stared down at the page in front of her. What would she write? The usual amusing little observations about what happened at work? Later she would use some of them in her column. But she knew some of them were becoming repetitive and she was beginning to wonder how much longer she could make her pieces fresh and interesting.

And what about her personal life? She could have described the outing to Bertorelli's: the food, the wine, the conversation. How happy Charlotte was. And me, she thought. Am I happy? I should be. I love Matthew and he loves me, but we seem to have arrived in some kind of limbo. I want life to move on and I'm not sure if he does.

I wonder if he knows how much it hurts me to constantly feel that I'm being held at arm's length. And me . . . no matter how deeply I love him I don't know if I can take much more of this. Oh, Matthew, my darling, what am I going to do?

Helen replaced the cap on her pen and closed her diary. She slipped it into a drawer. She wasn't sure if she would write in it again.

Chapter Seventeen

July

'Didn't you know that Helen has taken a few days' leave?' Marina looked at Matthew quizzically and sensing his embarrassment she smiled kindly. 'Perhaps you just forgot,' she said. 'I know you men – in one ear and out the other!'

'Erm . . . yes. Something like that.'

He stood there uncertainly. Stefano's was busy as ever, and with the early evening diners arriving Marina's attention had already strayed to the reservation book. She looked up and, as if surprised to see him still there, she said, 'Well, you know where she lives. I'd get along there if I were you.'

'Right. Thanks. I will.'

Matthew stepped out into the wet street. A watery sun was trying hard to break free from the clouds but the rain persisted. People looked miserable as they hurried to the bus stops and underground stations to begin their journey home. He was sure that Helen hadn't told him that she was taking any leave, but no doubt she would explain as soon as he got to the flat. The image of the young man who had been watching the place swam into his consciousness. The same young man who worked at the dog track. Matthew hoped to God that no harm had befallen her.

The inclement weather had brought an early end to daylight and the reflected light from shop windows shone on wetly gleaming pavements. Further out of town lights were showing behind drawn curtains in the modest flats and houses, but Helen's windows were completely dark. Matthew got out of the car and tried the bell anyway, but there was no reply.

Just as he turned away, one of the girls who lived in the downstairs flat arrived breathless and soaking and desperate to get in from the rain. 'You're a friend of Miss Norton's, aren't you?' she said. Before he had time to reply she added, 'Didn't you know she's gone away? I said I'd keep her mail for her. Now, if you don't mind . . .'

'Oh, yes . . . sorry.'

Matthew moved out of the way so that the cheerful girl could open the front door. As she stepped inside he almost asked her if it was all right to follow her in. He thought if he could only go upstairs to Helen's flat he might be able to solve the puzzle of why she had gone away without telling him. She might even have left a note pinned to the door.

Knowing the plan was irrational, he hesitated and the downstairs tenant was inside the porch and had turned to face him. She had her hands on the door ready to close it. She must have read his mind.

'Miss Norton didn't leave a message for you,' she said. 'I'm sorry.'

Intensely discomfited by the girl's obvious sympathy, Matthew managed a cheery, 'That's OK. I'm sure she'll write.'

He hurried back to his car and sat there soaked to the skin and dripping miserably. He wasn't at all sure that Helen would write to him. And he had no idea what he could do about it.

It didn't take Helen long to unpack her suitcase. She hadn't brought much because she didn't intend to stay here long. She walked over to the window and looked out at the traffic on Neville Street. When she had lived in Newcastle as a child she would never have thought that one day she would be able to afford a room in the Royal Station Hotel.

She wasn't sure whether she was supposed to close the heavy velvet curtains or leave that for the chambermaid, so she left them for the moment and turned to look at the elegant Victorian room while she decided whether to go down for dinner or order something from room service.

Room service, she decided. I'm tired after the journey and I want to get my thoughts together for tomorrow, and in any case I'm not very hungry. She couldn't help giving a small smile of satisfaction as she relived the journey home, so different from the journey to London all those years ago in the crowded carriage and with the packet of sandwiches that Eva had made for her. This time she had travelled first class and had gone to the restaurant car for lunch. If only Eva could have seen me, she thought, and immediately frowned when she remembered why she had come and that she was going to have to face her old friend in the morning.

She wondered if her aunt's housemaid would have changed much. She knew herself to be very different from the gauche schoolgirl who had once had to make a new life in London. Now she was confident and, she had to admit to herself, stylish. Her mother had brought them up to speak nicely but now even the slightest trace of a northern accent had gone.

Not long after she had rung for service and ordered a light meal the young waiter returned with a selection of sandwiches and a steaming pot of coffee. He placed the tray on a low table near the ornately tiled fireplace. Helen, knowing what it was like to 'wait on' for a living, tipped him generously. He closed the curtains for her and withdrew with a polite little bob of his head.

When she had eaten her fill she got into her pyjamas and, finding the coffee still passably hot, she filled up her cup and took it to bed with her. A mistake. The extra shot of caffeine chased away any hope she had of sleeping. She reached for her handbag which she had placed on the bedside table and took out the letter that had brought her here. Although she had already read it many times she read it again.

Dear Miss Norton,

I am glad you have written to me although I wish you had written sooner. You must have known that your aunt did not know where you were living and when I asked her maid, Eva, if you had left a forwarding address with her she told me you had not. Before I write anything further let me make it plain that Mrs Roberts does not know I have taken it upon myself to let you know what the situation is.

First of all let me assure you that your aunt is not being neglected. The problem is she may be being looked after too well. Does that sound strange? You must have heard the expression 'to kill with kindness'. The meals she is served are more than adequate; in fact they are much more than she needs and she has grown lamentably overweight. There is always a box of chocolates or fancy biscuits on her table and if she wants a snack between meals all she has to do is ring the bell.

At first I thought your aunt's maid was simply misguided but I no longer believe that. People who kill with kindness often have an agenda of their own and in this case it is obvious that they want to keep your aunt docile so that they can have the run of the house. You knew that Eva and her husband are living in, I suppose? But did you also know that one of her sisters is living there?

Your aunt spends her days in her sitting room until she is helped up the stairs to bed at night. And bedtime for her is growing earlier and earlier. I suspect that this is so that Eva and her husband can entertain their friends in the parlour.

You need not worry about the house being kept clean. It is. Eva is house-proud. I believe she likes to think of it as her own home and this is causing me a lot of worry. Perhaps I have been reading too many mystery novels but I can't help thinking that your aunt may be persuaded to write a will in her maidservant's favour, and once that is done, who knows what might happen. Forgive me if you think this too fanciful but I urge you to come and judge the situation for yourself. Especially as you are Mrs Roberts' only relative and should, I imagine, be her rightful heir.

Let me assure you that I will continue to visit your aunt at least once every week. I hope to hear from you soon.

Yours faithfully,
Alistair Salkeld

This was not what Helen had expected when she had decided to write to Dr Salkeld. She had imagined that Eva had simply grown tired of writing her little reports and if anything had been wrong she would have written straight away. That could still be the case. Dr Salkeld could indeed be letting his imagination overcome his sensible everyday self, but the letter had disturbed Helen enough to make her decide to come and find out what was happening.

Helen did not care in the slightest about being her aunt's heir. She had never imagined herself inheriting the house and would not have wanted to. But at the same time it made her very uneasy to think that her old friend Eva could be conspiring to influence her aunt to write a will in her favour. She didn't think, as the doctor obviously did, this was any more sinister than that but accepted most reluctantly that it was her duty to find out what was going on.

Duty? she thought to herself. Do I really owe this woman any kind of loyalty? Helen still felt bitter about the way her aunt had presided over the splitting up of the family and yet, as the years had gone by, she had come to accept that her mother's elder sister had been thrust into a situation she had not asked for.

If my mother and my aunt had been closer, Helen pondered, things might have been different. However, it was the very fact of their sisterhood that had brought Helen back to Newcastle. She knew in her heart that that was what her loving, forgiving mother would have wanted.

She put the letter back in its envelope and allowed herself a smile at the good doctor's expense. She remembered him to be clever and sensible, so it was amusing to think of him being carried away by the crime novels he read. She wondered whether he favoured the classic English detective stories that her editor Jocelyn Graves loved, or if he preferred the more 'hard-boiled' American fiction.

However, he had been concerned enough about his patient to reply to Helen's letter and also assure her that he called to see her aunt every week. No doubt he presents his bill for his visits, Helen thought, but why shouldn't he? If making money was his only reason for visiting Jane Roberts he wouldn't have urged me to come home and visit her.

Home . . . Helen thought as she tried to get to sleep. Do I still think of Newcastle as home? If I do then it is only the home I once shared with my sister and brothers that lives in my memory. Any home I have in the future must be where they are.

'I'm sorry but Mrs Cook is out,' the girl said. 'Who shall I say called?'

Helen stared at the podgy young woman who had answered the door. She looked young enough to have only just left school and yet had adopted the manner of an experienced maidservant.

Helen guessed that the girl must be Louie, Eva's sister, and that the Mrs Cook she referred to was Eva herself.

'That's all right,' Helen told her. 'It's Mrs Roberts I've come to see.'

The girl was obviously taken aback. Her worried frown almost turned into a scowl before she recovered and said, 'Oh, but Mrs Roberts doesn't like to have visitors.'

'Whether or not that is true I am going to come in and visit her. So will you please step aside?'

For a moment Helen wondered whether she was going to have to use physical force to get into the house, but after subjecting the youthful Cerberus to a determined stare, the girl gave way and stood back reluctantly. As Helen pushed past her into the narrow hallway the young maidservant who had become a child once more recovered herself enough to say, 'Who are you?'

'That need not concern you right now,' Helen said and she opened the door and walked into her aunt's front parlour.

She almost turned and walked straight out again. Despite the pleasant summer weather a roaring fire burned in the grate and the room was unbearably hot. It was also dim and shadowy. The heavy velvet curtains had barely been drawn and Helen had to stand still and accustom her eyes to the muted light before she could make out the figure of her aunt sitting in the armchair by the fire.

'Is that you, Louie?' her aunt said. 'I didn't ring but seeing you're here I would like a cup of tea and a slice of cake.'

Helen didn't say anything. Almost choking on the combined odours of coal dust and extravagantly applied furniture polish, she made her way through the over-furnished room to the window and drew all the curtains back as far as they would go.

Helen turned to find her aunt blinking in the light. 'Who's that?' she asked. 'You're not Louie.'

'No, Aunt Jane, I'm not.'

There was a moment of stunned silence then Jane Roberts said, 'Helen! What are you doing here?'

'I've come to see you . . . to see if you're all right,' Helen said, realizing at once how inadequate the answer was.

'I don't believe you,' her aunt said. 'Why should you care whether I'm all right or not?'

'Why indeed,' Helen replied.

She went to sit in the armchair at the other side of the hearth. It was only then that Helen saw how overweight her aunt had grown. Her features were lost in folds of pasty flesh and her floral dress strained tightly over the immensity of her body.

They stared at each other in silence while the fire crackled.

'You're not all right, are you?' Helen said eventually.

Her aunt's reply was subdued. 'Why do you say that?'

'Living like this. Cooped up in an overheated room on a summer's day.'

'I'm not strong enough to go out.'

'That's rubbish.'

'I had a stroke. You know I did. And yet you still ran off and left me,' Aunt Jane said with a spark of angry resentment.

Helen ignored that remark. 'You've made no attempt to recover properly. No attempt to get your strength back. You've just allowed yourself to become grossly fat and useless.'

Helen saw Aunt Jane flinch and then to her dismay her aunt blinked and squeezed her eyes shut as if she was holding back tears.

'They keep me like this,' her aunt said. 'Eva and Donald. They give me anything I want to eat. They say I should rest as much as possible. Louie goes to the library to get books for me – they have my magazines delivered. I don't have to lift a finger.'

'And look what it's done to you! Why have you let this happen?'

Aunt Jane gave a vast sigh. 'Because it's the easy thing to do.' She paused. 'And remember,' she said, the spiteful edge returning, 'You arranged that Eva should stay here and look after me, didn't you?'

'Yes, I did. I accept my responsibility. I'll have to sort things out.' She got up to leave. 'I must go now; I've got things to do.'

'Helen!' Her aunt's voice held a note of panic.

'What is it?'

'You won't say I sent for you, will you?'

The panic gave way to unconcealed fear. Helen was appalled.

'No, I won't, I promise you.'

'The child will tell them you've been here.'

'Don't worry. I'll be as nice as ninepence to her on the way out. She won't have anything to complain about.'

Louie was standing in the hallway, her young face creased with worry. Helen couldn't be sure whether she had been able to hear any of her conversation with her aunt but a friendly smile brought forth a slight relaxation.

'Are you Helen?' Louie asked.

'That's right.'

'But why . . . ?'

'I was in town and I thought I'd call and see my aunt. Now I must go,' Helen said. 'Why don't you make Mrs Roberts a nice cup of tea?'

'I will.' Louie was obviously relieved to be asked to carry out so mundane a task. 'But what should I tell our Eva?'

'Tell Mrs Cook I'll call back later.'

Helen smiled as convincingly as she could, then she opened the front door and made her escape. She needed fresh air and sunshine. The atmosphere in her aunt's house had been claustrophobic. Glancing at her wristwatch she saw that it was not too early to have lunch. Although lunch at the hotel would no doubt be very good she had no intention of going there. Even though she had much more than ninepence to spend, she was going to go to the Cosy Café.

A couple of hours later, when she was sitting at the kitchen table with Eva, it took all Helen's determination not to give way to nostalgia. During those dark days when she had first come to live with her aunt the young maidservant, not much older than herself, had been her only ally and although Eva had been reticent at first a real friendship had developed between the two girls.

285

Helen remembered how hard Eva worked and how she had always looked tired, not to say exhausted. Now she was plump and confident, smartly dressed in a fresh-looking blue-and-white print frock and her once lank hair neatly permed.

'Well, this is a nice surprise,' Eva said as she poured Helen a cup of tea. 'Poor little Louie didn't recognize you at first, and your aunt told me you were the last person she expected to see.'

So Eva had questioned Aunt Jane. Even though she had little sympathy with her mother's sister, Helen found herself hoping that she hadn't been intimidated.

Eva kept her head down while she poured the tea. 'I've sent Louie down to see our mam for a while so that we can have a nice chinwag before Donald gets back from work,' she said. 'I suppose you'll want to know why I stopped writing to you.'

'You suppose right.'

Eva began pouring tea into her own cup. 'Well, I know I should have done, but I have such a busy life keeping house and looking after your aunt, and really I didn't think there was much point in sending you reports when everything was going so well.' Helen remained silent and Eva, flustered, added, 'Of course I would have written if there was anything wrong. I hope you know that.'

'I'm not sure if you would, Eva. I imagine you didn't think I'd care. And that's my fault.'

In the ensuing silence Helen wondered once more why she had come here today. Conscience, she supposed, and the strongest of feelings that this was what her mother would have wanted her to do.

The table was set with a cheerful floral patterned tablecloth and there was a two-tier cake stand with sandwiches cut into crustless triangles on the bottom tier and homemade angel cakes on the top.

'Go on, take a sandwich,' Eva said. 'They're tinned salmon with a slice or two of cucumber.'

'No thank you, Eva. I haven't come to take tea with you. We need to talk.'

'Talk? Is something the matter? You look so serious.'

'It's about the way you're looking after my aunt.'

Eva looked uneasy. 'I hope she hasn't been complaining to you. She gets the best of everything, you know.'

'No, she hasn't been complaining. She's too frightened to do that.'

'Frightened?' Eva pretended indignation. 'I'm sure I don't know what you're talking about. And I'll have you know she gets the best of care. Anything she wants, waited on hand and foot, she is.'

'I know that, and it's all done to keep her docile, so that you and your family can take over her house.'

'Take over? I don't know what you mean.'

'Yes, you do. You keep her in the front parlour and then send her to bed early so that you can sit in there and act as if you own the place.'

Eva was outraged. 'It's that Dr Salkeld, isn't it? He's found out where you live and written to you. Telling tales. He's always telling me that I should encourage her to get out and about. Out and about! She can hardly move from her chair. I'm just about breaking my back getting her upstairs at night.'

'And whose fault is that? You're grossly overfeeding her.'

'She doesn't complain about that.'

'No, I can imagine she doesn't. But it's got to stop.'

'That won't be easy. She'll make a fuss.'

287

'I know it won't be easy but this way of life is killing her. Eva, you've got to go.'

'What!'

'You've got to find somewhere else to live.'

'But where?'

'You say Donald's working now? Well, you must find a house to rent, just as other people do.'

'But if we're living out who will look after your aunt at night time?'

'I don't mean that you're to live out, Eva. I mean that you're to find another job. I'll stay here until you do.'

'You stay? Where?'

'In my old room.'

'That's Louie's room now.'

'Send her home to your mother, tonight.'

'But she's used to living with us.'

'Well, take her back when you have your own place and for goodness' sake, stop this quibbling. My mind's made up. You've got to go.'

Eva's features tightened with fury. 'Well, well, Helen Norton. Who would have thought you could be so ungrateful?'

'Ungrateful?'

'You were pleased enough to leave me to do everything when you went off to London, and I don't suppose you gave a thought to your aunt from one day to the next.'

'I admit it.'

'So why the fuss now?'

'Because it's the right thing to do.'

Eva stared at Helen with pursed lips and then said, 'Well, in that case we'll get out of here as quickly as we can and you can look after the old tartar. And another thing, I'll take money instead of proper notice, if that's all right with you.'

'Whatever you say.'

Helen had checked out of the hotel after she'd lunched at the Cosy Café and she had brought her suitcase with her. She carried the cakes and sandwiches in to her aunt and sat with her while Eva banged about the house opening and closing drawers and cupboards.

When it came to bedtime no one appeared and Helen faced the task of getting her aunt upstairs, washed and put to bed. She found clean sheets tossed on to the bed in her old bedroom and guessed that Louie had already gone to her mother's. She didn't meet Donald Cook that night and he must have gone to work very early the next morning. And if he came back after work he stayed out of her way.

'Donald's found somewhere,' Eva told Helen grudgingly. 'There are plenty of houses vacant with so many people out of work. Not that a lady like you would care about that, I suppose.'

'I didn't mean you had to leave immediately,' Helen said.

'Didn't you? Did you expect us to hang around here knowing what you think of us? My dad's coming up with his handcart in the morning to help me shift everything, and don't worry – I won't take anything that doesn't belong to me!'

The next morning Helen had an errand to run and she left the house while Eva packed up. When she returned the handcart was loaded and ready to go. She had known from the start how painful this would be but she was not prepared for the silent tears they both shed when Eva took her leave. She handed Eva an envelope containing a more than generous settlement but they parted without a word.

Dr Salkeld called as Helen was serving a lunch of steamed fish to her disgruntled aunt and he smiled approvingly.

'They've gone already?' he said.

'This morning.'

'How will you manage?'

'It won't be for long. Just a few days, in fact, although I'll probably stay on for a little while until my aunt's new housekeeper settles in.'

'You've found someone already?'

'I confess I already had her in mind.'

'And who is she?'

'Margery Sutton; she's the mother of a friend of mine.'

Chapter Eighteen

August

Helen took a tram to the Central Station. She had reserved a seat on the morning Pullman. When she was queuing for a paper at the newsstand she saw one or two of the porters eyeing her uncertainly. She knew it wasn't the fact that she only had one suitcase; it was the state of that suitcase that made them doubt whether she would be able to tip them well.

The case had been given to her mother by one of the rich ladies that she had cleaned house for. It was a trifle shabby-looking but Helen had never seen the need to buy a new one. Eventually, one of the porters, who perhaps had recognized the quality of the case and knew that many well-off people kept their expensive luggage for years, approached Helen with a polite smile. She didn't really need a porter but she handed him the case and when he had escorted her to her table in the carriage she tipped him generously.

Helen surveyed the tables set with snowy linen, each one illuminated by a pink-shaded lamp. She was pleased to see that none of the other three seats at her table was reserved. For that she was thankful. She hoped no last-minute arrival would take one of them. She wanted to read her paper and drink several cups of coffee while the train steamed south-wards. She did not feel like engaging in polite conversation with a fellow traveller. As soon as she was settled a steward handed her the luncheon menu and told her that coffee would be served when the train was underway.

She looked out at the busy scene on the platform: people hurrying to catch their trains, couples and sometimes whole families saying goodbye. She glanced across the carriage towards the other windows. A train had been stationary on the other line ever since she had boarded. She saw the blinds were closed and guessed that this was the night train from London, the sleeper, and she wondered briefly about the people who had made that journey. As usual she found herself speculating about the lives of total strangers and wondering whether they would make interesting stories.

After a blowing of whistles and a slamming of doors the engine released a great hiss of steam and the train began very gently to pull out of the station towards the High Level Bridge. The rhythm of the wheels on the tracks changed as they left the station behind and after they had crossed the River Tyne Helen sat back and gave way to imaginative speculation about the sleeping train.

What if there was a young couple on that train? she thought. A couple running away from the police like in *The Thirty-Nine Steps* . . . Matthew had taken her to see the film and they had both enjoyed it, although they agreed that Alfred Hitchcock had taken many liberties with the novel's original plot.

Matthew . . . Was it fair of her to come here without telling him? But once she started telling him her family history it would be difficult to know where to draw the line. If she thought he was really committed to her it would be easier, but as it was she'd kept everything to herself for so long that it had become a habit that would be hard to break.

The snack bar on the platform was crowded and Perry found them the only table left vacant. Elise drew back. 'It's by the window,' she said.

Perry smiled, 'Don't worry, darling, no one knows us here. No one is going to go rushing to tell your father where we are. Now we've at least an hour before our next train so I'm going to order bacon and eggs, toast and marmalade and a pot of tea.'

'Oh, no. I never eat that sort of breakfast. My mother says it would be bad for my figure.'

'She may be right, but right now you need to keep your strength up.' He cocked his head to one side. 'Can you smell that bacon frying? Don't say you aren't tempted.'

'All right! I am! But you must let me pay.'

Perry made a show of taking the money reluctantly but Elise suspected that he had spent more than he could afford on their berths on the night train and also that he was the one in need of a substantial breakfast.

He went to the counter to give their order and his tall, slim figure seemed to merge into the haze of steam coming from the water boiler on the counter. Elise was aware of customers at nearby tables giving her speculative glances. She supposed it was because of the way she was dressed. She knew very well that her clothes were noticeably expensive here in this cheap snack bar where people came because they could not afford the restaurant in the hotel.

Flushing slightly with embarrassment, she turned to look out of the window at the train from which they had recently disembarked. People were still sleeping there or being woken up with trays of tea or breakfast to keep them going until they reached Edinburgh. Perry had explained that it was easier for them to change trains at Newcastle and he had been astonished at her reaction.

'Newcastle!' she had exclaimed.

'Yes. Why? What's wrong with that?'

For a short while she had not been able to answer him but she refused to give way to indeterminate memories. She shook her head. After all, what did Newcastle mean to her? It was years since she had any thoughts whatsoever about the place where she was born and where she had spent the first nine years of her life.

'Nothing's wrong,' she said. 'It's just that this journey is getting complicated, isn't it?'

'Not at all, my darling,' Perry had replied. 'And in any case you mustn't worry about any of that. Just leave everything to me.'

Elise watched as men wheeled trolleys along the platform and loaded bread and milk and other provisions on to the train. Soon it pulled away, and as it snaked around the curve of the platform and out of the station, Elise saw that the Pullman, with its distinctive dark red carriages, which had been standing on the next track, had gone.

Back to London, she thought. The people on the Pullman are going to London. What am I doing here? On impulse she rose from the table and turned towards the door. She was standing there hesitantly when Perry returned.

'What is it?' he asked. 'Do you need the ladies' cloakroom? It's over the bridge, I'm afraid, in the main concourse.'

'No . . . it's all right. I just . . .'

'Are you still worried that we'll be spotted?'

'No. I don't know what the matter is.'

'Poor darling. You're exhausted, that's all. I heard you

294

tossing and turning in the bunk below for most of the night. I wanted to climb down and get in beside you and take you in my arms and comfort you. But the damn things are too narrow for two to sleep comfortably so I lay there feeling guilty instead.'

'Guilty?'

Perry smiled down at her. 'Yes. Guilty for loving you so much. Guilty for wanting to marry you. Guilty for making love to you. Guilty for stealing you away from the bosom of your family when I know how much your mother dotes on you.'

Suddenly Elise felt all right again and she returned his smile. 'Oh, that's all right,' she said. 'It's Bertie she dotes on. Not me.'

'Well, sit down, then. Here comes the waitress with our breakfast and I want you to enjoy every mouthful.'

Elise ate with every indication of enjoyment. She was young, she was healthy and she had obviously begun to recapture the feeling of adventure and excitement that had spurred her on to agree to elope with him. Thank goodness for that. A moment ago Perry had been worried that she was going to bolt. If she'd been determined he would have had to let her go. He could hardly restrain her physically; that would be kidnap, wouldn't it?

And if she had gone? Would he have been heartbroken? Of course not. He was surprised to discover that despite the dire circumstances he found himself in he might even have felt relieved. He knew this was a hare-brained scheme and if he had not been so desperate he would have waited, courted her, even tried to win the approval of her parents by being a faithful suitor.

And there was always the possibility that Hugh Partington

295

might have paid him off, given him a large sum of money to stay away from her. That would have dealt with his immediate predicament but in the long term he would end up penniless again. No, the sort of money Elise Partington would one day inherit was worth waiting for. And even if her father lived to a ripe old age he would surely have too much pride to allow the daughter of one of the wealthiest industrialists in Europe to live in poverty.

It had not been too difficult to make Elise fall in love with him. She was completely inexperienced as far as the opposite sex was concerned and a bit of flattery combined with the excitement of their secret meetings had convinced her that theirs was a special relationship. The original plan had been to make sure that she did not fall in love with anyone else and to wait until she was eighteen before asking for her hand in marriage. If her father had refused permission then they would have had to wait until she was twenty-one, when almost certainly there would have been some sort of trust fund maturing.

However, his fascination with the dog track had made waiting impossible.

'Are we going to the dogs again?' Tom Chapman would joke when he came up to town on leave. It was Perry who had first discovered dog racing and introduced it to his old friend. The two of them would dress in old coats, caps and mufflers and pretend to be ordinary working men, adopting atrociously false Cockney accents that fooled no one, least of all the men they placed their bets with.

Tom, being cautious, stuck to the Tote, the official betting facility. But Perry was fascinated by the course bookies with their blackboards showing the odds they were offering on the various dogs. After checking the form in the racing paper he would then look at the race card to see how individual dogs had done in their previous races. He kidded himself that he was quite an expert, but after an initial run of good luck, he began to take risks on outsiders because the odds were good. It was a good way to lose your money.

Bad gamblers get desperate. They take bigger and bigger risks to recoup what they have lost. Perry was no different. Instead of cutting his losses he got into very muddy waters. He had found it all too easy to borrow money from dubious characters he met in the bar and their 'hail fellow well met' attitude soon evaporated when he began to lose in a big way.

He owed them much more than the actual sum he had borrowed, of course, because they expected interest, and their rates were extortionate. When he couldn't pay them back the threats started.

One night when he had been to the track without Tom, a car pulled up alongside him as he was walking home. A rear door opened and a smooth voice said, 'Get in.'

Before Perry could answer the driver of the car got out, came round and seized him, then pushed him into the back of the car.

'Don't worry,' the smooth voice said. 'We're not going to hurt you. Not if you pay back all the money you owe me.'

Perry peered through the darkness and as his eyes adjusted he saw a bulky man with a fedora pulled down, concealing most of his face. The little he could see was badly pockmarked. He had a cigar clamped in his mouth and the aroma of tobacco mingled with that of an expensive cologne.

'I don't owe you any money,' Perry said. 'I've never seen you in my life before.'

'No, it's some of my friends you owe the money to and they're beginning to lose patience with you. They're little men. They can't afford to go on backing losers. So, being a good friend, I compensated them.'

'You mean you bought up my debts?'

'That's right. So now you owe the money to me. And nobody ever welshes on me, I can assure you.'

'Who are you?'

For an answer the man grabbed Perry's arm, took the cigar out of his mouth and stabbed it on the back of Perry's hand. 'No need for you to know names.'

'Christ almighty,' Perry screamed. Tears of pain stung his eyes. 'That will leave a scar.'

'Don't complain. You're lucky I didn't burn your pretty face. How would you have explained that to Miss Partington?'

Perry's insides turned to water. 'She has nothing to do with this. You . . . you wouldn't hurt her, would you?'

'Not if I don't have to. By the time the scar on your hand fades I hope you will have settled your debts and then we'll all be happy. Now get out,' the man said. 'I know your situation but I also know that you have a chance to get your hands on some of the Partington fortune. Good luck to you. I'll be sending someone along to collect.'

The driver opened the door, dragged Perry unceremoniously out of the car and shoved him violently down to the ground. Perry heard the car door slam. As he hauled himself to his feet it sped away. He had twisted his ankle when he'd fallen and jarred his wrists when he'd attempted to save himself. The back of his hand was throbbing with pain.

There was no one else in sight. How long had it taken for his world to become a very frightening place indeed? While he was in the car time had seemed to become suspended.

In this state he couldn't face public transport and he didn't have enough money left for a taxi. He limped the weary miles back to his apartment, snivelling like the coward he knew himself to be. By the time he got home he had accepted that his only hope was to persuade Elise to elope with him as soon as possible.

However, the problem proved to be that although she loved the idea of being in love and had been thrilled when he playfully suggested that they should elope, she hadn't really taken him seriously. And that was why, even though he had promised himself that he would not, he had had to seduce her.

It was raining. Rain fell on the tracks as they hurried over the bridge and made their way to the platform where their train had just pulled in. There was no shelter here and the people disembarking looked gloomily up at the sky and unfurled their umbrellas. The few passengers waiting to get in turned up their coat collars or held newspapers over their heads.

Perry had waved away a porter and was carrying the luggage himself. Elise, feeling guilty because she had two suitcases whereas he only had a travelling bag, said, 'Don't worry, I can tip the man,' but Perry had hurried on.

'If there's a hue and cry the man might remember helping a handsome young couple and tell them where we were going,' he explained.

Once on the train he had somehow struggled along the narrow corridor until he found an empty carriage and then hurried inside, sliding the door closed after them.

'I thought we'd be all right at this time of day,' he said. 'People are coming in to town rather than heading for the country. I don't think we'll be disturbed.' He stowed the luggage in the overhead racks and then turned to look at her.

Seeing her rather pinched expression as she stared out of

the rain-streaked window, he took her in his arms. 'Isn't this exciting?' he said. 'In years to come we'll have such stories to tell our children!'

Elise broke away and flung herself down on to the seat. He understood at once that he had said the wrong thing and he sat down beside her and took both her hands in his. They were cold. He rubbed them and then raised them to his lips and kissed them.

'What is it, Elise?' he said. 'You do love me, don't you?'

'Oh yes! It's just . . . just that I wonder if you love me.'

'How can you say that? Would we be here if I didn't?'

'We might.'

'I don't know what you mean.'

For a moment he wondered if she had seen through him, come to realize that he was no more than a fortune hunter. Glancing at the scar on his hand he felt sick with fear. But her next words surprised and reassured him.

'I mean that you might feel that you have to marry me after we . . . after what we did.'

'If that's what you truly believe then I'll never forgive myself. I love you, Elise. I intended to marry you one day whatever happened. The fact that we got carried away and that I could have made you—'

'Pregnant.'

'That we might have conceived a child has only brought our plans forward. Don't you see that?'

'And you don't think I'm cheap?'

'Not that again, Elise. I don't think you're cheap, my darling. We did what we did because we love each other.' Perry controlled a spurt of irritation. His child bride – his prize bride – was proving hard work. It seemed she needed constant reassurance. 'Why don't you sit back and try to relax,' he said. 'Look, I bought you this magazine when I got my paper. It's called *Potpourri* and it seems very amusing.'

Elise took the magazine and turned the pages listlessly. Perry opened his newspaper. After a slamming of doors and a whistle the train began to pull away from the station. The final stage of their journey had begun.

Elise did not want to disturb Perry. Men liked newspapers, she knew that. Her father, patient and kind though he was, never liked to be disturbed when he was reading his paper. She flicked through her magazine but found nothing to interest her. She thought *Potpourri* a strange name for it. As far as she was concerned a potpourri was a collection of dried flower petals, leaves, herbs and spices that was used to scent the air, and the only article in the magazine that was remotely connected with that was a piece about flower arranging.

She closed the magazine and looked out of the window. The wind had risen and the rain was slanting across the glass. The countryside sped by in a watery blur. She closed her eyes. She was tired and the rhythm of the wheels on the track along with the warmth rising from the pipes under the seat was making her drowsy. She was too overwrought to sleep but she allowed herself to fall into a dreamy, trancelike state while she relived the circumstances that had brought her here.

If it hadn't been raining that day, the day that had changed her life, she might not be here at all . . .

She couldn't even remember the name of the little café Perry took her to or exactly where it was.

'You'll like it,' he'd told her. 'It doesn't look much from outside but inside it's very cosy. I often pop in for a snack. And sometimes even for breakfast.'

'Is it near to where you live?'

'Not too far, and it opens very early in the morning. Some of the customers haven't been home to bed at all and they sit there in their evening clothes devouring bacon sandwiches washed down with strong sweet tea.'

Elise had been intrigued and she had gone along willingly. Then on the way it had started to rain. A gentle shower that became a torrential downpour. Thankfully they reached the café before she was completely soaked. Perry went ahead to open the door but turned straight round again and grabbed her arms.

'We can't go in there,' he said.

'Why ever not?'

'There are some people I know – they'll recognize you. Word will get back to your parents.'

'What are we going to do?'

'We can't stand here in the doorway like this so we'll have to make a run for it.'

'But where shall we go?'

'My apartment isn't too far away. You're already shivering. Let's get you there and get you dry before you catch a chill.'

Before Elise could respond Perry took her hand and they ran through the rain, laughing like children until they reached the apartment block where he lived. Wind had blown rain across the tiled floor of the entrance hall and Elise almost fell as they skidded to a stop. Perry caught her and kept his arm round her as they waited for the lift.

'All right?' he murmured as they rose creaking to the top floor.

'I'm fine.'

She was out of breath and excited. She knew this to be a daring thing to do. To go to a man's apartment. To be there alone with him. The girls in the cheap romances that her school friends passed around the class nearly always had cause to regret being so reckless. Or so naïve.

The front door of the apartment opened into a tiny vestibule with dark oak panelling. Perry hurried them through into what turned out to be the living room. Brought up for most of her life in luxury she was surprised and dismayed at what she saw. The furniture was cheap and merely functional and to be honest the place looked none too clean. Perry must have seen her expression of dismayed surprise. He shut the door behind them and crossed to a table, gathered up some dirty dishes and disappeared into what must have been a scullery.

'I have no housekeeper at the moment. It's so hard to get staff, isn't it?'

'I have no idea.'

Elise had never had to think about the domestic situation at home. There were maids and menservants, a cook and a gardener and other people whose function she did not even know.

'But you can't just stand here,' Perry told her. 'I'll show you the bathroom. At least my towels are clean. You can get dried off and I'll find you something to wear.'

'Something to wear?'

'Of course. You can't keep those damp clothes on. We'll dry them by the fire and you can wear my dressing gown. How about that?'

Bemused, Elise allowed herself to be led to the bathroom. Perry left her there. She took off her outer layer of clothes, dried as much of herself as she could and towelled her hair. She sensed the door opening and peered out from under the edge of the towel to see that a hand had appeared. The hand was holding a dark blue silk dressing gown.

'Take it,' Perry's voice said. 'And pass out your damp

303

clothes. I've lit the fire and put the kettle on. We'll be very cosy.'

And indeed when she returned to the living room it did not look so shabby. Perry had drawn the curtains and lit some lamps with pretty shades. The gas fire, its ancient elements popping and spluttering, gave the room a cosy glow. There was a clean cloth on the table, a teapot, milk jug and cups and a plate of bread and jam.

Perry smiled ruefully. 'A bit like a nursery tea, I know,' he said, 'but I don't keep much food here. Now let's sit down and enjoy our little feast.'

Elise remained where she was standing.

'What is it?' Perry asked. 'Why do you look so surprised?'

'You . . . you've taken your clothes off. I mean you're wearing . . .'

Perry laughed as he spread his arms to show off the black silk robe he was wearing. 'I was wet too, you know. You wouldn't have wanted me to get pneumonia, would you?'

'No, of course not. It's just . . . just . . . Oh, I don't know.'

Elise tried to come to terms with and make sense of the strange situation she found herself in. She acknowledged that she was completely out of her depth. Her clothes were draped over a couple of chairs near the fire and steaming gently. Fleetingly she wondered what one of the heroines in the cheap romances would have done. Maybe the girl would have grabbed her dripping clothes, put them on and run out into the rain. Later, her virtue intact, she would catch pneumonia and die.

'Why are you smiling?' Perry asked.

'Oh, no reason.'

Elise had decided that she could at least wait until her

clothes were dry enough to put on before leaving. And eating bread and jam was surely no threat to her virtue.

'Well, I'm glad you're happy.' Perry poured the tea and added something to the cups from a silver flask. 'Just a spot of something to warm us up and chase the chills away.'

Whatever it was in the flask it did more than chase the chills away. Elise let go of any lingering doubts and began to enjoy the simple meal of bread and jam as if it were a banquet. She had a second cup of tea into which Perry emptied what was left in his flask. She still had no idea why exactly everything had seemed so amusing, but Perry had been so funny and so sweet and it had seemed entirely natural for her to go through to the bedroom with him and lie in his arms.

At one point she had turned away from him and curled up drowsily. She had felt his hand stroking her shoulder. 'How can I wake you up, my Sleeping Beauty?' he had whispered.

'Why not try a kiss?' she replied. She had begun to laugh and for a moment she thought she could not stop, then Perry turned her to face him and kissed her. What happened next had been so wild, so exciting, that Elise had wanted it to go on and on. Never to stop.

When Perry had told her that her clothes were dry and he would get a taxi for her and she must go home she had pleaded with him to let her stay.

'No, my sweet. When you get home you can tell your mother that you took shelter somewhere until the rain stopped. I'm sure that sounds reasonable.'

Reasonable or not, she couldn't help seeing that Perry looked anxious and she was touched. 'Don't worry about me,' she said. 'It will be all right.'

And it had been. It had been perfectly all right. Her

mother had not even noticed that she was late home. Her feeling of exhilaration lasted until bedtime and it was only when she was lying alone in bed that the excitement began to dissipate. For no reason she could think of she began to cry. She thought of all those silly heroines in those novellas again and realized that she had indeed been one of the foolish virgins.

He'll think I'm cheap, she moaned to herself. He won't want to see me again. How could he possibly love a girl that gave up her virginity so easily?

The next day at school she appeared pale and washed out. 'That time of the month?' Shirley asked.

Elise didn't answer her. She couldn't. Her friend's question had reminded her of something that might be a consequence of what she had done. The day dragged on and after school when she went to their usual meeting place in the park she was fully expecting him not to be there.

When she saw him she started weeping with relief. She saw that he was smiling the same tender smile as always. It's all right, she thought, he still loves me.

Perry saw that Elise's eyes were closed and he relaxed a little. He stared out at the rain-drenched countryside. Rain, he thought, the blessed rain. He had always planned to take Elise home that day. First he was going to take her to the café but he'd never had any intention of actually going in. He would have told her that he'd spotted someone he knew and then persuaded her that, as they'd come that far, they might as well go to his apartment. Once there he'd had every intention of seducing her but he had not been confident that she would succumb. The rain had made things so much easier. It had been perfectly natural for him to suggest they go home and get dry.

He looked at her now through half-closed lids. Who would have thought she would have responded so enthusiastically? Admittedly she had had a little help from the generous dash of whisky he had added from his flask. But even there he had taken a chance. Alcohol can relax your sexual inhibitions but equally it can inhibit them. He had been lucky. The inexperienced schoolgirl had revealed a passionate depth to her nature that you could never have guessed at from her cool, almost glacially beautiful exterior. He marvelled to remember how he had not found her sexually attractive. That had changed. Even though she would need constant reassurance, being married to Elise might not be such an onerous task after all.

It wasn't until after Helen had finished her lunch of Lamb Noisettes followed by Plum Pancake that she opened her newspaper. She had asked for a second pot of coffee and once the table was cleared she eased her shoes off – no one would see her feet under the table – and opened the *Daily Chronicle*.

The national news was depressing, with more shipyards closing in the North-East and unemployment rising. The international news was even worse, with reports from Spain of continued fighting between the Nationalists and the Republicans resulting in massacres and bombings. Young men from England who felt strongly about the cause were actually going to Spain to fight on the side of the Republicans.

Helen thanked God that Matthew was no longer a foreign correspondent. Once he would have been there in the thick of it, risking life and limb to report the truth of what was going on. Although it made him impatient sometimes, Helen considered it a blessing that the wound inflicted in Afghanistan had never healed satisfactorily and had left him with one leg shorter than the other and a pronounced limp when the weather was bad.

Sometimes she was not so sure that it was any safer being a crime correspondent. There were so many dangerous criminals in London and other big cities these days and when Matthew was investigating a story he seemed completely fearless.

She turned the pages until she found his name and discovered that he had returned, like a bloodhound, to a story that he had covered before.

DOG TRACK BETTING FEAR
Matthew Renshaw
Crime Correspondent

After months of inactivity due to the investigations of the police, rumours are circulating that the doping of greyhounds has started up again. Bookmakers as far afield as Birmingham, Manchester and Newcastle are reporting unusual betting patterns, with complicated bets on the same named dogs.

This is not petty crime. There are indications that the men behind this are out-and-out gangsters with one particular 'Mr Big' being one of London's most notorious criminals. This reporter will be conducting his own investigation. Watch this space.

Helen's smile was rueful as she closed her paper. Watch this space, indeed! Suddenly she realized how much she had missed him. His reluctance to fully commit was infuriating – agonizing – but what could she do? She loved him and, although it hurt her pride, she knew she was prepared to wait for as long as it took. She could never leave him.

Danny closed the newspaper and stared ahead thoughtfully. He was sitting at Myra's kitchen table where he had just finished eating his midday meal. Joe had already gone back to the kennels and Myra was washing the dishes in the steamy scullery.

'Are you going to sit there all day or are you going to give me a hand?' she shouted.

'Can't help, I'm afraid. Got to go out.'

'Huh! After that lovely extra helping of steak and kidney pie I gave you!'

Danny didn't reply. He had already gone. Despite what the dust and straw would do to his chest, he had to get along and see his brother straight away. He would have to tell Joe it was time to make plans.

Chapter Nineteen

'You mean you didn't even notice that Elise did not come home from school yesterday?'

Hugh Partington faced his wife in the confines of her boudoir. He was white-faced with fury.

'No, I didn't,' Selma replied. She looked and sounded defiant.

'You didn't wonder where she was when it was time for tea?'

'She does not take tea with me these days. I have a meal in the nursery with Bertie. She prefers to eat a little later.'

'Where?'

'What do you mean, where?'

'Where does our daughter eat her tea?'

'In the dining room, I suppose.'

'You suppose.'

Selma's defiance crumbled. 'Look, Hugh, I'm sorry. You can't know how dreadful I feel. How ashamed.'

'And so you should be. To have the servants tell us that our daughter is missing. That she did not sleep in her bed last night. That is truly shameful.'

A hint of defiance flared again in Selma's eyes. 'You didn't notice either, did you?'

'I'm not often home at teatime.'

'No, but you used to make a point of talking to Elise

when you did come home. Of asking her about school, or her friends, or the latest movies and stage shows. You haven't done that so much lately, have you?'

Hugh was silent for a moment and then he said, 'You're right. We are both to blame. We have neglected her.'

'It's hardly neglect.'

'Yes, it is. And it started when Bertie was born. All those years ago when you first asked me if we could adopt her I was afraid that this would happen. It seems she has packed her bags and run away.'

'She hasn't taken very much with her. She can't be intending to go far. Perhaps she just wants to give us a fright.'

'I hope you're right. But we can't just wait. She's only sixteen years old. We have to find her.'

Selma took a step towards him. 'You don't think she could have gone to her sister, do you?'

'To Helen? How would she know where to find her?'

'It would be easy enough. She could have gone back to Newcastle and asked that dreadful woman, Mrs Roberts.'

'Her aunt?'

'Yes. If Helen isn't with her she probably knows where she is.'

Hugh looked thoughtful. 'It's a possibility. Do you want me to go there?'

'You? Go there yourself?'

'Of course. She's our daughter, isn't she? I shall do what any father would do.'

'What if you find her and she refuses to come back?'

'Is that what you want, Selma? Would you be happy if Elise chose to leave us now?'

Selma dropped her head into her hands. 'Of course not. And you must go. Straight away.'

'I will. But promise me that you will tell no one what has

happened. I've spoken to the servants and impressed on them that this must not become public knowledge. We don't want scandalous stories in the press. For your sake as well as Elise's. We don't want anyone to think you've been – we've been – neglectful parents.'

Seeing how wretched Selma was, Hugh took her in his arms to comfort her. She burst into tears but he did not know whether they were tears of grief or tears of chagrin. 'Calm yourself, sweetheart,' he said. 'You must show a cheerful face for Bertie. I'll telephone the station and reserve a ticket but we're only guessing that Elise has gone to find her sister. I'd better get some discreet inquiries started, too.'

'A detective agency?'

'That's right.'

Selma straightened up, took a step back and shook her head. 'Oh, Hugh, how could she do this? After everything we've done for her, how could she be so ungrateful?'

Hugh went downstairs to his study to make the necessary phone calls but before he had even dialled the first number there was a knock at the door and a maidservant entered.

'I'm sorry to disturb you, sir,' she said, 'but there's a Mrs Chapman and her daughter to see you. Mrs Chapman says it's urgent.'

He replaced the receiver. He did not need to be told what this would be about. 'Show them in,' he said. 'And please go upstairs and ask Mrs Partington to join us.'

'Eloped? You think she has eloped? But that's preposterous!' Hugh said.

Darlene Chapman bridled. 'Preposterous or not, I believe that's what has happened and I thought it my duty to come and tell you.'

Mrs Chapman and her daughter Shirley sat facing Hugh

across his desk. Selma was sitting beside him but she shrank away, almost as if she did not want to be there at all.

'On what do you base this assumption?'

'Tell them, Shirley.'

Hugh thought the girl looked excited. She was enjoying the drama of the situation.

'She's been meeting Perry Wallace after school.'

Selma gasped. 'Perry Wallace!'

Hugh felt a mixture of shock and anger.

Shirley, looking gratified by the dismay she had caused, continued, 'She thought nobody knew but she was acting strangely so I followed her a couple of times. She was so besotted with him that she didn't notice.'

'Why didn't you tell someone straight away?' Hugh asked.

'That's what I said,' Darlene Chapman agreed.

'Well, you don't snitch on friends, do you? And besides, to tell the truth I thought it was all fairly harmless.'

'Harmless?' Hugh said. 'That unprincipled ne'er-do-well meeting my daughter? I don't call that harmless.'

Shirley looked uneasy. 'I simply didn't think that she would take him seriously. I mean, who would? Everybody knows what Perry is like!'

'Except Elise, it seems,' Selma said. 'Who would have thought she could be so stupid?'

'So why did you decide to tell your mother now?' Hugh asked.

'My brother Tom is home on leave.'

'What does that have to do with it?' Hugh asked impatiently.

'He told me how boring it's going to be now that Perry has left town. Then Elise didn't come to school today. I put two and two together. If I'm right I thought you should

313

know straight away. Elise is my friend. I don't want any harm to come to her. I want you to do something about it before . . . before it's too late.'

Despite Shirley's revelations and the assumption that Elise and Perry had fled to Gretna Green, Hugh went to Newcastle. He was hoping against hope that Selma's first instinct had been right and that Elise, unhappy with the situation at home, had gone to seek out her sister. It was too late to call on anyone when he arrived so he booked into the Station Hotel and called on Mrs Roberts first thing the next morning. A smiling middle-aged woman opened the door and Hugh reflected that Helen's aunt did not appear to be the unpleasant harridan of Selma's memory.

'Who shall I say is calling?' she asked and Hugh realized his mistake. This woman was a servant of some kind. The maid or a housekeeper, perhaps.

Hugh gave his name and waited in the hallway while the woman knocked and entered the front parlour. When she returned she looked anxious.

'I'm sorry to ask you this, sir, but there isn't any problem, is there? I mean, Mrs Roberts is still quite poorly, you know.'

'I didn't know she was ill. I'm sorry. And I just want to ask her a few questions. I promise you I'll not cause trouble.'

The woman looked at him speculatively for a moment. She must have been partly reassured by his manner because she said, 'Very well. I'm Mrs Sutton, Mrs Roberts' house-keeper. Would you mind if I stayed in the room with you?'

'Not at all.' Hugh thought how fortunate Helen's aunt was to have such a respectful servant.

Mrs Sutton ushered him into a brightly cheerful room.

There was a dried flower arrangement in the hearth and pots of geraniums on a table by the window. The curtains were tied back as far as possible to allow the sunlight to flood in. Mrs Roberts sat in one of the fireside chairs and she looked up at him anxiously. She was a large woman with flabby cheeks.

'What is it?' she asked without waiting for him to say anything. 'Have the boys caused trouble again?'

'The boys?' he asked. Hugh had completely forgotten about Elise's brothers who had been found places in Haven House.

'The twins. Have you found out why they ran away?'

'No, it's not that. May I sit down?'

'Please do.' The answer came from the housekeeper, who sat down on a chair near the door. Jane Roberts continued to stare at him anxiously.

'It's not . . .' she faltered, 'it's not Helen again, is it? She hasn't been trying to get in touch with Elsie after all these years? If so, I've had nothing to do with it, I assure you.'

Hugh shook his head. 'No, she hasn't. It's the other way round, actually. I need to know if Elise has tried to get in touch with Helen.'

'Elise? Elsie? How would I know? Helen doesn't live here any more. She moved out years ago.'

'But you'll have her address?'

'No, I don't.'

Hugh studied the woman's truculent expression. Was she lying? Surely she would know where her own niece was living? He felt helpless. Even if she did know, there was no way he could force the information out of her. He wondered if her attitude was the result of Selma's last meeting with her. By all accounts it had not been very pleasant. Was this to have been a wasted journey?

315

'Well, then,' he said as he rose to his feet reluctantly. 'I suppose I'd better go. But if you do hear anything from Helen or Elise I'd be grateful if you'd let me know. I'll leave you my card.'

Mrs Roberts made no attempt to take the card he was holding out so he put it on the mantelpiece. Mrs Sutton had already opened the door for him when he paused. Should he offer Mrs Roberts money in exchange for the information she might have? He was pretty sure Selma would have done. He turned to face her and was shocked to see that she had begun to cry.

'I've upset you. I'm so sorry.'

She looked up at him, tears streaming down her cheeks. 'Helen is a good girl,' she said. 'She came home to fix things for me even though I didn't deserve it. She didn't leave me her address. She doesn't want anything to do with me, and it's my loss. And if Elsie wants to find Helen again then good luck to her. I should never have taken your wife's money. I should never have allowed those children to be parted.'

'Please go now, Mr Partington,' Mrs Sutton said. 'And don't worry. I'll look after her.'

The taxi was waiting outside and Hugh got in and asked to be taken back to the hotel. He had achieved nothing here, but there was one more thing he must do before leaving Newcastle. He would ask the solicitor, Arthur Garwood, to engage an agent who would conduct more thorough inquiries.

However, he believed Jane Roberts was speaking the truth and that she did not know where her own niece lived. It had not occurred to him – why should it? – that someone else in the household might have the information.

Margery Sutton watched the taxi drive away then closed the door and went to make a pot of tea. After settling Mrs

Roberts she went back to the kitchen and poured a cup for herself.

He didn't ask me so I didn't have to lie to him, she thought. For Margery Sutton had Helen's address. She wrote to her regularly to give her news about her aunt's slow progress back to good health. Helen had never told her anything about her twin brothers or that she had a sister called either Elise or Elsie, so Margery reckoned that this was private information. Helen obviously doesn't want anyone to know, she thought. And if that's what Helen wants, God bless her, as far as I'm concerned that's the way it shall be.

Hugh stayed in Newcastle one more night. He had talks with Garwood and also went to the family house in Jesmond. It was years since they had been here. Selma had been shocked to discover that Helen had been watching Elise and they had fled to London. Selma was adamant that Elise should be kept away from her home town and any memories it might evoke.

After inspecting the house where he had lived as a boy and in which he had always been happy, he went to call on his old friend who had been Selma's doctor, Charles Harris. After dinner with the family, Charles took him into his study so that they could talk in private. He poured them each a generous glass of brandy and they lit cigars.

'What's up?' Charles said.

Hugh told him.

'I'm very sorry,' Charles said, 'but it does look as though there might be an elopement here. What next? Gretna Green?'

'No, I'll go back to London in the morning. I don't want to leave Selma on her own for too long.'

317

'Is she taking this badly?'

'She is, but . . .'

'But what?'

'I'm not sure what it is that is upsetting her.'

'Surely she's upset because your daughter is missing.'

Hugh looked uncomfortable. 'Her relationship with Elise has not been the same since Bertie was born.'

'Aah.'

'At first I thought it was the kind of thing that happened when children become adolescents.'

'The awkward age? That could be the case.'

'But if anyone was the awkward one it has been Selma, not Elise. She . . . she refers to Bertie as "our own" child.'

'And to Elise?'

'She simply doesn't refer to her.'

'So the poor girl has found comfort in the arms of a handsome young suitor?'

'An unscrupulous young fortune hunter!'

'And you believe they have gone to Scotland to get married?'

'I do, and before I left London I arranged for a detective agency to send someone there straight away. They'll have to live there for twenty-one days before they can get married. I know the local housewives make good money by providing secret accommodation for runaways, but I'm determined to find them and stop this marriage from taking place.'

'No matter what has already happened?'

'What do you mean?'

'By your account he is an unscrupulous rake and Elise . . . Elise is a vulnerable young girl.'

Hugh stared ahead miserably. 'If he has seduced her I just don't know what I will do.'

'She will need her mother.'

'I know, and I'm not sure any more if Selma will want anything to do with her.'

When Hugh arrived home the next day the first question he asked was whether there had been any news from the detective agency.

'Only to report that they haven't found them,' Selma replied.

'Well, they must keep looking. They will be there somewhere. Probably hidden in some farmer's cottage until the wedding day.'

'What will you do if they are found?' Selma asked.

'Go and bring her back.'

'And if she doesn't want to come?'

'She will. I'll offer him money and you'll see how quickly he will fall out of love with her.'

'Regardless of whether they are married or not, what if it is already too late?'

Remembering his conversation with Charles, Hugh knew exactly what she meant. 'She would need her mother.'

'Her mother is dead.'

Hugh was shocked into silence.

'That girl has shown us no gratitude whatsoever,' Selma said, 'and as far as I am concerned Perry Wallace is welcome to her.'

The shadows of the trees were already creeping across the lawn but Patricia was reluctant to leave the garden and go back into the house. The day had been exceptionally hot and she was more tired than she liked to admit.

'Let's sit here until she wakes up,' she said.

'But isn't it time for her bottle?' Matthew asked his

319

sister with a brief nod towards the sleeping baby in the pram.

'I don't believe in all that. I'll feed her when she asks for it and the nurse and her timetable can go hang.'

Matthew reflected that since the birth of baby Gillian, his sister had changed. Once organized and dutiful, she had become more relaxed. Motherhood suited her – softened her somehow.

'You will stay and have supper with us?' Patricia asked. 'Not that it's anything special. Just cold cuts and salad and a big pan of boiled potatoes to keep George happy.'

'I'd love to. What time will he be home?'

'About nine o'clock. He'll be off duty when the night shift starts.'

Matthew, slightly uncomfortable in the canvas chair, eased his shoulders and stretched out his legs, trying not to obsess about the fact that one of them didn't stretch as far as the other.

'You know, I've never really understood what George does there in the bowels of Broadcasting House, but it sounds frightfully complicated,' he said.

'It is, to ordinary mortals like you and me,' Patricia replied, 'but I'll try and explain a little. At the moment his job is to sit in a bay with headphones and a telephone and receive reports from cities like Berlin, Paris, Rome, Madrid and other places in Europe. These reports are fed to a recording channel before being used by news programmes.'

'Interesting,' Matthew said.

'Yes, it is. There's a lot of information coming in. Worrying information. Spain, for example, is in turmoil.'

'The civil war.'

'That's right. George reckons he's as well informed as any reporter.'

Matthew remained silent.

'You'd like to be there, wouldn't you?' his sister said. 'You miss the days of being a foreign correspondent.'

'Maybe.'

'But instead of going somewhere exotic you're setting off tomorrow morning on a tour of provincial cities to investigate the latest crooked betting rumours. Now that sounds complicated to me!'

'It isn't really. The bad lads are trying to avoid detection by spreading their bets countrywide. The bookies suspect something big is going to come off.'

'Something big? Explain.'

'For example, if four dogs are doped in one race leaving an outsider to come first with good odds, the winnings could top one hundred thousand pounds.'

'Substantial,' Patricia said. 'How do you know which race will be targeted? I mean, there must be dozens of dog tracks.'

'There are. And you don't know. But I have my suspicions.'

Patricia shivered and pulled her cardigan round her shoulders.

'Are you cold?' Matthew asked. 'Shall we go inside now?'

'I'm not cold. It just came home to me that you might be dealing with dangerous men. Perhaps you'd be better off going to Spain after all!'

She had tried to make a joke of it but Matthew could see that his sister was concerned for him and he was touched. Also he didn't want her to be upset, not so soon after the birth of her baby.

'Right this moment there's nothing I'd like better than a cup of tea. Be a sport and go in and put the kettle on. I'll put the chairs in the shed and I'll wheel the pram in.'

'Don't wake her up!'

'I'll try not to. But if she does wake up how about letting her Uncle Matthew give her her bottle?'

A short while later Matthew was seated at his sister's kitchen table holding his new niece in his arms and trying not to show how amazed and delighted he was that the child had settled and was quite content to let him feed her.

Patricia made a pot of tea and put the milk, the sugar and the cups on the table, but she was strangely silent.

'What is it?' Matthew asked eventually.

'Why haven't you brought Helen to see the baby?'

The question took him by surprise. He had known from the beginning that Patricia didn't entirely approve of his relationship with Helen.

'Mum was quite strict about that. She said no visitors when you came home from the nursing home.'

'She only meant until we'd settled into a routine. Matthew, you haven't even mentioned Helen lately. Is something wrong?'

'Not really.'

'What kind of an answer is that?'

'Helen went away on holiday.'

'Why shouldn't she?'

'She didn't tell me she was going to. I found out when I called at the restaurant to see her and Marina informed me that she'd gone. I went to her flat but she'd left no message.'

'Just up and off?'

'That's right, and I have no idea where she went or why she went without telling me.'

'Had you quarrelled?'

'No. At least I don't think so.'

'Come on! A quarrel is a quarrel! You shouldn't have to think about it.'

'Hush. You're disturbing your daughter.'

Gillian had stopped sucking and her eyes were wide open. She gave the impression of being surrprised and offended. Matthew and Patricia kept quiet and Gillian started feeding again. They sighed with relief.

'We haven't exactly quarrelled,' Matthew said after a while. 'But I know she's been getting impatient with me.'

'And actually I don't blame her. Matthew, you're going to lose her if you don't walk her up the aisle very soon.'

'The irony is that I'd already realized that. Although it took a good friend of hers to point it out. I don't want to lose her. I love her very much and I was all prepared to go down on one knee if necessary and beg her to marry me right now. But maybe I've left it too late. Maybe she's just got sick of waiting.'

'For goodness' sake don't give up so easily.'

Matthew looked at her in surprise. 'You would like me to marry Helen?'

'Yes, I would. I admit that I didn't take to her at first and I still believe that there's a side of her I don't know about, as well as things she isn't telling us – even you – but when I see you together I can only see how happy she makes you. And when you're alone like this you're a pain in the posterior. Go ahead and woo the girl properly, Matthew. You have your sister's blessing.'

Chapter Twenty

Before Matthew left the next morning he considered going to Helen's flat to see whether she had returned. He decided against it. If she was there they would have a lot to say to each other and he didn't want to rush it. And besides, he didn't even know whether she would see him. It would be better to wait until he came back from his tour of the provincial cites.

Usually when he set off on an assignment he was totally focused on the work ahead. But this time as he began his journey north he could only think of Helen and what he would say to her when he saw her again.

Hugh came into the bedroom and opened the curtains. 'Wake up, Selma,' he said.

She had been sleeping when he had got up and gone down for breakfast, and he seldom disturbed her. Every day he had all the national newspapers delivered and he liked to glance through them before going to the office. Selma stirred, yawned sleepily and half rose from the pillows.

'What is it?' she asked. Then as memory flooded back she sat up straight and asked, 'Is there any news?'

Hugh's laugh was bitter. 'You could say so,' he said. 'But not the sort of news we wanted.'

Only then did Selma see that he was carrying a newspaper. 'You'd better read it for yourself,' he said.

He handed her the paper but instead of sitting down on the bed as she expected, he began to pace up and down. Distracted, Selma said, 'Keep still, darling. You're making me nervous.'

'Just read it.'

'Read what?'

'You can't miss it. It's on the front page.'

Offended by his peremptory tone, Selma frowned then cast her eyes over the page before her. It only took a moment before she gasped and cried out, 'Oh no!'

'SOCIETY RUNAWAYS!' the headline screamed. Selma read on feverishly.

Rumours have reached this newspaper that Elise Partington, daughter of one of the richest industrialists in Europe, has eloped to Gretna Green. Her intended bridegroom is Perry Wallace.

Emerald Leighton, editor of our society pages, has been told by a reliable source that this handsome man-about-town and the ravishingly beautiful sixteen-year-old are desperately in love and determined to marry each other. However, Elise's father, Hugh Partington, is equally determined that they shall not, and is making every effort to find them before the starry-eyed young woman and her handsome but impecunious suitor face each other over the blacksmith's anvil and tie the knot.

We have decided to send our own reporters to Gretna in order to keep our readers informed of any developments in this romantic story.

By the time Selma had finished reading the report she was

shaking. She let the newspaper fall from her fingers and it slithered down over the silk bedspread on to the floor.

'Who has done this?' she asked. 'Who has told them?'

Hugh came over to the bed and, picking up the pages of the newspaper, rearranged them and folded it up.

'I could ask the editor, I suppose, but he'll probably say something about not revealing his sources. Especially if he hopes to get further information.'

'Information about what?'

'About what we are doing to bring Elise back.' Hugh sighed as he sat down on the bed. 'I thought I could trust our servants to be discreet.'

'You think it came from here?'

'Where else? You've probably never thought about this, Selma, but servants know just about everything that goes on in the households where they work. If you are fortunate they are loyal. It is a matter of pride not to spread gossip about the people who employ them. But in this case I think money is involved. A newspaper will pay good sums for a story like this and someone was tempted.'

'Are you sure, Hugh? I mean, couldn't it be Elise's school friend Shirley who has gone to the press?'

'I considered that but I don't think so. The girl is loyal to Elise and I'm sure she wouldn't do anything to embarrass her.'

'What can we do?'

'Nothing about what has already been printed. We certainly won't respond to any requests from reporters for information.'

'If only I'd known,' Selma said.

'Known what?'

'I should have listened to you all those years ago about how unwise it was to bring a girl like that into our lives.'

'Did I say that?'

'Well, not exactly, but you were more cautious than I was.'

Hugh remembered very well that the reason for his concern had been Selma's own quixotic character rather than the chance that the child might cause trouble. Now it gave him no pleasure whatsoever that he had been right to be concerned. He had grown to love Elise and his present state of anger was tempered by anguish and worry.

'You mustn't be too hard on her,' he said.

'How can you say that? After everything we have done for her, this is how she has repaid us. She has not shown the least gratitude!'

'Children are not required to show gratitude, Selma.'

'Adopted children are!'

'No, they're not. And in any case, over the years you have done your best to ignore the fact that Elise was adopted. Most of our friends in London have no idea.'

'Well, I shall make sure that they know now. I would hate them to think that any true daughter of mine would think herself so cheap that she should run off with a scheming fortune hunter like Perry Wallace!'

Hugh saw that there was no arguing with her and he also saw, with a sinking heart, that whatever the outcome of this sad affair was, Selma and Elise would never be reconciled.

The next morning Jocelyn was alone in *Potpourri*'s untidy office on the top floor of the house in Russell Square. Hearing footsteps ascending the stairs and expecting Charlotte to arrive breathless and apologetic for being late, she was surprised when Helen walked in.

'Welcome back, stranger,' she said. 'Good holiday?'

Helen's answer was a smile.

She's not to be drawn, Jocelyn thought. Am I going to let her get away with this? After all, we're supposed to be friends, aren't we? 'Go anywhere nice?'

She noted how grudgingly Helen gave an answer. 'Newcastle.'

Jocelyn could think of only one reason why anyone should go to Newcastle. 'Family visit?'

'Yes,' Helen said tersely, 'and to save you further questions, I have been visiting an aunt. She needed help to sort out a problem.'

Jocelyn was taken by surprise. She sat back and stared at Helen for a moment before she said, 'You have an aunt? Do you realize that that is the most you've ever told us about yourself?'

Helen lifted up the assortment of manuscripts and letters that were resting on the nearest chair, dumped them on the floor and sat down. 'I know,' she said. 'And you've never pressed me. Until now.'

'Ouch!' Jocelyn said. 'I'm sorry.'

Helen smiled. 'No, it's all right. I know what a pain I must have been. How uninformative.'

'Uninformative? Mmm . . .' Jocelyn said. 'An interesting choice of word. Let me check my thesaurus.' She made a show of reaching for one of the heavy books on the shelf behind her desk and pretended to flick through it. 'Uninformative leads to secretive, leads to enigmatic, leads to mysterious . . .' She closed the book and looked up laughingly. 'Have you any sinister secrets, Helen?'

'No. It's just that I've never liked talking about myself . . . my family . . . why I left Newcastle to come to London. It was all too . . . too painful.'

'Oh, I'm so sorry, my dear.' Jocelyn felt contrite. 'And here I am making fun of you. Forgive me?'

'Of course I do. But that's enough for today, all right?'

'It's enough for the moment and forever if that's how you want it. But now, you do realize you had Matthew in quite a state about this, don't you?'

'Matthew came here?'

'Of course he did. He couldn't understand why you had gone away without telling him. Or where and why you had gone. He tried to put a brave face on it but he looked utterly wretched. And it hurt his pride to have to ask us if we knew any more than he did. Whatever the reasons for your reticence, don't you feel just a little bit guilty about that?'

'Yes, I do. And I intend to sort things out with him. If he still wants to see me.'

Jocelyn saw how strained Helen looked and decided to change the subject. 'Have you thought about work at all while you've been away?' she asked.

'Do you mean the restaurant or my writing?'

'I meant your writing. But the restaurant comes into it. Forgive me, Helen, but you must have guessed what I'm going to say.'

'The restaurant pieces are repetitive and stale.'

'I wouldn't have put it quite so strongly. But they are a bit samey.'

'Do you want to drop them?'

'Perhaps. But if we do, I wonder if you would consider trying something else? Something similar. It would mean that you would have to leave Stefano's. Would you mind terribly?'

Helen laughed. 'I wouldn't mind at all! Oh, I've loved working there. I adore Stefano and I even have a soft spot in my heart for the formidable Marina. I've made friends with the other girls and some of the customers, and I've heard all their stories and learned so much about life but . . . but, oh, I don't know . . .'

'It's time to move on. I'm sure you're a very good waitress but that's not all you are. You're a first-rate writer and that's where your future lies. Exactly where, I'm not sure. And I don't know if you're sure either. I think you could write fiction if you wanted to but it would be taking a gamble.'

'I know. I've thought about it.'

'And?'

'I will when I'm ready.'

'When you've saved up enough money not to have to live in a garret like other hopeful young novelists?'

'Something like that. I have to admit it's been good earning enough to lead a fairly comfortable life.'

'So would you like to hear my suggestion?'

'Go on.'

'Leave the restaurant and get a job in the fashion department of a department store. Write a weekly piece about working there.'

'Diary of a shop girl?'

'I hadn't thought of a heading but that might do. What do you think?'

'I think it would be very hard work – the shop assistant part of it, I mean.'

'You're young and you're fit.'

'You would want me to work in a fairly well-known store?'

Jocelyn nodded. 'The store would remain anonymous just as the restaurant did.'

Helen looked thoughtful. 'I'm quite tempted. But there's a problem. I have no experience of shop work whatsoever. Even if any decent store agreed to take me on I would almost certainly make a fool of myself as soon as I started work.'

330

Jocelyn smiled. 'And that would make good copy.'

'You're a cruel woman. But, yes, I'll start looking around for a shop job.' She looked thoughtful. 'But I won't give in my notice at Stefano's until I have to.'

'That's wise. Are you going in today?'

'No. It's back to work tomorrow.'

'Then why not hang around and observe a day in the life of a struggling but dedicated editor? Seriously, you can do some filing – if you wouldn't mind, that is. Charlotte is completely addle-headed these days. Any thinking space she has left in that poor brain of hers is filled with wedding arrangements and finding a cosy little nest for her and Edward to set up home in.'

'I heard that!' Jocelyn and Helen looked round to see Charlotte standing in the doorway. She was clutching a shopping bag that looked full to bursting. She looked as rumpled as usual but her smile was radiant – and forgiving. 'I know you don't mean to be unkind, Aunt Jocelyn. What you say is just your idea of humour. So I still fully intend to share these delicious pastries with you – and Helen, too, if she's staying.'

'You're a delightful child,' Jocelyn said. 'But what else have you got in that bag? It can't be full of pastries.'

Charlotte dumped the bag on top of the pile of papers on her desk. 'Oh, all sorts of stuff. I'm meeting Edward in the gardens at lunchtime and I thought I'd make some sandwiches.' She started delving into the bag. 'The pastries are here somewhere. Got them! I'll put the kettle on, shall I?'

'Well, it's a little early for a tea break but please do.' While Charlotte had been rummaging in her shopping bag a newspaper had fallen out. Jocelyn noticed it lying on the desk and called out, 'Why on earth did you buy that gossipy rag?'

'For the gossip, of course! A runaway romance, would you believe! The girl I was sitting next to on the bus was reading it and I couldn't help reading over her shoulder.'

'Bad-mannered child.'

'I know. That's more or less what she said. But when she got off the bus she gave me her paper anyway. Do you want a look while I make the tea?'

She picked up the newspaper and offered it to Jocelyn.

'No, thank you.'

'Well, I'll leave it here in case you change your mind.'

She dumped the newspaper on Jocelyn's desk and hurried out to the little kitchen where a moment later they could hear her filling the kettle. Jocelyn was surprised to see Helen reach for the paper and even more surprised to see her grip on it tighten as she read one of the stories on the front page.

'You look shocked,' she said. 'What is it?'

Helen continued to read for a moment and then she looked up and smiled. 'Oh, it's just the latest piece of sensationalism. I'm surprised that they print this stuff. But I'm not shocked. Not at all.'

But she was shocked; Jocelyn could see that clearly. And when she had smiled the smile had not reached her eyes.

'I know I said I'd help you with some filing but I still haven't unpacked properly or done my washing. Would you mind if I just went home now?'

'No, don't worry. But think about the new job, won't you?'

'New job? Oh, the department store. Of course.'

When Helen rose from the chair she was clutching the newspaper and when she bumped into Charlotte in the doorway she made no attempt to return it. Neither did she say another word before Jocelyn and Charlotte heard her hurrying down the stairs.

'What happened?' Charlotte asked. 'Why did Helen rush off like that?'

'I don't know, but I think it must be something to do with what she read in the newspaper. What exactly was the story that caught your eye?'

Charlotte looked puzzled. 'It was all about some runaway heiress. A foolish child who has fled to Gretna Green with a man who is probably a fortune hunter. I don't see why that should upset Helen. Do you?'

'No, I don't.' Jocelyn sighed. 'And if ever we're going to find out it will be in her own good time.'

Myra liked to read the gossip columns in the newspapers. She talked about the people featured there as if they were her personal friends. Dukes, duchesses, princes and playboys, stage stars, film stars and the fabulously wealthy – she could have written several biographies. She squirrelled away the known facts about these people and speculated on the facts that were not so well known. Doc Balodis didn't understand her obsession.

'They are just people like you and me,' he would tell Myra.

'I know that,' she would reply, 'but their lives are so much more interesting. Some of them are just like characters in a book or a film. Reading about them takes you out of yourself for a while.'

Danny could empathize with that. He had always enjoyed reading: books, magazines, newspapers, anything that came to hand. He read fiction for the sheer pleasure of it and he suspected that, just like their landlady, he needed to escape from humdrum everyday life now and then.

Myra would read her newspaper whenever she had time to sit down with a cup of tea and a cigarette. Danny, who was often at home during the day, especially if the weather was bad, would sit at the table with her and get on with whatever he was reading. Myra probably knew very well that Raymond was deeply involved with dangerous criminals but she was good-hearted and she had always been kind to Danny and Joe, so if she sometimes interrupted him to relay some sensational titbit Danny would listen patiently.

'I hope they don't find them,' she said that day.

Danny looked up and tried to work out what she was talking about. It was no use. He hadn't actually been reading the book he was holding. He had been thinking, as he often did these days, of how he was going to get Joe away safely from the dangerous way he was living. 'Don't find who?' he asked.

'The runaways. She's only sixteen and they've eloped to Scotland so they can get married without her father's permission. Romantic, isn't it? Look—' she pushed the paper across the table to Danny. 'Read it for yourself. I'll put the kettle on for another cup of tea and we'll have the rest of the apple pie with it.'

Myra stubbed her cigarette out in the overflowing ashtray and went into the scullery. A little later when she came back with the tea and the apple pie she looked around the room in astonishment. Danny had gone and he'd taken her newspaper with him.

Less than an hour later he was outside Stefano's. He knew Helen had been away from London but he didn't know whether she was back yet. Lately Danny had lost track of his sister. The lights in her upstairs flat had remained out and he had not seen her going into work. She must be away, he had concluded. He couldn't imagine where or why, especially as her boyfriend had not gone away and didn't seem to know where she was either.

So why was he standing here now debating with himself whether he should just march in and ask for her? He almost did. But in the end he decided that what he had to say was better said in private. He cursed the instinct that had made him come hurrying off to find her as soon as he had read the report in the newspaper. He didn't even know whether Helen already knew about what Elsie had done.

No, he had better go back to the dog track. He still had the problem of Joe to sort out. And that made things complicated. How could he go to Helen after all these years to talk about their younger sister without mentioning his twin brother and how they had been living? I should have thought this through, he decided as he turned to go. Maybe I'll try Helen's flat again tonight, or maybe I won't. After all, I don't suppose there is anything either of us can do.

Chapter Twenty-One

Daily Chronicle, 20th August 1936
GREYHOUND DOPING – HOW IT'S DONE
Matthew Renshaw
Crime Correspondent at large

Here in the great northern cities there is no evidence of the doping of greyhounds. The recent advances the police have made in the matter of detection seem to have put an end to the practice. For the moment.

However, there are rumours that certain unscrupulous men are about to pull off a major illegal enterprise which could net them thousands of pounds. So what do they do? There are several options. They could dope the favourite with a sedative to make sure that it loses and the second favourite wins.

Or, more complicated, they could dope three of the fancied dogs with a sedative, leaving two outsiders winning at high-value forecasts by finishing first and second. A forecast simply means betting which dogs will finish first and second. Then there is the outrageous option of doping every dog in the race except the dog you want to win it, usually a high-priced outsider.

And how do they do it? Here they need the cooperation of the kennel boys and girls. Most of these young people are completely honest, but it's a low-paid job and there are some who will happily take a backhander. They've persuaded themselves that they are not harming the dogs and that a capsule wrapped up in a nice juicy piece of meat will do no lasting harm.

To avoid suspicion bets will be spread around the country. Which, if you remember, is why I've been talking to the bookmakers in the provincial cities. My investigations have convinced me that the rumours are true and that by the time the dogs have been tested after the race the criminals will have collected their winnings and be long gone.

So where will this happen? And when? There are so many dog tracks that it's hard to say with any certainty. But my own recent investigations have led me to believe that I might know the answer. I'm on my way back to London.

Helen bought her usual newspaper on the way to work and started reading it on the bus. So Matthew had been out of town, she thought. She wondered whether he would get in touch with her when he came back, or whether he'd been so upset by her cavalier treatment of him that he would never want to see her again. Why on earth had she done it? Why had she risked losing the man she loved with all her heart?

Feeling far from happy, she turned the pages of the newspaper to see if there was any news of her runaway sister. Elsie, she thought, what have you done? Helen pushed her own heartache aside and gave way to nagging worries about her younger sister.

There was a small item but it didn't tell her anything new. Apparently there had been no sightings of the couple despite the fact that reporters from several newspapers had gone to Gretna Green and it was 'rumoured' that Hugh Partington had set private detectives on them.

Oh, Elsie, my pet, what can you be thinking of? Helen wondered. Are you so foolish that you have allowed your head to be turned by the first handsome ne'er-do-well that has paid you attention? Or perhaps you were unhappy. It's not uncommon for girls to marry the first boy who asks them simply to get away from an unhappy home. And what if Hugh Partington fails to find you in time and you actually marry this man? Will your romantic dreams come true? Will he be kind to you once he gets his hands on your money? And what if the Partingtons cut you off without a penny? Will Perry Wallace keep his marriage vows or will he desert you?

Helen closed the paper and put it in her shopping bag. She was surprised to find herself smiling. With all these worrying thoughts swirling round in her mind she knew she should feel more anxious than she did. Why am I not thoroughly despondent? she wondered. And then she realized with a small flowering of hope that whatever Elsie had done and whatever happened next, she might have made it possible for Helen to contact her. The best thing that can result from this mess, Helen thought, is that I will see my sister again.

'I take it you've read that?' Doc Balodis indicated the newspaper lying on Raymond's desk. It was open at the page showing the article written by the crime correspondent.

'Too clever by half, isn't he?' was Raymond's snarling answer.

'He's coming back to London.'

'Well, then?'

'He's worked it out. He'll come here. Tonight, probably.'

'So?'

'Are you going to go ahead?'

'Why not? He can't prove anything.'

338

'He can share anything he knows with the police. They'll test the dogs.'

'And that will be too late. The birds will have flown.'

'But not you. You and I aren't going to make enough out of this deal to vanish like they can. You'll be closed down here. Ruined. Almost certainly we'll end up in jail. Well, you will.'

'What do you mean by that?'

'I don't have to hang about. I'm small fry to them. I can collect my winnings pronto and go.'

'There's friendship for you!'

'We were never friends.'

'No we weren't, were we?' Raymond shook a cigarette from the pack on his desk and lit it with the one he had just finished. This joined the other cigarette ends in the overflowing ashtray.

Balodis dragged a chair up close to the desk and sat down. 'It's not too late to call it off,' he said.

'It is too late and if I did they'd kill me.' Raymond's forehead was beaded with sweat and Doc Balodis realized he was deadly serious. 'Think about it,' Raymond went on. 'They've got too much money invested in this to write it off. I've got no choice. But I'm not as stupid as you think. I've spread my bets in places they don't know about. I'll make enough to get away. Leave all this behind.' He laughed. 'Start a new life. That's what they do, isn't it?'

'Does Myra know?'

'Of course not.'

'And the lad?'

'You mean Joe? He'll do what he's told. He doesn't need to know anything more than that.'

'So you'll leave him to face the music?'

'Why not?'

'No compunction?'

'It's a hard old world, isn't it? Now give me the pills and go back to the house and tell Joe to come over as soon as he's finished his meal.'

So it was going to be tonight. Doc Balodis took a small brown bottle from his pocket and placed it on the desk. If only Raymond knew, he thought, he could have got these pills, or something very like them, himself. There had been no need to pay him a fortune for something very like the capsules that could be bought over the counter for travel sickness. But Raymond wasn't as clever as he thought he was. That was why he had got himself into such a mess.

Time for me to go, Doc Balodis thought. Time for me to go.

In the room they had shared ever since coming to London Joe had just finished reading the item about dog doping. He was sitting on his bed and he looked up at his twin who was standing over him. 'Why have you shown me this?' he said.

'Did you think I didn't know?'

'Know what?'

'What you've been doing. Taking money to fix the races by doping the dogs. You never talked about it and you tried to hide the money you made, but did you think I didn't wonder why you could look after both of us so well?'

Joe dropped his head and stared down miserably at his hands still clenched around the newspaper. 'I never harmed the dogs, you know. No bits of straw under their eyelids, none of that stuff.'

'I know that, Joe. I know you would never do anything like that and I can't blame you for what you did because it's my fault as well. If I'd really cared about what was happening I would have stopped you.'

At this Joe looked up. 'That's not so easy.'

'What do you mean?'

'Raymond made it clear that if I tried to stop now there would be no way he would protect me.'

'Protect you from who?'

'The guys behind it, of course. Or the rozzers for that matter. He said I'd end up in jail.'

'That's why we've got to go. Get out of this.'

'When?'

'Right away. You've read that.' He nodded towards the newspaper. 'That reporter thinks something big's going to come off. Very soon. The police are on to it, and so is he – Matthew Renshaw, I mean. If the law doesn't get you he'll make sure they do. He's not stupid. He must have worked out what's going on and he'll have a pretty good idea of who's doing it. I've told you, Joe, we've got to go.'

'Go where?'

'Where do you want to go?' Danny tried to make Joe smile. 'Is there anywhere you fancy? The seaside? The country? Abroad?'

'Abroad? What are you talking about? How could we go abroad?'

'In spite of the fact that you like to spend your money on flashy clothes I know you've got a fair bit saved up. We could get on a train and go anywhere in England, or we could get the ferry and go to France. I quite fancy the South of France – be good for my chest down there.'

'But what would we do when the money runs out?'

'Find jobs. Waiting on in a beach café, clearing up in a bar, washing dishes in a hotel. There are always jobs like that.'

'We don't speak French.'

'Yes, we do. We were top of the class at school, remember?

It'll come back to you. And anyway, there's always fruit picking. Lots of foreign workers go there for that and if you work hard you can earn enough to keep yourself for months.'

Joe looked uncertain. 'Do you think we could get away with it?'

'We vanished once before, remember. We can do it again. Besides, I don't think we have any choice.'

Suddenly Joe looked up and smiled as though a burden he had been carrying for years had dropped away from him. 'OK, I agree. We go. But when?'

'Why not tonight? Just act normal until everyone is asleep and then we'll get up and go.'

'Just like last time,' Joe said.

'Yes, just like when we left Haven House. And that worked, didn't it? Now come on, we'd better go down for our meal or Myra will wonder what's going on.'

Danny, uneasy that Joe had been away so long, decided to go and see what was happening. Doc Balodis had told Joe that Raymond wanted to see him after their meal. He wasn't his usual droll self and he didn't lavish his usual exaggerated praise on Myra's cooking.

Myra had noticed, too. 'What's up with you?' she asked. 'My steak and kidney pie give you indigestion?'

The doctor looked as though he had to bring back his attention from a troubling place. 'Not at all,' he said. 'The pie is perfect. Raymond doesn't know how lucky he is.'

Myra gave him a sharp look. 'Whether he does or he doesn't is none of your business.'

After that Doc Balodis had said very little and as soon as the meal was over he went up to his room where they could hear him moving about. Danny thought he could hear

342

drawers opening and closing and that made him thoughtful.

Danny had expected Joe to come back for a cup of tea before going to start work in the kennels but the next person who walked in was Raymond.

'Where's Balodis?' he asked.

'Gone up to his room,' Myra replied. 'Funny mood he was in. Do you want Danny to go and get him?'

'No. Let him stew. And clear off, Danny boy, let a man have his meal in peace.'

Raymond had tried to smile when he said this but the twist of his mouth was wolfish and his glance shifty. That's when Danny had decided to go across the road to the track.

He found Joe in the kennels. He was sitting on an upturned bucket and staring down at the straw-covered floor. He looked up when Danny's shadow fell across him, held out a piece of paper and said, 'It's tonight.'

Danny knew what his brother meant. He took the piece of paper and looked at the names of the dogs scribbled there.

'He doesn't trust me to remember them,' Joe told him. 'But I have to destroy that as soon as I've done it. Like always.'

'Have you done it?'

'Poor old Daddy's Girl.'

'What are you talking about?'

'The dog, she doesn't stand a chance anyway, but I'm supposed to dope her along with the others on that list. And I'm not going to. I'm not going to dope any of them.'

'You told him that?'

Joe shook his head. 'I didn't have the nerve. I just took the names from him and came here. Time's running out. The owners will be here soon to lead their dogs into the traps.'

'Can the owners tell if their dogs have been doped?'

'Not if it's done properly. They think he runs an honest track. If the race doesn't go as planned Raymond will kill me.'

'No, he won't, because we won't be here.'

Joe looked up at him hopefully. 'We're leaving now?'

'That's right.'

'But what about our clothes? The money?'

'We can't go back to Myra's. Raymond's there now. We'll just have to leave with nothing. We did that once before, remember?'

'But where shall we go?'

'Don't worry about that. We won't be sleeping rough tonight, I promise you.'

Helen called at Eli's on the way home and bought bread rolls, cheese, salami, olives and some pickled red cabbage. She preferred it to sauerkraut. She also bought two large slices of creamy, comforting vanilla cheesecake – two slices because she was hoping that Matthew would come to see her tonight. If he doesn't I'll eat both of them, she thought, just to console myself.

She bathed as usual to rid herself of the restaurant smells and pulled on a pair of slacks and a silky blouse. She didn't want to look as though she had dressed up especially. In her imagination, if her bell rang she would hurry down – well, not exactly hurry, that would be undignified – to the front door. She would look up at Matthew in surprise – in *pleased* surprise – and say . . .

What on earth would she say? Here her usually fertile imagination deserted her and she knew very well that she would probably fling herself into his arms and sob with relief and gratitude that he still wanted to see her.

She didn't have to wait very long. When her doorbell rang she forgot all about dignity and she raced down the stairs, fumbling at the lock in her eagerness to open the door.

'Matthew—' she began and then stopped in a state of total shock when the door swung open to reveal her brothers standing there.

After the initial shock and tearful greetings Danny did all the talking. He told Helen they had left Haven House because they were worried that they would take the blame for an accident in which another pupil had been killed. Helen would have liked to know more about it but he hurried on to tell her of their time living on Mrs Norris's smallholding and how they had had no choice but to leave when she died.

Joe smiled for the first time since they had arrived. 'I liked the old girl,' he said. 'And I think she was pleased to have company but she never knew there were two of us. We thought if anyone was looking for us they would be looking for twins, so as far as she knew there was only one of us – called Jake.'

Again Helen would have liked to have known more but Danny, with a sense of troubled urgency, hurried on to tell her of their arrival in London.

'Joe got here first,' he said.

'And I'll never forgive myself for that.'

Both Helen and Danny looked at Joe in surprise. He shook his head. 'If I'd told Danny to leave the farm first he wouldn't have got soaked to the skin like that. It ruined his health. His chest's never been right since then.'

'That can't be helped now,' Danny told him. 'And anyway, you've worked hard and looked after me ever since.'

The brothers looked at each other sombrely and the seconds ticked away. Eventually Helen said, 'When are you going to tell me what exactly you've been doing?'

'I've been working at a dog track,' Joe said and Helen suffered a twinge of unease.

Matthew's reports of crooked dealings and the doping of greyhounds were fresh in her mind. 'Go on,' she said.

Her brothers looked at each other again and then Danny carried on with their story. When he had finished, when he had told the tale of how Joe had found the job and how he had been persuaded to help fix the races, Helen was appalled.

Joe stared at her miserably. 'I owed it to Danny to look after him,' he said.

Helen remembered how it had always been that way. Even when they were small children, fearless Joe had looked out for his more placid brother. She ignored the entreaty in Joe's eyes and addressed her question to Danny.

'But you've told me that you've known where I was for some time – that you've been keeping an eye on me, as you put it, ever since you saw me that day in Russell Square.'

'He never told me,' Joe interjected. 'Not until just before we came here. He didn't tell me he knew where Elsie was either!'

'So why didn't you come to me sooner?' Helen continued. 'You must have known that I would help you.'

'I wanted to come,' Danny said. 'But we couldn't. You would have asked us about the accident that made us run away from Haven House.'

'Are you going to tell me now? Tell me why you thought they would blame you?'

A worrying look passed between the brothers and it was Joe who answered. 'Because we were enemies,' he said.

'Enemies? Why?'

'Tod Walker was a bully and he was out to get Danny from the very first day. Everybody knew I hated him. We couldn't be sure whether anyone saw what happened or not, and if they did, would they say anything.'

'So Joe decided that the best thing to do was to leave that night,' Danny said.

Helen stared at their anxious faces. She wished she could have simply accepted their explanation and moved on. But she had to know. 'It wasn't an accident, was it?' she asked.

'It could have been,' Danny said. 'It wasn't planned. When he started his usual bullying on the cliff top it could have been him that pushed one of us.'

'But that didn't happen.'

'No.'

'One of you went too far. One of you pushed him deliberately.' This was a statement, not a question.

'Yes,' they said in unison.

'Which one?'

'Me.'

'Me.'

Again they had spoken together and Helen, looking at their obdurate expressions, knew that it would be a hopeless task to try and get the truth out of them. And in any case she wasn't sure if she wanted to know. She loved them both equally fiercely and she had no wish to come between them – to damage their loyalty to each other. She decided it was time to ease the tension.

'Let's eat,' she said. 'And then we can talk about what we're going to do next.'

The twins soon demolished the feast that Helen had bought in the hopes that Matthew might call. While they were eating she made up the bed in the spare room. 'You'll have to share,' she told them, 'unless one of you volunteers to sleep on the sofa here in the sitting room.'

'We'll take turns,' Joe said and he grinned.

Helen was amazed at how quickly he seemed to have been able to forget his troubles. But Danny was more subdued.

'There's something else you ought to know, Helen,' he said. 'I think your boyfriend is on to Joe.'

'My boyfriend?'

'Matthew Renshaw. I know you're close. I've seen him bring you home. I've . . . I've watched you from across the road.'

'So it was you!' Helen said.

'What do you mean?'

'You haven't always been as clever as you think you are. Matthew spotted you. He recognised you from the dog track.'

'No, I knew he'd seen me, but he must have mistaken me for Joe. He doesn't know there's two of us.'

'Whichever one of you he thought it was, he also thought that you'd followed him because of his investigations. He thought he might have put me in danger.'

'So what are you going to tell him?'

'I don't know.'

'If you tell him the truth he would put it in his report. He would tell the police. Unless you asked him not to.'

'I couldn't do that. I couldn't ask him to cover anything up for my sake. He's too honest. I wouldn't want him to abandon his principles.'

'If Joe and I go you won't have to say anything. Just let us hide out here for a while until we decide what to do. Perhaps you could give us enough money to get away somewhere.'

'No. You're not going anywhere. Without me, that is. If we go anywhere – and I think we must – we go together.'

And that means I must abandon any hope of putting things right with Matthew, Helen thought. Matthew whom I love with all my heart. But I love my brothers, too, and they need me. I've spent all these years wishing and hoping that we can be together again. And even if it means that I can never see Matthew again I'm not going to part with Joe and Danny now.

The next morning the newsboy on the corner was shouting something that Helen couldn't understand. She never had been able to make out his garbled speech and she wondered if anyone else could. The only word she could make out was ''Orrible!' A small queue waited to buy their morning newspaper and as they moved on Helen saw the news board and the words written on it.

'SLAUGHTER AT DOG TRACK!'

She waited her turn and while she did so realized that what the boy was shouting was: ''Orrible murder! Man beaten to death!' Numbly she handed over her penny, glanced at the headlined story then stuffed the paper in her shopping bag. And instead of going to catch her bus to work she went back to her flat.

Danny and Joe were up and dressed and making tea and toast for themselves as she had told them to do. She had also told them to make as little noise as possible until they heard the tenants of the flat downstairs leaving and to stay put until she came home from work. She had promised to come home early.

They looked up in surprise. 'Forgotten something?' Danny asked.

'No. Pour me a cup of tea while I read something in the paper and then you'd better read it too.'

Daily Chronicle, 21st August 1936
DOG TRACK DEATH MYSTERY
Matthew Renshaw
Crime Correspondent at large

Police are investigating the suspicious death of Raymond Costello, the owner of the South Park dog track. His body was found in his office late last night by Myra Thomson, a woman claiming to be his fiancée. He had been badly beaten.

As my readers will know, I was at the dog track last night in connection with my inquiries into an illegal betting syndicate. An unusual pattern of betting had drawn me there, but as far as I could tell, if there was a plan to dope some of the dogs, it was not carried out.

This is pure speculation but if something went wrong, maybe Mr Costello paid the price with his life. Certainly he met a violent end. Miss Thomson claims that she knows nothing about Mr Costello's business associates. But the police are determined to track these men down and they are anxious to talk to a Dr Balodis who Miss Thomson says was a friend of Mr Costello. They also wish to trace one of the kennel lads, Joe Jackson, who seems to have gone missing.

'Jackson?' Helen said.

'That's the name I gave to Raymond when I asked for the job,' Joe said. 'Didn't want to use our real name.'

Helen handed him the newspaper. She thought that for all they were dressed like slightly flash men-about-town they looked very young and vulnerable as they sat next to each other on the sofa reading Matthew's report.

So that's where Matthew was last night, she reflected. It's just as well he didn't come to see me, for I wouldn't have been able to let him come in. Nor would I have had an explanation that he could understand. She took the newspaper back and looked at the story again.

'This report only mentions Joe,' she said.

'I never worked in the kennels,' Danny told her. 'Like I said, Mr Renshaw only knows about one of us.'

'But this Miss Thomson might have mentioned that there are two of you.'

'Perhaps she didn't,' Danny said. 'After all, it's only Joe that was involved with the doping.'

At this Joe gave an anguished cry.

'What is it?' she asked.

'This is all my fault,' he said.

For a terrifying instant Helen thought he was going to confess that he had been there when Raymond Costello was murdered and that he had somehow been party to the savage beating the man had received. But when she saw his anguished bewilderment she was angry with herself for considering the possibility, even for a moment.

'How is it your fault, Joe?' she asked.

'I didn't dope the dogs last night. The deal went wrong. They had to teach him a lesson.'

'I don't see how killing him teaches him anything.'

'It's to warn others not to cross them,' Danny said. 'That's the way they think.'

Helen saw that Joe was weeping silently, the tears running down his good-looking young face. 'Listen, Joe, this is not your fault. It's Mr Costello's own fault for getting mixed up with these crooks.'

'I should have told him I wasn't going to do it.'

'You know we couldn't do that,' Danny said. 'He would

351

have handed you over to them. We had to get away for our own safety.'

'Danny's right,' Helen said. 'And I'm not going to let any harm come to you now. So stop worrying.' She stood up and gave them what she hoped was a confident smile. 'I've got to go out now; I've got things to do and people to see. And if the bell rings, keep quiet and don't open the door.'

When Helen left they were still sitting huddled together like frightened children. If I had managed to keep us all together when our mother died it would never have come to this, she thought. But I didn't and I've got to make up for it now. I've been given this chance to help my brothers, and I can only pray that fate will be kind and that one day the three of us will be reunited with Elsie.

As she hurried to the bus stop she tried not to think that the only person who might call at the flat was Matthew and that she wouldn't be there – not today or ever again.

Chapter Twenty-Two

'I'm sorry, Matthew, I really don't have any idea where Helen is.' Jocelyn Graves looked uncomfortable but Matthew knew she was not the sort of person who would lie to him.

'Did she come to see you?'

'Only once after she got back from Newcastle.'

'Newcastle?'

'She has family there – well, an aunt at least.'

'Could she have returned there?'

'No, she would have told me. She just said she felt the need to get out of town. She was going to look for a house to buy somewhere and she would be in touch when she was settled.'

'What about her work?'

'She's decided to bring the À La Carte column to an end. That's part of it, I think. She felt her work was getting stale and she needed to find inspiration for something new.'

'And you are willing to wait and see what she comes up with?'

'Of course. Look, Matthew, I have to tell you this – even when Helen does get in touch with me she may not want me to tell you where she is.'

'And that's your own fault!' It was Charlotte who had spoken and Matthew turned towards her desk to find her glaring at him. 'I told you to get on with it, didn't I? I told you that Helen and you were made for each other and that you ought to stop shilly-shallying and get married otherwise she would get sick of waiting and you would lose her. And I was right. What do you think, Aunt Jocelyn?'

'I'm not sure.'

'Why do you say that?' Matthew asked.

'Helen isn't the sort of person to simply run away. If that was what it was, I think she would have had the decency to tell you. There must have been another reason.'

'And it must have been something important,' Charlotte said. 'She told me that she was very sorry but she can't be my bridesmaid after all.'

Charlotte looked so glum that despite his own feelings Matthew found it in his heart to be sorry for her. 'I'm sorry,' he said.

Charlotte made an effort and smiled. 'Don't worry. Mother has come up with Stephanie, the daughter of an old school friend of hers. They've just come back from India and they're keen to get into the swing of things. The girl's a bit feather-brained but she's good-hearted and she's grateful to me for taking her under my wing.'

'So life goes on,' Matthew said.

Charlotte frowned. 'Of course it does. I mean, just because you've made a mess of things doesn't mean I have to postpone my wedding until Helen surfaces. She wouldn't expect me to; she told me so when she called in here.'

Matthew turned to Jocelyn. 'When she does get in touch will you let me know?'

Jocelyn stared at him gravely. 'I've already told you. That depends on whether Helen wants me to.'

For a while nobody spoke. Matthew became aware of the patter of rain against the windowpanes and the sounds of the traffic in the square below. Charlotte had resumed her typing and Jocelyn was trying not to show that she wanted to get back to reading a manuscript that lay on the desk in front of her.

'Well, I'd better be off,' he said.

'Yes . . . I'm really sorry I can't help you,' Jocelyn replied.

A little awkwardly he turned to go and he sensed immediately how relieved the two women were. Just as Marina had been relieved when he had given up trying to get her to tell him exactly what Helen had said when she gave notice at Stefano's.

'How many times do I have to tell you?' Marina said. 'She came in and she gave notice immediately. She said she was very sorry to let us down like that but she was leaving London straight away.'

'And she didn't say where she was going?'

'Mr Renshaw, I am not lying to you. She didn't say and as a matter of fact I didn't ask. I was too busy thinking who I could get in to take her shift at such short notice and where would I find another waitress as good as she was.'

Matthew didn't know what else he could do. He had been to Helen's flat several times. No one answered when he rang her doorbell and the girl in the ground-floor flat, whose coming and going was admittedly erratic, was a little hazy as to whether Helen had come back from her holiday or not. They had not seen her but they thought they might have heard her moving around. Or at least she had heard people moving around.

'What do you mean, "people"?' Matthew had asked her.

'Well, actually . . .' she paused and looked embarrassed. 'I think I've heard more than one person up there – at the same time, I mean. Oh, dear . . .'

355

Matthew had turned and left abruptly. He knew what the girl was suggesting and he didn't want to allow for the possibility that she could be right.

One evening in September he found himself sitting at the kitchen table in his sister's house and pouring out the full story. His baby niece was asleep in her pretty nursery upstairs and Patricia was preparing a meal for herself and George, who would be home any minute from his job at the BBC.

'What shall I do?' Matthew asked.

Patricia stopped stirring whatever it was in the pan and turned to look at him. 'Matthew, I have no idea what to say to you.'

He looked at her in surprise. It was so unlike Patricia not to be able to come up with some kind of advice – even if it was the kind of advice he would ignore. Then he saw how tired she looked and a surge of guilt swept over him. Baby Gillian, although adorable, was very demanding. She was a robust and healthy child who seemed to need an inordinate amount of feeding. Whenever her daughter obliged by sleeping for a while Patricia dashed about catching up with her household chores or simply sat down and tried to get her strength back.

'I'm sorry, Patricia,' Matthew said. 'You don't need to hear my troubles. What's that you're cooking, by the way?'

Surprised, Patricia answered, 'A sauce for the spaghetti – bolognese, as a matter of fact. There's enough for you if you want to stay.'

'I do, but that's not why I asked. You go and lie down on the sofa for a while. I'm perfectly capable of making spaghetti bolognese.'

'Really, Matthew? Would you?'

'Go on. I'll wake you when everything's ready.'

'If madam baby doesn't wake me up first,' Patricia said

with a smile. She handed the wooden spoon to Matthew, gave him a grateful peck on the cheek and headed for the sitting room.

Patricia was upstairs feeding Gillian when George came home. The meal was ready but Matthew kept everything warming and his brother-in-law opened a bottle of wine. They sat at the kitchen table. Matthew encouraged George to talk about his work for the BBC and George told him the latest news from Spain. There was a new Republican government and the Nationalist army had just closed the border with France.

When Patricia came downstairs they decided to stay in the kitchen for their meal, and Matthew and George dished it up and insisted that Patricia relax. They also changed the topic of conversation to something more light-hearted. But by the time Matthew said goodnight he knew the answer to his question.

Although he still had a limp, his leg gave him little trouble these days. He would go into the office tomorrow and demand to be reinstated as a foreign correspondent. If they said no then he would resign. He knew that his reputation was such that there were other newspapers that would be glad to take him on. And if not, then he would go freelance. There was nothing for him here in England. He would go to Spain.

14th September 1936
Dear Shirley,

We did it! We got married at the blacksmith's anvil and I am now Mrs Perry Wallace!

By law we had to live here in Scotland for three weeks before we could get married and we knew that they would come looking for us. Other runaway

357

couples hide away on farms or in tiny little hovels owned by local people, but we guessed that my father would have the countryside combed, as they say, so what did clever Perry do? He got in touch with an old school friend of his who owns a crumbling old mansion just the right side of the border.

The house must have been grand once but now it looks shabby and neglected. Perry's friend, Archie, lives there with his mother who is quite gaga. I think they stay there because Archie is ashamed of her, but he's a very dutiful son and he told us that he's hoping to find a wife who not only has enough money to rescue the house but who will also be kind to his mother.

'But what if you find such a person and you don't fall in love with her?' I asked.

Archie laughed and said that he didn't expect to be as lucky as Perry.

Perry was quite cross with him about that, although I'm not sure why.

Honestly, Shirley, I wish you could have seen the place. It was like a spooky old mansion in a movie, with dark panelling and stags' heads and even suits of armour. Perry had warned me that the food would be dreadful, and he was right. Fishcakes and sausages were served regularly at mealtimes and Perry and Archie joked that some of the meals the old cook dished up were just like those they had at school. But the wine cellar was well stocked and Perry has begun to teach me about wines. He says I'll have to know such things when we are back in London and start entertaining.

We will be living in Perry's apartment at first and I do hope that you will come to see me there – and

Annette, too. I read in the *Tatler* that Ernestine is living in Switzerland. When I told Perry this he laughed and said that would be because her husband wanted to be near her Swiss bank accounts, but Archie said that it could be because if there was another war Switzerland would remain neutral just like it did last time. I imagine Ernestine will like living in Switzerland. Who wouldn't? But if she visits London I hope she'll come to see me, too.

Just fancy, Shirley, two of us are married and in spite of all those ancient titles I can't help feeling that I am much luckier than Ernestine is. Perry is so clever and handsome and I'm sure he really loves me. You should hear the things he says to me when we are in bed. No, perhaps you shouldn't! They are not the sort of things suitable for the ears of a young innocent girl!

Oh, Shirley, I had no idea that married love could be such bliss! Perhaps I'd better end this letter before I run out of exclamation marks!

I shall send one of the maids down to the village to post this tonight; however, as we are catching the milk train to Newcastle in the morning and getting the first connection to London, I may be back in town before it reaches you. Whatever happens, by the time you read this there will be no need to keep things secret. Perry says that we must do the right thing and face my father straight away.

On that rather scary note I will end this letter.

With love from

Elise

(Mrs Perry Wallace!)

★

Selma read Emerald Leighton's society column with growing outrage.

> The runaway lovebirds are back in town. Perry Wallace and his new wife, the enchantingly beautiful Elise, have come back to face the music although I have it on good authority that Selma Partington is refusing to have anything to do with them. Oh, dear, does this mean that Elise will be cut off without a penny? This sentimental old columnist hopes not, but everything depends on Papa Partington, who I'm told is not averse to setting up a meeting in his office.

Once more Hugh had brought the offending newspaper up to bed for Selma and he watched her unenthusiastically while she read the piece he pointed out.

'How do they find out these things?' Selma raged when she had finished. 'I've done exactly as you said. I have refused to talk to the press and I have even kept quiet about my feelings when meeting my friends.'

'That's one thing you don't do, my darling,' Hugh said. His smile was strained.

'What are you talking about?'

'You don't keep quiet.' He raised a hand to stop her angry reaction to his words. 'Oh, I don't mean you go round gossiping. I mean that when we talk together – like at this moment – your voice is raised so loud that I'm sure they can hear you down in the kitchen.'

'You exaggerate.'

'I do, but it's almost true. You are so used to servants coming and going quietly about their duties that sometimes I think you are not even aware of their existence. You have quite forgotten the wisdom of the old saying, *pas devant les domestiques*.'

Selma looked weary. 'So we still have a traitor in the house?'

'It's the logical explanation.'

'Then what can we do?'

'Try to be even more discreet.'

Without realizing what she was doing, Selma began to crumple the newspaper savagely. Hugh took it away from her. 'Don't,' he said. 'You'll get newsprint all over your hands.' Selma shot him a look that seemed to say that was the least of her worries and he continued. 'This will soon be over, my darling. I've arranged for them to come and see me tomorrow.'

'What will you say?'

'That depends on what they – on what Perry Wallace – has to say. Selma, think about this, are you sure you don't want to be there?'

'I'm positive.'

'Don't you want to see your daughter?'

'I never want to see Elise again.'

'That's very unforgiving of you.'

'I'm sorry, Hugh; I've made my mind up. Just think of the scandal and how that could affect Bertie.'

'He's only a baby.'

'But these things don't go away. Whatever Elise does now she's damaged goods. I don't want anything like that to embarrass our son as he grows up. And another thing, I know you don't want me to talk to the press right now and you're absolutely right. But after a while I shall let it be known, just to close friends, who will tell their friends, that Elise was adopted and that no matter how much we tried to make a good life for her, in the end she reverted to type.'

Hugh saw that there was no use in trying to persuade Selma to change her mind, and in any case he wasn't sure if he wanted her to. Even though he had not been entirely in favour of the idea when Selma had asked him if they could adopt Elise, he had grown to love her as much as a father could love a daughter. Yet he, too, felt betrayed by what she had done and he, too, did not want any scandal attached to their own child for whom he had such high hopes.

'I'd better go now,' he said, 'but I'll tell your maid to bring some coffee, shall I?'

Selma nodded and raised her cheek for a kiss. Still so beautiful, Hugh thought as he took his leave, and I still adore her. And now I shall have to work out what I am going to do about this most troublesome child. As he ran through the possible options, the most worrying thought pushed itself to the forefront of his mind.

Elise never knew how she came to be adopted by us in the first place, he remembered. What would she say if she knew that her former happy childhood came to an end because it was our car that ran over and killed her mother?

Perry was feeling optimistic. When the invitation came for them to meet Hugh Partington in his office he reasoned that at least they were not going to be ignored and that if Elise's father intended to deal harshly with them he would have done so through solicitors; he would not want to see them personally. However, his confidence began to ebb a little when he saw how formally they were greeted.

Elise's father had chosen to see them in the boardroom. When they were shown in he was standing at the far end of a massive table and when Elise would have hurried forward to greet him he raised his hand.

'No, Elise,' he said. 'I want you to wait in my office until I have talked to Perry. Miss Phillips will take you there and get you some coffee.'

Elise's face was strained as she left with her father's secretary but she gave Perry an encouraging smile. As soon as the door had closed behind them, Hugh Partington sat down and made a vague gesture for Perry to do the same. Hugh had taken the seat at the head of the table, naturally, but Perry was not sure where exactly he was meant to sit. Surely not at the other end of the table? After hesitating for a moment he walked along and took the chair three chairs down from where Hugh was sitting. If he sat there, he reasoned, they would be able to look each other in the eye.

Hugh was examining some papers spread out on the table in front of him. He didn't look up and Perry became aware of the tick of the imposing boardroom clock on the mantel of the fireplace behind Hugh. Perry's gaze strayed to the ponderous oil paintings framing the walls. No doubt they are very valuable, he thought, but they are all quite hideous. Perhaps they were deliberately chosen to be unappealing so that those who attended the board meetings would not let their attention stray. This thought made him smile and he was startled when Hugh Partington gave a slight cough and said, 'Something has amused you?'

'Erm no . . . I mean, the paintings. They . . .'

Hugh looked at the paintings on the wall opposite Perry and shook his head. 'I've never thought them humorous but perhaps you are a bit of an art critic?'

He made the words 'art critic' sound like something else entirely: dilettante, amateur, dabbler – someone not entirely genuine. Perry flushed. He knew immediately that he had been wrong-footed and this meeting was not going to be an easy one. He realized how futile it would be to try and explain why the paintings had made him smile so he simply kept quiet and waited for Hugh to continue.

Hugh shuffled his papers into a neat pile and looked Perry in the eye when he said, 'In case you're wondering, these documents have to do with the trust fund I set up when we adopted Elise. I have decided to allow her a modest allowance until she is twenty-one. Then her trust fund will mature.'

'Elise is adopted?'

'You didn't know?'

'No.'

'And if you had known would you still have married her?'

'What are you suggesting?'

'It isn't a mere suggestion. I'm telling you that I believe you married Elise because she is the daughter of a very rich man and one way or another you hoped to profit from that.'

'One way or another?'

'I'll come to that. But had you known she was adopted you might not have believed that she was such a good investment – especially now that I have a son of my own who will naturally inherit the major part of my fortune.'

'Mr Partington, I love Elise, and as far as money is concerned all we hoped for is that you would give her some sort of marriage portion so that we could live comfortably together.'

Hugh's withering look made Perry squirm uncomfortably. 'A marriage portion large enough to get you out of your present difficulties, no doubt.'

'My difficulties?'

'Surely you didn't think I wouldn't have you investigated? You owe a great deal of money to a very dangerous man. A man who has already threatened you.'

Instinctively Perry looked at the back of his hand where the scar, although fading, looked as though it might be permanent.

Suddenly Hugh Partington's icy disdain gave way to fury. 'If you have put Elise in danger you will learn that I can be a much more dangerous enemy than the so-called king of London's underworld.'

Perry believed him but he also knew that it was time to stop all pretence. 'So will you help me?'

'I take it the modest allowance I suggested would be totally inadequate?'

'Yes.'

'You need a large amount of money straight away?'

'Yes.'

'So what are we going to do?'

'You're asking me?'

'I mentioned that I thought you'd hoped to profit one way or another.'

Perry looked at him questioningly.

'And I'm surprised you didn't try the other way first. That is, come to me and suggest that you could be bought off.'

'There wasn't time.'

'Ah, I'm glad you've decided to be honest. But why do you say that?'

'You didn't even know that Elise and I were seeing each other.'

'No, by God, if we had we'd have put a stop to it.'

'Exactly. She's only sixteen and you could have sent her off to finishing school in Switzerland or France. I would have had to pursue her and convince you that I was a serious threat. That might have taken months – years even, and I needed the money as soon as possible.'

'So you set out to make a young girl fall in love with you and took her away from her parents in order to pay off your gambling debts.' Hugh raised his hand. 'No, that wasn't a question, Mr Wallace, that is the truth of the situation, and now that we are being completely honest with each other you had better tell me how much you need.'

Perry's eyes widened. 'You're going to help me?'

'Yes, but there are conditions.'

'I expect there will be.'

Hugh nodded. 'One way or another you have to remove yourself from my daughter's life. If you remained married I would not trust you to treat her well. You are a reckless gambler. You would return to your ways. Once she has her money you would spend it all and leave her penniless and then, who knows? You might desert her in order to find another rich woman. No, Mr Wallace, you have to go.'

'Leave her?'

'Yes.'

'When?'

'As soon as possible. Today, in fact.'

'Today? But what shall I tell her?'

'Leave that to me. Once you walk out of this door you are never going to see her again.'

'But what am I to do?'

'I will give you enough money to settle your debts and also disappear. I'll make you a small annual allowance. Go abroad. Find a job. That would be a novel experience for you. But wherever you go you must never get in touch with Elise again. If you do the allowance stops, as it will if you get married again.'

'Married again? But—'

'After three years Elise will be able to divorce you for desertion. My legal team will handle that. So now that we understand each other it's time for you to go.' Hugh Partington slid a piece of paper across the table towards him. 'Take this.' Perry took it, saw that it was a bank draft and his eyes widened. 'What's the matter?' Hugh asked.

'You have been very generous.'

'If we never see or hear from you again it's worth every penny. You will receive instructions about your allowance during the next few days, but after you settle your debts I want you out of London as soon as possible.'

'Elise . . . if she comes back to the apartment . . . ?'

'She won't. Not if you write what I dictate to you.'

Hugh pushed a clean sheet of paper across the table and handed Perry his own fountain pen. When Perry had finished writing the two men parted without another word.

Elise looked up anxiously when her father came into his office. She had made herself comfortable in a deep leather armchair and Hugh's secretary had provided her with coffee and magazines.

'You've been ages!' she said.

Hugh sighed and went to sit behind his desk.

'Where's Perry?' she asked. 'Have you had a good talk? Is everything settled?'

'Everything's settled.'

'Oh, good.' Elise suddenly became aware of the distance between them and, letting the magazine she had been reading slide to the floor, she rose and took a step towards him. 'Daddy . . .' she said.

'No, sit down, Elise. We have to talk.'

'And Perry?'

'Later. Sit down.'

She looked at his solemn expression with dismay. 'Are you very angry with me?' she asked.

'Yes, I'm angry.'

'And Mother? Is she angry, too?'

'What do you expect?'

367

Elise felt hot tears begin to gather and she blinked to try to stop them. 'Daddy, I'm so sorry. So very sorry, but I love Perry and he loves me. We just had to be together.'

'Even if it meant hurting those who loved you?'

Elise brushed the tears away from her cheeks with nervous fingers and hurried on, 'Oh, I know what a shock it must have been for you, and I'm really, really sorry for the upset I've caused, but now that it's done I hope you'll find it in your hearts to forgive me. I love Perry so much and he loves me and he makes me so happy.'

'Elise, stop this! You stupid, stupid little girl. You have no idea what you're talking about!'

Elise was shocked by the force of her father's anger. 'What do you mean?' she asked. 'Are you saying that I'm too young to know what it means to be in love?'

'For God's sake, stop this babbling about love. Perry didn't marry you because he loves you. He married you because he needed money. Perry Wallace is an old-fashioned fortune hunter and I don't suppose for one moment that he even knows what love means.'

'That's not true! He's . . . he's wonderful. The things he says . . . the things he does.'

Her father's face darkened. 'You little fool. What you're saying is that he seduced you and I'm ashamed of you, do you hear that? Ashamed!'

Elise began to cry in earnest and her father made no attempt to comfort her. After a while when the sobs subsided he got up and came over to hand her a clean white handkerchief.

'Dry your eyes,' he said, 'and keep the handkerchief. You'll need it when I tell you how much Perry Wallace loves you.'

★

At first she didn't believe him.

'You're only saying these things,' she said. 'It's some kind of trick to make me leave Perry.'

It gave Hugh no pleasure to assure her that what he had told her was true. 'You'd better read this,' he said.

The note was brief to the point of brutality. In it Perry told her that anything her father said about him was true and that it would be best if they parted immediately. She must not come back to the apartment but do whatever her father told her to do.

As Hugh expected there was another storm of weeping and he waited patiently for it to stop. He wanted desperately to take her in his arms and comfort her, but he resisted the temptation, because if he did he didn't know how he would have the strength to carry out the next part of his plan.

'So what am I to do?' Elise said at last. 'Am I to come home with you now?'

'No, Elise. You're not coming home. You betrayed our trust and your mother doesn't think that the bridges can be mended.'

'And you? What do you think?'

'I think the same.'

'But where am I to go?' There was a note of panic in her voice.

Hugh picked up the internal phone and spoke to his secretary. A moment later the door opened and Miss Phillips ushered Helen Norton into the room. Hugh answered Elise's question.

'You must talk it over with your sister.'

Part Four

The Years Ahead

Chapter Twenty-Three

December 1938

Margery Sutton and Dr Salkeld came with Helen to the funeral. The day was cold and damp and the church unheated. As soon as the service was over Dr Salkeld excused himself, saying he had to make some house calls. This meant that Helen and Margery were the only people, apart from the gravediggers, who saw Jane Roberts being lowered into her last resting place.

The vicar blew his nose and intoned his prayers. He smiled sympathetically at Helen when she took the trowel and threw the required clod of earth down into the grave to land with a dismal thud on her aunt's coffin.

'Come along, Helen,' Margery Sutton said. 'There's no need to stay longer. Let's get home and have a hot cup of tea.'

'You go and wait in the car,' Helen said. 'I have something else to do.'

Jane Roberts' housekeeper guessed what Helen meant and she squeezed Helen's arm before making her way along the sodden paths that led back to the entrance to the churchyard. Helen returned to the church porch where she had left a small bouquet of lily of the valley.

A short while later Helen, who had been dry-eyed throughout the funeral service, was weeping as if her heart would break as she stared down at her mother's grave. She stooped to clear a tumble of dead leaves which were obscuring the memorial stone and placed the flowers, which had been her mother's favourites, on the untidy grassy mound.

I've neglected you, she thought. But what could I do? I cannot come to your grave every week as some bereaved do.

'Don't think of her lying there in the cold earth.' Helen had not heard his footsteps and she turned, startled, to find the vicar standing behind her. 'Your mother is in heaven and even more important she lives on in your heart. Now say your prayers and go in peace.'

Margery had made sandwiches and baked cakes in case Dr Salkeld had been able to come back with them, and now they looked at the laden table in the dining room with amused dismay.

'Dr Salkeld said he would try to call in and see you before evening surgery,' Margery told Helen. 'This won't be wasted.'

'Even so, I think you have overestimated the amount the good doctor can eat,' Helen said.

'Not at all,' Margery replied. 'When he visited your aunt he would sometimes stay for a bite to eat and a gossip. I think he's lonely. Now why don't you go and sit by the fire in the front parlour? I'll make up a tray.'

'No, why don't we sit in the kitchen?' Helen replied. 'It's warm and cosy in there – and more convenient.'

She could have added that the last place she wanted to sit was in the room she most associated with her aunt. In all the

374

time Helen had lived in this house she had only known her aunt to visit the kitchen a handful of times. The room was like neutral ground.

Helen and Margery Sutton had much to discuss. Jane Roberts had left Helen the house as she had said she would, but Helen knew she would never want to live in it. She would put it up for sale and Margery had agreed to stay on and oversee everything.

'What about the contents?' Margery asked.

'If the people who buy the house don't want them, send them off to the salerooms.'

'Is there nothing you want to keep?'

'No. I mean yes. There is something. I don't know if it's still here but there was a picture – very sentimental – two cherubs and a garland.'

'It's in the front bedroom.'

'Well, I know it's not important or valuable, but when I first saw it I thought it was the only object in the house that my mother would have liked. Somehow that was comforting.'

'I'll parcel it up for you. It should be small enough to go in your case.'

'Thank you. When this is all over what are you going to do?'

Margery looked thoughtful. 'When I told Dorothy that Mrs Roberts had died she wrote immediately and asked if I would go and live with them in Singapore.'

'But that's wonderful,' Helen said.

'No, it isn't. I told you years ago that I doubted if I would settle there. As far as I can tell from Dorothy's letters, it's a very different way of life. Dorothy loves it but I don't think I would. And besides, what will happen if there is a war? It's looking more and more likely, isn't it?'

'I'm afraid so. Well, would you like to come and work for me?'

Suddenly Margery Sutton couldn't look Helen in the eye. She busied herself pouring another cup of tea and taking an inordinately long time to stir in a spoonful of sugar. 'Well, actually, I've had another offer,' she said.

'Of work?'

'You could call it that.' She laughed.

'For goodness' sake, tell me,' Helen said.

'Angus – Dr Salkeld, that is – hasn't been able to find a satisfactory housekeeper since his wife died.'

'And he wants to offer the position to you?'

'He's offered more than that.'

'You mean . . . he asked you to . . . ?'

Margery nodded. 'Marry him.'

'And you've said?'

'I would tell him once all this business was settled.'

'But you're going to say yes?'

'Oh, I think so, but it doesn't do any harm to keep them guessing, does it?'

'Well, that's wonderful, Margery. Is there anything in the sideboard we can drink a toast with?'

'Only the sweet sherry your aunt was so fond of.'

'That will do. You sit there while I go and get it.'

Helen was staying at the Royal Station Hotel. When Margery had telephoned to tell her of her aunt's death she had come north straight away, but she could not bring herself to sleep in the house where she had been so unhappy. In the morning she would telephone the solicitor and tell him to go ahead with the plans to sell the house.

She had already had an appointment with him when he had told her the terms of her aunt's will, which were very simple. Helen was the sole heir. He had also given her a letter which Helen reread now when she was lying in bed and couldn't sleep.

In it her aunt had told her something which Helen had suspected for some years. That it had been the Partingtons' car that had knocked down and killed their mother. Also that the Partingtons' chauffeur had been in no way to blame and that Mrs Partington had been prompted to help them by the sheer goodness of her heart.

Helen only half-believed that. No doubt the wife of one of the richest men in England felt it her duty to help the bereaved family, but she had been childless and had seen this as an opportunity to take the youngest child into her home and adopt her. Helen remembered the night that Mrs Partington had come for Elsie, how she had lifted her on to her knee and comforted her. How she had wanted to leave as soon as possible, leaving all Elsie's belongings behind, including the homemade doll Maisie.

Helen had kept that doll and when Elise, as she wanted to be called, had come home with her she had presented it to her only to find that her younger sister didn't remember the doll at all. However, seeing Helen's ill-concealed dismay, she had said, 'Oh, how sweet. I shall keep her forever!'

Elise had never spoken about her feelings for her adoptive parents and Helen, guessing that she was deeply wounded by their abandonment of her, had decided to wait until her sister felt ready to talk. She had accepted that this might never happen and now, reading her aunt's letter, she decided not to reveal its contents to either Elise or her brothers. What would be the point of it? They had made a new start and they must let the unhappy years go.

Before settling for the night she telephoned Danny and asked him how he was coping.

'Very well,' he said. 'Joe's been trying out some new recipes for Christmas; he's really taken to this cooking business, you know, and Elise actually got round to choosing the fabric for the new curtains although she's made no move towards getting the sewing machine out. As for me, I could run this place blindfold. Oh, and there's a parcel for you.'

'Parcel?' Helen felt a flutter of apprehension. 'They've sent it back?'

'That doesn't mean they've rejected it.'

'It did last time.'

'But the letter was encouraging, wasn't it?'

'Mmm.'

'There'll be a letter inside again. Do you want me to open it and read it to you? Helen . . . are you still there?'

'I wish you hadn't told me,' she said, 'because now I don't know what to do. If I say yes, I may have to put up with the disappointment while I'm alone here.'

'Or the elation,' Danny said. 'Yes, you're probably right. I shouldn't have told you and I won't open it and read the letter. Goodnight, Helen. We're all looking forward to your coming home.'

'Danny, wait! I can't bear it! Open the damned parcel and read me the letter. Disappointment or elation, I'm a big girl. I can deal with it.'

Helen heard a clatter as Danny put his receiver down and then the rustle of paper. A moment later he was back on the line and he gave her the news she had been waiting for.

'Don't say anything right now,' she told Danny. 'And don't tell the others. Promise?'

'I promise. Goodnight, Helen, and God bless you.'

There was no sleeping after that. They've accepted my

novel! Helen thought. Accepted it! And they want me to go up to town and discuss things with them.

By the time Helen boarded the morning Pullman her head was full of hopes and dreams for her future as a writer and her only regret was that she could not share her exciting news with Matthew. In the two and a half years since she had seen him she had never been able to forget how much she loved him, and on many a night she had lain awake trying to work out if there was a way they could be together. But in her heart she knew this was impossible.

Joe had been involved in the last big crime story Matthew had covered before he had resumed his former job as a foreign correspondent. There was still a chance that the police would want to question Joe and she had to protect him. That was why they had left London with no one but Jocelyn Graves knowing where they had settled.

Helen gave her order from the luncheon menu, asked for a pot of coffee and opened the newspaper she had bought at the station. Matthew was still in Germany where he had been since November. She had read his reports on the night they called Kristallnacht, or the Night of Broken Glass. He had described how Nazi Storm Troopers and German citizens had launched a massive, government-coordinated attack on Jews throughout Germany. The mobs burned synagogues, destroyed businesses, ransacked Jewish homes, and brutalized the Jewish people. Matthew had written that in his opinion the Night of Broken Glass illustrated the radical nature of Nazi policies towards the Jews.

Helen knew Matthew to be fearless and outspoken. She could only hope that so long as there had been no declaration of war he would have the sense to keep himself safe. But what if war came, as it surely must? What would he do then? Helen could not imagine him coming home to England if other men of his generation were called to fight. He would think it his duty to be there, and if he could not fight at least he could let the world know the truth of whatever was happening.

Today Matthew's piece presented a round-up of what was being written in the German press. Apparently Herr Hitler was preparing his people for a very long war.

'I'm glad you came home for Christmas, Matthew. The old folk haven't actually said so but I know they've been fretting for you.'

Matthew was helping his sister Patricia dress the Christmas tree in her front parlour. Or rather he was trying to stop his niece from pulling the ornaments off the tree the moment her mother had put them on.

'Look,' he said, after Gillian had successfully evaded him and pulled down a whole string of tinsel. 'Why don't we let her help?'

'Help! Are you joking?'

'I could show her how to put the decorations on rather than pull them off.'

Patricia frowned. 'But she'll just put them anywhere.'

'Surely it doesn't matter if she does? But if you really want the tree to look classy, I'll lift her up and show her where to put them.'

His sister looked at him appraisingly. 'I should have thought of that. This marriage and motherhood business has turned my brain to mush. I think I'll go and make us a pot of tea. You can take over till I get back.'

When she returned with the tea tray she paused in the doorway and watched as Matthew lifted her daughter up to put the star on top of the tree. It was a difficult task for chubby little hands and the star hung there slightly crookedly, but Matthew hugged Gillian and told her it was just perfect.

'You really ought to have children of your own,' Patricia said. 'Pity you let that girl get away, isn't it?'

'Don't start on that,' Matthew said. 'Not again.'

He looked so despondent that she felt guilty. 'I'm sorry. I know you've been trying to find her. I just wish I could help you.'

After the excitement of dressing the Christmas tree Gillian had fallen asleep in Matthew's arms and he laid her down on the sofa and covered her with a soft nursery rug. Patricia took the tray to a table near the fireplace and poured them each a cup of tea.

The sky outside was dark and the fireside scene inviting. Matthew momentarily gave way to a pang of longing. This is what home should be like, he thought. And I should have a home of my own to come back to rather than imposing myself on my sister or my parents each time I am in England.

When they were settled in the fireside chairs Matthew said quietly, 'Actually there is something you could do.'

'Just tell me!'

'Have you ever come across a magazine called *Potpourri*?'

'Yes. It's quite good.'

'Helen used to write for it.'

'She what?'

'She used to have a column in *Potpourri*. It was about life in a restaurant. The title was À La Carte.'

'I used to read it. Sometimes it was hilarious. And always utterly believable. But of course it would be − she wasn't making it up. She really worked as a waitress! Matthew, I *knew* there was something you weren't telling me about that girl!'

'There was a good reason. She was writing about a real

restaurant and it couldn't be identified, so she had to remain anonymous.'

'*You* knew.'

'Not for a long time. And of course I promised to keep her secret.'

'And now that you've told me how can I help you?'

'By reading *Potpourri*.'

Patricia frowned. 'But the À La Carte column hasn't been in the magazine for some time.'

'I know that. But something has taken its place.'

'Beside the Seaside! That's it, isn't it? It's the diary of a seaside landlady. You think Helen is writing that?'

'I'm sure of it. I've been having the magazine sent to me and I've been reading it every week trying to make out where she's living.'

'But Matthew, it might not be a real place. She's a writer, isn't she? She could be making it up.'

'Not Helen. The place will be real enough and the rambling house she fell in love with and wanted to bring to life again will be real, too. I've searched each piece for clues but she's clever. She makes the resort sound like many another resort and the people who come to stay like holidaymakers anywhere.'

'And you want me to see what I make of it?'

'Yes, I do.'

Patricia shook her head. 'Honestly, Matthew, if you haven't been able to work it out I don't see how I can.'

'You've heard the old saying "two heads are better than one"? And there's something else. She may have made a mistake at last.'

'Tell me.'

'She mentioned a billeting officer coming to inspect the premises.'

'Oh, that's a great clue. It just narrows it down to the whole of the south coast of England, doesn't it?'

Matthew looked rueful. 'More than that, probably. Much of the east coast, too.'

'The expression "needle in a haystack" comes to mind,' Patricia said.

'I know, but please read it anyway.' He sighed. 'If she makes another mistake I'm sure your keen, far from mushy, brain will spot it.'

'All right, Matthew. I'll do my best to help. But now let's talk about Christmas and making this a good one, not just for Gillian but for our parents, too. They never complain but I can tell that they sense that their world is changing and, like so many these days, they're worried about what's to come. They lived through one war and now we're probably going to have to help them live through another.'

Danny had the champagne on ice when Helen returned. Joe had made a celebratory buffet and set it out in their family room, although he hadn't been told exactly why. He just assumed it was because Helen was coming home. And Elise, also in ignorance of the true reason for the celebration, had finished the task she had been given of putting the Christmas decorations up.

They were all pleased to see Helen and she was pleased to be home. The house was warm and welcoming and furthermore they had never felt like strangers there. From the moment she had walked into the old house she knew it was where they were meant to live. She had had enough money saved to buy the house outright but it needed much doing to it, and also it seemed she was going to have to be the main breadwinner for her family.

Quite a few of the grand old houses nearby had turned

themselves into guesthouses or small hotels. So that's what Helen had decided to do. At first she did almost everything herself, but gradually the others learned to help. Joe became a surprisingly good cook, Elise a reluctant chambermaid, and Danny took the reservations, ordered provisions and kept the books.

This left Helen free to get back to her writing. Jocelyn had been delighted when she got in touch and at first kept her busy with book reviews. When she came up with the idea of a diary of a seaside landlady Jocelyn had welcomed it. And she had also kept Helen's secret. So had Charlotte, who had continued to work at the magazine after her wedding although she was longing for the day when Edward would earn enough money for her to give up work and start a family.

During the first winter away from London Helen had finally got down to the task of writing a novel. She had never forgotten the old house she had seen on one of her trips to the countryside. Her imagination fired by thoughts of the generations who lived there, she wrote a fictional history of the house. It was dramatic, romantic and totally over-indulgent, and the publisher she sent it to told her so.

The accompanying letter also said that she simply didn't have the knowledge to write historical fiction and that if she wanted to do so she must be prepared to do proper research.

Then, almost in tears, Helen had come to the end of the letter. The last paragraph told her that there was nothing wrong with her actual writing; in fact it was of a very high standard, and that if she cared to try another kind of novel they would be pleased to look at it.

She had thought long and hard about that advice and had eventually decided that the sort of story she wanted to tell would be set not in historic times but in the world of today. She remembered the films she and her mother had been to see together, and the sort that they had most enjoyed had been the detective stories, the thrillers.

That's what I'll write, she thought. But it won't all be doom and gloom. No matter what straits she finds herself in, my detective will have a sense of humour. So Helen had determined to be a writer of detective fiction and tonight they were celebrating her first success.

When Danny told his brother and younger sister why he was opening a bottle of champagne they cheered and they hugged Helen and told her that they had always known she could do it.

'And this is just the beginning!' Joe said. 'You bet Mr Hitchcock will come calling and ask you if he can make a film of it. And when he sees our Elise and how beautiful she is he'll want to make her the star.'

They carried on laughing and joking until they heard the paying guests come in. They were two young men who were working at the radar installation.

'They'll want their supper,' Joe said. 'I'd better get back to the kitchen.'

'I'll set up the table,' Elise said and she checked her hair and make-up before hurrying through to the dining room.

'And I'll lock up,' Danny told Helen. 'So why don't you go to bed now? You must be exhausted.'

'Thanks, Danny, I am rather tired.'

It was only after she had left the room that it dawned on Danny how subdued Helen had been throughout their little celebration. Of course she would be tired after her journey, he thought, but in his heart he knew it was much more than that. There should have been someone else here to share Helen's success tonight. Someone who would almost certainly have been with her had she not chosen to flee from London in order to protect her brothers.

She's breaking her heart, he thought, and I can't let this go on. There must be a way of making Joe safe, and if there is I'd like to bring Matthew and Helen together again.

Chapter Twenty-Four

Christmas had been busy. Usually free of paying guests at this time of year, they had had no choice but to stay open for the men from the radar installation, now numbering five. They in turn had been disappointed not to get home leave. Helen decided she would make the Christmas celebrations as merry as possible.

Danny helped Joe in the kitchen and Helen cleaned rooms and changed beds along with Elise. She had already started writing another book and she resented the time spent away from her typewriter, so she resolved to take on domestic help as soon as possible. Especially as another visit from the billeting officer had made it clear that she could expect to have every room filled with military personnel.

'What you do will be vital,' he had told Helen. 'First-rate food, a warm bed and cheerful company are good for morale.'

After Twelfth Night the jolly mood dissipated. Their paying guests came and went on their different shifts and never talked about their work. Joe was happy enough in the kitchen and was intent on filling the store cupboard in case there were going to be shortages. Danny helped him with this but Helen noticed that her twin brothers were a lot more subdued than usual. In their spare time they would sit quietly and talk to each other, breaking off the conversation if anyone came too close.

But if the twins were subdued, Elise was positively downcast. Throughout the Christmas celebrations she had been the most high-spirited, laughing, dancing and flirting with the youngest of their paying guests, although never letting him believe that she was seriously interested in him.

Helen was not surprised when her younger sister's mood changed so noticeably. She had suspected that much of her relentlessly cheerful behaviour had been an act designed not so much to convince the others as to persuade herself that she was having a good time.

On Christmas morning a card had arrived from the Partingtons. It was enclosed with a letter from their solicitor saying that as they had no idea what her present tastes might be they had deposited a generous sum in her bank account with which she was to buy herself a present. This had been their way ever since Elise had come to live with Helen, so she should not have been surprised. She just hasn't entirely accepted her new life yet, Helen thought, and she cursed the Partingtons for their cruel treatment of the girl they had been so eager to take away from her real family.

As winter gave way to a reluctant spring Elise took to walking on the beach after she had finished her morning duties. She never asked for company but one day, when she had stayed out longer than usual, Helen put on her warmest coat and went to find her. It wasn't hard. The chill wind had driven even the hardiest walkers away and Elise was the only person standing on the damp sand, her hands stuffed in her pockets as she gazed out across the white-capped waves. She didn't turn as Helen joined her. She simply said, 'I wonder where he is.'

'Who?'

'Perry.' She paused. 'My husband.' Then she began to laugh – or was she sobbing?

Helen glanced sideways and was concerned to see tears streaming down her sister's face. She took a handkerchief from her pocket and offered it wordlessly.

'Thank you,' Elise said. 'But I'm not crying, you know. It's this wind – makes my eyes water.'

'If you say so,' Helen said. 'But is this what you do every day? Come here and stare out across the Channel?'

Elise answered the question with one of her own. 'How far do you think it is from here to France?'

'Depends where in France you want to go. And where you start from. About twenty miles at the narrowest point. You're not thinking of going to look for him, are you?'

'No. I don't want to see him again. Ever. He's an unprincipled, dishonourable cad and sometimes I think I hate him for what he did to me. But, oh, Helen, it was so wonderful while it lasted. Can you understand that?'

'Yes, I think I can. And I also think you should put him from your mind altogether. You're young, you're beautiful and you have a wonderful life ahead of you.'

Elise turned and gave a disbelieving smile. 'Life as a chambermaid?'

'I've been thinking about that. It's too late to send you back to school but what about college? There must be something you would be interested in studying.'

'Don't you need me to help you in the house?'

'We can afford to get staff in now. So, think about it, Elise. And for God's sake let's get home. I'm bloody freezing!'

After that conversation Elise seemed to cheer up a little and now and then she even asked for company on her morning walks. Then in March, on her nineteenth birthday, another letter arrived from the solicitor. There was no birthday card from the Partingtons enclosed and at first Helen thought that was the reason her sister looked so distraught.

They were sitting at the table in their family room having a coffee break after giving the guests their breakfast. Their new domestic help, Mrs Fearon, was clearing the tables in the dining room and her husband, a former army cook who had been wounded in the last war, was learning his way round the kitchen. Danny had brought in the mail on a silver salver.

'A letter from London, for you, madam,' he said to Helen in a voice like that of a butler in a movie. 'I imagine it's from your publisher.'

'And this looks as if it's from your solicitor, madam,' he said, turning to Elise.

The last envelope on the salver was a blue airmail envelope. 'From your Australian pen pal, I think,' he said to Joe, who grinned as he reached for his letter then stuffed it in his pocket to be read later.

'And no mail for me,' Danny said. 'But then I never write to anyone, do I? Perhaps I should respond to one of those pen pal requests in the newspaper like Joe did. You never know what might develop.'

Joe looked embarrassed. 'Leave it be, Danny,' he said. 'Nothing has *developed* between Muriel and me. We're just pals.'

Suddenly Elise cried out, 'Oh no!'

'What is it?' Helen asked.

'Perry,' she said. 'He's dead. They found him on the beach.'

'The beach?' For a moment Helen thought that her sister's husband had been found on the beach where Elise liked to walk every day. Had they been meeting secretly?

390

'Which beach? Where?' Joe asked.

'Biarritz.'

'What was he doing in Biarritz?'

'I can guess,' Danny said. 'The casino.'

Elise nodded. 'He couldn't keep away from gambling.' She stared at the letter. 'Apparently he got mixed up with the wrong crowd, ran up some debts and asked my father to settle them.'

'And Mr Partington refused,' Helen guessed.

'That's right. So now he is dead and the French police don't think there's much chance of finding whoever it was who killed him. Poor Perry.'

They looked at her in surprise. After her initial outburst she had calmed down. She passed the letter to Helen. 'You can read it if you like. My father's solicitor thought I ought to know what had happened, especially as now I won't be put through the inconvenience of having to divorce Perry. Inconvenience? That's all it means to people like that.'

Helen skimmed through the letter then glanced up at Elise. 'Are you all right?' she asked.

'Strangely enough I'm fine. I'm sad, of course, but I'm not heartbroken. Poor, poor Perry. Now I can put the whole unhappy episode behind me.'

1st September 1939

I have neglected my diary lately but I feel that I ought to mention the mood of unease, not to say downright dread that pervades the air. Germany has invaded Poland and although Mr Chamberlain has issued an ultimatum to Germany saying that they must withdraw, the Government is preparing us for war.

Matthew is in Berlin. I wish he wasn't.

*

3rd September 1939

This morning Mr and Mrs Fearon joined us while we listened to the wireless. At quarter past eleven our Prime Minister, Mr Chamberlain, announced that the deadline of the final British ultimatum for the withdrawal of German troops from Poland had expired and that 'consequently this nation is at war with Germany'.

Nobody spoke. It was what we were expecting but it was frightening to have our worst fears confirmed.

As far as I know Matthew, along with other British nationals, is still in Germany. What will happen to him?

Over the next few days Danny saw how feverishly Helen searched through the newspaper and then threw it aside in anguish. There had been no reports from Matthew Renshaw since the day after war had been declared when the Royal Air Force launched a raid on the German navy.

Danny could imagine him phoning his last report through to London and also the consequences of his action if he was discovered. As surely he must be eventually. The telephone lines would be tapped or cut altogether, and as far as Danny could see it would be pretty pointless for Matthew to stay there. If he has any sense he'll get home somehow, Danny thought.

Then what will happen if he does? Am I going to allow Helen to go on tormenting herself like this? No matter what Joe and I will have to face up to, we have no right to keep her away from the man she loves.

A week later Danny saw Helen throw the paper aside. She hurried out of the house without bothering to put her coat on. He picked up the paper and scanned it quickly to see if he could find what she had been reading. The report was brief.

You may be wondering why we have not heard from our correspondent Matthew Renshaw. As you may remember, he was in Germany when war was declared. We have it on good authority that he, along with other British Nationals, is quite safe and that they are making their way home.

'What is it?' Elise asked and Danny handed her the paper.

'Who is Matthew Renshaw?' she asked when she had read it.

'He's the bloke Helen is in love with.'

'Since when?'

'Since before we all got together again.'

'But why have we never seen him?'

'There are good reasons and I promise you I'll explain it all, but right now don't you think you should go after Helen and see if she's all right?'

Elise had had the good sense to take Helen's coat with her and when she found her on the beach she slipped it over her shoulders.

'Thanks,' Helen said.

'Now it's your turn to gaze out across the sea,' Elise said. 'But in your case I'm hoping and praying that he will come home.'

Helen turned to look at her sister in surprise. 'What do you know about it?' she asked.

'Very little. But Danny has promised to explain. Now come home, won't you? At times like this you ought to be with your family.'

George had been working on what he called the graveyard shift in the sub-basement control room at Broadcasting

House. When he got home just before nine in the morning Patricia was clearing up the mess their daughter had made on her high chair. He dropped a kiss on Gillian's head and took Patricia in his arms.

'What's this?' she said anxiously. 'Bad news?'

'No, sweetheart. It's good news. Our people in Paris phoned in to say a British contingent is making its way by train to one of the Channel ports. They couldn't or wouldn't say which one, but it's looking good.'

'And Matthew is part of this contingent?'

'He is.'

'Thank God for that.'

Patricia allowed herself the luxury of weeping in her husband's arms and when she had thoroughly soaked his jacket she looked up and said, 'I know you must be tired, darling, but I want you to go straight round and tell the old folks.'

George found his handkerchief and wiped Patricia's face. 'Why don't you and Gillian come with me?' he said. 'Then we can all have another good cry – together!'

The day after Matthew's first report from London appeared in the newspaper Danny and Joe knew it was time to make a decision. During their rest time in the afternoon they retired to the room they shared on the top floor. At first they simply sat on their beds staring at each other across the narrow space that divided them. Danny was the first to speak.

'I'm sorry, Joe,' he said.

'It's all right. I would have gone anyway. I've been thinking about it for some time.'

'If there'd been any other way . . .'

'Forget it, Danny. You've protected me long enough.'

'Surely that's the other way round. You protected me.'

'Oh, yeah, I worked to provide for us both, but I owed you that. It was my fault you got ill.'

'No, it was my own fault. I shouldn't have been so stupid as to go out in the rain. You wouldn't have done. And another thing. I guessed what you were up to as soon as I realized that you were more flush with money than you ought to be. I should have stopped you doping the dogs but I just went on having an easy life. A good life. At your expense. There's not much to choose between us, Joe.'

'Except for one thing.'

'Don't. Don't say anything. Not now.'

'I have to, because it's another reason for what I'm going to do. I was responsible for Tod Walker's death that day. Oh, yeah, he asked for it. Or that's what I told myself when I shoved him as hard as I could towards the cliff's edge. I wanted him to go over. I wanted to put a stop to the grief and the bullying. I wanted to protect you.'

'I know that. That's why it's as much my fault as yours.'

'You didn't do the shoving though, did you?'

'No, and I'm sorry.'

'What do you have to be sorry for?'

'Oh, just sorry that it happened and that you've had to live with it all these years. And sorrier still that you're going away.'

'I told you. I would have anyway. And I'm going sooner than you think. I want you to be with me when I break it to Helen.'

Danny told Joe that of course he would be with him when he told Helen, but he decided that he would never tell him that there had been no need to push Tod over the cliff. No need because he hadn't bothered him at all. Danny had his own quiet way of dealing with trouble and he'd been pretty sure that like all bullies Tod Walker would have left him alone once he realized that he didn't react. No, it would be pointless and cruel trying to explain that to Joe now. Best to leave it in the past.

Matthew had only been back in London for two days when he got a phone call at the office asking him if he would join the caller for lunch at Stefano's.

'Who are you?' he asked.

'Someone who knows Helen Norton.' The caller rang off.

Matthew racked his memory and tried to place the voice but couldn't. However, the moment he walked into the restaurant and saw the good-looking young man waiting in the bar area he recognized him as the missing kennel lad.

'You . . .' he said. 'Joe Jackson.'

'Actually, I'm not. I'm not Joe and my name isn't Jackson, but why don't we go to our table and I'll explain.'

Danny had chosen Stefano's because he thought that might convince Matthew that whoever this person was that was calling really did know Helen. He led the way to the restaurant area and on seeing Marina he said, 'I believe you have a table for Mr Norton?'

Marina showed them the table and left them with the menu. Danny was aware that Matthew was staring at him. 'Norton?' he said. 'That's Helen's name.'

'Yes. Joe and I are her brothers.'

Matthew looked bewildered. 'I didn't know she had any living family . . .' he began.

'Ah, that was the trouble. She did have a family. Two brothers—'

'Twins!'

396

Danny nodded. 'And a sister. There are four of us.'

'Was it you or Joe I saw outside Helen's flat?'

'Me.'

'And at the dog track?'

'That was Joe.'

'So it was Joe that was involved in the dog doping.'

'Yes.'

'Did Helen know?'

'Helen didn't know where we were or what Joe was doing. She didn't know I had been following her. That I had found her.'

'Found her?'

'It's a long story and I'm going to tell you most of it. Then what you do is up to you.'

When it was time to go back Elise and Danny met at Charing Cross. They had come up to London together, simply telling Helen that they needed a day out to cheer themselves up. They had been vague about where they were going and left Helen with the impression that they were going along the coast to somewhere like Whitstable where they had found a good fish restaurant. They felt guilty about misleading her but they each had their reasons.

When they arrived in London they had been surprised to see the sandbags protecting the public buildings, wardens wearing tin helmets, and the number of men in uniform in the busy streets. Women, too.

'This makes the war seem so real,' Elise said.

'I know. Elise, are you sure you want to do this?'

'Absolutely.'

'Good luck then.'

After that they had parted, Danny to go to his meeting with Matthew in Stefano's and Elise to meet up with her old friend Shirley Chapman. When they returned home and were sitting round the table in the family room, Elise told Helen where she had been and why.

'You want to be a nurse?' Helen said.

'I do.'

'You never said anything to me.'

'That's because I wasn't sure if I'd be accepted. A matter of pride.'

'When did you first think of it?'

'I started thinking on the beach that day when you told me I should do something with my life. I thought very hard and couldn't come up with anything at first but when it became clear that war was inevitable and I faced the prospect of being summoned to work in a munitions factory, I thought a little harder. I knew that if we had to go to war, I wanted to do something to put people together again rather than blow them to bits. Nursing it would be.

'Then by sheer coincidence I got a letter from Shirley Chapman saying pretty much the same thing. You knew I'd been writing to her?'

'I did.'

'And you didn't mind?'

'Of course not.'

'Shirley is the only one of my old school friends who bothered to keep in touch. I always had the feeling that Annette didn't like me very much, and as for Ernestine, she's so taken up with high society that I don't believe she writes to any of us.'

'So your friend Shirley also wants to be a nurse?' Helen said.

'She does. And we both had an interview today with a very fearsome lady. The result being that we've both been accepted for nursing training, although we don't know yet

398

which hospital we'll be going to, or even whether we'll be able to stay together.'

'So Danny came with you to London?' Helen said.

'Erm, that's right. It was good having him there.'

'When will you be going?'

'I was told to settle my affairs.' Elise smiled. 'What on earth does that mean?'

'It means you should get your life in order,' Joe volunteered. 'Because you might not be coming home for a while.'

Elise's smile faded. 'Yes,' she sighed. 'I know that. Anyway, I'll be getting a letter any day now with a list of what I need to take with me and telling me where to go.'

Nobody spoke for a while and, seeing how downcast Helen looked, Elise said, 'I will be allowed to come home and see you all now and then, you know.'

Helen made an effort to smile. 'Of course you will. And I'm very pleased you have made the choice you have. Our mother would have been proud of you.'

Elise looked sad. 'I don't remember her as well as you do, you know. But I remember she worked hard and there was always something to eat and she always managed to be cheerful. Things went wrong for all of us when she died.'

'But Helen got us together again and things began to go right again,' Danny said. 'And if we have to part now, at least we'll be able to keep in touch.'

Helen, alerted by something in Danny's tone and by the way he had glanced briefly at Joe, said, 'What is it? There's something you haven't told me, isn't there?'

The twins looked at each other again and after a nod from Danny Joe reached into his pocket and drew out a brown envelope. He handed it to Helen.

'Go on – have a look,' he said.

The envelope contained more than one document. Helen spread them on the table and after a stunned moment she looked up.

'You've joined the army,' she said.

'Yes. I decided not to wait until I was called up. It was going to happen anyway, so I decided I might as well get it over with.'

'When are you going?'

'Tomorrow. To Aldershot. That's my travel warrant,' he said, pointing to one of the documents on the table. 'And Danny has helped me to get my affairs in order!'

He said that with a grin but again Helen thought there was something passing between the twins that they did not want her to know about. Danny caught her speculative look and smiled.

'But I suppose you know that you're not going to get rid of me!'

'I don't want to.'

'What if I'd wanted to be a hero like Joe? Oh, I went along for the medical just in case, but whereas Joe passed A1 I was deemed completely unfit to be a member of the armed forces. So I'll be staying here to help you run our own little garrison and make life as cheerful and comfortable as possible for anyone who is billeted with us. And talking of them, it's time to get on with the evening meal. Action stations, everyone!'

'No,' Helen said. 'Mr and Mrs Fearon are perfectly capable of managing on their own. Elise and I will set this table while you, Joe, go along to the off-licence for a bottle of champagne.'

'Champagne?' Danny said. 'We don't have any caviar.'

'We don't need any,' Helen told him. 'Because you, Danny, are going along to Bill's Fish Bar for cod and chips for four. And mind you ask for extra batter.'

Very early the next morning, before anyone else was up, Joe and Danny had breakfast in the kitchen and then they walked together to the station. Joe had said goodbye to his sisters the night before and had insisted that he didn't want them to see him off.

'I'll probably blub like a baby if you do,' he'd told them, 'and that's not the sort of memory I want to leave you with.'

While they were waiting for the train Joe said, 'Do you think he'll come?'

'I do.'

'And will he feel obliged to turn me in?'

'I think that's unlikely.'

'Because he's in love with Helen?'

'Well, there is that, but he's also an intelligent grown-up man who realizes that you would be much more useful serving King and country as a soldier than mouldering in prison for crimes you committed when you were just a kid.'

'I haven't just joined up because of that, you know.'

'I know that, Joe. I'm your twin brother, remember? I know you wanted to do the right thing.'

'How much did you tell him?'

Danny knew what Joe meant. 'Nothing about Tod Walker. I said we ran away from Haven House because we were miserable there.'

'And he believed you?'

'Why shouldn't he? We were only kids and we'd just lost our mother. But try to forget about that, Joe. Go off and be a hero!'

Danny stayed on the platform and watched as the train carrying his twin brother off to war drew away. Whatever happened in the future, he knew that Joe would never entirely forget what had happened on the cliff top. The memory would haunt him for the rest of his life.

'You look dreadful,' Danny told Helen when he returned to find her hunched over the table in the family room.

'Thanks a lot!'

'Too much champagne. Joe should never have bought two bottles.'

'It's not just the champagne, you know,' Helen said. 'I didn't sleep very well.'

'I don't think any of us did.'

'Well, Elise is asleep right now. You know how difficult she finds it to get up in the mornings. I don't know how she's going to cope with nursing training.'

'Don't worry. She'll cope. Like she said, she has too much pride to give in and make a mess of things. Do you think you could manage a cup of coffee? I know I need one.'

Helen spurned the toast he had made but while she sipped her coffee she smiled at her brother and said, 'How did you get to be so wise, Danny?'

'Whatever you mean by wise I think it's because I've had more time to think. With not being able to be as physically active as Joe I've had to put my energy into my thinking processes.'

'Maybe you're right,' Helen said, 'but when you were little you were always the more thoughtful of the two.'

'Perhaps I was just lazy. Letting Joe go ahead while I followed. Are you feeling any better, by the way?'

'Yes, a little.'

'Well, why don't you wash and dress and go for a walk along the promenade. The fresh air will be good for you.'

'I'd like to, but the guests will be down for breakfast soon.'

'And the Fearons will be arriving any minute. Off you go and give me the chance to see if I can manage without Joe. You'd be doing me a favour.'

'All right. But promise to let Elise wallow in bed a little longer. This could be her last chance of a lie-in.'

When Matthew arrived at the house in Folkestone her brother Danny opened the door.

'I'm glad you came,' he said.

'Did you think I wouldn't?'

'Who can tell? It's been a while since you've seen each other, hasn't it?'

'And whose fault is that?'

'I thought we agreed to let all that stay in the past.'

'Are you going to let me in, or are you going to keep me here while you question me?'

'You can come in and wait if you like. I'll even give you some breakfast. But Helen has gone for a walk along the promenade. Why don't you go and catch up with her?'

Trying not to show how irritated he was by Danny's admittedly reasonable manner, he turned and almost fell down the steps, righting himself at the last moment. If he says anything, anything at all, I'll punch him, Matthew thought and immediately felt ashamed of himself.

No matter that Helen's brothers had been responsible for all the misery since she had left him; they were trying to do the right thing now. Or at least this one was. And if he was to be believed his twin brother would already have departed to join the army. That meant he still had to meet Helen's sister, Elise, who, amazingly, was Hugh and Selma Partington's adopted daughter. The girl who had eloped with that rotter

Perry Wallace and whose story had been all over the newspapers.

Poor girl. Afraid of scandal, they had dumped her pretty quickly. But that was just as well, Matthew thought. For Helen – wonderful, adorable Helen – had been able to step in and retrieve the lost girl, making sure that her family was together again. To do this she had sacrificed her own happiness.

As he strode along the quiet morning streets Matthew was determined that that state of affairs was going to change.

He saw her from a distance. She was standing still, with her coat collar turned up and her hands in her pockets as she gazed out across the sea.

'Helen,' he said quietly when he was close enough.

She turned towards him and her eyes opened wide with dismay. 'Oh, no,' she said.

He couldn't help smiling. 'That's a nice greeting. I was hoping you'd be pleased to see me.'

'I am! It's just that you shouldn't . . . I shouldn't . . . I can't explain.'

'You don't have to. I know why you ran away. Danny came to see me and told me about Joe working at the dog track and how he got drawn into the doping and how you felt you had to protect him.'

'Of course I had to protect him. He's my brother and I'd already let him down once.'

'No, you hadn't, Helen. It wasn't your fault that your family got split up, and you've certainly done enough for them now. So will you please be quiet and consider doing something for me.' As he spoke he took her in his arms and turned her round so that she was facing him.

'What,' she said. 'What do you want me to do?'

'First of all I want you to kiss me, and then I want you

404

to promise never to run away from me again, and to make sure of that I want you to marry me.'

Helen laughed. 'In that order?'

'In that order.' He lowered his face towards hers but before their lips met he stopped. 'You do realize that I will be going to France, don't you?'

'As a reporter with the British army?'

He nodded.

'Must you?'

'You know I must.'

'Yes, I do,' she said.

As they kissed her joy was tempered by the bitter-sweet realization that they would soon be parted. They would have to face the years ahead with courage and pray that one day they would all be together again.

The Promise

Benita Brown

*In his last moments he offered up a prayer to the Almighty.
'God, keep my daughters safe from harm . . .'*

Marion Brookfield is just eighteen when she makes a promise that will change her life for ever. When her father, a journalist, is murdered by a vagrant, she vows to put aside her own dreams and care for her younger sister Annette.

Orphaned and penniless, the girls believe they have found a refuge when charming businessman Victor Bateman proposes to Marion and they move into his luxurious home.

But Marion's friend Daniel Brady is conducting his own investigation into Henry Brookfield's death. He learns the journalist was closing in on the ruthless head of a child prostitution racket when he was killed. And now his precious daughters may not be so safe, after all . . .

Praise for Benita Brown's powerful novels:

'I didn't want to put it down . . . A must for Catherine Cookson lovers' *Coventry Telegraph*

'Real heroines, genuine heartache . . . What more could you want?' *Northern Echo*

978 0 7553 3476 6

headline

The Dressmaker

Benita Brown

'Mrs Winterton, Melissa has the makings of a fine dressmaker, better than I could ever be. I want you to look after her . . .'

Emmeline Dornay's dying wish is for her daughter Melissa to have a home. But when the funeral is over, Melissa discovers that her future looks bleak. Wealthy Lilian Winterton *will* honour her promise and put a roof over Melissa's head, but only if she can earn her keep.

As an unpaid seamstress in the grand Winterton household, Melissa is ignored by the family and mistrusted by their servants. And when scandal occurs and the blame lands unfairly at her feet, she is thrown out on to the streets. Left with nothing but her needle and thread, Melissa finds her dreams are in tatters. But can the rags of her life be sewn into riches . . . ?

Praise for *Fortune's Daughter*, longlisted for the Romantic Novel of the Year Award 2007:

'If Catherine Cookson were alive, she'd be giving Benita Brown a pat on the back for this' *Northern Echo*

'A wonderfully evocative tale' *Lancashire Evening Post*

'A romantic tale of rivalry and deceit' *Newcastle Upon Tyne Journal*

978 0 7553 3474 2

headline

Starlight and Dreams

Benita Brown

Growing up under the critical eye of her father and stepmother in the wrong part of a Northern seaside town, Carol Marshall longs for freedom. The picture house is where she goes to dream, to pretend she's someone else: someone special. Then Carol wins a competition for a local girl to play a part in a film, and she's whisked away to London to be swept up in a world of glamour and excitement.

But all that glitters is not gold. And the journey to stardom is paved with danger, loneliness and vice. Carol is poised to get everything she ever wished for. But at what price . . . ?

Set against the backdrop of Britain's golden era of cinema as the nation recovers from war, this dazzling novel of ambition, passion and betrayal will enthral you and break your heart.

Acclaim for Benita Brown's novels:

'A romantic tale of rivalry and deceit' *Newcastle Upon Tyne Journal*

'You won't be able to put it down' *Yours* magazine

978 0 7553 5290 6

headline

Now you can buy any of these other bestselling books by **Benita Brown** from your bookshop or *direct from her publisher*.

FREE P&P AND UK DELIVERY
(Overseas and Ireland £3.50 per book)

Starlight and Dreams	£6.99
A Dream of Her Own	£6.99
Her Rightful Inheritance	£6.99
In Love and Friendship	£6.99
The Captain's Daughters	£5.99
A Safe Harbour	£5.99
Fortune's Daughter	£6.99
The Dressmaker	£5.99
The Promise	£5.99

TO ORDER SIMPLY CALL THIS NUMBER

01235 400 414

or visit our website: www.headline.co.uk

Prices and availability subject to change without notice